Woman.

Wife.

Smuggler.

Spy. . . .

"I have gone by many names.

Some of them are real . . . but most are carefully constructed personas to get me through checkpoints and across borders. They are lies scribbled on forged travel documents. . . . Splashed across wanted posters. My identity is an ever-shifting thing. . . . Tonight, I am Hélène and I am going home."

Praise for Ariel Lawhon's

CODE NAME HÉLÈNE

"Captivating.... [Lawhon] sweeps readers into Nancy's wry, fast-talking, first-person account of her adventures.... Lawhon's gripping narrative gives 'Hélène' her due." —*Shelf Awareness*

"Masterful.... Exhaustively researched and vividly woven.... As much an epic love story as an engrossing narrative of an unlikely anti-Nazi combatant.... Lawhon has proven herself a master at her craft, and she does readers a great service with *Code Name Hélène.*" —*Chapter 16*

"Magnificent.... This astonishing story of Wake's accomplishments will hold readers in its grip." —*Booklist* (starred review)

"Readers will be transfixed by this story of a woman who should be a household name." —*Library Journal* (starred review)

"Riveting.... [A] stunning, moving story." —Bookreporter.com

"Gripping.... Lawhon's vivid, fast-paced narrative will keep readers turning the pages, and a detailed afterword makes plain how much of the account is factual. This entertaining tale does justice to Lawhon's larger-than-life subject." —*Publishers Weekly*

ARIEL LAWHON

CODE NAME HÉLÈNE

Ariel Lawhon is a critically acclaimed *New York Times* bestselling author of historical fiction. Her books have been translated into numerous languages and have been LibraryReads, One Book One County, Indie Next, Costco, Amazon Spotlight, and Book of the Month Club selections. She lives in the rolling hills outside Nashville, Tennessee, with her husband and four sons. She splits her time between the grocery store and the baseball field.

www.ariellawhon.com

ALSO BY ARIEL LAWHON

I Was Anastasia
Flight of Dreams
The Wife, the Maid, and the Mistress

Code Name Hélène

Code Name Hélène

A NOVEL

ARIEL LAWHON

ANCHOR BOOKS
A DIVISION OF PENGUIN RANDOM HOUSE LLC
NEW YORK

FIRST ANCHOR BOOKS EDITION, FEBRUARY 2021

The Library of Congress has cataloged the Doubleday edition as follows:
Names: Lawhon, Ariel, author.
Title: Code name Hélène : a novel / by Ariel Lawhon.
Description: First edition. | New York : Doubleday, 2020.
Identifiers: LCCN 2019025941 (print) | LCCN 2019025942 (ebook)
Subjects: LCSH: Wake, Nancy, 1912–2011—Fiction. World War, 1939–1945—Fiction. | GSAFD: Biographical fiction. Spy stories.
Classification: LCC PS3601.L447 C63 2020 (print) | LCC PS3601.L447 (ebook) | DDC 813/.6—dc23
LC record available at https://lccn.loc.gov/2019025941

Anchor Books Trade Paperback ISBN: 978-0-525-56549-9
eBook ISBN: 978-0-385-54469-6

Map of Nancy Wake's France by Mapping Specialists

www.anchorbooks.com

Printed in the United States of America
10 9 8 7 6 5 4 3 2 1

For:

My husband, Ashley. Forever. And for always.

Also,

Sally Burgess, who told me we could no longer be friends if I didn't write this story next.

And,

Elisabeth, who makes the dream come true. Every. Single. Time.

War is too important to be left to the generals.

—FRENCH PRIME MINISTER
GEORGES CLÉMENCEAU, 1917

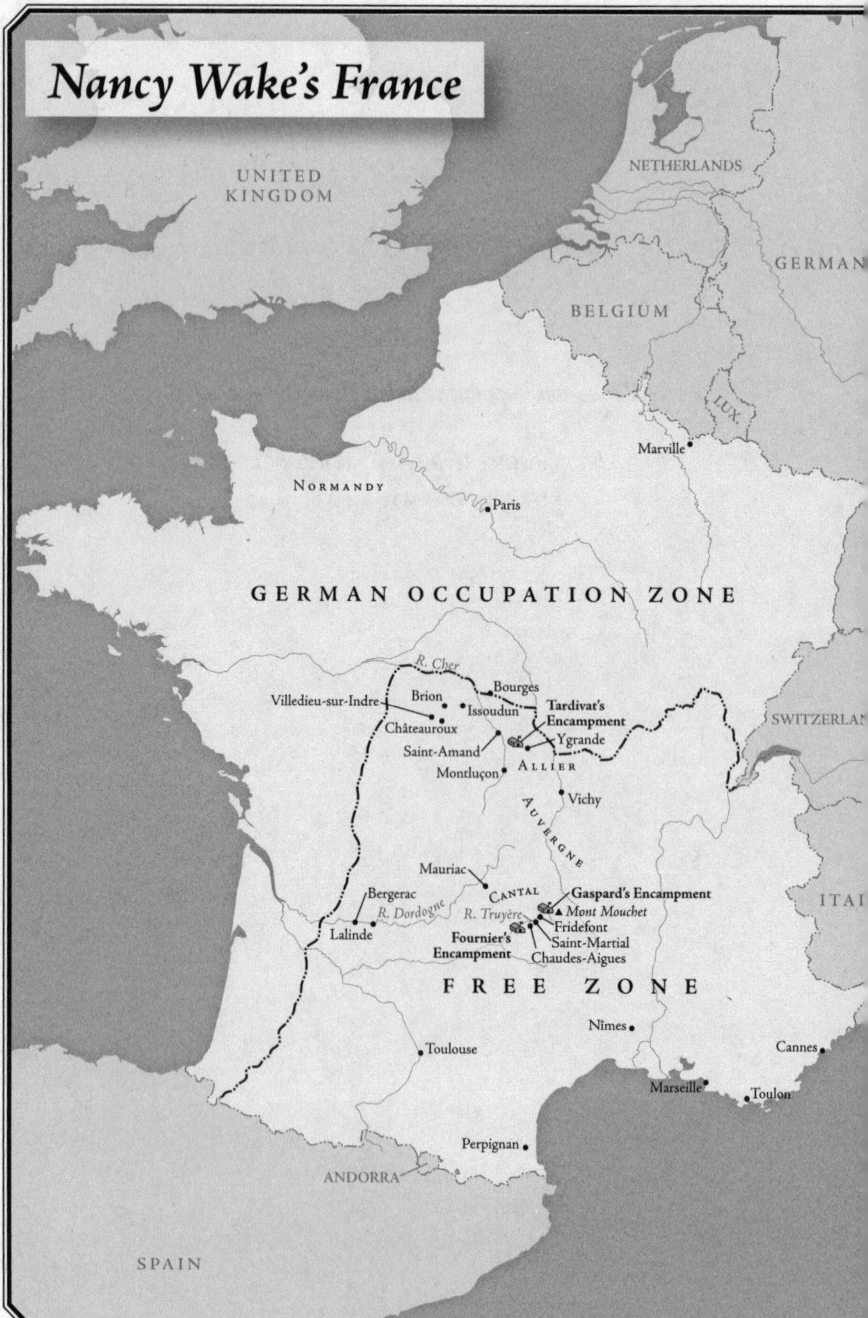

Nancy Wake's France
UNITED KINGDOM
NETHERLANDS
GERMAN
BELGIUM
LUX.
Marville
NORMANDY
Paris
GERMAN OCCUPATION ZONE
R. Cher
Bourges
Villedieu-sur-Indre
Brion
Issoudun
Tardivat's Encampment
Châteauroux
Saint-Amand
Ygrande
ALLIER
Montluçon
SWITZERLA
Vichy
AUVERGNE
Mauriac
CANTAL
Gaspard's Encampment
Mont Mouchet
Bergerac
R. Dordogne
R. Truyère
Fridefont
Lalinde
Fournier's Encampment
Saint-Martial
Chaudes-Aigues
ITA
FREE ZONE
Nîmes
Toulouse
Cannes
Marseille
Toulon
Perpignan
ANDORRA
SPAIN

NANCY GRACE AUGUSTA WAKE

Also Known As

the fighter

"Madame Andrée"

the smuggler

"Lucienne Carlier"

the spy

"Hélène"

the target

"The White Mouse"

PART ONE

Nancy Grace Augusta Wake

The power of a glance has been so much abused in love stories, that it has come to be disbelieved in. Few people dare now to say that two beings have fallen in love because they have looked at each other. Yet it is in this way that love begins, and in this way only.

—VICTOR HUGO, *LES MISÉRABLES*

Hélène

BENSON MILITARY AIRFIELD, ENGLAND

February 29, 1944

I have gone by many names.

Some of them are real—I was given four at birth alone—but most are carefully constructed personas to get me through checkpoints and across borders. They are lies scribbled on forged travel documents. Typed neatly in government files. Splashed across wanted posters. My identity is an ever-shifting thing that adapts to the need at hand.

Tonight, I am Hélène and I am going home.

It is February 29. Leap Day. The irony of this is not lost on me, because I am about to jump out of an aeroplane for the first time. I've only just been lifted into the belly of the Liberator bomber like a clumsily wrapped package. Me in slacks, blouse, and silk stockings beneath my coveralls, tin hat, and British army boots. The camel-haired coat and parachute pack don't do much to help the ensemble. But this isn't a fashion show and I'm not here to make friends, so I don't care that every man on this plane is looking at me as though I don't belong. Besides, I'm hungover. And I think I might throw up.

There are only four of us on this flight: an RAF pilot, a dispatcher, "Hubert"—my partner on this mission—and myself. A motley crew indeed. I settle into the jump seat across from Hubert and we watch with trepidation as the aperture in the floor closes. There's a grinding of gears and the clank of metal and then we're locked inside. I very much regret that third bottle of wine I shared with the boys last night. Headquarters delayed the mission by an entire day so we would have extra time to memorize key details of our cover story, which meant that, for the second night in a row, we raucously celebrated our looming departure and likely death. By the end of it we were singing "Blood on the Risers" at the top of our lungs, and now I can't get the stupid song out of my head.

"Gory, gory what a helluva way to die . . . ," I hum, only to find the pilot staring at me with a bemused grin. I shrug. It's the truth. This *would be* a helluva way to die. Too late now, though, because all four engines shudder to life with an angry bellow.

I begin counting as the plane rumbles across the aerodrome. Ten. Twenty. Thirty—good grief, when will this thing ever get off the ground?—forty. And then my stomach drops as we lurch into the air like a drunken seabird. The Liberator heaves and rumbles its way into the low-hanging clouds over the English countryside, sounding all the while as though someone has tossed a pound of bolts into a meat grinder.

Once we're through the clouds and the engines dim to a lesser roar, the dispatcher looks at me and shouts, "Witch?"

Under normal circumstances I would be offended, but Witch is my code name for this flight. I nod in the affirmative.

He turns back to his control panel and radios Command. "Witch on board"—a pause and then a glance at Hubert—"Pudding as well. Approximately two hours until the drop."

Poor guy, it's not his fault. He's not been given our real code names, much less our *actual* names. Need to know, etcetera, etcetera. I make a face at Hubert and he grins. We'd argued over which of us had the worse handle. Mine is sexist but his is stupid, so in the end we declared it a draw.

"At least the plane is heated," I say, but Hubert has settled into his jump seat, closed his eyes, and is trying to sleep. If he hears me he doesn't let on. Hubert is not what you'd call a conversationalist.

I grow queasier as the Liberator bounces ever higher and I'm trying to decide whether to throw up now or later, when the dispatcher drops into the jump seat next to me.

"You don't look like a witch. Is that really what they call you?" he asks.

"Sometimes they put a *b* in front."

He's American and Texan and therefore a gentleman, so it takes him a moment to realize this is a joke. "My momma would yank a knot in my throat if I used either word for a lady."

"Lucky for you I've rarely been accused of being a lady," I say with a wink, and I haven't been married so long that I don't enjoy watching him blush.

The dispatcher looks at me a bit closer, taking in my strange attire. "We ain't never dropped a woman before."

"We?"

He nods toward the pilot. "We make this run three or four times a week. But you're the first girl we've ever tossed out."

"Get used to it, Tex. There are about ten coming up behind me."

"Well, I hope you can do what the men haven't."

"Which is?"

"Get this war straightened out. I'd like to go home."

He returns to his radio and I try to find a comfortable position. Unfortunately there is no such thing as sleep when you're in the belly of a bomber rocking back and forth, trying not to puke. It's enough for me to swear off booze altogether. Well, maybe I'll just take a break. This is war, after all, and a girl has to find comfort where she can.

After several minutes of quietly willing my stomach to settle, something lands in my lap. I open my eyes and see a brown paper bag. Inside is a Spam sandwich.

Heaven help me.

I look up to find our pilot leaning halfway out of the cockpit, one hand on the yoke and the other extended toward me holding a canteen.

"Here!" he shouts. "Drink this. It will help."

"That's very kind, but—"

"Coffee is the best cure for airsickness," he says, and then, "Drink it. You look awful."

The truth is I feel several degrees worse than awful, so I unbuckle and scramble onto my knees to reach for the canteen. The pilot is big and sturdy. Deep, soulful eyes. I don't typically go for the mustached type, but his is nice. If I weren't hungover and married, I'd think him quite attractive. He offers me that same bemused smile, then returns to his duties when I've relieved him of the canteen and situated myself in the seat once again.

The coffee is hot and black, thick as tar. I take half of it slowly, like medicine, and then use the rest to wash down the sandwich. At least he has been generous with the mayonnaise. Only when I've finished, my stomach is settled, and my ears are no longer popping does it occur to me that he has sacrificed his dinner for my sake.

As I wipe the crumbs off my lap I notice that the dispatcher is staring at my outfit. I look ridiculous. I know that. But everything I need for the next six months has to be carried into France, on my person, tonight. And there is no way to accomplish that without appearing homeless. Or possibly deranged.

Finally, he shakes his head, perplexed, but I'm used to it. I have that effect on men. Across the way, Hubert is sound asleep, head lolled to the side, snoring. I'm not sure what he's wearing underneath his coveralls, but I'd bet it's nondescript and civilian. Perhaps not so expensive as mine, but Hubert isn't the flashy type. He errs on the side of Stoic Brit with a Stiff Upper Lip. But his French is excellent, which is why he's on this mission.

I don't exactly sleep but I do finally settle into the flight, and an hour later the dispatcher taps me on the shoulder.

"We're thirty minutes out from the airfield. But stay buckled. The descent will be bumpy."

"Turbulence?"

"Nah. The Germans like to send their greetings as we come in over the coast."

"Are you telling me that they will be shooting at us?"

"Yes, ma'am. But don't worry. We've done this a hundred times and we ain't been hit yet."

I am about to audibly curse Major Buckmaster for withholding this bit of information when the first deafening boom shatters the air above us. *Bumpy* is, in fact, not the right word at all for what we experience. I'd have gone for horrific. Gut-mangling. Possibly lethal. The Liberator is tossed around like an empty bean can by fire from the antiaircraft artillery below—the *ack-ack* guns, as our dispatcher calls them—and I wonder if perhaps my life as a saboteur won't come to an abrupt halt right here, fifteen thousand feet above French soil. My temples pound. My stomach clenches. And a fine sweat rises across my brow. However, my life remains intact and the only thing I lose is my dinner, right there on the floor of the aeroplane. Our pilot is none too pleased to see that I've returned his offering of coffee and Spam sandwich in considerably worse condition than he gave it to me. I'd extend him my sincerest apologies, but I'm too busy wiping my mouth on the sleeve of my coveralls. Hubert, awake now thanks to the gunfire, is shaking his head as though I've already failed my first important mission.

"Listen, if you don't want to do this we can take you back," the dispatcher says, eyeing the lumpy puddle near my feet.

"And go through all this nonsense again? The hell with that. Just get me to the drop point and let me off this bloody plane."

Before long, we leave the worst of the *ack-ack* fire behind and descend in a smooth, rapid glide over a dense forest. I see bonfires and a strange blinking light as the hour hand on my watch ticks over to one in the morning. It looks as though we're about to descend into the rim fires of hell, complete with a control tower to guide us in.

"What is that?" I ask, pointing out the window.

The dispatcher shrugs. "Could be your guys. Could be the Germans. We never really know for sure. And we don't stay to find out. The goal is not to get shot down, see?"

"Well, if it's not the Germans, they'll certainly see us coming. Someone has lit up the whole damn forest."

The SOE warned us that the Maquis are notoriously lax when it comes to security. But I never thought they'd announce our arrival by lighting up the drop zone like a carnival.

Hubert is on his feet, calmly attaching the static line of his parachute to the drop line connected to the plane. There's no room in the drop zone for both of us to land safely at once, so he's to go first.

We barrel toward a clearing atop a nearby hill, flying a mere four hundred feet above the treetops. The ground is alarmingly close and I begin to ponder any number of things, rational and otherwise:

whether I'll accidentally shoot myself with the revolvers tucked into each pocket of my slacks when I land, how well they packed my chute back at headquarters, what Henri is doing right now, whether I've brought enough supplies to get me through my next menstrual cycle, whether Picon misses me, whether the expensive brassiere I'm wearing will last until the end of my mission, what to do about the blister forming on the side of my big toe. I go over the memorized list of railway junctions, bridges, underground cables, and fuel depots that must be destroyed, the addresses of safe houses along with contacts and passwords, and the names of every Resistance leader known to London. There is far more hidden inside my brain than in my backpack or purse. Thus, the cyanide pill tucked inside the second button on the cuff of my left sleeve. I wonder, fleetingly, if I'll be forced to use that pill and what cyanide tastes like.

"T-minus sixty seconds," the dispatcher shouts toward the cockpit, and our pilot gives him the thumbs-up, then pulls a long red lever to his right. The aperture, ten feet from where I'm sitting, begins to lower with a whine and cold air rushes into the Liberator, pulling the breath from my lungs. I am thankful, once again, for my ridiculous, heavy coat.

When the hatch is fully open, the dispatcher turns to us and begins counting down. "Twenty seconds!"

I watch Hubert stand at the open hatch with the utmost calm. He is a soldier after all. Air jumps are nothing new to him. Whereas I've done only the one, back in London, and that was from a hot-air balloon.

"Ten seconds!"

Hubert squats, arms spread as though he's about to jump over a hedge. He tugs on the drop line once to make sure it's secured to his chute.

And then the countdown comes so quickly I can barely catch the words. "Five, four, three, two, one. *Jump!*"

Hubert is gone into the night and a second later the drop line goes taut. His chute has deployed, and I watch it inflate like a balloon beneath us. The dispatcher is staring at me in disbelief. "Why are you just sitting there? Go!"

"Wait!"

"No time! He's out. You gotta go!"

I raise one palm and shove it toward his face while I unbuckle myself with my other hand. He's muttering profanities as I unzip my purse and dig through the contents, looking for my tube of Lizzie Arden lipstick. For once, I'm not concerned about my forged travel documents or the one million French francs neatly stacked inside. Nor do I double-check that I still have the list of targets that must, no matter what, be distributed once the Allied forces land in France. I am frantic to find that slender tube of courage. Victory Red. The color of war and confidence and freedom. Finally, my pinkie brushes against the cool, familiar metal and I pluck it from my purse along with the silver compact Buckmaster gave me as a parting gift. We've now passed the drop zone and the Liberator turns back around in a lazy, rumbling circle, but I meticulously apply the lipstick.

"What on earth are you doing?" the dispatcher shouts.

"Putting on my armor."

And suddenly I am calm. Collected. I feel like myself once again. I doubt our dispatcher will sign up to drop any more women into war zones, because he looks positively apoplectic as I stand, slide the lipstick and compact back into my purse, smack my lips, and then tuck the purse into my coveralls and belt my coat.

"Hey, Tex, has anyone ever refused to jump?" I ask.

Try as he might, he cannot hide his grin. "Just one guy. Sat down and buckled himself back in as soon as the hatch opened. Didn't say a word to us the entire flight home."

"Figures." I step toward the aperture, attach my rip cord to the drop line, and check it just as Hubert did. "Thanks for the ride."

The drop zone is in view once more. God knows where Hubert is down there, so I stand at the edge of the aperture and try to summon my courage. It is not normal to throw oneself from hurtling pieces of machinery. It goes against mankind's most basic instinct to survive. But I have trained for this—have known it was coming—for months. Besides, my husband is down there, somewhere, and I cannot get to him unless I leap. In the end that is where I find my fortitude, the thought of Henri, waiting for me. And now there is no time left for hesitation, so I give the dispatcher a nod, take a long breath through my nose, and remember what our instructor said: elbows in, legs together. Then I step out of the plane and into the dead of night.

This is nothing like jumping from a balloon. The Liberator is gone with one last angry roar, and I am greeted not by silence, as before, but by a cacophonous whoosh of air. The ground hurtles toward me and my rip cord catches on the drop line. There is a violent jerk followed by a rib-crushing tug, and I huff out a strangled breath as the straps of my parachute pack snap tight across my chest. My legs swing out in front of me like those of a dangling marionette. Then I surge upward for a split second as the oblong silver parachute flares out, slowing my descent. Only then am I engulfed by total silence, but I have no time to appreciate it because the treetops are less than fifty feet away. I plunge toward a thick copse of trees, their dark, bare, scraggly branches reaching toward me like the hands of gathered skeletons. I pull, hard, on my right steering line and my legs swing away as the parachute turns, but I'm dropping too fast to avoid the trees altogether. The left corner of my chute catches on the farthest limb of a giant oak—as though it has plucked me from the sky with the tip of its bony finger—and I am yanked tighter into my harness. The sound I make is neither intelligible nor ladylike. And then I am swinging eight feet above the forest floor, trying to catch my breath, trying to find my bearings, as my lines untwist and I rotate in a lazy circle. North. South. East. West. Impossible to determine at this time of night. I force myself to wait, to dangle quietly beneath the tree. I can make this drop to the ground if I'm careful, so I yank the metal loop on my straps. Nothing. I try again. Gah! The release mechanism is locked. I have no more success on the next three tries, so I'm hanging there, trying to figure out how I'll reach the knife strapped to my garter belt—hidden beneath coat, jumpsuit, and slacks—when I see the red glow of a burning cigarette in the shadows directly beneath me. Once I catch my breath, I can smell the tangy scent of burning tobacco. I hear two heavy footsteps as someone moves forward.

"I hope all the trees in France bear such beautiful fruit this year," says a deep, male voice in French.

The weapons of warfare are different for women. Rarely do we have the luxury of bullets and bombs. Our tools are benign. Silk stockings and red lipstick. Laughter. Cunning. The ability to curse in foreign languages and make eye contact without trembling. But the most effective weapon by far, I believe, is charm.

So I laugh at him, then reply easily in his own language. "Enough of that French bullshit. Cut me down."

I am grateful beyond words to hear him return the laughter. "Hubert warned me about your tongue."

"Did he?"

"*Oui.* He said it was harsh enough to strip paint."

He's found Hubert then. Friend, not foe. Or so I hope. One can't ever really be sure these days. The Frenchman is roughly my height, very handsome, and quite thin. Though that could be due to the Occupation Diet and not a genetic disposition. Regardless, he shimmies up the tree in a pair of worn slacks and a collared shirt, then out onto the branch above me with a small knife clenched between his teeth. Nothing about the way he's dressed or how he moves gives any hint of his identity. He could be a German sympathizer about to slit my throat, for all I know.

"Ready?" he asks, setting the knife against the rope attached to my release mechanism.

"Yes."

Three quick saws and I drop to the ground with bent knees. My boots sink into the thick mulch that covers the forest floor, but I am unharmed. The Frenchman is still up in the tree, tugging at my chute, while I slip out of my harness, hat, coat, and coveralls. He finally pulls it free and lets it float to the ground. I am cold, I can see my breath curling into the air before me, but I refuse to shiver or put on my coat.

"Do you have a shovel?" I ask, staring up at him.

He looks at me as though I've asked for an engagement ring. "Why?"

"To bury the chute." I hold up the harness I've just shed. "And this."

He drops smoothly to the ground beside me, folds his knife, tucks it into his pocket, then takes his sweet time lighting another cigarette. "We aren't going to bury it."

"I was given strict instructions—"

"Fabric this soft? This sheer?" He gives me one of those looks his countrymen are famous for and caresses my parachute. "You'll want it later. Trust me."

I suppose I could try to yank the giant sheet of nylon from his hands, but it would only make noise and we haven't exactly been quiet thus far. I watch him fold it instead. Only once it has been tucked under his arm does this strange little Frenchman finally take the time to study me. He looks me over, from red lips to shoulder-length black hair; from expensive coat—now folded and draped over one arm—to the Louis Vuitton purse dangling in the crook of an elbow. He moves on to the buttons that run down the front of my blouse, then to my slacks, his gaze finally lingering on my feet.

Then his gaze returns to my eyes. "How did you, of all people, come to be here?"

I offer him my very best smile. The one meant to disarm, because I am not yet fully convinced that Hubert isn't somewhere on the other side of the hedgerow with his throat cut and this man part of the Milice.

"Now, *that*," I say, "is a very long story."

Nancy Grace Augusta Wake

Eight Years Earlier

THE PONT ROYAL, PARIS

1936

The French are better at day drinking. Likely because they've had more practice, but I'm determined to learn. It's a good thing Stephanie is already waiting for me at the Pont Royal. I can see her on the terrace at our usual table, arm draped over the ornate railing, a long-stemmed goblet held between two slim fingers.

I rush across the street and into the bar only to find it crowded with the usual clientele: packs of tweed-suited Gallimards. The Pont Royal is best known for catering to the editors who work at Éditions Gallimard and journalists from all the daily papers. It's an excellent place to make connections and a better place to eavesdrop. Not yet three o'clock in the afternoon and every single one of these men is halfway through a glass of cognac, ashtrays spilling over. They all sport the sloppy smiles of men who have knocked off work early to talk shop away from the office. I weave my way through the tables, pushing through clouds of cigar smoke, and out onto the terrace.

There is an empty goblet on the table, along with the one in Stephanie's hand, and I marvel that she has already gone through a round of cocktails in the thirty minutes it's taken me to walk from my little flat on rue Sainte-Anne.

"Sorry I'm late." I drop into my chair and balance a large handbag on my lap. I look around the terrace, noting that, for once, she has not delivered on a promise. "Where is he?" I ask.

"On his way."

Stephanie leans across the table to brush a light kiss against each of my cheeks. Born in Paris to Yugoslavian parents, she is both quintessentially French and curiously exotic. Although married to a Spaniard, she maintains her maiden name. This is a point of honor for her, a Rubicon that shall not be crossed, a stake driven so far in the ground that it can never be uprooted. Naturally, I take great joy in provoking her.

"*Bonjour,* Madame Gonzales."

Stephanie raises the goblet to her lips. It's filled with amber liquid, and a curl of sugared lemon peel dangles from the rim. She glares at me while taking a calculated sip, then spits out her maiden name, along with a lemon seed. *"Marsic."*

Only then do I notice that she is drinking an Earthquake, far and away her preferred cocktail, and a potent one at that. Clearly, I have catching up to do.

The terrace is packed, and I crane my neck, searching for the waiter. It isn't until I wave him down that I notice half the men sitting around us are staring at Stephanie. No surprise there. She is undoubtedly beautiful, but in the Slavic way, with almond-shaped blue eyes the color of hydrangeas, and wavy blond hair. But it's her smile that she charms them with. Poor fools. She'll have them picking up our entire tab by the time we leave.

"I cannot believe you had this much liquor on an empty stomach," I say, envious. I'm a two-pot screamer myself, helplessly sloshed after the second drink.

"I was nervous."

"I have known you for three years and never once have I seen you nervous about anything."

"Not for myself." She rolls her eyes. "For you. For the interview. It is important, *non*? And besides, you were late."

I nod meaningfully toward my handbag. "I would have been here sooner, but I fell madly in love on the way over and decided that I had to have it at once." The purchase was very spontaneous, *très*

Parisien, and I am both shocked at myself and flush with excitement. "Regardless, you're the only person I know who calms rattled nerves with an *Earthquake.*"

"This drink is a balm to the soul," she says, running the pad of one finger along the curled lemon peel on the rim of her glass. "That stupid English name doesn't do it justice. Say it in French. With proper pronunciation."

I wouldn't know a lick of French if not for Stephanie. Nor would I know how to wear a scarf, smoke a Gitane, drink cognac, or wear red lipstick. She is my tutor in the pursuit of becoming a Parisienne, and I am her devoted student.

"Fine. *Tremblement de Terre.*" I can hear the slight twang in my voice, the Australian accent I've worked so hard to hide, but it's passable. A stranger on the street would understand what I've said.

"Much better, *ma petite.*" Stephanie claps her hands as though I'm a child in need of encouragement. "You are coming along nicely."

"I'm learning the key is not to bother with all those bloody feminine and masculine rules of yours—all the *le* this and *la* that—it just gives me the shits."

I wait patiently for her to laugh or reply, but she is transfixed by something on my lap. "Nancy," she says, "why is your handbag moving on its own?"

"Oh!"

"Please tell me that is not a dog," she says as I lift the tiny, wire-haired terrier from my purse. His ears are pointed, his hair is white, his eyes are black, and his tongue is pink. He bears a startling resemblance to a cartoon. Or a coin purse.

"His name is Picon," I say, setting one hand to my heart, "and I believe he will be the great love of my life."

The little dog licks my wrist as though to confirm the sentiment.

Stephanie is aghast. "Why was he in your purse?"

"Because he wouldn't fit in my pocket."

"What I mean to say is, *why* have you brought him with you?"

"Well, he's hungry, for one thing. And I couldn't very well leave him at home. Besides, I only bought him half an hour ago." I lift the ball of puffy white hair—hardly bigger than my hand—and nuzzle him into the crook of my neck. "I had the strangest sensation while crossing over the rue de Rivoli a little while ago, as though someone was watching me. I turned and there he was, in the window of that little shop between the cobbler and the chocolatier—you know, where the street dips down and the puddles collect after every rain? It was love at first sight. He feels it too. I can see it in his eyes."

"Put it down. It's going to *pisse* on you."

"Picon would never!"

"Picon?" Stephanie says. "As in the aperitif?"

"Exactly so. And one day I will get him a wife and I will name her Grenadine and they will live happily all of their days."

Stephanie presses her lips together, trying not to laugh, so I do it for her. My laughter has always been sudden and combustible and loud. She shakes her head at the sound. Stephanie takes my laugh quite personally, as though I invented it to threaten her own staggering appeal. Yes, she's married—to a man we call Count Gonzales, though none of us actually know his first name—but it only makes her more attractive somehow. Unattainable. Men hardly *look* at me when she's in the room. So I won't apologize for any advantage I can get.

"What?"

"It's not fair, you know, that laugh of yours. I'd give anything for it. And see! It's already earned you an admirer." She motions behind me with a tilt of her chin and there's a brief flash of something in her eyes—mischief, or jealousy, perhaps—but it's gone before I can identify it.

At first, I think she means one of those ridiculous, uptight Gallimards, so I turn to stare him down. But instead of an angry editor I find a handsome man with a crooked smile. He's sitting at the far end of the terrace, at a table by himself, wineglass in hand, and he is staring at *me*.

"Oh, good grief, don't *look*. Have I taught you *nothing*?"

But it's too late. This curious man has seen me. So I tip my head to the side, brazenly meeting his gaze.

"That is Henri Fiocca," Stephanie says, "the most notorious heartbreaker in all of France."

"Not just Paris? But *all* of France? That's quite an accomplishment." I laugh again, louder, and his eyes tighten with curiosity. "He's too pretty to be a journalist," I say, turning back to Stephanie.

"He's not."

"What then? A model? An actor? Minor royalty like your husband?"

"He's an industrialist."

I scratch Picon between the ears. "Which could mean anything from canned goods to the opium trade."

"He's in shipbuilding."

"Sounds boring."

"I think the word you're looking for is *lucrative*."

"And you know this how?"

"He does business with the Count. And I hear stories." This is how she always refers to her husband—*the Count*—never by his actual name. With pride yes, but never intimacy.

"Mr. Fiocca is very beautiful."

"*Oui.* But he is trouble."

In all the time I've known Stephanie she has never warned me off a man, and I find this quite suspicious. I'm about to ask what she means when the waiter finally arrives at our table.

"Qu'est-ce-que je peux vous servir?"

It takes a moment, but I answer in somewhat broken French, *"Vin rouge et une . . . ah . . . planche de charcuterie."* I give Stephanie a questioning glance to make sure I've gotten my order correct. She nods, pleased with her tutelage.

"Anything else?" the waiter asks, in English now, to accommodate my broken French. He grins at Stephanie. "Madame?"

"A friend will be joining us soon," Stephanie says, motioning to the empty seat beside her. "He will have a glass of Château Barthès Rosé." She smiles at the waiter and I fear he will drop to one knee and propose on the spot. The poor man stumbles away in a daze.

"How did you find him?" I ask. "Every journalist in the city has been looking for him since Milo ran that picture. Hell, how did you even learn his name?"

Two weeks ago, my editor at Hearst published a photograph of an unknown man on his knees, face turned to the sky, bleeding onto the cobblestones of Vienna's Old Square. The headline screamed: *Terror in Vienna!* And every journalist in the city has been scrambling for an exclusive ever since. Stephanie claims to have acquired it for me.

She shrugs. "The Count has connections."

It answers nothing, and I am about to press her but—damn him—our waiter is back, in record time, stepping between us. He holds a tray in one hand and makes a show of arranging everything on the table before offering a small bow and disappearing.

The delicate scent of fresh bread, fine cheese, and cured meat wafts up from the table. This is a thing, I have found, that is present only in France. The food smells *different* here. It is *pervasive.* And it makes me wonder if I've ever truly smelled my food before. Little Picon, who has been still and quiet in the crook of my arm, begins to squirm and whine, so I pluck a small piece of shaved ham from the platter and feed it to him with my fingers.

Stephanie grimaces. This is the one area in which she defers to her Yugoslavian heritage. The woman cannot stand the French habit of taking pets in public. "That is disgusting," she says.

"He's hungry."

"Then put it down and let it eat off the floor. Like a proper dog."

I open my mouth to protest, but a champagne glass magically appears on the table in front of me.

"What is this?" A different waiter stands beside me dutifully.

"Le soixante-quinze," he says, "courtesy of that gentleman in the corner."

The French 75. It is the Pont Royal's signature cocktail and the most expensive item on their drinks menu. I have always wanted to try one.

Clever man. This drink is an invitation—and an elegant one at that. Much as I sensed Picon this afternoon, I can feel Henri Fiocca staring at me. I lift the champagne glass and turn to consider him again. I take a sip. My mouth is instantly awash in the bright notes of gin, lemon, and champagne. Expensive. Top-shelf. Henri Fiocca is showing off. The bubbles tickle my nose and I cannot help but smile.

"Tell me about him," I say to Stephanie without taking my eyes off this graceful stranger.

She obliges. "*Français.* Obviously. A good bit older than you, I think. Don't let that alarm you. The best ones are always older. Comes from a wealthy family from Marseille. Notorious with the women."

She recites this curriculum vitae even as I take another appreciative sip. He has dark, curly hair, brown eyes, a square jaw, and the sort of cheekbones that could make a girl weep with envy. Broad shoulders. He's sitting down so I can't tell for sure, but I suspect he's quite tall. Taller than me, at least, and this definitely works in his favor. I absolutely hate having to wear flats just because a man didn't have the good sense to grow a few inches taller.

Fiocca stares back, waiting. Hopeful. *Patient.* And this surprises me, because at first glance I would have taken him for the sort of man who likes to pounce. But no, he's letting me decide. And I am so very tempted. One more sip and I close my eyes to relish the swirling citrus fizz on my tongue. I am about to stand and make my way to Fiocca's table, when Stephanie demands my attention.

"Nancy," she says, and there is a note of urgency in her voice that has me turning back to her.

"What?"

She's staring at the door that leads onto the terrace. And—ha!—there's no mistaking the man who stands there. The Count has convinced him to come after all. What part Stephanie herself played is still unclear. She could have convinced or seduced, blackmailed or charmed, for all I know. There's no telling with this ridiculous miracle-working woman.

"He's here," she breathes, as though she can't quite believe it herself.

Janos Lieberman certainly knows how to make an entrance. Or perhaps it is that he, himself, is so striking he commands attention. Janos doesn't have a unique face, per se. He's pleasant-looking but not remarkable. Dark hair. Dark eyes. Dark stubble across his solemn face. It's the jagged pink scar cutting its way from earlobe to eyeball that makes him instantly recognizable. The whip split him clean to the bone and nearly took out his left eye in the process. Even from this distance the stitch marks are still evident, little pocked craters at even intervals along his cheekbone. The scar looks like a broken zipper, and he will be forever marked by its ferocity. You cannot help but stare when you see him.

Stephanie is on her feet, halfway to the door before I can collect my wits. And then she's greeting him, kissing both cheeks, and leading him back to the table before the Gallimards can pounce.

This is the man I have come to meet, not Henri Fiocca—appealing as he may be—so I turn back to the Frenchman and tip up my glass, downing the rest of this glorious French 75 in three luxurious gulps. I give him a polite nod of gratitude and dismissal.

Henri Fiocca raises an eyebrow, then offers a sigh of disappointment. His shoulders drop, and I find this both amusing and sad. Such a pity. I turn back to the table, where Stephanie and our guest now stand before me. This is important. I give them my full attention.

"Nancy," she says, practically quivering with excitement, "meet Janos Lieberman."

He extends his hand and I receive it gladly. It's an enormous hand, dry and callused and oddly cool despite the warm afternoon. "Thank you for coming," I say.

Janos takes his seat but says nothing.

"Don't worry, I warned him about you." Stephanie gives me that smile, the one that could be an apology or a declaration of war. Then she hands him the glass of rosé. "Here, I took the liberty of ordering you some wine."

It's an interesting choice of drink for a man, but not without calculation on Stephanie's part. Men are particular about their liquor. And most people have a strong preference between red or white wine. Rosé in late afternoon is the easiest, safest thing to order for a total stranger.

He takes it without question. "Thank you."

Stephanie situates herself between the Gallimards and our guest. She's trying to block their view, to prevent them from studying his scar, but half the men on this terrace have recognized him already. There is a buzz in the air. They know he isn't just one of the countless Austrians who have spilled across the border into France this year, but rather the face of Vienna's persecution epidemic.

Hearst insists that, in my articles, I refer to men like Janos as "political refugees," but the truth is they are Jews, running scared. This one in particular. He's got that hunted look in his eyes. Clothes wrinkled from wear. Cuticles picked raw. He needs a shave. Hell, he needs a *friend.* It was Janos who insisted we meet in a public place, after all, and I can't say that I blame him. But I can tell by the way his hands are shaking that he is afraid to talk. The Gallimards know it too. Some are wide-eyed with interest. Others show thinly veiled disgust or horror. Many try to hide their animosity behind pursed lips and lit cigars. It's no wonder. Janos has chosen to share his story with me, and they have reason to envy that fact.

"They recognize me from that damn photograph," Janos says, his Austrian accent heavy, as he glances around the terrace. He sets a hand self-consciously against his left cheek. I expect him to wince at the touch, but he doesn't.

Janos lifts his glass from the table and I watch his Adam's apple bob up and down as he takes a sip of the wine. It makes him look vulnerable. Exposed. Like a teenage boy trying to be braver than he is. After a moment he shakes his head. "This was a mistake. I shouldn't have come."

And just like that, I can feel my story slipping away. I do the first thing that comes to mind. "Look at me," I tell him.

He does.

I set the pad of my index finger against his scar. My touch is curious, not seductive, like a doctor examining a wound, and I hold his gaze the entire time. "Who did this to you?"

"The Brownshirts."

"And who took that photograph?"

Janos shudders, as though the piece inside him that holds everything together has broken loose. "It doesn't matter. He's dead now."

Instinctively I lean toward this opening that he has created. Here is my story and I am determined to catch it as it falls from his lips. I can see him filling his lungs, gathering courage, and I do not turn away, not as he braces himself, not even when one of the Gallimards makes a crude remark behind me.

"Please," I say. "Tell me what happened in Vienna."

* * *

Henri

Damn.

He likes the way she laughs.

He likes the rest as well, but it's her laugh that has him standing with one foot in the street and one foot on the curb, staring at the terrace, where she sits with her friends. No one could blame him for waiting an hour longer, hoping she would change her mind and accept his company after all. Henri waited until he felt like a fool and then he decided to leave. But now she's at it again, head tilted back, eyes squeezed shut, palm flat against her heart, that little dog in her lap, laughing as though she has an endless supply, as though laughter is a thing that can be wasted, scattered wantonly in the street. It fills the air—rich and lusty—and he'd go back in and buy her another drink if he thought it would do any good. But no. He offered, and she declined. He likes to think she was a bit sad about it, however. Perhaps he flatters himself. Still, Henri hesitates, and she must sense it, because that beguiling woman turns and finds him lingering here at the corner.

He nods once, embarrassed.

She smiles, again, and in the moment before she turns back to her friends, those pale mischievous eyes tighten at the corners and he sees something flash in them.

Curiosity.

But a blink is all it takes to break the connection, and just like that his opportunity is lost. She looks away and he leaves for good.

Damn.

* * *

VIENNA

St. Stephen's Square

"What are we looking for?" Frank Gilmore asks as we make our way through a tangle of vehicles that have stopped outside Vienna's famed St. Stephen's Square. I look up, toward the great, Gothic towers of the Stephansdom, and I push forward, intent. Janos said it happened near this cathedral, the very place where Mozart and many of the Hapsburgs were married. Such a violent act for a holy place.

"A man with a whip," I say over my shoulder.

His legs are longer than mine and he catches up quickly. "Nancy, are you sure—"

"It was a long train ride, Frank. If you wanted to back out, you should have done it twelve hours ago."

"And miss the chance for a romantic getaway with Nancy Wake? Never!"

I snort. "This isn't a date."

"It could be." There's laughter in Frank's eyes when he winks at me. "I am an equal-opportunity romantic."

"I believe the word you're looking for is *incorrigible*."

Long-limbed. Freckled. Toothy. Hair the color of old potatoes. Frank Gilmore is a caricature of himself. The combination of his physical attributes makes you think he should have been a redhead but swam the wrong direction in the gene pool. I've always suspected he's a bit disappointed about this. I think he would have worn that ginger badge with honor. Regardless, Frank is one of the best photographers in Paris. I brought him because he's fearless. Rumor has it he once hung upside down from the girders of the Pont de Passy just to get a picture of King George as he sailed beneath on his royal yacht, the *Britannia*. Turns out George was napping under a canopy and all you could see in the photo were his swollen feet. It was never published, but Frank became a legend. The print now hangs above the toilet in his flat. Frank says it makes him laugh every time he uses the loo. It's one of the many reasons I find him endearing.

Like me, Frank is a freelancer. And if I've learned anything since bluffing my way onto the roster at Hearst, it's that we carrion birds of the publishing world must flock together. He didn't hesitate when I called him yesterday and proposed this adventure.

After a few minutes of weaving our way through traffic and onlookers, Frank and I make it to Vienna's Old Square. There's a huge crowd of people standing in a circle before the Stephansdom and somewhere, in the middle of it, a woman is screaming.

I look at Frank and he nods. He lifts the camera from where it hangs on a strap around his neck and slips into the crowd on my right.

I am average height and average weight, but still, it takes me a long time to push my way through the wall of bodies to see what's going on. I'm not the sort of woman you'd call angular, but I do have sharp elbows and I put them to good use as I maneuver my way into the open. I am struck by three things at once.

The bonfire.

The Brownshirts.

And the waterwheel.

The fire burns right in the middle of the square, fifty feet from the cathedral steps, filling the air with rancid smoke and turning the ancient cobblestones black. Around it saunter seven Brownshirts holding rifles. Two more Brownshirts heap contents from one of the nearby shops onto the fire. They are the *Sturmabteilung,* Hitler's private military, the men he brought with him to power, the men who answer to him alone. And here they are, just as Janos said, tormenting Vienna's Jewish shopkeepers.

No, not tormenting.

Torturing.

An old woman is tied spread-eagle to the massive waterwheel. It rattles and clanks through the square in a large, undulating circle, pushed along on each side by a Brownshirt. They turn her round and round as she cries and screams. Her long salt-and-pepper braids swish back and forth across her shoulders as her shawl drags on the ground beside her. I am ashamed to admit that I had not believed Janos. Not truly. His story seemed so outrageous, so unbelievable, two nights ago at the Pont Royal.

He must have known how hard it would be for someone like me to truly understand. And I think he must have pitied my ignorance as we sat there warm and fed and content. To me this was a story to pursue. But to Janos it was a nightmare to escape.

"Go to Vienna's Old Square on a Friday afternoon," he said.

"They like to begin their spectacles a few hours before Shabbat begins. It gets worse every week."

Finally, the waterwheel rolls to a stop and I am frozen, immobile, as a Brownshirt steps forward. He looks like the sort of man who was laughed at as a child, teased mercilessly, as though he's been assembled with spare parts and put together in haste. Large head on narrow shoulders. Sparse hair combed away from a high forehead. Eyebrows so thick and black it looks as though they've been drawn in charcoal by a child's clumsy hand. Lipless mouth. Sunken eyes with dark circles beneath. Huge ears with long lobes that slide right into the sides of his neck. The rest of him is hidden beneath that brown uniform and those tall brown boots, so I cannot guess at his height or strength. But in his hand there is a whip, and I know that this is the man I have come to find.

He walks toward the waterwheel and the woman tied to it. I expect there to be some speech, some bit of pomp and circumstance. A warning, at least. But no, he simply attacks. I hear the whip before I see the strike. There is a single crack, like the sound of breaking rock, and then a red stripe opens across the old woman's back, splitting her dress diagonally, splitting the air with her screams.

The man has found his rhythm now and he strikes again. Then again. And again.

Crack.

Crack.

Crack.

Four red lashes across her back. There is a rushing in my ears and a rising in my stomach. I don't know what to do. I stand in silent, horrified witness along with every other person in the square. Two Brownshirts still hold the wheel upright but the others pace in front of the crowd, rifles up and ready, waiting, hoping someone will intervene. They are eager for an opportunity to shoot.

The man with the whip begins to shout, cracking the air with emphasis. *"Juden Verboten! Juden Verboten! Juden Verboten!"*

Jews forbidden.

Jews forbidden.

Jews forbidden.

There's a sharp intake of breath beside me but I do not turn to look. I force myself to be still, to listen instead. And I hear the truth. Most of the shopkeepers in this square are Jewish. They will all be driven out, or worse. They are not welcome. This fact is written across the square, in red paint, now that I have the eyes to see it, now that I look beyond that wheel. Over half the shop windows are dripping with red paint, *Juden* daubed on them in a sloppy, hateful scrawl.

The two soldiers beside the wheel make one last half rotation, leaving the woman upside down, panting heavily, body stiff, braced for another blow. Her dress has fallen down around her waist, and her bunched, torn undergarments are on display before the crowd. It is not enough that they have wounded her, they intend to shame her as well. We can all see the pale skin of her thighs, the trembling of her muscles, and the blue, corded veins that are knotted in bunches at the back of her knees.

"Juden Verboten," the man says, loudly, clearly one last time.

"Who is that?" I ask the shopkeeper beside me, not taking my eyes from the Brownshirt in charge. I pray this stranger speaks enough English to understand me, and I make a mental note to brush up on basic German.

"Obersturmführer Wolff."

"Obersturmführer?" The Germanic languages are a mystery to me, all hard edges and rough grunts. I don't know what this word means.

He spits onto the cobblestones. "Nazi."

Oh. *Oh.*

Slowly, carefully, I pull my notepad and pen from my skirt pocket and begin writing. It's the only thing I can do. I write because I am afraid I will forget the specifics, remembering only the horror. I write details. Brownshirts. Whips. Waterwheels. I write about red paint and red welts. I write names and ranks the best I can remember and spell them. I write without ever looking at my notepad because that is too conspicuous. I let my hand travel messily across the page, searching for Frank, praying he has captured this on film. I scan each face, looking for his close-cropped potato head.

The square is now still, and that's what reveals Frank in the end.

But not just to me. The man they call Wolff hears the shutter of Frank's camera at the same moment I do. It's an unmistakable sound in this deathly quiet air. Frank, trying to get one last photo.

Chunk. Click.

It is the sound of proof being exposed, and Wolff's large, round head follows the telltale noise to the doorway of an empty storefront where Frank has taken refuge. He is squatting on the threshold to get a better angle, his entire body leaning forward. He is the last person to realize that Wolff has seen him, and all I can think about is how Janos said the man who took his picture is dead.

Frank's name is rising in my chest, hurtling toward my lips, when he finally lowers the camera. He scrambles to his feet, lips moving frantically as though running through his options. Fight. Flight. Faint.

Wolff drops his hand to his side and unfurls the whip. He lets it drag behind him on the ground like the tail of a rat as he walks toward Frank. I might not be romantically interested in him, but I've never respected Frank more than I do in this moment because he does not flinch. Does not run or make a fist or lose his nerve. He grips the camera in two hands and holds it tight against his chest like a shield. Back straight, jaw clenched, lip curled in defiance.

Frank waits.

I can almost see him counting off Wolff's footsteps in the seconds it takes for them to come face-to-face. No words are exchanged. No threats. No violence. Wolff simply looks Frank up and down. Notes the pale shade of his skin and the freckles strewn about his face like ink on parchment. And Wolff makes a decision about the worth of this one man's life. The scales weigh in Frank's favor, apparently, because Wolff reaches out with his free hand and grabs the camera.

Frank grips it tighter, his knuckles turning white as he strains to hold on. *No.* His entire body screams the word, resisting.

Wolff raises the whip.

And I see it there in Frank's eyes, the calculation. He cannot retain his grip on the camera and block the whip at the same time. He must choose. Wolff yanks again, and the camera is ripped out of Frank's hands. It's like an appendage being rent from his body. A violent separation.

A serpentine invasion of the soul. Hatred. Pure and holy *hatred.* That's what I feel as I watch Wolff turn from Frank without ever speaking a word and strut toward the bonfire, those tall brown boots clipping against the uneven stones of the Stephansplatz. He lifts the camera and turns before the crowd, as though displaying a piece of evidence before a jury. He shows it, slowly, to every pair of watching eyes. And then he hurls it to the ground with all his strength.

Frank's camera shatters on contact and fills the square with the sound of cracking metal and breaking glass. Wolff bends down and pulls the long ribbon of film from its compartment, exposing it to the light. He tosses the film onto the fire, where it curls in on itself like burnt hair, then kicks each remaining piece into the coals.

"Nein Kameras," Wolff shouts, one long spindly finger pointing at the bonfire.

I'm so busy watching the camera burn, breathless, that I don't even notice one of the Brownshirts approach me. I don't pay any attention as he reaches out and yanks the notepad from my hands. One moment it's there and the next I'm left with three long paper cuts against the index finger of my left hand. I feel the sting first and the rage second.

Frank, however, has seen this, and he has forgotten his camera, his outrage, and is rushing toward me. He knows me well. And it's a good thing too, because I'm filling my lungs. I'm stepping forward. I'm reaching for the notebook. And then I am engulfed entirely in the wiry arms of Frank Gilmore. He looks to be all tendon and bone, but Frank is built like a steel cable. Once wrapped around me, he is immovable.

"Don't," he hisses in my ear. "It's not worth the whip."

I struggle against the surprising strength of his grasp. I want my notebook. I want revenge. But Frank is right. Wolff will not spare me simply because I'm a woman. Today's demonstration is proof of that.

Frank's voice drops to a whisper, barely audible, in my left ear. "You never forget a damn thing, Nancy," he says. "Write your article anyway."

We stand there as our belongings and the contents of the old woman's millinery shop are consumed by fire, the air thick with the smell of burning wool and silk. One beautiful hat after another is tossed into the flames, first turning black around the edges, then collapsing inward only to combust with defeated little puffs, as though silenced by outrage.

We watch as Wolff and his Brownshirts saunter from the square. We watch as the crowd waits, antsy, for them to climb onto their motorcycles. Every ear is tuned to the rumble of engines and the squeal of tires as they speed away, victorious. Then three men rush forward and lower the waterwheel to the ground. They murmur soothing things to the old woman. They gently cover her exposed body. We watch them cut the ropes that bind her wrists and ankles from the wheel and carry her off, limp and whimpering.

"Your camera…" It's all I can think to say, the only words I can summon.

"Can be replaced." I feel Frank shrug around me.

"But the photos…"

He clears his throat but doesn't answer. So Frank Gilmore isn't as stoic as he'd like to appear, then.

My voice is that of a stranger. Distant. Tremulous. Weak. "What just happened? I wouldn't treat an animal that way, much less a human."

"That's because you *are* human, Nancy. They are not. Or at least not anymore."

The crowd begins to disperse, whispering and wringing their hands, but still Frank holds on to me, so I drop into a squat and slip out of his arms. Enough of that. I stand there, hands on my hips, glaring after the motorcycles.

I can hear the alarm in his voice when he asks, "What are you thinking?"

"If this is happening in Vienna, what's it like in Berlin?"

BERLIN

The Brandenburg Gate

We follow the sound of chanting. To his credit, Frank didn't abandon me at the Westbahnhof train station in Vienna. He could have.

His camera is destroyed, and without photos there's no chance of him getting paid. He has no reason to wade further into this mess. But God bless him, Frank is British, and therefore a gentleman. He refused to send me into the lion's den alone.

It is eight hours by train from Vienna to Berlin but only one mile from the station to the Brandenburg Gate, so we make the trip on foot. I'm glad for the exercise, for the chance to stretch my legs. I've spent twenty of the last thirty-six hours on a train, with Frank, no less—he snores—and I'd give my kingdom for a warm bath and a soft bed. I miss my pillow. I miss Picon. Poor baby is staying with Stephanie and must think I've abandoned him. But there is work to be done and all those things can wait.

"Dare I ask what we're looking for this time?" Frank is far less enthusiastic now. He hasn't mentioned romance since Vienna. "And will there be a whip?"

"I don't know," I say, answering both questions at once.

Wolff is a Brownshirt. He came from here. His entire worldview originated here. And I cannot report on what's happening without seeing it firsthand. Frank might not have a camera anymore, but he can stand as witness. And as we melt into the crowd I am grateful for his presence.

It is an odd thing to be amidst a sea of people and not understand a word they speak. I have been on my own since I was sixteen—for eight years now—traveling and living abroad, first in New York, then London, and now Paris. But the only language I've ever tried to learn is French. It feels right to me. I like the way each word rolls off my tongue. It is light and artful. Like toile. Like champagne. German is something else entirely. It originates in the throat. It's a rumble and threat. Guttural and deep, and it sounds ominous as we are swept along in this mass of bodies headed toward the beating heart of Berlin.

Frank keeps trying to hold my hand—protectively, I think—and I swat it away. "I'm not afraid," I say, as a way to soften the sting.

"You should be. I am." He moves his grip to my elbow and I feel the drag as he begins to slow down. I can feel his hesitation with every step. He wants to turn back.

But I lean forward, jaw stiff. "Then that's how we differ. Because I am *angry*."

He shakes his head. "You are a terrifying woman, Nancy Wake."

I laugh because I don't think of myself as terrifying at all. But I'm glad he does.

Frank, however, doesn't find any of this funny. "That doesn't mean you have to be reckless," he says. "We don't even know what's going on here."

"And running away won't tell us."

He gnaws at the inside of his bottom lip. "What you call running away I call escaping," he mutters. He lets me lead him forward through the crowd but he never releases my elbow.

There are at least three dozen risers set up around the Brandenburg Gate. They circle the great swath of open area in front of the monument, and the crowd spills into the space, most people rushing forward to be at ground level before a large wooden podium that squats before the gate.

"Over there," I say, urging Frank toward the nearest riser on the left. Once seated, we are about twenty-five yards from the podium. Close enough to see clearly but not be noticed in return.

"What now?" he asks as we settle onto the hard wooden seats.

"We wait. We see what happens."

As it turns out, we wait for a very, very long time. Through lunch. Through the afternoon. Hungry. Tired. Thirsty. We watch the area fill with more living bodies than one would think possible. We watch the flags unfurl, the uniforms arrive, and the orchestra assemble. We watch, and in our exhausted state we try to remember, to file everything away as best we can. I know I won't recall the details on my own, so I make a game out of it.

"Test me," I say, closing my eyes and turning my face to the sky. The sun is warm on my cheeks and my hair. I can feel a tingling at my scalp as my dark strands soak up the heat.

"On what?" Frank whispers.

"Everything. I need to remember this. And I don't dare bring attention to us by writing it down."

It's a diversion from the boredom, so he decides to play along. "Okay. Um. All right, the gate. How many columns?"

"Twelve. Six on each side. Together they form five passageways through the gate."

"And what sits on top of the columns?"

"A massive stone cap."

It's not the answer he's looking for, because he adds, "And on top of that?"

I think for a moment, hunting for that detail. I've spent hours staring at the gate already. It should be easy to recall, but instead I have to reach into the white spaces of my mind. This is why the game is so important. Memory is tricky, easily bleached by hunger and exhaustion. After several moments of groping around, I see it once more.

"A bronze sculpture," I say.

"Of?"

"A chariot drawn by four horses."

Perhaps Frank finds the game calming as well, because his voice sounds less tense when he asks, "The open area in front of the gate is surrounded by what?"

"A colonnade. It's very Romanesque. A place where Caesar would have pontificated."

He snorts. "Be careful what you ask for. The world doesn't need another Caesar."

"Tell that to the Germans."

Frank doesn't like this line of thought, apparently. "Keep going."

"On the other side of the gate is a boulevard that leads straight to the City Palace. It's lined on both sides by linden trees. They're all full and puffy and the leaves haven't started to turn yet."

We go on like this for some time and I sit there all the while, eyes closed, answering his questions about crowd size (well over five thousand at this point), orchestra size (full, though there is one trumpeter who must have been recently drafted, because he cannot play a note—they should have given the poor man a set of bells), weather (bright and sunny but not enough wind), smells (sweat, shoe polish, grilled sausage and sauerkraut from the food carts, and something else, something tinny and metallic and very human—excitement perhaps, or maybe fear), and sounds (chanting, cheering, and chatter; the revving of engines in the distance, honks and squeaks from the orchestra warming up, singing, whispers, tired children crying somewhere behind us, and now, finally the swell of anticipation—a kind of static electricity in the air).

Our presence here is accidental—we had no way of knowing there would be a rally—but it is illuminating. Hitler's entrance is specifically designed, and timed perfectly. Frank and I literally have a front-row seat to this madness. Hitler waits until we are half-delirious from heat and hunger and exhaustion. Until we have sat through hours of political theater and endless martial songs. Ranks of goose-stepping soldiers. He waits until our ears are throbbing from the triumphant notes of the orchestra playing Wagnerian overtures. Drums. Marching. Chanting. Our bodies slipping into a trance of sensory overload. Hitler waits until the blue hour—that moment when the sun is down but the sky has not yet turned dark. No moon, no stars. The twelve enormous marble columns of the gate are illuminated with floodlights while the sky behind it turns a royal, majestic blue. Some might even call it divine. It's all part of the theatrics, of course, designed to make him look bigger and more powerful than he really is. It is designed to make him look invincible. Godlike. And I'm sure he does look like that to this waiting, eager, throbbing mass of humanity. Because they lose their collective mind when he steps onto the podium, arms raised, anticipating their worship.

"What the flaming hell is that?" Frank whispers in my ear as a tattered, stained flag is raised above the podium.

"Oh," I say. "That explains why he's holding the rally here."

He just looks at me, waiting for an explanation.

"Three years ago, Hitler led a torchlit procession through this gate when he seized power."

"Okay, but what is *that*?" He points again at the tattered, stained flag.

The first words Hitler speaks are shouted into the microphone with psychotic zeal. "The *Blutfahne*!"

The blood banner. It takes me a moment to realize I've not said the words aloud. So I speak them in disbelief. I thought it was a myth. Some sort of exaggeration promulgated by Hitler to advance his own grandiosity. To witness it with my own eyes feels like witnessing a prophesied abomination. Something warned of in the Bible.

"It looks like a piss-poor flag," he says.

"It is. But it's the first one he commissioned." We are witnessing one of Hitler's most venerated rituals, the solemn consecration of the colors.

Frank leans close to my ear, afraid of being overheard. "Why are they touching the other flags to it?"

One by one, uniformed soldiers step forward and extend flags attached to long wooden poles and brush them against the blood banner that waves ominously above Hitler's head.

"Those are swastikas. Each new flag is touched to the blood banner in blessing. That first flag is said to be steeped in the blood of those who died during Hitler's first, failed coup over a decade ago. They say that fifteen of his supporters were killed that night and he soaked the flag in their blood as tribute to their loyalty."

"That's disgusting."

"No. It's evil. But look at them. They don't care."

The crowd is cheering, reverential. All eyes on him. Everyone on the balls of their feet, palms raised in salute.

"How do you *know* all of this?"

"I interviewed Hitler once."

Frank looks at me, stupefied, as though I've just admitted to a candlelit dinner with Lucifer himself. "You did *what*?"

"It was one of my first assignments for Hearst. Three and a half years ago. They sent me to Vienna to interview the new German chancellor. I'd only heard the name Adolf Hitler once or twice at that point. I had no idea what he would become."

"I want to hear that story, if we make it out of here."

I shrug, ashamed to admit that I underestimated the impact he would have on the world. At the time he was just an assignment, a crazy man pontificating in Germany. Because I was female and unknown, Hitler allotted only thirty minutes for the interview. The entire thing took place in a barbershop while he was being shaved with a straight razor. I still remember the scrape of that blade against his neck—the way it slid over the tender skin of his throat—and the snip of the scissors as his mustache was trimmed. The barber lifted the razor every time the chancellor answered one of my questions, so as not to nick him. Once, I thought I saw his hand tremble. I made eye contact with Hitler only twice: when I introduced myself and when he dismissed me. He did not thank me or say good-bye.

It all seems like a lifetime ago. I've been living wild and free ever since, traveling Europe, having my fun. I've been blind and deaf to most of what's been happening around me. Then I met Janos Lieberman. He was Vienna, surrounded by this growing cancer the entire time, and I wouldn't know half of what Adolf Hitler has done since that interview if not for him.

"Sieg Heil!" the crowd begins to chant in unison.

"Jawohl!" he screams in reply, that rasping, staccato voice echoing through the air. "Berlin!"

This is how people are brainwashed, I think. *This is how they follow a monster.* Everyone around me is mesmerized, their eyes glazed over, their breathing slow and rhythmic. And the longer he speaks, the more the crowd is hypnotized. They lean into his words, consuming them. Hitler shouts, they nod. His Lilliputian mustache quivers, his fists punch the air, he jabs and gesticulates, and they devour every word. They love him. They *worship* him. He is flanked by Brownshirts, each of them as putridly self-satisfied as Wolff, and I scan their faces for that whip-wielding monster but am relieved to find him absent.

"Sieg Heil!" they scream, frantic. Obsessed. Saluting and clapping. Believing every word, receiving every command they've just been given. Men. Women. Children. All of them swallowing it whole so they can be corroded from the inside out.

Frank reaches for my hand again and his voice is trembling when he says, "Can we go now? What more do you want to see?"

"Nothing," I say, and we slip off the risers, invisible to everyone around us, for their eyes are on Hitler alone. "I want to see nothing else."

Hélène

THE AUVERGNE, FRANCE

March 1, 1944

It is dark as pitch, I have no idea where Hubert is, and this strange little Frenchman is trying to get me into his car.

I slide my hand closer to my coat pocket and therefore the revolver hidden inside. "I'm not going anywhere until you tell me who you are and where to find Hubert."

"My name is Henri Tardivat. And I am *trying* to deliver you to him."

I have room in my life for only one Henri and it's not this man, so I make a mental note to call him Tardivat and then ask, "Why?"

"I am your contact."

I do not tell him that our contact's name is Maurice Southgate and that we have been instructed, in no uncertain terms, not to use a vehicle of any sort. London has assured us that the Germans have commandeered most of the civilian vehicles in this area. Barring the option of a train, we are to bike or walk to our rendezvous point. Since we see neither trains nor bicycles available at the moment, however, our remaining option feels less than ideal in the dead of night in unknown territory. And then of course there is the issue of my coconspirator. I cannot leave without him.

"I'm not getting in that car without Hubert."

Tardivat tips his head to the side, pulls at his cigarette, then blows the smoke out his nostrils. "Are you always so difficult?"

"I assure you, this is the agreeable version of myself."

There is a rustle in the bushes beside Tardivat. "It's true," Hubert says, voice deadpan, as he steps out of the hedgerow. "This is about as pleasant as she gets."

"About time," I mutter as he brushes dried leaves from his coat. He looks altogether calm, standing there in the dark, as though there's nothing odd about this meeting.

"I sent this chap to collect you," he says.

"And why didn't you come along?"

"I was burying my chute." Hubert eyes the pile of silver nylon under Tardivat's arm with concern. He scowls at me for breaking The Rules.

There's no time to explain, so I say, "We need to find our friend and be on our way."

"About that." Tardivat snuffs out his cigarette between thumb and forefinger, then flicks it into the bushes. "Maurice Southgate sends his regards. He's in a bit of trouble with the local Gestapo. He won't be meeting you tonight."

Hubert's face is hidden in shadow, so I cannot see his expression, but we exchange a quick glance nonetheless. The fact that he knows Southgate's real name is a good sign, but we can't be sure how he came by it.

"What exactly does that mean?" Hubert asks.

"Southgate got caught up in a German raid near Montluçon and has likely been arrested. Or killed. I'm not sure which."

I am exhausted, cold, and hungry. My dinner was far from satisfactory, but I still regret leaving it on the floor of the Liberator. "And you know this because . . . ?"

Tardivat shrugs in that nonchalant French way, as though we have all the time in the world to stand in a damp forest in the middle of the night and chat. It's infuriating. I want to grab his shoulders and shake him so hard his teeth rattle.

"He sent word to me," he says. "Be grateful. Otherwise there would have been no one to greet you."

Hubert tightens the belt around his coat. The air is growing colder. "And our other associate?" Southgate was only one of two men we were supposed to meet at the drop zone. The other is Denis Rake, our radio operator.

"A no-show."

"I suppose you're the one who lit the fires?" Hubert asks.

"Standard procedure. The planes have to be signaled somehow. You aren't the first lot to fall out of the sky, you know."

Indeed, we're not. Counterintelligence missions have gone up seven hundred percent in the last year. And yet what London cannot prepare you for are the myriad decisions that must be made on the ground when things do not go according to plan. To trust a stranger or not. To bury your chute or allow it to be purloined. To accept a ride or hike instead.

But Tardivat is losing patience. "Listen, do you want me to take you to Gaspard or not? If so, you need to get in the car. Because I'm not walking. His encampment is over twenty kilometers away in Mont Mouchet, and there are other places I have to be tonight."

There is no need to confer. For better or worse, Tardivat knows a great deal about our affairs. At the moment he is our only option.

"Lead the way," Hubert says.

While Tardivat is stuffing my parachute into the trunk of his car, I tug on the sleeve of Hubert's coat and whisper, "Denden?"

It's our code name for Denis Rake. He refused to parachute into the Auvergne with us, demanding instead to be flown onto a private landing strip two days ago on a small Lysander. The man does not jump from planes or like guns, and he'd be no use to the war effort whatsoever if he wasn't the best radio operator this side of the Atlantic Ocean. However, we were assured that Southgate and Rake would meet us here and together we would find the maquisard leader known as Gaspard to begin operations. I now wonder if we've all fallen into an elaborate trap.

Hubert shakes his head. "No idea."

We slide into the backseat of the small, two-door Renault and I know that somewhere in the deep pockets of Hubert's trousers are a pair of service revolvers identical to mine. And I'm certain that, like mine, his hand hovers nearby, ready to fire them into the back of Tardivat's skull should things go badly from here.

Whatever else I might think of Henri Tardivat, he is a superb driver. Within moments he's navigated us through the forest floor and onto a narrow, winding back road—all with the headlights off. He whistles softly to himself and hangs one arm out the open window. The air is brisk and it smells of old leaves and frost, but it keeps us awake as we drive.

"Don't worry," he says sometime later, when Hubert protests him turning onto another byway, "the Germans stick to the Routes Nationales."

"Why?"

"You'll see."

And indeed we do. The farther we drive into the Auvergne, the rougher the terrain gets. In the ten years that I have lived in this country, I have heard this area referred to as the Fortress of France, but I never knew why until now. The little car climbs ever higher through the hills without so much as a groan of protest as those same hills turn to mountains, many of them over six thousand feet. The byway disintegrates into a dirt road that is pitted and meandering and almost impossible to navigate. We wind through seemingly endless plateaus and around volcanic rock formations, occasionally drifting perilously close to gorges whose bottoms we cannot see in the dark. Wooded slopes spring up on all sides and the road softens beneath a blanket of pine needles. I must confess that it is perfect terrain for the maquisards to wage their unique brand of guerrilla warfare. And instructions from London notwithstanding, walking would have been exhausting and a bicycle utterly worthless.

It is three o'clock in the morning when we pass through an opening in a low stone wall and pull up to the château at Mont Mouchet. It sits alone in the middle of a large field without so much as a single ornamental hedge or tree out front. It is old, solid, large, and square. Pieces of pale stone are crumbling off the corners, but otherwise it appears intact and impenetrable. All the lights on the first floor are blazing and the circular driveway is packed with crushed rock and an endless supply of small flatbed trucks and rusty Renaults. There must be thirty or more, parked at haphazard angles all around the château. Cars, cars everywhere, when London said they were rarer than sugar in wartime.

"Stolen," Tardivat offers before I can ask. "Though to be fair, the maquisards only target known collaborationists. They'd be confiscated by the Germans anyway. We might as well get some use out of them."

"Where do they get the petrol to power so many vehicles?" Hubert asks.

"Most of those are *gazogènes,* coal-fueled vehicles. And coal is easy enough to come by in these parts." Tardivat peels himself out of the car and stretches. "Wait here. Gaspard does not like surprises."

We watch as he saunters across the drive, hops up the front steps, and pounds on the broad double doors. Once he's slipped inside, I turn to Hubert. "Do you think he's going to kill us?"

He leans his head against the back of the seat and yawns so wide that his jaw pops. He closes his eyes. "If so, I hope he's quick about it. I'm exhausted."

After several moments, the front doors swing open again, and the small Renault is illuminated by a rectangle of yellow light.

"He's waving us in," I say. "For better or worse, here we go."

Hubert and I grab our packs, situate our weapons within easy reach, and walk into the house, only to find it occupied by fifty of the most surly, suspicious-looking Frenchmen I have ever seen. A quick introduction proves them to be dirty-minded, foulmouthed, and irritated by our presence. A den of thieves indeed. But they are not Germans, and that is an immeasurable relief.

"Gaspard will arrive in the morning," Tardivat says. "You can wait up with this lot or you can try to get some sleep. Your choice."

A brief glance at Hubert and the decision is made. "Sleep."

He nods to a long, lean maquisard standing at the foot of the stairs. "This is Judex, Gaspard's chief lieutenant. He will see you up to your room."

"And what of you?"

Henri Tardivat grins and offers me an exaggerated wink. "You are not the only ripe fruit that must be plucked out of a tree tonight, madame."

I want to hate the man, but I can't quite muster the animosity, even when the maquisards leer. The truth is I've never met an Henri whom I didn't like.

Tardivat evades my retort by escaping through the front doors.

The interior of the house is much like the exterior. The floorboards are battered but none of them squeak, the plastered walls are chipped in places but not discolored, the tapestries frayed but numerous, and the furniture, though old, is stolid and austere. Who and where the original tenants are we're never told, but I can surmise that they are an unshakable lot. We follow Judex up three flights of stairs and down a long hallway to the only empty bedroom in château Mont Mouchet. He opens the door, then leaves without a word.

There is a single window, a washstand, and a double bed. There is no chair, couch, or even a rug on the floor for one of us to sleep on. Hubert curses, I groan, and we glare at each other in a standoff for several seconds, but there's no point making a scene.

I am too exhausted to argue. "Give me the left side and you can sleep on top of the covers," I say.

"That's a very specific request."

"Left is my psychological side."

"I do not believe there is any such thing as a psychological side of the bed."

This is what happens when your partner is a former soldier turned academic. Creativity takes a backseat to logic.

"Of course there is. My husband sleeps on the right side of the bed and I have the left. *Psychologically* speaking, I cannot sleep otherwise. That's my offer. Take it or leave it."

"I fear your husband would kill me if he knew."

"My husband is not the one you need to fear tonight. Just stay on your side."

He shrugs. "Fair enough."

Our backpacks, along with my purse, are stuffed under the bed, and we claim our respective sides in silence. I hand Hubert my coat and crawl under the blankets, trying not to think of who might have used this bed last or what took place within. Both of us secure a loaded revolver under our pillows. I pull the sheets up to my chin,

Hubert burrows beneath his pile of coats, and we are asleep in seconds.

We wake sometime later to raucous shouting and slamming doors. The entire house vibrates, and I can hear little trails of plaster dust sliding down the walls. It is not yet dawn but there are ribbons of pale sky along the horizon.

"Do those buggers never sleep?" Hubert groans beside me.

"I'd wager Gaspard has arrived."

"Should we greet him, then?"

I shake my head and my hair rustles against the coarse linen pillowcase. "No," I whisper. "They think we're asleep."

Hubert is silent for a moment, pondering. "We have the advantage, then."

"He'll know we're here—"

"Which means they're discussing us."

"But," I say, "I'd bet they left Judex on the stairs. They're a ruddy awful lot of pigs but they aren't entirely stupid."

Hubert is at the window, peering down in a matter of seconds. "As I recall, you were quite adept at the ropes course in Kent."

"So?"

"We're in luck. These horrid men have supplied us with a perfectly adequate trellis that reaches all the way to the ground."

Despite excelling at the ropes course, I did not, in fact, enjoy the training exercise. Nor do I particularly like putting it into practice as I shimmy down three floors of rickety trellis after Hubert. Despite the age and questionable construction of the wooden slats themselves, the wisteria vines are strong and established and—thanks to a late winter—mercifully bare of leaves. We are on the ground in no time.

"These poor fools need all the help they can get," I whisper as we creep around the side of the château toward what appears to be a kitchen. "Worst security I've ever seen. There's not a guard in sight."

"They left Judex on the stairs. They probably have lookouts at the windows. It's impossible to sneak up on the house."

"But not," I say, "to sneak *around* it."

The kitchen windows are low and open, and the smells of coffee and porridge drift out from them and into the predawn air. My stomach complains and I count the hours since eating that ill-advised Spam sandwich. Hubert shakes his head at the sound as though to say, *Get that under control,* and we settle into what was once an herb bed. At the moment it is occupied by sparse little plants that have turned dry and brittle with neglect. We try not to snap any branches as we take our spots.

Hubert looks a little puzzled by the rapid, colloquial French that's bantered about inside. He's the pure, academic sort who learned from professors and textbooks, whereas I learned the language from Stephanie and Henri and the streets themselves, so I translate as needed. Soon enough I can distinguish Gaspard from the others even though I cannot see him. He is loud and brash and domineering. He cuts off his lieutenants constantly, dismissing their ideas and observations. Arrogant. Surly. Self-satisfied. He sounds like a bully and I dislike him immediately.

"Oh," I whisper, the sound of my voice little more than that of a breath. "They're talking about us now."

"And?"

"He has no interest in cooperating with London."

"Then why the bloody hell are we here?"

"He believes he will be receiving aid from de Gaulle's Free French forces in North Africa." I listen a bit longer, then snort. "It is seen as disloyalty to take aid from *les Britanniques*."

The conversation inside the kitchen notches up rapidly and I lean my head against the wall to listen. If Hubert cannot keep up, I'll fill him in later.

"What do we do with these two *Britanniques,* then?" one of Gaspard's lieutenants asks. "Tardivat drove off and left them here."

"Get rid of them. I don't care how."

A pause and then, "We suspect the woman is carrying a lot of money with her."

There is a long silence and I can hear a coffee cup sliding across the table. A slurp. "How much?"

"We don't know. But she is very calm. Sure of herself. Both of them carry large packs."

"Radios perhaps?"

"Non."

Gaspard asks, "Are they armed?"

"We believe so."

Fingers tap an eager staccato against the table. When he finally speaks again, Gaspard's solution is stunning in its nonchalance. "One of us will have to seduce the woman, then kill her and relieve her of the money."

There is a great deal of foot stomping, hooting, and volunteering at this proclamation.

Gaspard sounds intrigued. "She is attractive?"

"Très sexy!" a man says, laughing, then goes on to describe my finer points, not the least of which apparently include straight teeth, shiny hair, a small waist, and *gros seins.* I glance down at my breasts in curiosity. Interesting. I've always thought Frenchmen preferred a diminutive bosom.

Hubert shakes his head, horrified. Apparently, he understands a bit more country French than he lets on.

Several of the men suggest that I might be shared among them before I'm dispatched. One of them offers to go collect me at once. There is some talk about how they will get into the room without getting shot and what to do if I resist or if Hubert tries to intervene.

"Assez!" Gaspard shouts, bringing order back to the room. "I will do it."

"And the man?" one of his lieutenants asks.

"Kill him too."

Nancy Grace Augusta Wake

HEARST NEWSPAPER GROUP, PARIS HEADQUARTERS

1936

"We can't publish this," my editor says. He slides the stack of papers back across his desk toward me with the tip of one finger as though they are contaminated.

I blink at him. I am exhausted and unwashed and not my sharpest at this particular moment. The entire article was written longhand on a notepad I bought at the Anhalter Bahnhof train station as Frank and I left Berlin. I returned to my flat long enough to type it and change my clothes before delivering it to Milo Caron, my editor. I expected any number of things after he read the article, but rejection wasn't one of them.

"I don't understand." I look at Frank, sitting beside me, and then back at Milo.

"I cannot submit your article," he says again, but slower this time as though I am stupid.

"Why not? It is a *great* article."

"Because I've got a man in Berlin right now. A man I sent *on assignment* to cover this story."

"And you've got a woman in your office *right now* with a finished article!" I slam my fist down on the desk and instantly regret it because a bolt of pain shoots into the back of my elbow. *Shit.* I have *got* to work on my temper. I cradle my elbow in my other hand, rubbing the bone with my thumb.

"Hearst is an award-winning syndicate, not some tabloid like *7-Tage.* This is an important story. I sent my best guy."

"Guy?" I ask with enough fury in my voice that Frank shrinks back several inches. "Did your *guy* go to Vienna? Did *he* see whippings?"

Milo runs a thumb over his chin. Scratches the stubble. He doesn't answer my question. "No one who reads our newspapers will take your article seriously."

"Why not? They took you seriously when you published that photograph on the front page. That's what sent us to Vienna. And then to Berlin. The entire world has now seen what the Brownshirts can do with a whip."

"I published photographic *evidence.*"

"It's the truth," Frank says. "I saw every bit of it myself."

"Which is why you took photographs, I presume? Photographs I can submit alongside it as *proof.*" He glares at each of us in turn.

"I took pictures and they were *destroyed.* Along with my camera. Smashed to bits in Vienna. Just like she said. In. Her. Article."

Frank's face is red and splotchy and I'm delighted to see that it is not embarrassment but anger that's lit him up like a campfire. But I cut him off before he can continue. "If three eyewitness accounts aren't enough for you, what is?"

"Do you need counting lessons? I see two people here."

I brush a piece of lint from my skirt. "Me. Frank. And Janos Lieberman."

Milo's face pales a bit at the name. I'm not supposed to know it. Janos was never named by the paper.

"You may have published the photo, but I got the interview. Me. Not your *guy* in Berlin. It's written and ready for publication as well." I stand and prepare to leave. "But it's become quite clear that you are not interested in my work. Which is a pity, because, as you well know, these articles are printed in a dozen cities throughout the U.S. I can only imagine what William Randolph Hearst would think if you lost this particular scoop. No matter, though. I'm sure there's some other *tabloid* that would be willing to publish my interview."

Milo's voice takes on a conciliatory tone. "Where is Lieberman?"

"Gone."

"Where?"

"Across an ocean, far away."

"Which ocean?"

I feign stupidity. "How many of them are there again? I don't know how to *count*."

There is an art to French cursing that I'm nowhere near perfecting, but I'm once again inspired to apply myself when Milo explodes in the most impressive display, first excoriating me for insubordination and then for my actions themselves. "You let him leave the country?"

"No. I *helped* him. His story in exchange for a transit visa."

"You know where he's gone? How to reach him?"

"Of course."

"Put me in contact."

"Submit it," I say, sliding my article back in front of him, "or I sell Janos's interview to the highest bidder. I'm just a *freelancer* after all."

Frank gallantly opens the door for me and I slam it on our way out.

"That was ballsy," Frank says when we're standing outside, looking up at Milo's fifth-floor office window.

I rub my temples and close my eyes. My eyelids feel like they're lined with sandpaper. I can't decide whether I want to eat an entire loaf of bread smeared with butter or throw up on the sidewalk. "It was stupid."

"Maybe. But at least he didn't win. That's something."

"You're a good egg, Frank; you know that, right?"

"By which you mean you're awfully fond of me but not the least bit attracted."

I give him a lopsided smile. "No hard feelings?"

"Nah. Just a bit of bruised pride. Nothing some good old French brandy won't fix."

"I'm really sorry about your camera."

He chucks my chin with his knuckles. "Cameras can be replaced. People can't." And then Frank Gilmore plants a sloppy kiss on my forehead and turns to leave.

"Hey!"

He looks over his shoulder. "Yeah?"

"You realize that all the articles and photographs in the world won't be enough to stop what's coming, right?"

A shadow crosses his face. "I know."

"So what do we do?"

"When the time comes, we fight."

I am weeping and puffy-eyed when Stephanie finds me. The only thing I hate more than crying is to be *found* crying. But here she is, waltzing into my bathroom with Picon under one arm and a towel under the other.

"Get up," she says. "We're leaving."

"What are you doing here?" I drop lower into the tub. Thank God for bubbles.

"You did want the dog back, no? Because I'm not keeping him."

"Of course. I mean, what are you doing in my *bathroom*? How did you get my key?"

"You gave it to me before you left." She looks at the ceiling and sighs, as though I am an imbecile. "And I have come to collect you."

"For what?"

"An excursion."

"I don't have the heart to go out tonight, Steph."

Picon whimpers at the sound of my voice and Stephanie lowers him to the ground. He skitters across the floor, his little nails clicking against the tile, and rises up on his hind legs beside the tub, trying to see me.

"I have something a little grander than a night on the town in mind. And you need it. You look awful, *ma petite*."

I lean my head back against the lip of the tub, close my eyes, and let my arm hang over the edge. Picon licks my puckered fingertips and I scratch him behind the ears. "I have always loved the way you encourage and nurture others. Especially while they are under duress."

"It is true."

"It is mean."

"I am not known for being nice."

"Well, I am not known for enjoying insults."

There is a sound that only French women can make. It is one of impatience and exasperation and is spoken with breath, not words. I envy them this skill.

"Enough," she says. "Get dressed. I'm taking you on holiday for a week."

I open one eye. Lift a brow. "Holiday?"

"You need to get away, to take your mind off things."

"A week? What about your husband? Besides, I have work to do. I..." I don't know exactly what I want to say, so I lift one hand and wave it around, flinging water drops across her skirt.

"You submitted your article. Your work is done. And the Count is in Spain on business. He's left me with nothing to do but spend his money, and I don't want to do it here. Get up."

"No."

"Nancy, you're being ridiculous—"

"I'm not getting up while you're in this bathroom. I do have a little bit of dignity, you know."

I've never seen the whites of Stephanie's eyes before, but they are on full display when she rolls them. "Good grief. We have the same parts."

So blunt. So French. Are they embarrassed at nothing? Regardless, I cross my arms and sink even farther beneath the bubbles. We are not *that* close of friends.

She mutters something about prudish Australians as she drops the towel on the floor and retreats into my tiny living room. But now I'm intrigued.

"And just where exactly do you plan on taking me?" I shout after her.

"Marseille."

MARSEILLE

It looks like a painting. Marseille is a city of hilltop villas and sleek yachts. Tile roofs. Beryl seas. Tanned legs. Twisting, narrow streets. Its central thoroughfare, the Canebière, leads from the glinting waters of the Mediterranean straight into hills that drip with grapevines. It smells of salt water, baking bread, and bouillabaisse. Of fresh basil and day lilies. There are fish markets and casinos. Hotels and dance halls. Bistros. Beaches. Cafés. Tiny little parks that are half the size of a city block. And flowers everywhere. It is a cascade of color. It is overwhelming in the most delicious way.

"I'm never leaving," I tell Stephanie as I roll onto my side and rub Picon between his sweet, floppy ears. We lie beneath an umbrella on the beach as the sun begins its downward slide.

"I told you so," she says, stretching out on her towel.

"You were right. I'm not afraid to say it. This was a brilliant idea."

We arrived at eight this morning, having taken the night train. Stephanie booked us a private compartment and we arrived well rested and eager to see the city. The streets were empty, except for a few tradesmen and gardeners headed to work. On the Canebière, workmen were hosing down the sidewalks with perfumed water.

"That seems a bit excessive," I said as we dodged a particularly aggressive spray on the way to our hotel. There were a few stragglers still out from the night before, dressed in their evening finery, and they walked through the water, filling the streets with laughter.

"It's a port city, *ma petite.* Lots of fish. The smell is otherwise very"—she waved her hand around, searching for an English word—"aggressive."

After chucking our suitcases into the room, she took me directly to the nearest shop and made me buy a new bathing suit. Now I feel as though I'm lying about in my underwear. I've never worn a two-piece bathing suit before. But Stephanie insists that since I possess a double portion of bosom I should wear a suit with double the pieces. I've given up arguing with her. Besides, compared to everyone else on this beach—Stephanie included—I look fully clothed.

We begin to gather our things when we can no longer feel the warm tingle of sun on our skin. All around us people are coming in from the water, stretching on their towels, and loading up what's left of late-afternoon picnics.

"You'll like this next part," Stephanie says as she pulls a light sundress over her shoulders.

I push onto my elbows and squint up at her. She stands in front of me, blocking the sun, looking for all the world like an angel in some Renaissance painting. "What comes next?"

"We play."

We spend every other day in Marseille much like the first, with one notable difference: we sleep until noon. I wake each morning to birdsong and bright light drifting through my open window. The sun is warm, the breeze is fresh, and I am pleasantly sore in new places from days spent walking through steep, narrow streets and up grassy hills. In the last six days I have learned to gamble—I prefer blackjack to craps—let out a mainsail, eat oysters on the half shell, buy lingerie, press grapes, and, most important, *relax.* Slowly all the knots in my shoulders have softened, my worries have faded.

On our last morning in Marseille we have mimosas for breakfast, scallops for lunch, and then we spend another long, lazy day on the beach. I am sun-soaked and waterlogged, and after a short midday nap beneath my umbrella, Stephanie convinces me to go exploring one last time.

We visit the Calanques, tall white cliffs that tower over the Mediterranean and span twenty kilometers between Marseille and Cassis. One section, near the city, is shorter than most, and we sit for an hour watching a group of young, handsome men swan-dive into the blue water below.

"That," Stephanie says, pointing to a crumbling stone fortress on an island far out in the bay, "is the Château d'If. It was once a great fortress. Then it became a prison. Now it is a tourist attraction. Perhaps one day we will come back, and we can rent a boat and take a closer look. I have never been inside."

I like the idea of traipsing along the high walls and through the towers and I tell her as much. Picon lies on my lap, spread out flat on his back, exposing himself shamelessly. I rub his little pink belly and giggle when his tongue lolls out the side of his mouth.

"And that," Stephanie says, after a while, turning to point up the mountain where a basilica sits at the highest point overlooking the city, "is the Notre-Dame de la Garde. It is Marseille's best-known symbol. You will not find a more beautiful building in this entire city. Perhaps in all of France. I am told that merely stepping inside will make you religious."

"Then I will appreciate it from here," I say, and she laughs.

On our way back into the city, we walk by the Marseille Cathédral de la Major and the Vieux Port. Everywhere I look there are brightly painted buildings and flower boxes bursting with blooms. Cafés. Yachts. Vendors. Shops filled with more little luxuries than I could ever afford in ten lifetimes. Our time here is like being in a dream and slowly, one hour at a time, I forget the horrors that I witnessed in Vienna and Berlin.

"Do you think Milo will submit your article?" Stephanie asks as we walk back to our hotel.

Her question yanks me out of the dream I've been floating in. "I don't know."

"If he doesn't, I will have the Count speak with him."

"Your husband knows Milo?"

"He knows everyone, *ma petite.* How do you think he was able to get Janos that transit visa?"

"I have long since stopped wondering about such things. You work miracles. I just take it as fact at this point."

We continue down the Canebière for some time in silence. Picon sits in the crook of my arm yapping at every dog, cat, and bird he sees. "What are we doing tonight?" I ask.

Stephanie throws her arms into the air and spins in a circle. "Tonight, we dance!"

"You can't be serious?"

"What is life for, *ma petite,* if not for dancing?"

"Welcome to the playground of Coco Chanel and Somerset Maugham," Stephanie says, waving one long, elegant arm as we stand before Le Bar de la Marine.

The bar faces the Vieux Port, Marseille's natural harbor. It is three stories tall, has stuccoed walls, a huge courtyard filled with wrought-iron tables, and flower boxes that spill over with twisty vines and fragrant pink blossoms. Snippets of unfamiliar music drift from the open windows. Somewhere, inside, a band is warming up.

"What are those instruments?"

Stephanie tilts her head to the side, listening. "Strings. Tambourine. And an accordion." She dismisses my groan with the wave of a hand. "There would be no tango without the accordion. You will learn to love it in the end."

Oh, surely not. "Stephanie. I don't know how to tango."

My wicked little friend grins. "Yet."

As it turns out, learning the tango is a bit like learning French itself: I do much better when I ignore the rules. Not to say that I don't *move properly,* but rather that I go by instinct. Yes, the dance fails if I don't point my toe at my partner's spine on an outside step. But if I stand there thinking about how I'm *not* properly pointing my toe, then the whole thing really does go tits up. So I feel my way through. Thankfully, Stephanie had us arrive at Le Bar de la Marine an hour before most of the other patrons. I have the opportunity for a basic lesson before I'm thrust into the fray. And, as with the language, I find the learning process far more enjoyable when I am cheek to cheek with a handsome Frenchman.

We discover in short order that this particular establishment has no lack of willing dance partners and, before long, I've had enough brandy and turns around the dance floor to feel comfortable with the basics. Stephanie, damn her, was right again. We dance and drink and laugh the night away, hardly speaking five words to each other all the while.

I cannot actually remember the last time I laughed this hard. My partners are good-humored when I step on their toes and when I miss the count. They tease me, gently, in French. And I *laugh.* Soul-filling, heart-lifting laughter. I feel as though I'm floating, as though my bones have gone soft, like I don't have a care in the world and *yes,* I'm aware that likely has as much to do with the brandy as it does with dancing, but I don't care. This is my last night in Marseille and I mean to enjoy it.

Before this trip I did not own a single evening gown, but I now have one and it is *perfect.* The dress is satin, floor-length, purple, and looks fabulous with my borrowed pearls. It is open in the back, all the way to my waist, and my dance partner finds this feature a little too fascinating. He keeps trying to slide his hand beneath the fabric, and I keep having to warn him about a knee to the groin.

"Did you know," I say casually, at the end of a lazy twirl, "that scar tissue forms inside a man's testicles every time he gets hit in the groin? It just stays there, building up over time, clogging up the knackers."

It's somewhat dim in the dance hall so I can't be sure, but I think his face pales a bit at this. If nothing else, his hand stays where it's supposed to from then on. We are on our second tango together—my ninth of the evening—and I am pulled against his lean chest when a little prickling begins along the back of my neck, as though I am being watched.

I count off the steps in my head, trying not to break our rhythm as I look around the room. Slow. Slow. Quick, quick. Slow. *Whirl.*

Again.

Slow. Slow. Quick, quick. Slow. *Whirl.* Dip.

I am bent over backward, my partner's mouth dangerously close to caressing my neck, when I see him.

Henri Fiocca.

Even upside down he is every bit as beautiful as he was that night at the Pont Royal. Wide brown eyes. Heavy lashes. Full mouth. Dark brows. High cheekbones. Once vertical again, I am only somewhat surprised to see a stunning blond woman on his arm. Fiocca is wearing a nicely tailored suit and a pocket square. The blonde is wearing as little as she can get away with. He is staring at me and she is glaring at him. Stephanie did warn me about that—*notorious with the women.* So, as my partner whirls me around once again, I do my best to pretend that I never saw him at all.

* * *

Henri

He knows that laugh.

He'd recognize it anywhere, in fact. Full-throated and warm. Self-deprecating, as though she's laughing at herself and inviting everyone else to join in. The very sound of it makes his ears warm. It's that woman from the Pont Royal. The one with the black hair and the blue eyes.

"Why won't you dance with me, Henri?"

Oh. Marceline. He has completely forgotten her. Just like that, one breath of laughter from that woman, and he's lost all interest in his companion. No. That's not fair. He wasn't interested to begin with. Only bored. And lonely. And Marceline, as ever, was persistent. She wanted a night out, so he reluctantly obliged. Even though he knows better.

"I'm a terrible dancer," he says. It's a lie, of course. But Marceline has been trying to run her stockinged foot up his pant leg for the last hour, and there's no telling what would happen if he submitted to a tango—find himself unwittingly affianced by next month, no doubt.

"Then you'll have to take me out again." She curls her lips into a perfect rose-colored pout, then a corner of her mouth twists higher when she sees that he's noticed.

Henri's father loves brazen women like this. Loves being chased. He wants to be convinced of the challenge, to deem it worthy. Because that's what it is, in the end, when a woman throws herself at you. Just a challenge. A game. Bait and switch. She reels you in and then you spend the rest of your life trying to catch her. It's exhausting. And insubstantial. Once you've gotten a woman like Marceline, what do you actually do with her? That's not a question his father has ever been able to adequately answer, and he's gone through four wives as a result. The real trouble, however, is that he wants Henri to like the same kind of woman. To like Marceline *specifically.* But this is just one of the many ways in which he is not in the least bit like his father.

That laughter echoes above the music again and Henri cannot help but smile. Marceline thinks the smile is for her and she leans closer. He is in danger of being kissed, so he pushes back from the table.

Again, that pout, but disappointed now instead of provocative. And a question in her calculating eyes.

"Excusez-moi," Henri says, "I must visit *les toilettes.*"

A narrow escape. He doesn't enjoy lying to women but has been known to use the tool occasionally in the act of self-preservation. He does visit the men's room before going in search of the raven-haired girl from Paris.

Le Bar de la Marine is crowded tonight and it's easy to blend into the throng as he edges his way around the room. Henri scans the tables and the clusters of partygoers who lean against the bar and gather in the doorways. He looks for bent heads kissing—afraid she might be among them. And he looks for dark heads thrown back in amusement. For bright white teeth and soft curves. Nowhere. He can't find her anywhere. Henri is beginning to wonder if he imagined the sound, if he summoned it with his longing. But then he hears the familiar cascade again.

She's only ten feet away, on the dance floor, in the arms of some other man in a poorly tailored suit. She is either new to the tango or he is a terrible dancer, because there is nothing fluid about their movements. And not for lack of proximity. The man is holding her close enough to make Henri's jaw clench but there is no chemistry between them. He feels both relief at this discovery and an intense dislike for the man.

She is counting off the steps, trying not to miss them, when her partner bends her backward into a dip one beat too early. Her lips purse in annoyance as her long, slender neck bends in a gentle arc. Her hair spills like ink onto the floor. And she sees Henri. He is certain she sees him because there is a tightening at the corners of those wide blue eyes. Recognition. She remembers.

"A friend of yours?" Marceline asks, hand sliding into the crook of his arm. There is a possessive note to her voice that irritates him, and he struggles not to pull his arm away. For the second time tonight Henri has failed to notice her presence.

"We have a mutual friend." Again, the truth, but just barely.

"She does not dance well."

No wonder his father *loves* Marceline. A pretty face and a caustic heart.

He shrugs. "Come, I did not mean to abandon you."

The music winds to a close and the band takes a break. Henri leads Marceline away and the dance floor clears enough for him to see his laughing girl return to her table across the room. And—ha!—Stephanie Marsic is there as well. Not that he is surprised. She has been insisting for months that he meet this friend of hers. Her presence is the opening he needs. Though, given the number of men surrounding their table, a short one. Now or never, he decides.

"I think it's time I get you home." Henri knows there is a wide gap in understanding between his meaning and Marceline's interpretation, but he lets it stand.

Her smile is broad, lips curling victoriously around her teeth. She collects her clutch from the table and he helps with her wrap.

"But I must say hello to someone first." Henri leads her across the room, careful to guide her by the elbow and not hold her hand.

Stephanie looks up as they cross the empty dance floor and waves him over. Then she is on her feet, kissing both of his cheeks before he's had the chance to greet her properly. Their table is littered with wineglasses and partially smoked Gitanes, and Henri sees, out of the corner of his eye, that his laughing girl is wearing a dress the color of plums. Her gown is open at the back and a long string of pearls is looped around her neck, but worn backward so they caress her spine. It's never occurred to him before that he could be jealous of a piece of jewelry.

"Madame Marsic, a pleasure to see you again." He returns the kisses. "How is your husband?"

"The Count is away on business. As usual." Stephanie darts a glance from his face to Marceline's. And then to her friend. Back to his. She motions to the table. "Won't you join us?"

"We were just leaving," Marceline says, all smile but no joy.

"Pity." Stephanie matches the note of frost in Marceline's voice. "But, Henri, you *must* meet my friend."

She is even lovelier up close. Large eyes—he sees now that they are green, not blue as he thought. Broad mouth. Dark brows. High cheekbones. She extends one long arm and he takes her hand, fighting the urge to turn it over and kiss her palm.

"Nancy Wake," she says in the strangest accent, and it takes him three long heartbeats to place it. Not British. Not Irish. Not Scottish.

Australian. An exotic bird indeed.

"Noncee," he says, trying to pronounce it correctly. "Henri Fiocca."

"A pleasure to meet you." The barest hint of a smile suggests what might be a dimple forming in her left cheek.

"It's all mine." And it is, clearly, because he's still holding her soft, warm hand in his.

Henri lets go with a start and she extends her hand to Marceline. "Nancy," she says.

Marceline curls both hands around his arm rather than accept the greeting. "Time to go, Henri."

"This is Marceline," he tells them on her behalf, since she refuses to do so.

Nancy's smile grows wider—and there it is, the fully formed dimple—just the one—and he is transfixed by its singular perfection. She lifts her wineglass from the table and tips it toward him.

"Have fun with that." She laughs, then turns back to the table, shaking her head.

The last thing Henri sees as Marceline drags him across the dance floor and toward the door is Nancy's arm draped across the back of her chair, wineglass, now empty, dangling upside down between two fingers.

A long string of shiny black taxis sits at the curb outside the bar and he steers Marceline toward the nearest one. He opens the door and helps with her dress. She scoots across the seat, patting the worn leather, expecting him to join her.

"Good night," he says.

Fury, jealousy, and disappointment flash across her face in turn and he thinks that perhaps she is not so pretty after all.

"Henri," she snaps, but it is an order he does not intend to follow.

"Thank you for joining me tonight." He hands the driver more than enough money to get her home, then shuts the door.

* * *

Fiocca and his date walk away and Stephanie watches me staring after them.

"What was that about?" I ask.

She shrugs.

"Why is he here?"

Another shrug. "He lives in Marseille."

"Are you kidding me?" I glare at her. "You did this on purpose! You invited him to the Pont Royal in Paris. You brought me to Marseille. This entire thing was a setup."

Stephanie grins, not even bothering to deny it. "I thought he would be a fun challenge for you."

"Did he know?"

"Of course. I've been after him for months."

"And tonight? You set this up as well?"

"No. But I knew he favors this place. I played the odds."

"What about that woman? Is she a part of this? Some idiotic way of making me jealous?"

"*Are* you jealous?"

"No."

"Liar." She laughs. "If you'd gone over to him at the Pont Royal, that woman wouldn't be an issue right now."

"I was there to interview Janos!"

"Yes. But also to meet Henri. You just didn't know it."

"I hate him." I throw my hands up. "And I hate you too."

"No, you don't."

Damn, damn, dammit. What I really hate is that she can read me so well.

"Fine." I stand up. "Challenge accepted. That's what you want, right?"

I'm so mad, so blood-boiling *mad*—at Henri, at Stephanie, at myself—that I am marching toward the entrance before I've had the chance to form any sort of plan. I push through the double doors and find Henri Fiocca standing with one foot in the street, closing the door of a taxi. He gives the roof two hard thumps and it pulls away from the curb. It takes him a moment to notice me and I study his profile, trying to read his thoughts, but then he's turning, and he sees me. Surprise. Then recognition and, I think, pleasure. Or relief, perhaps. A soft emotion. Something tender and open, and it catches me off guard. I keep expecting him to pounce. With hands tucked into his pants pockets he shifts, head tilted to the side, to consider me. And then he smiles.

Oh no you don't. That famous charm will not work on me. And I wonder just how badly I'd damage that pretty face if I punched him.

"What are you doing here?" I demand, stomping right up to him until the end of my nose is only a few inches from his collarbone. He's a good bit taller than me and I try not to like this fact as I tilt my head up, waiting for his answer.

"Noncee." He nods, giving me the greeting I haven't afforded him. "That's a strange question."

"I don't understand how you do it."

"Do what?"

"Charm every woman you meet. First Stephanie and now that b—" I'm trying to be gracious, so I hedge. *"Blonde."*

"Marceline?"

Her name is irrelevant. "Why did you bring her tonight?"

"She rang me up. Asked for a night on the town."

"She just *rang you up*?" I try to mimic his nonchalant tone, the purr in his voice.

"Yes." He sighs, as though this is some grave burden he's doomed to bear.

I glare at him. "Happens often, does it?"

"Every girl, except for the one that I want, rings me up." And then Henri Fiocca, the most notorious heartbreaker in all of France, gives me a meaningful look, daring to lift an eyebrow.

It takes a moment, one long stuttering heartbeat, to gather my laughter, but then I unleash the full force of it on him. I laugh so long and so hard that he stands there waiting for me to compose myself. But he doesn't look offended. On the contrary. Henri Fiocca looks *besotted.* I am unsure how I gained the advantage in this situation, but I am determined to make the most of it.

"If you want my company, Mr. Fiocca, *you* will ring *me* up."

I leave him at the curb, astonished.

By the time I return to our table, Stephanie has abandoned her cigarette and is blowing smoke rings into the air with a cigar she's confiscated from one of her many admirers. I listen to the music, relishing the feel of it rumbling across the floor and into my feet. I'm filled with the swell of it. Or perhaps I'm filled with elation from my encounter with Henri. He wasn't taking that woman home after all. Sending, yes. Taking, no. There is a huge difference between the two, and I can't decide whether to be pleased or irritated with myself that it matters.

Stephanie is watching me, waiting for me to tell her everything. But I'm not ready to talk about Fiocca. Instead, I ask, "How can you smoke those wretched things?"

"They're hideous, aren't they? I abhor the smell."

"So why do it?"

"Because it is unexpected."

"I don't understand."

"Sit down." She waves one hand at me in irritation. "That's the point, *ma petite.* A Parisienne always does the unexpected." She puffs for a few seconds and then blows another smoke ring from between perfectly painted red lips. "It levels the playing field. Men don't know what to do with a woman who can clip her own cigar."

Stephanie has been slowly doling out her secrets since we met and I, the eager pupil, gobble them up. "Teach me," I say.

She flicks a glance over my shoulder. "Perhaps tomorrow."

"But—"

I am interrupted by a waiter who is right beside me, a single drink on his tray. He places it on the table with a flourish. *"Le soixante-quinze françois,"* he says.

The French 75.

Fiocca.

I will not let Stephanie see me smile. I will not. I... *dammit.*

"Be careful, *ma petite,* you are in danger of falling in love with that man." Stephanie taps her ash into the tray. She looks at me knowingly from beneath a fan of dark lashes.

"Nonsense. I've only seen him twice."

She gives me her best pitying glance. "Are you immune to love at first sight?"

"It's a myth. No one falls in love that quickly." I tap my chest, hard, with one finger. "I *refuse.*"

"Go on. Refuse. The heart does what it wants. How do you think I wound up married to a Spaniard that I never see?"

I consider the cocktail instead of responding. I lift the glass and twirl the stem between my fingers. Once again, the combination of gin, lemon, and champagne is exquisite. It's a bright flurry of anticipation on my tongue. And, to his credit, Henri Fiocca lets me enjoy seven full sips before he arrives at our table.

"Will you dance with me?" he asks, extending his hand.

I have not refused a dance yet and have no good reason to now, so I accept his hand and let him lead me to the far edge of the dance floor, away from the band and out of the thickest chaos. I have *felt* the man looking at me twice now, so I expect to feel something at his touch as well, and I am not disappointed. But it isn't a physical tingling or an elevated heart rate. Nothing so melodramatic. It is internal. Emotional. Once my hand is wrapped firmly in his, I feel... *calm.* My entire frenetic self begins to idle. As though I've been given permission to rest. It is a foreign sensation. Henri pulls me close against his chest with one arm, then takes my free hand in his and weaves our fingers together. There's no point fighting against the dance, so I drape my arm across his back and rest my palm between his shoulder blades. He sways for a moment, finding the rhythm, and then he whirls us into the dance.

"It is not a crime to enjoy the company of a beautiful woman," he says, picking up our conversation from where we left off outside.

It takes great restraint not to roll my eyes. "Could you *be* any more French?"

"As a matter of fact, no. I am guilty as charged, on both sides, for many generations." We dance quietly for a moment before he adds, "You say that like it's a bad thing."

"Not bad. Just..."

"What?"

"Well, not to put too fine a point on it, Mr. Fiocca. But you are trouble."

"I am not. And please, call me Henri."

"Stephanie told me so. In those exact words, no less, *Mr. Fiocca,*" I stress.

"Can you at least drop the *Mister*? And Stephanie is mistaken."

"After seeing you with that blonde? I think I'll be keeping the *Mister* for now, thank you very much."

"I have known Marceline since we were children. We used to be friends."

"And lovers?"

"For a short time." He leans closer to my ear and whispers, "Just because I spent the evening with Marceline does not mean that I am trouble. Nor does it mean that I have feelings for her."

I snort.

"You think I lie?"

"I think it is your native tongue. Besides, it's actually *worse* to spend time with someone you don't like. To lead them on."

He moves closer, resting his forehead against mine. "You were doing it too. You're in the most romantic city in France. You've danced all night. And from what I saw, there wasn't a scrap of chemistry between you and your last partner. But still, you danced. Besides, I wasn't leading her on. She knew up front what she was getting. A night out. Nothing more."

I open my mouth. Snap it shut. "It's not the same. A full dance card is not the same thing as..."

"What? A full evening?"

"It's different."

"No. It isn't. Let me tell you a thing I learned from Victor Hugo."

"Oh, *please.* Victor Hugo? Are you going to quote some obscure bit of French poetry now? Try to win me over with that accent of yours?"

Henri leans so close that his breath curls into my ear. "Would it work?"

"No."

"Good. Besides, I wasn't going to quote poetry. Just the truth."

"I thought they were the same thing." I hate my traitorous body for curving into his. And I hate him a little more for teaching me exactly what a tango is supposed to feel like.

"Nonsense. Most poetry is garbage."

"Enlighten me, then. What did the great Victor Hugo tell you?"

"He said that when a woman is speaking to you, you must listen to what she says with her eyes. And your eyes, *Noncee,* say that you are attracted to me. *That* is the difference between this dance and your last."

"So? It means nothing."

"It means a great deal, given that the attraction is mutual."

"It's not an unusual phenomenon for you, I'm sure. You're not exactly the sort of man who spends your evenings alone. I've seen the company you keep."

"Marceline is not interested in *me.*"

"Charm and looks don't exactly grow on trees."

He flings me out to the end of his arm, then curls me back in with a snap, and I am stunned to notice that my feet do not get tangled at all. "Nor does money. Which is her ultimate motivation."

"That is rather unfortunate."

"It is also very French. Women in this country have expectations, you know."

"And women in mine do not?"

"I suspect women from your country are very, *very* different."

"I don't believe you know a thing about women from Australia."

"I am trying to learn. Which is why you should have dinner with me. I know a quaint place not far from here. It's still open. They serve the best bouillabaisse in the city."

"No."

"You're not hungry?"

"I am absolutely *starving*."

"Then eat with me."

"I don't think I'm your type, Mr. Fiocca."

He seems puzzled by this. "Shouldn't I be the judge of that?"

"Come on, it's obvious."

"How."

"You like blondes. I clearly don't fit the description."

"Who said I like blondes?" He moves the hand at my waist to tuck a piece of hair behind my ear, letting my dark strands slide between his fingers as he does so.

"I imagine that's all you ever go out with. Night after night. It's probably a *parade* of blondes."

"One woman does not equal a parade."

I shake my head. Laugh at him for the tenth time this evening.

"You really won't go to dinner with me?"

"No."

"Why?"

"I don't remember getting a phone call from you."

"I don't have your telephone number."

"If you want my number you can find it."

"No dinner. But you'll dance with me?"

"I dance with anyone who asks, but I only dine with those who call."

I am a woman who has been possessed, my entire life, by great luck. I was delivered, at home, in the winter of 1912 by a Maori midwife in Wellington, New Zealand. And seconds after peeling the caul from my face, she turned to my mother and said, "The child will be lucky, from this day until the day she dies." It is the only tender story my mother ever told me about my birth, but it has proven, over and over again, to be true. Particularly in the area of timing. No sooner do I make this pronouncement than the song ends with a flourish and I step out of his arms.

"Good night, *Mr. Fiocca*."

Hélène

CHAUDES-AIGUES PLATEAU, CANTAL, FRANCE

March 1, 1944

Hubert and I sit up in bed, hands folded behind our heads, ankles crossed, discussing the various ways in which I might kill Gaspard.

"Perhaps I should snap his neck?" I yawn, again, lamenting the long night and inadequate sleep. From this angle I can see only the tops of the tallest trees out of the window. They are all dark and bare against the newly woken sky.

"You could shoot him," Hubert offers.

"Too much blood spatter."

He turns his head on the pillow and gives me a withering look. "Don't tell me you get queasy at the sight of blood?"

I am a devoted fan of the male species. They are brave, brilliant, offer endless entertainment, are good for moving heavy objects, and make the act of procreation a great deal more enjoyable. I'd hate to see a world in which they did not exist. But sometimes they can be spectacular idiots.

"Insinuate such a thing again and I will smother you with a jam rag."

The room grows brighter every moment, and I stare at Hubert long enough to watch the color bloom in his cheeks and then spread to his temples like a rash.

"You don't have to be vulgar," he says, finally.

"And you don't have to be stupid. Show me a girl who gets wobbly at the sight of blood and I'll show you someone who hasn't hit puberty. Dealing with *blood* is one of the most basic realities for every woman alive."

The man I am to call Hubert for the foreseeable future is married to a lovely yet banal woman. I doubt they have ever discussed the physical realities of what it means to be female or what she must put up with for that one week every month. I've known Hubert for six months now and he still has no idea what to do with me. He does the only logical thing and changes the subject.

"You probably shouldn't kill Gaspard," he says.

"Why not? This is the most interesting thing that's happened since we left London. I've never killed a man and I'm itching to try. He seems like a good place to start."

The corner of Hubert's mouth twitches and I know that we've made our peace. "He's our contact."

"He's a dog with two dicks."

Hubert says nothing, so I try to explain. "That means—"

"I know what it means." He clears his throat and I take the win. This is the closest I have ever come to making Hubert laugh, and I am feeling victorious until he says, "You don't have to do that with me, you know."

"What?"

"Curse."

"I didn't take you for the easily offended type."

"I'm not. Spent years in the military, remember?"

"So why the lecture?"

"You use profanity as a weapon. A way to be disarming. To charm or sometimes offend, depending on your audience. It's how you demand parity and respect with your male coworkers. But you already have my respect. You did from our first day of training. I just wanted you to know that. Before Gaspard makes an appearance." His face is perfectly expressionless, and if not for his slow blink and the gentle rise and fall of his chest, I might suspect he was dead.

"You respect me?"

"Immensely."

"But you do not like me?"

He grins. "Not in the slightest."

I am looking at Hubert, intrigued, when a stomping and rattling begins downstairs. The clatter of pans. Chairs scraping across old wood floors. The whoosh of air going up the flue as someone lights a fire. Laughter and grumbling and the groan of rusty pipes as a man pulls the chain in the loo downstairs.

"Sounds like Gaspard is up and about," Hubert says.

"How long before he puts his little plan into action?"

"Depends."

"On?"

"What he finds when he comes in here."

"You don't think he'll wait for us to make an appearance downstairs?" I ask.

Despite our current situation, Hubert would not be my first choice as bedfellow. He is starched and humorless. Possessed of excellent insight into human character but without imagination otherwise. Yet Buckmaster paired us together for a number of very specific reasons. Some of them are still a mystery to me, but one in particular became evident early on in our acquaintance: I am not hard of hearing by any stretch, but Hubert has bat-like abilities in that area. The answer to my question comes a breath later when I hear someone stomping up the stairs.

I pride myself on being a woman who gives credit where credit is due, so I say, "Well done. But how do you know it's him and not Judex?"

"Whoever is coming up those stairs is a good bit heavier than any of the men we met last night."

I listen as the footfalls grow closer. He's right. Indelicate clomps belonging to someone who is secure enough in his position to not mind giving away the sign of his approach.

"Besides," Hubert adds, "Judex hasn't left the landing all night. The third step from the top squeaks every time he moves."

The benefits of having a bat for a partner are becoming more and more evident by the second. I make a mental note never to argue with Maurice Buckmaster again.

I did not earn my place with the SOE by being unintelligent. Both of my service revolvers are cocked and ready beneath the bedspread. I slide my left hand under the quilt and wrap my palm around the grip. And that's another of the reasons why Buckmaster paired me with Hubert: I'm a better left-hand shot than he is. Hubert, for his part, is holding both of his revolvers behind his pillow. He might look relaxed, but one twitch of an elbow and our looming guest will find himself with a perfectly round hole in the middle of his forehead, with another to match, in his breastbone, two seconds later.

"Think he'll knock first?" I ask.

"Unlikely."

And once again Hubert is correct. The door is kicked open so abruptly that it shudders on its hinges, sending a fine film of dust onto the floor. I assume that Gaspard expected to find us *in flagrante delicto,* given his look of surprise when he sees that we are on the bed, fully clothed, and unperturbed by his arrival.

"What is this?" he demands.

He is a big, barrel-chested brute of a man. Olive skin. Small, black eyes. A great heap of stiff dark hair that sits atop his head like a bottlebrush. A beard that hasn't been trimmed in months. If he were a dog, one would think he had the mange.

"As if we could sleep. You and your men sound like a herd of buffalo down there," I say.

He glares at me.

"Oh. Buffalo. Right. It's an animal native to the United States. Big. Lumbering. Terribly ugly. Smells like old shit left in the sun to bake."

Gaspard, for all his faults—and there are many—rallies quickly. "Bison," he says, "is another word for that animal."

I tip my head to the side. Interesting.

"But," he continues, waving a hand at us, "what is this? You two. In bed. *Dressed.*" His expression changes more quickly than I would have thought possible. It goes from bewilderment to obscenity in a heartbeat.

I brush the index finger of my left hand against the barrel of my service revolver. "What did you expect?"

"My men said you were pretty."

"So you assumed I am a prostitute? That I prefer sex to sleep?"

"Non." I can see the tightening of Gaspard's eyes as he recalibrates

the situation. Decision made, he turns his attention to Hubert. "But I see the problem now. Your friend is not much of a man."

The thing I love most about Brits is that they are not easily perturbed. Certainly not by pompous Frenchmen. Hubert looks at Gaspard as he would a bit of dung stuck to the bottom of his shoe.

"We are here to assist with your efforts against the Germans," Hubert says, "not cavort in the bed linens."

Gaspard gives me a pointed look. "What are bed linens for if not cavorting?"

"Sleeping," I say.

He takes a step across the threshold. "Perhaps you just need a different sort of man?"

"Alors tu veux coucher avec moi?"

Clearly the man is not accustomed to seducing a woman before an audience, but I am forcing his hand, so the effect is painfully awkward. Just as I intended. I can feel Hubert vibrating with suppressed laughter beside me.

"What man would not want to sleep with you, madame?" Gaspard says, clumsily, answering my question. I have been looked over by worse than the likes of him, and I don't so much as break eye contact as he peruses what little he can see above the quilt.

I tip my head toward Hubert. "That one for starters."

"Then he is a fool."

"The one in front of me isn't much better."

"Meaning?"

"That I do not think much of what I see."

Gaspard is unrelenting. He moves a hand to his belt buckle. "Then perhaps you would like to see a bit more?"

"No doubt even your best effort would be unsatisfactory. Besides, I have no desire to be *murdered* in my sleep and then have my money *stolen.*" I wait a moment as Gaspard's face pales. "I would have expected a better plan from a man with your reputation."

"How could you suggest such a thing?"

"I heard it with my own ears."

"Impossible."

"Insinuating that I am a whore is one thing. But calling me a liar is something else entirely." I flip back the quilt, allowing Gaspard to see the revolver held in my left hand. Hubert follows my lead, bringing each of his guns out from behind the pillow. We stare at Gaspard until he drops his eyes.

"This is war. I am not ashamed of being strategic," he says with a shrug.

"I would not fault you for strategy. But I cannot forgive stupidity."

There is not a single thing about Gaspard that I like. He is cursed with hubris and disdain for others, but he does think quickly on his feet. "You mentioned money," he says. "How much? Enough to arm my men?"

The Eighth Commandment forbids me to lie. I learned this in Sunday school, had it drilled into me by Miss Maggie Monroe. But I believe that even she would take no issue with me as I tell Gaspard that I have only enough cash on my person to buy lunch, and a poor one at that. I do not feel guilt for the outright fabrication, nor do I give it a second thought.

Gaspard considers Hubert and me, now standing, service revolvers at the ready. "What a disappointment," he mutters.

Of all that he has said, this bothers me most. I have been called any number of things by men in my thirty-one years, but disappointing has never been one of them.

"You have no money," he spits—literally *spits* onto the floor. "And you have no radio operator. You are of no use to me. Tardivat will answer for bringing you here."

Gaspard would choke on his own teeth if he knew the amount of cash hidden in my purse, but I would sooner swallow the whole lump dry than give him a single franc.

Hubert taps the barrel of his revolver against his thigh. "You will not accept our help. And we find you abhorrent. What now?"

Gaspard shrugs. "You are no longer my problem."

"I really wish you had let me kill Gaspard," I tell Hubert as we sit on a low rock wall surrounding a small cemetery, ten kilometers from the château.

"Waste of a bullet."

"Oh, I don't know. I think dispatching Gaspard would have been a great boon to the war effort. Might have even earned us a medal. Unlike our current enterprise." I wave an arm at the country lane that stretches in either direction. "For all the good we're doing, they may as well have parachuted us into Brighton."

"It's only been twelve hours."

I snort. "Slow start."

We left Gaspard's encampment on foot several hours earlier. Threatening to kill us was somewhat expected. Trying to send us off with an empty belly was unconscionable, so we made him endure an awkward breakfast in which we ate more than our fair share of porridge with raisins. It was almost entirely tasteless, but it did stick to our ribs and we haven't been hungry since.

Hubert chose this inauspicious resting place to assess our situation because the lane runs straight for a good distance in either direction of the cemetery. We're not likely to be ambushed by Gaspard's men or anyone else in this location. The lane is covered here by a broad canopy of bare branches, and little pools of light filter through, making the ground look like a patchwork quilt that has been pieced together badly. It is as pleasant as a cemetery can be, I suppose.

"How far to Chaudes-Aigues?" I ask.

Hubert examines the Michelin map he keeps folded in a tiny square and tucked into his boot. After a moment of turning the map this way and that, then finding his bearings based on the sun's position, he points south, down the lane. "Roughly fifty kilometers."

"Small mercies. We can make it before dinner. Weather and road permitting, of course. Although we'll have to go through introductions again with this Fournier, and I'm looking forward to that about as much as shaving my legs with a cheese grater."

Women. Hubert doesn't say the word aloud, but I can see him shaking his head in consternation. Well, let *him* try to shave his legs a single time, much less every two days for the rest of his life, and see how he feels about the process. Or the analogy.

Our orders were to rendezvous with Gaspard because his group is the largest in the area. We could have never known in London that it is also the most arrogant, overconcentrated, unintelligent, and ill-prepared group of men in the entirety of France. I don't like having to shift to an alternate plan any more than Hubert does, but there are other groups, all of whom need assistance as well. And having been rejected by Gaspard, we move on to the next name on our list. A list that is stored well within the folds of my own gray matter. Hubert might have exceptional hearing, but I have fabulous recall. Names. Dates. Facts. Locations. I can remember all of it with uncanny skill. However, I have only two details regarding our next contact. His name is Henri Fournier, and his group is based near the town of Chaudes-Aigues.

"What do you think is wrong with the French?" I ask.

"A great deal," Hubert says. "But you must be more specific."

"Not a single one of them can seem to name their sons anything but Henri. Here an *Henri,* there an *Henri,* everywhere an *Henri, Henri,*" I say in singsong voice. "I'll have to call our new contact Fournier. It's too confusing otherwise."

"I don't care what you call him. We just need to get there." Hubert drags himself off the stone wall and begins to stretch, but no sooner does he have his arms over his head than he freezes. He looks as though he's surrendering to an enemy force. Very slowly Hubert turns his head to the south and stares down the lane.

"What?"

"A car is coming."

I squint down the road but cannot see a thing other than dirt and shadows. "A German patrol car?"

"Probably." He gives me a single nod and then vaults over the low stone wall and squats down behind it.

We have a bit of time, so I ready myself. I drop my purse and backpack behind the wall next to Hubert. Set both revolvers in my lap and cover them with my coat. Sit up a bit straighter. Put on my "pretty face," as my husband calls it. Cross my legs. And wait.

Before long a little Renault sputters into view, weaving this way and that to avoid potholes. It's headed toward us at an urgent clip and a cloud of dust blows up in its wake. I know the driver has seen me when the car begins to slow. And then it's screeching to a stop, spitting bits of gravel against the wall beside me.

The driver rolls down his window and sticks his head out. "Choosing a suitable grave, are you, Duckie?" he says in the most perfect, aristocratic English.

"Good God, I hate you. You shameless piece of shit!" I jump up from the wall and wave my revolvers in delight. Denis Rake, our radio operator, has finally decided to make an appearance.

Rake unfolds his long, limber body from the car, looking every bit the ballet dancer. "I would have it no other way, Duckie. What an odious world it would be if you actually *liked* me."

The nickname he's given me stems from our first meeting, in England, and Rake has never once called me by my given name. He looks at my raised weapons without the slightest bit of concern. "It's not as though I deserted. There's no need to gather a firing squad."

I set down the revolvers and launch myself into his arms, giving him a hug and then a sloppy kiss on each cheek. There are no words to describe my delight at seeing him, so I don't attempt to find any.

"About time you got here," Hubert says as he scrambles to his feet from behind the wall.

"Ah, there you are. Letting our girl do the work as usual."

I gather my stuff and begin loading it into the backseat of the car. "Where have you been? We thought you were dead."

"My dear, swarms of Germans were chasing me everywhere. It's a miracle I got away."

A cock-and-bull story if I've ever heard one. Rake has a lover somewhere in the country, and everyone knows he flew in a few days early for a rendezvous.

"Hogwash," Hubert mumbles under his breath.

"The real question," Rake says, "is why the bloody hell the two of you are out here, in the middle of nowhere? Tardivat told me to meet you at Gaspard's compound at Mont Mouchet."

I let Rake know what happened with Gaspard as quickly as I can, along with my feelings toward the man and where we're headed now.

He shakes his head and turns to Hubert. "You should have let her kill him."

Hubert tosses his bag into the backseat beside mine, then climbs in next to it. "I'm sure she'll get her chance. I have a suspicion Gaspard isn't going anywhere."

CHAUDES-AIGUES PLATEAU, CANTAL, FRANCE

Château de Couffour

I decide immediately that I like Fournier. He and a number of his men have taken up residence in the Château de Couffour, a home so old it makes Gaspard's residence look like new construction. It is situated outside Chaudes-Aigues, a large town in the mountainous Cantal region that sits at the bottom of a winding river valley and is surrounded by imposing hills and plateaus for fifty kilometers in every direction. At any other time, the region would be considered scenic. The sort of place you'd spend a long holiday at the peak of summer. As it stands, under German occupation, it is difficult to traverse and remote enough to keep the enemy at bay. Crisscrossed by deep rivers, heavy with snowmelt, and not easily accessible by any major roadway, it is the perfect location from which to wage guerrilla warfare. Perfect for hiding from enemy forces and—most important to us—clandestine airdrops from London.

These maquisards are not formal soldiers. They are citizens, average men driven into the wilderness to escape either the Germans or the *relève*—the forced conscription of French nationals into the German workforce. They have left their homes and their families to make one last, desperate stand against Hitler's invaders. I respect them, and I want to help them.

Like Gaspard, Fournier has considerable forces, but unlike him, they are not concentrated in the immediate vicinity. He has broken his men into groups of fifty and one hundred and settled them throughout the Chaudes-Aigues plateau. In the forest mostly, but also in small towns and villages along every roadway, in order to keep an eye on German troop movements. Fournier is no idiot, however. For himself he has chosen the remote, comfortable Château de Couffour, a fifteenth-century castle somewhat restored to its former glory. Of the seven original towers, only one remains, but it is three stories tall, is in excellent condition, and has a pointed, conical roof and a spiral staircase. There are eleven other rooms in the château, one of which happens to be an expansive and fully stocked wine cellar. He tells Hubert all this within moments of our arrival, and I get the impression that he is trying to convince us to stay. It's not a hard sell.

"It's brilliant!" I say, giving Fournier my nod of approval. Then I stick out my hand. "You and your men may call me Madame Andrée."

He glances from me to Hubert. Then back to me. Then to Denis, and I see the confusion register on his face. Once again, he turns to my tall, confident partner, a man so *obviously* military that he must be in charge.

"Andrée is the *chef du parachutage*," Hubert says. "Talk to her."

Fournier's eyes snap back to mine but they are narrowed slightly. *"Pardon,"* he says. "I did not mean to offend. We are glad to have you. And your associates."

Hubert and Denden introduce themselves, giving the code names they've been assigned for our interactions with the Maquis. Fournier is the exact opposite of Gaspard. Short and bald. Diminutive in stature and voice. There isn't a blustery bone in his body. His eyes are wide, curious, and clear as well water. Fournier listens to us without interrupting.

"Your arrival could not be more timely. I have run out of money."

"Have you been working with another agent?" Hubert asks. "Victor? Or Patrice, perhaps?"

"I do not know these men," Fournier says. "I spent my own money to arm my men. Everything I made in thirty years of business. It's gone," he adds with a shrug. "But I do not regret it."

It is one thing for me to hand out freshly printed francs, courtesy of the British government. But this man has spent every cent he's earned fighting the Germans. His is exactly the kind of group we have come to help.

"Tell us what you need," I say.

Fournier wastes no time in making a list. The group of fifty men situated in and around the château has only the most rudimentary arms and little to no ammunition. They need money. They need boots. Socks. Food. They need everything. But there is a system in place and I must abide by it. I will not distribute so much as a firework until I've assessed his group for myself.

"I believe we can help," I tell Fournier. "But first we would like to meet your men."

Once our tour is complete we convene back at the Renault. As ever, Hubert's face is unreadable, but I know his mind is racing. Our starting point has been established, but it is daunting.

I turn to Rake. "All your equipment is in working order?"

He nods. "Yes."

"Good. Let's see if we can get through to London tonight and let them know we've made contact with the Maquis. We'll test out that radio of yours by requesting a shipment of arms for Fournier."

God bless Denis Rake. He pulls his radio equipment out of the car and marches it right into the château. Hubert and I gather our bags and choose separate rooms in the tower. I don't have time for a much-needed bath, so I just wash my face, apply a bit of perfume, and brush my hair. A quick nap—no more than thirty minutes—and a bit of lipstick and I'm right as rain again.

Hubert and I meet Rake and Fournier in the study an hour later. It's nearing dusk and Rake is bent over the table inspecting a little notebook littered with markings I can't read.

"What is that?"

"Shorthand."

"In what language?"

"Hungarian."

"You speak *Hungarian*?" Hubert asks.

"Bit of a long story, that," Rake says, running a thick finger over the squiggly lines.

"Okay, then, rain check. What are you looking for?" I ask.

"The time of tonight's transmission." He taps the page, finding what he's looking for, then stuffs the notebook back into his boot. "I am expected to come through to London at a different time on each day of the month. This is my first time radioing in, see, and I want to make sure I've got it right." He looks at the clock. "It is March first. They'll be listening for our transmission at fifteen minutes past eight."

Rake, Hubert, and I are all startled at the sharp sound of Fournier's clap. "Excellent!" he says. "We can eat dinner first."

"It's not quite as easy as that," I say. "We have to determine our drop zones, name them, and transmit the coordinates before we can request a shipment. It's already growing late, and I have to code the messages before Denden can send them."

Once again, Fournier proves himself to be my favorite kind of Frenchman. He shrugs. "It's dinner for two in the study, then."

"Three!" Hubert drops into a chair beside the large, ornate desk where Rake has situated his radio and props up his feet.

In the end, Fournier cannot curb his enthusiasm and decides to join us, bringing in two large platters of simple but freshly cooked food: roasted rutabagas, turnips, and Jerusalem artichokes, sprinkled with a bit of salt, along with a loaf of rustic bread and—much to our delight—a bottle of wine.

"Most people boil their roots," he says, setting the platter, four plates, and our forks on the table. "But I think roasting brings out the flavor. It's better with onions and garlic. But you can't find such things in this part of the country until later in the spring. And then only wild ones in the forest. We make do."

We mumble our gratitude as we tuck into dinner and after a few minutes Fournier tactfully clears his throat. "I do not mean to interfere, but I have a suggestion about where you might want to place your drop zones."

Hubert lifts his head to meet Fournier's gaze. "You know the area. You need the supplies. It's not interference. By all means, tell us."

"Let me get my map," Fournier says.

"No need." He spreads his map out on the table beside our plates.

Fournier studies the map, turning it around several times, before setting the tip of his index finger on our location. "We are here," he says, then scoots his finger over an inch. "And this the closest plateau. It is elevated, flat, visible from the air, and perfectly clear of trees, brush, and debris."

Hubert considers for a moment. Then his eyes tighten. "Yes. But it is cut off on three sides by the River Truyère. We could find ourselves trapped between rapids and plateau in the event of a German ambush."

Fournier nods solemnly. "That would be a very real concern had I not already instructed my men to identify and prepare routes of escape at several points along the river."

If Hubert is frugal with his words, then he is positively stingy with his smiles. But the corner of his lips does curl up at this news and he gives Fournier *the nod*—his very specific show of respect.

Rake and I work into the evening, nibbling on our dinner as we go. It is provincial, but not without flavor, and the wine helps tremendously. We consult Hubert's map, identifying all the possible drop zones within a ten-kilometer radius. We name each of them after fruit—Strawberry, Lemon, Apple, Orange, etcetera—then record and code their exact map references. After a bit of trial and error we finally have our list.

We watch as the little wall clock turns to eight fifteen and Denis begins tapping out his first message in Morse code.

"Turn on the radio," he says, after what seems like an eternity. "The BBC French Service."

Fournier fumbles with the dials and we listen in silence to the scratchy sounds of classical music broadcast over the airwaves.

"I let London know we have made contact. And I transmitted the coordinates for our drop zones."

"How will we know they received them?" Fournier asks.

"Just wait," Rake says.

Our dinner is gone and our plates shoved aside when, finally, at nine o'clock, the music fades out and an announcer comes on. "And now, for some personal messages," he says.

What follows this announcement is the most seemingly random litany of nonsense we have ever heard. Song lyrics. Nursery rhymes. A biblical genealogy, car parts, three entries from a dictionary, and then the phrase we have been waiting for: "A cricket chirps in Kent."

"We've gotten through!" Rake shouts and I swear to God I think I actually see Hubert smile. Fournier looks like he might stand on the table and dance.

Now that contact has been confirmed, I hand our first message to Denis Rake and he turns back to his transmitter. He begins to methodically tap out our request in Morse code:

Hélène to London. Contact made with group leader two. Wants boots, Sten guns, ammunition, grenades, and cash for fifty men at Lemon. The cow jumped over the moon.

It was Buckmaster's idea to use fruit. He thought it would be easier for me to name the drop zones after vegetation than vehicles, which was Hubert's preference. The bit of nursery rhyme was my idea—just to irritate Buckmaster—and is known only to Rake and myself as a security measure. Regardless, London now knows that we are here, what Fournier's group needs, and that the message is in fact coming from me.

Once more we turn our attention to the radio and, half an hour later, we hear the announcer say, in the most deadpan voice possible, "A frog is croaking in the mountains." Now we can be sure that in the English countryside, in a manor house stuffed with radio operators working on rotating shifts around the clock, our transmission has been recorded. And then a call has been made to Buckmaster's London office. Our request has been received and approved.

They can call me a frog or a witch or a stinging nettle for all I care. Help is on the way.

"Okay, then," Rake says, laying his headset on the table. "With any luck, we'll have our first shipment tomorrow night."

I don't realize how exhausted I am until I drop into the narrow bed in my room. Sleep rushes toward me in a heavy wave, and my last waking thought is that of Henri and the fact that I am now, finally, back in the same country as my husband.

London comes through in spectacular fashion the next night. We wait atop the plateau henceforth known as Lemon once the sun has gone down. It is well after midnight when we hear the great lumbering engines of a Liberator bomber.

"Think it's that same crew we had on the way in?" I ask Hubert.

"Possibly," he says, eyes trained on the dark western sky, and I imagine he hears fifteen different things that are lost to me.

Fournier and his fifty men wait along the tree line as Hubert,

Denis, and I stand beside the bonfire. A single fire is all I've allowed. I'll be damned if I'll have festival lights greeting our pilots. The ones I had on landing were more than enough. And as I pointed out to Fournier, though the plateau is the perfect drop zone, it is also visible for miles around. No need to draw unwanted attention.

Before long, the Liberator is in sight—a great black hulk against the lesser darkness of the sky. It's all rattle and clank and bombastic noise as it makes its first pass over the airfield. Fournier's men cheer and then they curse, thinking the plane has missed us. But it circles back a moment later and then the first silver parachute deploys. Six more follow, and below each of them dangles a massive wooden crate.

The crates are on the ground in seconds. They are swarmed by Fournier's men, who've been given strict instructions to only open the boxes but not remove anything. I have to inventory the weapons first. Then we must clean and degrease everything before they can be distributed. I learn, on this first night, what a laborious process that is. The weapons are packed in Cosmoline, a sticky, greasy goo that is impervious to heat, cold, and moisture. However, the weapons won't work properly until the wretched substance has been removed from stock to stem.

Our eyes are heavy, and our fingers numb, when Hubert hears the trucks. A quick conference with Fournier confirms that he is not expecting anyone else to meet us here. We are surrounded by weapons, but half of them are still packed in grease and a not a single one is loaded. It's like dying of thirst in the middle of the ocean. Water, water everywhere and not a drop to drink.

I reach for my service revolver, only to remember that I took it out of my holster an hour ago and set it atop my pack because it was hard to squat beside the crate with it strapped to my thigh. Stupid woman. My pack is, of course, sitting there, wide-open, on the other side of the bonfire.

"Hubert?" I say, looking to my pack and then to him.

"I only brought the one."

I dive for my pack as five trucks crest the plateau, blinding us with their headlights. All around me I can sense Fournier's men slip into the shadows and disappear. Most of them aren't armed—that's why we're here, after all—and those who are have little in the way of ammunition. They wait. And they watch.

One by one the engines cut off, but the headlights remain on. My pack is only three feet away, and my revolver sits in plain sight. But reaching for it now could get both Hubert and me killed.

The creak of a car door. A thump as it slams shut. Then an enormous man steps into the broad yellow beam of the headlights. His face is hidden in darkness, but I can see that he is wearing tall brown boots. A brown shirt. And a German military cap. He holds a pistol in one hand, and a whip hangs from his belt.

Nancy Grace Augusta Wake

LE TRAIN BLEU, NORTHBOUND TOWARD PARIS

1936

I wake to gentle rocking and cool air on my face. Stephanie sits beside the open window, blowing smoke from her Gitane into the fresh air of the French countryside. The blue velvet curtains are pushed against the wall behind her head, and little strands of hair cling to the fabric like gilded cobwebs. Picon sits on her lap licking pastry flakes from her dressing gown. When he sees that I'm awake he hops down, skips across the plush carpet, and leaps into my berth. Picon wags his tail ferociously and pulls himself into a tiny ball beneath my chin.

Stephanie and I didn't speak last night when we left Le Bar de la Marine. Or when we returned to our hotel. Assuming that I was drunk on lust, she left me to my thoughts. And when I left the hotel fifteen minutes later, she no doubt thought I was off to rendezvous with Henri. Needless to say, she was stunned when I returned a short time later with two train tickets and a determined expression.

"Pack your things," I said. "We're going back to Paris—"

"Tonight?"

"Right now."

"You cannot be serious. We're booked on the first train tomorrow. Don't you want to sleep?"

"The Blue Train leaves the station in less than an hour and I'll be on it with or without you."

She ceased arguing at this. I knew that the only way I could convince Stephanie to leave Marseille twelve hours early was to book a private compartment on the Calais-Mediterranée Express, Paris's infamous and elegant express night train—Le Train Bleu, as it is called for its lavish blue sleeping cars. The price of admission was enough to make me flinch, but it got me hard and fast away from Henri Fiocca. Money well spent, as far as I'm concerned. The man makes me... *nervous*. He's too handsome. Too confident. Too persistent. So, we boarded the train just after midnight and went to sleep in our separate berths, surrounded by cobalt velvet and gold trim.

Stephanie glares at me now, but I know she can't be too angry. She's always wanted to ride the Blue Train and has taken full advantage of the experience by having breakfast brought to our car. A tray littered with hot coffee, croissants, ripe berries, fresh cream, polished silver, and pressed linen napkins sits on a stand in the middle of the floor.

Now that Picon is no longer there to clean them up, she brushes a crumb from her lap and says, "Please tell me you did not give Henri Fiocca your phone number."

I stretch out until the tips of my toes and the palms of my hands are pressed against the walls at each end of my berth. I hold my breath and let my sore muscles burn with the strain.

"Of course not."

"Good, at least you've learned *something* from me."

"I'm not such a poor student as that, you know."

Stephanie takes a long drag and turns her chin toward the window. The smoke slips away in a thin, silver stream as she stares at me from between slitted eyelids. "Did you not find him attractive?"

"He is a ridiculously virile male specimen. I look away."

She makes one of those nondescript noises that French women are famous for and picks a piece of tobacco from her tongue with perfectly filed nails. "Not rich enough?"

"I don't care about his money."

"Liar."

"Oh, stop," I say. "If you don't know me better than that, our friendship isn't worth much."

"His money isn't important to you *at all*?"

I consider this and tell her the absolute truth. "The fact that Henri Fiocca has money is more *pleasantly unimportant* than if he had none."

"It's not just that he has money, Nancy, he's—how do the Brits say it?—*bloody loaded*."

Her imitation of a British accent is more Liverpool than Knightsbridge, but I applaud the effort with a bit of clapping as I try to hide my smile. But after a minute I sit up and point a finger at her. "And *that* is why I left. I refuse to be like that blonde he was with last night, falling out of my dress and desperate for his attention… for his money." I shrug, finally getting around to what I really mean. "He thinks I'm a sure thing."

I can't tell whether she's impressed or frustrated by my resistance. "What happened on the dance floor? It looked as though the two of you hit it off in spectacular fashion. I've never seen you dance so well."

"He's a tall, handsome Frenchman who knows the tango. What do you think happened?"

"Ah." She looks at me with pity. "You fell in love. I did warn you about that."

"No," I object. "You *challenged* me. But I know better than to expect anything but play from a playboy. I will not become a notch on his bedpost."

She grins slyly. "So you will run instead? Have I not convinced you that he's a worthwhile conquest?"

"It is Fiocca's job to convince me, not yours."

PARIS

Rue Sainte-Anne, 2nd Arrondissement

"I can't believe it worked." Frank Gilmore slides the *New York Evening Journal* back across my kitchen table. "Milo submitted your article." He taps the date. "This was published two days after we met with him."

"It didn't work at all, actually," I say.

"What do you mean?"

I tap the space where a byline should be. It's blank.

"Where's your name?" Frank demands.

"Where indeed."

Poor Frank. He has never considered the possibility of not getting credit for a job well done. "I don't understand."

"It's not that complicated, really," I say. "I'm a woman."

"So?"

"So Hearst does not publish the names of its female journalists. Particularly its freelancers. 'That's just how it is,' I was told at the beginning, when they hired me."

"But that's—"

"Bullshit. Yes. I know. Milo likely didn't even file my name with the article."

"He's an *arsemonger*," Frank spits. "This is your victory. You should be able to take it."

I should have negotiated this byline. I should have *demanded* it. But the truth is I didn't even think Milo would concede and file it at all. Besides, this is the first time in the three years that I've been writing for Hearst that I have seen one of my articles in print. Of course, *this* would be the one on the front page, above the fold. I submit them, and I know they're published because I get paid, but they are always printed in the United States in cities with strange-sounding names like *Houston* and *San Francisco* and *Detroit.* Until a courier delivered this paper an hour ago, it has always felt like a job I have in theory, but not in reality. Milo wired the editor of the *New York Evening Journal* and asked him to send a copy as proof that he'd done my bidding. I am told the editor sent this copy with a friend who was traveling to Paris from Lakehurst, New Jersey, by way of Frankfurt and the *Hindenburg.* "Quicker than the mail," Milo said in his accompanying note.

"Without your name it doesn't count!" Frank argues, growing more incensed by the moment. "You are being *erased* from history even as you're writing it!"

"I had an option early on, of choosing a male pen name," I tell him.

"Why didn't you?"

"I decided that if I couldn't get credit for my work, as myself, I wasn't willing to give it to a man who doesn't even exist. Besides, I needed the paycheck desperately. And when I signed on it was either take their terms or go back to Australia."

Frank opens his mouth and I know where he's going, so I stick my finger right in his face. "Don't you dare say, 'But what about George Eliot?' Don't you dare! Mary Ann Evans made her choice and so did I."

All the while Stephanie has been listening to our conversation without comment. She's positioned herself at the seat closest to the window, so she can blow her cigarette smoke out onto rue Sainte-Anne instead of my tiny four-hundred-square-foot flat. I smoke when the mood strikes me—usually when I'm angry—but Stephanie smokes *a lot.* Perhaps too much. She'd be furious with me if she knew how I'm starting to worry. But she's not looking at me right now, or wondering what I'm thinking. She taps her ash into one of the empty pots in the wrought-iron flower box fixed beneath the window. I planted geraniums in them last summer but they've long since shriveled with neglect. I meant to replace them this year with something a little more low maintenance, like ivy, but never got around to it. Stephanie doesn't seem to notice, however, but rather pours another finger of brandy into each of our glasses. We've been drinking for an hour and I've got that pleasant, tingly feeling in my head, like I could dance or nap. One or the other. A coin toss, really. Present company prevents me from doing either, however.

"Nancy doesn't actually *enjoy* journalism," Stephanie says. "And can you blame her?"

"I guess not." Frank looks at me as though I've just been accused of not enjoying chocolate. Or sex. "But the whole thing is a damned pity. You're so good at it."

I hate being pitied. So I change the subject. "I don't *dislike* journalism. It's the travel I love. What other job lets you jaunt off, anywhere in the world, on someone else's dime? If I have to write an article now and again in exchange—even if I don't get credit—so be it."

Frank looks as though he might argue with my logic but thinks better of it. I suspect that—even though he's far fonder of his camera than I am of my typewriter—his motives are similar. We've both been to a dozen countries and counting. Besides, it's not my skill as a wordsmith that makes me an excellent journalist, it's my curiosity.

"How did you get into this, then?" he asks.

"I was living in London at the time," I say, lifting my glass from the table and swirling the amber-colored brandy until a tiny whirl forms at the bottom of the glass. I watch, mesmerized, until the liquid settles. Stephanie brought a bottle of Rémy Martin from Count Gonzales's private collection to celebrate the occasion, and it has been on the window ledge just long enough to taste like black cherries set in the sun to ripen. I roll it around my tongue before finishing the thought. Warm and sweet and rich. Aged vanilla with cloves but woodsy as well, with a hint of cedar and orange peel. It's like bourbon, only better, somehow, as though bourbon got dressed up and went out for drinks.

"I absolutely loved it, of course," I say. "... Until winter arrived. The boat I'd taken from New York docked early that fall and I spent those first days watching the changing of the guard at Buckingham Palace, buying frivolous trinkets up and down Piccadilly, lying about beneath the trees in Hyde Park, and marking the time according to the chimes of Big Ben. London sounds romantic—and it is, mostly, until it turns gray and soggy in late November. I'd left sunny Australia and gone through New York that summer, so I wasn't prepared for London winters. But I was quickly running out of money and I knew that I had to get a job or go home. Home was not an option—I wanted to keep traveling—so I checked out of my hotel and acquired a room at a charmingly disreputable boardinghouse on Cromwell Road and enrolled at Queen's College for Journalism. They had a course I was able to finish in a few months—mostly typing and shorthand—and the second I had my diploma I started answering advertisements for freelance journalists in the newspapers. The first call I received was from an editor at the London bureau of the Hearst Newspaper Group and, thanks to my newly acquired diploma, they wanted to see me."

Frank has that look on his face, like he can't decide whether to shake his head, laugh, or call my bluff.

"The editor liked the marks I'd gotten in typing and shorthand," I continue, "but he was more interested in Egypt than anything else."

"Egypt?" Stephanie asks. "What did that have to do with anything?"

"He wanted to know if I'd ever been and how much I knew about the country in general. The Middle East was a growing area of interest for Hearst and they were looking for a writer who could enlighten their readers in the areas of Egyptian arts, literature, and science."

Frank nods with sympathy—the poor bloke just gets nicer the more he drinks. "So, you were buggered?"

"Not in the *least.* I told that man, without so much as a blink, that not only had I been to Cairo four times, but that I could read and write in Egyptian. Fluently."

Stephanie laughs so hard I fear she might choke on her brandy, and Frank looks at me agog.

"You did not," he says.

"I most certainly did."

"Didn't he ask for proof?"

"Of course. And I gave it to him." Both of them are perched on the edge of their seats, and I think that even though I don't particularly enjoy the process of *writing,* I do love the art of *storytelling.* "He asked for a demonstration and when I agreed, he handed me a pen and notepad, pulled a book from his shelf, flipped it open, and began reading a random passage."

"And what did you do?" Stephanie asks.

"I started to write, in delicate squiggles, swirls, and curls across the page, backward, from right to left. He was awestruck as I continued my hieroglyphics for a full page. And when he finished, I read the passage back to him verbatim."

This is where I lose Frank. "Bullshit," he says.

"Excuse me?"

He throws up his hands. "*Bullshit.* I'm not a complete knob, you know. Modern Egyptian writing is in Arabic, not hieroglyphics."

"So?"

"So there's no way you could have fooled him."

"Can *you* read Arabic, Frank? Or hieroglyphics?"

His eyes narrow and he hesitates. "No."

"Well, neither could he. So when I read the notes I'd written in *Pitman shorthand* back to him, without error, he was convinced." I wait until they've both finished laughing before I add, "Had that particular test been graded, I no doubt would have gotten excellent marks for resourcefulness."

"But terrible marks for honesty," Frank adds.

Stephanie waves off the observation. "Honestly, Nancy, you're so good at this kind of thing, you should have been a criminal."

"If I hadn't gotten the job, I would have seriously considered it. But as it turned out, he offered one on the spot, with a single stipulation."

"Which was?" Frank asks.

"That I move to Paris. The Hearst European Bureau was understaffed."

"Brilliant!" he shouts, raising his glass in salute.

"It is worth noting that I met our dear Stephanie only a week after my arrival. I was having a drink at Luigi's, admiring my new city from the terrace, when a row started at the other end of the bar. The crowd parted just in time for me to see Stephanie throw a pitcher of water at her husband's head while cursing simultaneously in French and Yugoslavian."

"The Count deserved it," she says without apology.

"He left, Stephanie stayed, and I thought it would be interesting to befriend a woman who could so easily clear a room."

There is a great deal more to that particular story, of course, but Stephanie has long since sworn me to silence. I am considering whether to accept the next round of offered brandy when the phone rings. I feel more than a little light-headed, so I decline a refill and bring my empty glass with me as I cross the room and lift the receiver from the box on my wall.

"This is Nancy." My voice isn't slurred, but I can hear my thrumming Aussie accent more than usual.

"Bonjour, Noncee."

Well. This is interesting. Henri Fiocca has finally called. I'm not the kind of girl to wait by the phone. But it has been a week. I was beginning to wonder if he'd lost interest.

"Mr. Fiocca," I say, voice lowered so my friends cannot hear me. I am suddenly self-conscious about sharing this conversation.

"I thought we established that I would like you to call me Henri?"

"You requesting a thing does not mean it's established. You should already know me better than that."

"I have been *trying* to know you better, but you keep resisting."

I laugh. "And for good reason too."

"I—"

"Hold on a moment," I say, placing a hand over the receiver. I look at Stephanie and Frank. "This is important." Not that I want Fiocca to know that, of course. I look at them, pointedly, until they take the hint and begin collecting their things. I move my hand and say, quietly, "Would you mind calling back in fifteen minutes? I'm in the middle of something."

"I—yes, of course."

"Excellent." I hang up.

Frank isn't quite stumbling drunk when I kick them out of my flat—more of a gentle sway, like a palm tree. Stephanie, as usual, is stone-cold sober. She winks at me, mouths the word *Fiocca,* then wiggles her fingers in farewell, flashing a triumphant grin as I close the door in her face. She had twice as much to drink as either of us and she isn't the slightest bit pickled. I am determined to learn her methods if for no other reason than an innate desire to be the last man standing. Because I am tottering quite badly.

I lean my forehead against the door, listening to the sound of their retreating footsteps, then I exhale when all is silent once more. So much for running from Henri Fiocca—he's caught up to me rather quickly. What on earth am I going to do about that man?

"Absolutely nothing," I say out loud as I make my way to the kitchen for a big glass of water. "He's not some problem to be solved. He's . . . he's . . ." I look at Picon for an answer, but he's curled up on the rug, fast asleep in a patch of sunlight.

Hell if I know what Henri Fiocca is exactly.

Dead sexy.

Intriguing.

Wildly impressed with himself.

Tall. Strong. Yet gentle in the way that only big men can be. And his *voice.* It is an aphrodisiac. Which is a strange realization, to be honest, because I always thought I was susceptible to a Scottish accent. And yet here I am, falling for a Frenchman.

"Aaargh. I will *not.* It's ridiculous. I don't have time for this."

Which does nothing to explain why I'm brushing my hair until it crackles and applying another coat of lipstick as though he's about to walk through the door at any moment.

Fifteen minutes later on the dot my phone rings again.

"Hello. This is Nancy," I say again, knowing full well who is on the other end.

"Noncee."

I take a slow breath through my nose and press my shoulder to the wall. I curl the phone cord around one finger. "I suppose you got my number from Stephanie?"

He chuckles. "Of course."

"Hmm. Remind me to thank her."

There is an odd pause on the other end and for a moment I think that he's nervous, that he doesn't know what to say next. Fiocca clears his throat and asks, "Why did you leave Marseille? I came to Le Bar de la Marine the next night, ready to dance, but you were not there."

"That's when I was scheduled to leave. I have a job, you know. And a life."

"You didn't mention leaving that night. Why?"

I could lie. That's what I typically do when put in these situations. But something about Henri Fiocca makes me want to discard the typical and run headlong at the truth. "You seem to think I'm a sure thing," I say, "like some blonde who tags along after you."

"I was quite clear about my preference for brunettes."

"Yes, well, it's their preference for you that I find alarming. I'm not interested in competing for your attention."

"Let me assure you," he says, voice dropping lower, "you have my full attention. There is no competition."

I'm sure he says that to all his girls. But the fact that we are on the phone and not face-to-face has me feeling bold. "Prove it," I say.

"Have dinner with me tonight and I will."

"No."

"But..." He clears his throat. "You said if I called you would dine with me. A promise is a promise."

Something occurs to me, a few beats too late. "You're in Paris?"

"*Oui.* On business." He does not fall for the change of subject. "Dinner?"

The news of his proximity has thrown me. "I will not dine with you *tonight*." A pause to gather my thoughts and then, "I'm meeting a few colleagues at Luigi's. We have a lot to catch up on."

"Dinner tomorrow, then?"

There's no way out of it now. "Yes."

"When may I collect you?"

There is an art to setting a time for such a date. Early in the evening tells a man that you have no intention of going to bed with him. Late in the evening declares yourself open to other intentions. There is only one reasonable option in a situation like this.

"Eight o'clock," I say. Neither early nor late.

I can hear the smile in his voice as he recognizes what I've done. This is a game. Winner take all. "And your address?"

I give it to him.

"Tomorrow, then, *Noncee*."

He hangs up first this time and I stand there for a moment, the receiver pressed against my ear, lips pursed, unable to determine whether I am excited or terrified.

PARIS

Ristorante Luigi, 8 Rue de Buci

I wear my favorite armor to Luigi's: red lipstick. The fact that I'm also wearing a swishy dress and shiny black pumps doesn't hurt. Nor does the carefully curled hair or the heavy swipe of mascara. It's something I've already come to think of as the Fiocca Effect, this desire to be *noticed.* The dress itself isn't anything special, just a light blue cotton with a scoop neck, neatly belted, but it's enough to get Frank Gilmore's attention. He notices me leaning across the bar, giving instructions to Enzo, the barman. Frank waves me over to the raucous, crowded table in the corner but I hold up one finger. *Wait.*

"Don't forget," I tell Enzo.

He responds with a nod and there's a mischievous twinkle in his eyes as if he'd like to say, *About damn time,* but he's a smart man and he keeps his mouth shut.

Contingency plan in place, I make my way to the back of the room. A collective roar of "Nancy!" goes up and I survey the table crowded with my fellow freelancers. Journalists and photographers, every one of them male.

"I was just telling them about your job interview, Nance," Frank says, pulling out a chair for me. He's sobered up nicely since this afternoon. Probably went home and passed out for several hours. "Those damn hieroglyphics of yours."

"Well, don't let me interrupt you." I pull Picon out of my purse and listen as Frank continues. I scratch Picon's fuzzy chin and he licks my pinkie finger.

A few minutes later Frank gives me a questioning glance. "What kind of shorthand was it?"

"Pitman."

"Pitman shorthand," he finishes. "She'd written the entire thing backward, in *shorthand.*"

My colleagues laugh and cheer, and I watch as Frank positions himself for his grand finale. "And it's just that kind of ingenuity—no, *brilliance*—that earned our girl the lead article on the front page of the *New York Evening Journal*!"

And with that he pulls the newspaper from inside his suit coat and brandishes it with a flourish. It does not escape my attention that his thumb is covering the place where my name should be. I'd been in such a rush to evict him earlier that I hadn't even noticed the paper was gone, hadn't given it a second thought since speaking with Fiocca. Frank Gilmore, kind man that he is, is trying to give me the credit Hearst would not.

I'm not sure how it is elsewhere in the world, or even elsewhere in Paris, but our little group of freelancers is unusually supportive. Sure, we're all out there scrambling for our stories, following our leads, and keeping them to ourselves when necessary, but once the story is printed, we celebrate one another. And, as is customary, the winner buys the first round of drinks. I'm the only girl in this motley group of seven, and the only one who prefers brandy to beer. I wait until Frank summons the waiter, and we put in our orders before I tell a story of my own.

"Did anyone bother to ask Frank why the article was printed without a photograph?"

They all look at him and the color seeps across Frank's great big potato head. It's a wonder the strain doesn't turn him ginger on the spot.

"It's because his camera was smashed to bits in Vienna by one of those bastard Brownshirts. I saw it with my own eyes."

Our friends look at him closer now, nodding. Respectful. That is a battle scar to be proud of. And this is how it goes among the journos. We tell stories, mostly about politics and politicians, and all the surrounding wars. Skirmishes. Assassinations. Elections. But sometimes we tell stories on and about ourselves as well. We regale one another with tales of our humiliations and humanity. Frank did me the honor of showing the others that I am clever, so I return the favor by making sure they know he is brave.

I pause as our waiter deposits our drinks on the table and only when he's gone do I finish my story. "Frank didn't even flinch when that *arschloch* yanked the camera from his hands, smashed it onto the cobblestones, and kicked the pieces into the fire. He should have been right there with me on the front page." I raise my glass, wink at him, then repeat his words from earlier that day. "It's a *damned pity* he wasn't. To Frank!"

"To Frank!" they respond, tipping their glasses toward him in salute.

It's only after all the glasses have been clinked and he's been slapped hard enough on the back to rattle his teeth that a second, and now very familiar, drink is set on the table beside my brandy. A French 75.

I knew it! I absolutely *knew it.*

Then comes the whisper, low and filled with humor in my ear. "I take this to mean that you were expecting me?"

My breath catches in my throat and I hold it for three long seconds. "I knew you wouldn't be able to stay away."

"Is that so?"

My smile is victorious. "You are nothing if not predictable, Fiocca."

"You did ask me to prove it, *ma chère*."

I knew, as soon as I mentioned my meeting at Luigi's to Henri on the phone earlier, that he would send the drink. If pressed, I might even admit that I'd done it on purpose. Maybe I don't want to wait until tomorrow to see him. Maybe. And, since I'm being honest—especially given how little time I've actually spent with the man—I rather suspected he'd show up in person to place the order. So I told Enzo not to let him off the hook when he arrived. As a matter of fact, I *ordered* Enzo to send Henri over with the drink himself. It's why I wore this blue dress.

Frank has noticed Henri's presence and his eyes narrow. It's amazing how quickly my attention has shifted from my colleagues to my . . . I'm not entirely sure what to call him, but, as he sets his hand casually on my shoulder, I am aware that Henri is something more to me than any other man at this table.

"Who's your friend, Nancy?" Frank asks.

"This is Henri Fiocca."

Frank glances at Henri and then at the hand that rests on my shoulder, thumb lightly brushing the side of my neck. Intimate. Possessive. "And what are your intentions with our dear Nancy?" he asks Henri. It's a bold, defiant question and I love Frank all the more for it. He won't be brushed off quite that easily.

I turn my head to look up at Henri. I'd like to know the answer to that as well.

His voice and his face are perfectly calm when he says, "I have traveled all the way from Marseille—over six hours by train—to deflower her."

But then he dips his chin and winks at me.

"Well, if that's your goal you'll need to go in search of a different garden," I say. "That bloom has long since been plucked."

My poor friends are scandalized to hear such talk, Frank more than any of them. But Henri throws his head back and roars with laughter. His shoulders shake, and he presses his free hand to his chest, as though he can't quite find enough oxygen to replenish his empty lungs. And that, right there, is what turns the tide in his favor. I won't go as far as to say that he's *proven* anything to me, but I am willing to let him try.

I pull a handful of francs from my billfold and hand them to Frank. "That should be enough to cover drinks," I say. Then I stand, sling my purse over one shoulder, tuck Picon under my arm, and swallow the last of my brandy in a long pull that leaves my throat burning.

Fiocca's eyes widen but he says nothing as I lift the French 75 from the table. "Good night, boys," I tell my friends.

They all stare at me but no one protests. I've done stranger things and, honestly, their chances of picking up female companions are greater if I'm not present. I can see that Frank understands, though, and he surrenders. He gives me a single nod, I blow him a kiss, and then I'm out the door with Henri Fiocca.

We're already halfway down the street before it occurs to me that I've just stolen a cocktail glass from Luigi's. Oh well, I'll bring it back tomorrow, along with a tip for Enzo. Fiocca is nearly a head taller than everyone around us and I am very glad that I've worn my tallest heels. Still, I have to peer up at him and I'm unsure what to say, so I take a sip of my French 75 instead. This makes him smile.

"Easy, there. You're crossing streams."

"What?"

"First the brandy, now gin *and* champagne. You'll be asleep on a park bench by seven o'clock, at this rate."

"So that's the trick? I did wonder how you Frenchies hold your liquor so well."

"It's just *one* of the tricks. I'll teach you the others one day."

Fiocca lifts his hand and I think he might touch me, perhaps brush my cheek or tuck a bit of hair behind my ear. But he scratches Picon behind the ears instead.

"And who is this?"

I say with all seriousness, "The great love of my life."

"Ah, a rival. What is his name?"

"Picon."

"And how do you do, sir?" Henri says, offering his knuckles for a sniff.

Picon obliges and then licks them twice. Henri bows his head slightly in gratitude. "A pleasure to meet you as well."

And what am I supposed to do with that? I mean, really. How could anyone *not* fall for such a man?

Henri returns his fingers to the soft dip between Picon's ears and continues his ministrations. My poor little dog nearly goes limp from pleasure. His tongue lolls, his hind legs twitch. After a moment, Henri says, "Perhaps the gentleman won't mind a bit of friendly competition?"

"He could be persuaded to share, under the right circumstances."

"Care to detail what those might be?"

"I'm afraid you'll just have to discover them for yourself."

"Well, you have made it quite clear that you are not interested in having dinner this evening, but perhaps you will walk with me instead? The Seine at dusk is, I believe, the eighth wonder of the world."

"Is that so?"

"Perhaps the ninth." He winks.

"A walk sounds lovely. But I am wearing uncomfortable shoes."

"Then we will walk slowly."

Without waiting for an answer, Henri plucks Picon out of my arms and sets him gently on his shoulder, splayed out like a bear rug, one set of legs down his back and other down his chest. He holds my little dog there with one hand, giving him a reassuring scratch, and then offers me his other arm. I am delighted by this unexpected, gentle act, so I slide my hand into the crook of his elbow and Henri steers us toward the river while I sip my drink.

"I do not think it is legal to walk and drink at the same time. Surely there is some law about this," he says.

"Then you will have to bail me out of jail, Mr. Fiocca, because I have every intention of finishing this delightful cocktail."

"I don't plan to surrender you to the Sûreté. They will have to pry you from my arms."

"Is that where you expect me to be?"

"A man can hope."

Luigi's is only a few blocks from the Seine and once we are through the early crowds headed toward dinner, the river walk opens up before us like a golden cobblestone ribbon. Henri hears my quick intake of breath and pulls my hand tight against his side.

"I have lived in this city for three years. How have I never walked the river at sunset?"

"There is much to see in Paris, *ma chère.* It takes a lifetime to fully appreciate everything it has to offer."

The sky is a deep, cloudless blue, broken only by the startling gold and pink of a sinking sun, but I am equally stunned by the term of endearment he's just used. It's the second time tonight. "It's a bit early to be calling me *dear,* don't you think?"

He shrugs. "I am French. And you are beautiful. It makes sense to me."

I was not at Luigi's long enough to order dinner, so I begin to feel quite warm and happy as I take another sip of my French 75. Henri glances at me sideways as I hold the near-empty glass up to the last light of the sun and watch the colors refract across my fingers.

"I am glad you like it," he says.

I am hungry and happy and slightly buzzed, so I tell him the truth. "No one has ever called me *dear* before—not even my parents. I do like it."

Henri lowers his head until his lips brush across my cheekbone and he whispers in my ear, "I meant the drink, but I am glad to see that you appreciate my efforts to prove my affection as well."

I cannot remember the last time I well and truly blushed. My face matches the sky.

He brushes the knuckles of his free hand against my cheek. "A girl who blushes. Now, that is a pretty sight."

I look at him for a long time but don't respond.

"What are you thinking?"

"I am thinking . . . ," I say, "that I am actually quite hungry after all."

"Me too."

And then Henri Fiocca kisses me right there on the river walk. It's not that I haven't been kissed before. I am twenty-four years old and I am not innocent. But still. I have never been kissed like *this.* It is thunder and rose petals at once. Static electricity and delicate intimacy. His lips are warm and soft and sweet. He goes slow at first and then he's hungry. Ravenous, in fact. Henri Fiocca is consuming me. Tasting me. I think, if his hands were free, he might lift me off the ground altogether. I imagine us falling into the river. I imagine us falling in love. Getting married. Having babies. Growing old. I imagine silk sheets and ripe strawberries. Sweat. Swearing. Begging. It lasts ten seconds, but it may as well be a lifetime for all that I've planned out. I am Mrs.—damned—Fiocca by the time he pulls away.

Henri looks as me as though I have single-handedly invented womankind. As though I am Eve herself. He looks at me as if I am sun, moon, and stars all rolled into one. A galaxy. I am terrified of how I might be looking at him, as though all my thoughts are written right there on my face.

"Shall we find somewhere to eat?" he says.

I consider it a great testament to my character that I do not suggest him as the main course.

* * *

Henri

"Would you like to come in?" Nancy asks.

It is well past midnight and they stand at the door of her tiny flat. His laughing girl is quite solidly drunk. She is bright and funny and has a wit sharp enough to scratch diamonds, but the poor girl cannot hold her liquor. It goes straight to her head in the most charming and unnerving way. At the very least, she's had too much for one day. At worst, it is Henri's fault and he has allowed her to go too far around the bend. He takes full responsibility for the fact that she is leaning against him, warm and soft, inviting him not just into her home but, he suspects, her bed as well. So he tells her the truth.

"Yes, I would very much like to come in."

He's not entirely sure what she had to drink before he arrived at Luigi's—at least the one glass of brandy—but she has since had a French 75 during their walk and another while they waited for a table. Then they shared a bottle of Chenin Blanc during dinner at Le Foquet's. He does the math: at least one glass of liquor, two cocktails, and two glasses of champagne over a five-hour period. That would be enough to make an experienced drinker feel fuzzy around the edges.

Henri had only the champagne and a few sips of her 75, so he isn't addled at all. He has, however, learned any number of things about Nancy this evening. Each more fascinating than the last. She is the youngest of six children. She left home at sixteen. She has traveled much of the world alone. She loves brandy but hates beer. She carries her little dog in her purse but would sooner shave her head than own a cat. She cannot sing, whistle, or clap in time to music. She cannot ride a bicycle. She hates goat cheese—you should have seen the way she pushed it to the edge of the charcuterie tray with her fork and then wiped the tines on her napkin—but will eat a pound of feta in one sitting.

He did his best to make her laugh throughout dinner just so he could hear the sound. He introduced her to gratinéed scallops poached in white wine and served over mushroom purée on the half shell. They talked, and they ate. And they drank—far too much, he realizes now.

Nancy fumbles with her key, trying to fit it in the lock. "Let me," he says, gently pulling it from her hand after her third attempt.

Henri turns it easily and helps her into the flat. She sets her purse on the floor so Picon can climb out and then she kicks off her shoes. Nancy sways to some music in her head as she takes his hand and leads him toward the bedroom. It's only a few steps from the front door to her room and it's a good thing too, because she won't stay upright much longer.

Her bedroom is small but the bed is large and it's piled high with blankets and extra pillows. Nancy turns on the lamp and Henri turns down the bed. Her eyes are heavy and her smile is soft and she isn't startled in the least when he scoops her up and sets her on the mattress. Then he pulls the covers up and tucks them beneath her chin. Only then do her eyes register a hint of surprise.

"You aren't coming to bed with me?"

"Non."

"Why not?"

"You're drunk, *ma fille qui rit.*"

"So are you."

He laughs. "I've never been that drunk."

"Henri?" Her eyes, heavier now, open once more but with a struggle. "What does it mean?"

"What?"

"Ma fille . . ."

He bends low over the bed and brushes his lips against the soft curl of her ear. "My laughing girl."

Her voice is barely a whisper. "Is that what you think I am?"

"Filled with laughter? *Oui.*"

"No," she clarifies. *"Yours."*

"Indeed, I do." A second kiss, this time on her temple. "Clever girl. I see that you've caught on."

And then she has slipped beneath the folds of sleep, her breath a gentle wisp of air between parted lips. "Good night, *Noncee,*" he says.

Henri stands there a bit longer than is polite, watching her sleep, and is jolted from his trance only when he feels something nudge his ankle. Little Picon stands beside him, tail wagging.

"Have I won you over, then, good sir? It's your mistress I'm more interested in, but I'll consider it a win if I've earned your trust."

Thanks to their walk earlier that evening, his suit coat is covered in fine, white dog hairs, so he slides out of it and arranges it near Nancy's feet. Then he plucks Picon from the floor and settles him in the center of the small nest. Picon yawns, little pink tongue curling at the end like a soupspoon, and burrows deeper inside.

Henri sets her keys on the nightstand, turns off the lamp, and makes his way to the kitchen. It takes him several minutes, but he finds a pen in one of the drawers and—offering a prayer for forgiveness—scribbles the number to his hotel onto the wall beside her phone.

"Good night, *Noncee,*" he whispers, again, into the darkness, and then he walks out of her flat, locking the door behind him.

* * *

PART TWO

Madame Andrée

The best people possess a feeling for beauty, the courage to take risks, the discipline to tell the truth, the capacity for sacrifice. Ironically, their virtues make them vulnerable; they are often wounded, sometimes destroyed.

—ERNEST HEMINGWAY

Madame Andrée

CHAUDES-AIGUES PLATEAU, CANTAL, FRANCE

March 2, 1944

"Gaspard! What the *hell* are you doing in that uniform?"

My French is best when I'm angry, and the words ring across the plateau, furious and clear. His head snaps up and I can feel those beady little eyes zero in on me beneath the brim of his cap. He goes perfectly still.

I recognize him now that he's stepped into the bright ring of firelight. What I can't make sense of is why he's dressed as a Brownshirt. Hubert is beside me now, weapon leveled at Gaspard's head, bending toward my pack. He grabs my revolver and hands it to me in a single, smooth movement. For all his appearances of being gangly and uncoordinated, the man can move like a quicksilver when the urge strikes him.

I feel better with the revolver in my hand. I've grown to like the solid weight of it; the wood grain in my palm and cool gunmetal against my finger. This fascination with weaponry is one of the many surprises my new life has brought, and I am not unaware that, despite all my training, this is the first time I've ever pointed my revolver at a living person. Undaunted, I pull the hammer back with the pad of my thumb.

"Explain yourself," I tell Gaspard.

All around us the shadows begin to move as Fournier's men step from their hiding places at the tree line and shift toward the bonfire.

Those who have weapons raise them and those who do not stand in solidarity with their brothers. Fifty poorly armed men now seem a great advantage against five.

Gaspard is an odious pig of a man, but he is not stupid. He recognizes that he is outnumbered and lowers his weapon.

"You," he says with such loathing that he may as well have spit a glob of mucus onto the toe of my boot.

"What are you doing here?" Hubert demands.

"We thought you were Germans. We meant to kill you and take your weapons."

"Yes, but did you plan to *seduce* us first?"

Oh, how badly Gaspard wants to shoot me! His entire body is quivering with rage. But Hubert takes a step forward, not quite placing himself between us, but letting Gaspard know he'll have to go through him to get to me.

"And finding that we are not, in fact, Germans?" Hubert says. "What is your plan now?"

Gaspard flicks his tongue to the corner of his mouth. "I intend to depart in peace."

"I believe nothing you say while in that uniform." I nod toward his waist. "Where did you get that whip?"

Seeing no other way out of his predicament, Gaspard finally relents. "We ambushed a German supply line four days ago near Le Puy. We took their weapons and vehicles. Then we stripped these uniforms from their stinking corpses." He raises a hand, palm out so as not to alarm us by the movement, and then slowly lifts the collar of his shirt to reveal a bloody bullet hole.

From the corner of my eye I can see Hubert study my face. *Do you believe him?* That's what his expression says. He is waiting for me to decide. They all are. Not a single one of the Frenchmen who flank me has so much as moved a muscle. The realization that I am well and truly in charge is so startling that I have to keep my lips pressed together so my mouth won't hang open.

I am not ready to let Gaspard off the hook this easily, however. I glare at him for a moment longer, and only when the plateau is so quiet that I can hear the crickets chirping again do I turn to Hubert and nod, once. Then I release the hammer on my revolver and place it back in the holster at my thigh. None of the men around me follow suit. Though I have declared a truce, they will not let their guard down.

"You won't find what you're looking for here," I tell Gaspard.

Visibly relaxed, he turns from me and surveys the six open crates scattered across the plateau and the piles of weapons beside them. After a moment he returns that calculating gaze of his to me. "I see much here that I desire."

"You had your chance to work with us."

"Come, Madame Andrée, do not be unreasonable."

It is the weak-minded man's retort. A thing he says when thwarted by a woman. An excuse. A bit of intellectual poverty. He doesn't like me, therefore I am unreasonable. A *femme stupide.*

"Va te faire foutre," I say.

His eyes widen. His jaw clenches. I get the impression that no woman has ever dared speak to him like this. "You're not the only English rat crawling these hills. I'll get my weapons from someone else." He pauses here, then leans in for the kill. "*Non,* you're no rat like Victor and Patrice. You are *la Souris Blanche,* aren't you?"

The White Mouse.

Merde. Gaspard knows.

I ignore the question and remain perfectly still, without emotion as I say, "There is one thing I require before you get your filthy carcass off my mountain."

He snorts. "I don't take orders from you."

"You will, in fact. And you will learn that soon enough. But first, the uniforms. Yours. And those of your men. I didn't care for them on the Germans and I like them even less on you."

"As-tu perdu ton putain d'esprit?"

"My mind is quite intact. And if you are not a collaborationist, as you claim, you will have no issue surrendering those uniforms to be burned. You can leave here without them or you can face a firing squad. The one behind me will do just fine."

"Boudin," he spits.

I sigh. "Have you no imagination at all? Ugly? Is that the best insult you can come up with? I would expect more creativity from a man who wants to lead others into battle."

The four men behind him are shifting uneasily as we glare at each other. But I am out of patience. I pull my revolver from my holster and raise it once again. "The uniforms. Now." Gaspard opens his mouth to argue—or, perhaps, to deliver a better insult—but I pull the hammer back with my thumb. "*Please* give me an excuse to shoot you. I regret not doing so last time I had the chance."

Hubert takes a step forward, followed by a handful of Fournier's men. "Do as she says."

Gaspard is out of options, but he doesn't tremble at the edge of the firelight. He walks directly toward me and looks me right in the eyes as he tosses the whip onto the fire.

"Do you know what it means? That whip?" he asks as the edges begin to blacken.

"No."

He chucks the brown hat into the flames as well and then goes to work on the buttons of his shirt, never once looking away from my face. "It's a sign of Hitler's favor. Something he gives to his officers. They are called *Obersturmführer*. Senior Storm Leaders. They are the ones he has pulled from prisons and gangs and mental institutions. Murderers. Rapists. Thieves. Child molesters. They are chosen specifically for their depravity and then given whips so they can be let loose upon whatever victims please the Gestapo. Usually Jews. The man I took this from had a pocket full of children's teeth."

I think of Vienna and the waterwheel, of Obersturmführer Wolff. "What was his name? The man you took this from?"

"I didn't ask," Gaspard says through gritted teeth.

The world will be a better place without Wolff, but I want to be the one to kill him. I want that satisfaction. I am torn between hope that he is rotting in the ground somewhere, unable to hurt anyone else, and jealousy that Gaspard might have gotten to him first.

Behind him, Gaspard's men begin to peel their uniforms off, though they are not quite so bold about it. They hover beyond the ring of firelight. They ball their clothing and throw it as near the fire as they can get. Hubert kicks each piece into the flames.

But Gaspard is in a rage now, pulling off his boots, yanking at his belt, bending over so I can see the top of his broad, hairy arse. "I don't regret killing them!" he shouts.

"Nor should you."

"And I don't regret using their filthy, disgusting uniforms to get what I need to arm my men, so I can kill more of them."

He stands before me now, in his skivvies, in the cold night air. His jaw is clenched, his eyes wild.

"Just don't make an enemy of me in the process," I say.

He leaves, then, without a word, and his men skulk off after him, wearing nothing but socks and underwear. Hubert and I remain still as the engines roar to life. Fournier joins us from where he's been watching on the other side of the fire. None of us speak as they drive away. My arm aches from holding the revolver. I am cold. I am exhausted from being up half the night. And yet I stand there, unable to hide my grin as I imagine Gaspard and his men walking back into Château Mont Mouchet. Fournier is shaking with mirth beside me. Hoots, whistles, and laughter float up from the tree line. Someone claps.

I can feel Hubert's gaze burrowing into the back of my skull, so I turn and face him. "What?"

"I assume that you have a plan when it comes to Gaspard?"

"I do, in fact."

But even he cannot quite suppress the wry smile that tugs at the corner of his mouth. "And is humiliating him part of it?"

"Oh, no. That was just for sport." I return my revolver to its holster and stretch my arm. "He is a reckless, arrogant brute. A liability to everything we're doing here."

"Agreed. But what is your *plan*?"

"I will bring him to heel."

Hubert is quiet as I drive back to Château de Couffour. The sky is only now beginning to lighten and Denis Rake is sprawled out on the backseat of the little Renault, one arm draped across his face like a swooning Victorian. The effect is somewhat ruined by his snoring, however. I am tempted to open the window and wake him with a blast of cold air, but he's exhausted—we all are after unpacking and cleaning weapons late into the night. Our orders from London were to arrive at the plateau at ten in the evening and be gone by four the next morning to avoid detection. Easier said than done, as it turns out, but Fournier's first group of men has their weapons, and everyone seems to be happy. Except Hubert. He's scowling at the windshield.

"You make me nervous when you think," I tell him.

"And you make me nervous when you don't."

"What is that supposed to mean?"

"You let Gaspard go."

"What was I supposed to do? Arrest him? Shoot him? He's an absurd, arrogant, disgusting prick, but he's not a collaborationist."

"He's trouble," Hubert says.

"Indeed. But he also commands four thousand men spread across the Auvergne. We can't be starting a civil war between him and Fournier. We're on the same side of this bloody war."

He goes quiet again, popping his knuckles one by one, first the fingers on his left hand, then the right. "Still, I don't like it—"

"Oh." I've finally realized what's troubling him. "He knows our location—"

Hubert nods. "It's no secret at all, the plateau and Château de Couffour are only—"

"Five kilometers apart."

"Maybe a bit less."

"Which means Gaspard can find us easily."

"Or lead someone else to us," Hubert says.

"You think he'd really report us to the Germans?"

He shrugs. "I have no idea what that man might do."

The sun won't be up for another hour and the sky has that wet-wool look, like rain is coming in from the west. The road is full of potholes and the steering wheel on the Renault is loose. But I turn my head and look at Hubert anyway. His gaze is fixed on mine and he sits there, hands now still and resting in his lap, waiting for me to come to the same conclusion that he's already reached.

My mind is numb and flaccid after being up all night. It takes only a moment longer and I'm furious with myself for not taking stock of the situation earlier. *"Merde!"* I scream, pounding the flat of my hand against the steering wheel. "We have to move camp."

It was too much to hope for, I suppose, being able to weather the war safe and sound inside the Château de Couffour. But at least our host is coming with us.

I like Fournier. He was a hotel executive before the war and then fled to the country when the Germans invaded, bringing his cheerful wife and a small fortune with him. The money, long gone, was put to good use arming his maquisards, but his wife is kept hidden and safe in a remote village whose location he refuses to share even with me.

I stuff my possessions into my pack as Hubert stands at the door of my room. We did allow ourselves one last, comfortable sleep this morning when we got back from the drop zone. But it's late afternoon now and we have to be on our way. At least Fournier provided us a lunch of bread, soft apples, and fresh milk. There's a cow hidden somewhere on the property and she must be happy and well fed, because the milk was thick with cream.

"I should have known we couldn't stay," I grumble as I zip my pack.

"Large manor homes make easy targets," Hubert says.

"Yes, but they also come equipped with proper beds and fully stocked wine cellars."

I give one last, longing look toward the mattress and follow Hubert from the château. Denis Rake is waiting for us in the backseat of the Renault. He is unshaved, unhappy, and underwhelmed with our new plan.

"You mean to tell me we are actually going to camp out in the woods with these men?" He scowls at me, unaware of how comical he looks sitting there, holding the transmitter and radio to his chest like a couple of teddy bears.

I toss my pack onto the seat beside him, climb in, and start the engine. I offer my best, most charming grin—the one Henri loves—making certain to flash my dimple. "Not at all. Camping implies a short period of time. One week. Perhaps two. We're going to be *living* out there, rough as guts."

Although I can't be certain, I suspect that Rake is assailing me in Hungarian by the way he spits out a slew of guttural words.

"Any idea what he's saying?" I ask.

Hubert shakes his head in the seat beside me. "Not a word."

"Probably best."

And then we're off, following Fournier as he leads us to a remote encampment. Though his headquarters are at the Château de Couffour, his men are spread out, in small groups, throughout the Cantal. He's arranged each with a leader who answers directly to him and dispersed them widely so as not to be vulnerable to attack. Still, each of Fournier's camps has specific needs and I must assess them one by one in order to arm them properly. It will take weeks.

We drive for over twenty minutes, maneuvering our way through the foothills and then up, ever higher, until we reach the spot chosen by Fournier as our base for the foreseeable future. This is the farthest end of the Chaudes-Aigues plateau and is home to one of his larger groups, populated by over two hundred men. The plateau commands all the other surrounding mountains and valleys, and Fournier's Maquis control every path, track, and road that leads up to it. His men are embedded in the strongest position in the entire district and they use it to their advantage. Despite being remote, its elevation should provide an excellent radio signal for our daily transmissions to London.

Fournier directs us into a clearing and cuts his engine. We climb out of our vehicles and find six smoldering cook fires and a handful of men eating what I fear might be the remains of a horse. Once they recognize Fournier, a series of whistles are sent up and dozens more men materialize between the trees. Some hold weapons, but most don't. As I look around the clearing, it occurs to me that there is not a single shelter or tent to be seen, only these men, wearing what they have. The ground is damp, the men are haggard, and everyone is staring at us. I feel out of place in my wool slacks and red lipstick.

"I'll just explain to them who you are," Fournier says, then jogs off to speak with one of his lieutenants.

Hubert is an army man and accustomed to harsh conditions.

Even still, his shoulders slump and he glowers at the cook fire. He mutters something under his breath and stomps off after Fournier.

"You can't be serious," Rake hisses in my ear. He is an aristocrat, fond of his luxuries, and is dubious about this entire situation. "Where are we going to *sleep*?"

I flash him a wicked grin. "I call dibs on the car."

"Fine, but what are we going to *eat*?"

We both look back to the campfire, where Hubert is standing, now pointing angrily at the carcass. "Not that," I say.

"Have you ever seen Hubert so worked up?" he asks.

"I didn't actually know he was capable of emotions." And yet there he is, face red, voice a low rumble.

Rake snorts. "I still find it funny that Buckmaster put you two together."

"Because I have all the emotions?"

"On a regular basis."

We watch Hubert, amazed.

Finally, at a loss for any other explanation, Rake shrugs. "He must love horses."

"Madame Andrée!" Fournier shouts, waving me over.

"Come along, then," I tell Rake. "We're being summoned."

As we trudge through the clearing Rake takes in the various groups of men scattered near the trees, then leans in and whispers, "They're all staring at you."

"Jealous?"

He glares at me. "Have they never seen a woman before?"

It's true. Fournier's men are staring. They have been since we stepped out of the Renault. The more men who have entered the clearing, the more curious eyes I've felt upon my person. They are shameless in their surveyal. "Not in a long time, I'd wager."

"Careful, Duckie, that could be an issue."

I march ahead, chin high. "Only if I let it."

When we reach the fire, Hubert turns to me, hands tucked deep into his pockets, and says, "We have a problem."

"More than one, apparently, by the look on your face. But start with the most urgent."

"Your friend does not like the ... ah ... *arrangements* my men have made for feeding themselves," Fournier says.

"Arrangements?" I ask.

"Normally my men maintain a steady diet of forest mushrooms—*cèpes,* they're called—along with whatever game they can catch. Mostly fish and quail. With the occasional old horse thrown in for good measure," he says, and I shudder, then brave a glance at Rake. That confirms our suspicions. "But the Cantal is littered with small farms and villages."

"So?"

"So," Hubert interrupts, "these men have been raiding farms at night, stealing pigs and chickens. Pillaging root cellars." He points at the carcass beside the first. "Did you not notice it's still wearing a *saddle*?"

I hadn't, in fact. I was too distracted by the grotesque, bared teeth inside the blackened skull.

Hubert continues. "They pluck clothing right off the line and milk the dairy cows before their owners can get to them. They've become a plague throughout the Cantal."

Fournier is clearly embarrassed at this revelation, but he tries to defend his men nonetheless. "And who do you think is protecting those very farms and villages from the Germans? My men! What are they supposed to do? Sit out here and starve to death?"

It's clear most of these men don't speak English. Their heads whip back and forth from Hubert to Fournier to me. They are uncertain who is in charge. I look at each of them in turn and say very clearly, in French, "Leave us alone, we need to speak with Fournier."

None of them move. In fact, from the way their spines stiffen and their fists clench, it looks as if they are growing roots right into the ground. To be given an order by a woman? The insult!

"Allez!" Fournier snaps, and they look at him, startled, before glaring and stomping off.

"You cannot let your men steal from their neighbors," I say. "Or you will be fighting two wars. Much more of that"—I point to the saddle—"and your countrymen will be after you with pitchforks."

He gnaws at the side of his lip and looks somewhere beyond my left shoulder. He cannot bring himself to make eye contact as he says, "I can't afford to feed them."

And this is why I volunteered to come back to France, to be tossed out of an airplane, to sleep on the ground and be deprived of basic luxuries. "But I can," I say.

His eyes lock into place at this bit of news. *"Pardon?"*

"Well, to be specific, England can afford to feed your men. But the money will come through me."

"I don't understand," he says.

"Starting today, I want you to instruct your men as follows. Let them take whatever they like from the Germans. Food. Clothing. Vehicles. Lifeblood. All of that is fair game. But they are not to steal one more thing from their countrymen. Every time you take from your neighbors, you erode their trust. And we *need* them. Living out here is no excuse to take advantage of the only allies you have. We need their loyalty and their information. Understand? They see and hear things we don't, and we can't have them keeping it from us out of spite. I will request money for you and your men along with the weapons, and I will distribute it among your groups according to need. They can buy their provisions from these farmers at market rates. Do you understand?"

He nods.

"There will be no exceptions to this rule."

He nods again.

"Good. Go tell your men."

He blinks at me once and then trots off, assuming I mean *right this moment.*

"Well." I huff out a breath and turn in a slow circle, staring back at the little clusters of men gathered around the clearing. "This will be interesting."

I wake just before dawn with a full bladder and the uncomfortable realization that I am surrounded on all sides by two hundred sex-starved Frenchmen. In my experience, this particular species is undaunted even when regularly serviced. But the men around me haven't seen or touched a woman in months, possibly years. Rake was correct. This could be an issue.

The greater problem, however, is the urgent need to relieve myself. There is little chance of falling back to sleep now, so I decide that I may as well kill two birds with one stone.

Hubert teased me mercilessly back in London when he heard that I planned to bring my red satin pillow, a toothbrush, and a hefty supply of toothpaste with me on this mission.

"Bloody waste of space!" he said. "You'll drop straight to the ground with all that weight in your pack."

I'd patted his stomach and laughed. "It doesn't weigh half so much as your spare tire."

And that had been the end of it. Until last night, when he caught sight of me blissfully brushing my teeth beside the stream. I like to think he was sick with envy when I laid my head on that pillow inside the Renault while he laid his on a clump of dry grass beside the campfire.

The fire has gone out now, and my companions are snoring. This will never do long-term, but we will figure out better accommodations later. I sit up and stretch my aching back, push my hair away from my face, and peer out of the car window. I am the only person awake. There won't be a better time, so I push the door open, grab my pack, and pick my way through the camp. I head toward the gentle, trickling stream beyond the pines.

The stream bank is dotted with clumps of waist-high brush—gorse, I think—and I move carefully, looking for a good spot. It's at times like these that I wish I'd been born a man. How wonderful it must be to shift your trousers and *stand up* to pee. But no, women have to go bare-assed and vulnerable. In the cold! Not to mention the issue of aiming. Just thinking about the indignity makes me angry. I've been in this situation before and I didn't like it any better then. Best to just get it over with.

I squat.

And then I wait.

It takes only a few seconds, but, as expected, the bushes around me begin to shake. The men hiding inside are trying to get a better view. I knew it. I just *knew* it. I could feel all those leering eyes watch me as I headed to the stream last night. They'd marked my preferred location and formed a plan. Part of me can't blame them. My presence has created quite a stir. They are curious. And incorrigible. But still, this is unacceptable.

I slide my hand into my pack, withdraw my revolver, and stand. I like to think they are disappointed to see that my trousers are still in place.

"You can come out now," I say.

The bushes continue to wriggle but no one emerges.

"If that's how you prefer to do this."

I aim my revolver at the ground in front of the nearest patch of brush and fire a single shot. It's like startling a pack of geese. Men spring out of the earth all around me. Some throw themselves on the ground and begin scrambling away. Others shoot straight up, several feet into the air. A handful dart into the woods, but most freeze when I yell, *"Arrêtez!"*

I'm fairly certain that one man has pissed himself—his trousers are dark and damp around the crotch. Pity. He won't fare well against the Germans if that's what happens when he hears a gunshot.

And that's when Hubert, Rake, and Fournier burst through the trees, weapons raised, heads whipping back and forth, trying to find the cause of the commotion.

"What the bloody *hell,*" Rake says, looking at me agog. Half his hair is sticking out to one side and there's a bit of drool at the corner of his mouth. "Are you dead?"

"Good morning, gentlemen," I say.

"We thought someone had been shot," Hubert says.

"Someone was about to be."

Fournier is the only one who seems to have caught on to what's happening. He isn't smiling, exactly, but there is amusement in his eyes. "We thought we were being attacked."

"Call them back," I tell Fournier. "Every single man who just left. I want everyone in the clearing in two minutes."

He nods, then whistles, clear and loud, and we all tromp back to stand beside the fire pits. I am surrounded by dozens and dozens of men, the vast majority newly woken, and I look at their faces carefully. I can tell who was in those bushes based on who will not meet my gaze.

I set my pack on the ground, stow my revolver inside, and speak very clearly in French. "Since we're all together, I'd like to set a few ground rules."

They stare and blink. Rub their eyes. Scratch their crotches. Stretch and yawn. Some look at me suspiciously. Others smirk. I'd like to box every single one of their ears.

"Fournier is your commanding officer," I say, my voice loud enough to echo off the trees. "But my colleagues and I are the ones who will supply you with weapons and teach you how to use them. *Do you understand?*"

Heads nod reluctantly.

"Along with those weapons will come money for food. *Do you understand?*"

Heads nod, a bit more interested now.

I turn in a half circle, trying to make eye contact with as many men as possible. "But if you make me angry, I will not give you weapons. And I will leave you out here to starve. *Do you understand?*"

Heads nod.

"It really, *really* makes me angry when desperate, *surchauffé*, unwashed little men try to get a glimpse at my bare ass while I pee. *Do you understand?*"

Heads nod, emphatically.

"I will have my privacy. *Do you understand?*"

Nodding, nodding, nodding.

Hubert tries to wrestle his grin into submission, but Rake is positively shaking with mirth.

"I will go to the damned toilet in peace. *Do you understand?*"

Heads nod.

Fournier chortles out loud. I glare at him and he clears his throat, doing his best to make it seem as though he's coughing.

"Follow me into the bushes again and I will shoot you twice, once in the ballocks and once in the skull. *Do. You. Fucking. Un. Der. Stand.?*" Heads nod once more. "Good. Now get out of my sight."

They flee, like their own mothers were after them with a switch, and before long it's only myself, Fournier, Rake, and Hubert left around the burned-out fire. At least the horse carcass has been removed.

"I am tired and hungry and cold," I say. "And I swear if any of you teases me about this, I'll kill you too."

Hubert shrugs. "I actually thought it was quite impressive."

Rake nods, eyes glinting. "My own ballocks crawled right up inside my body. I'll have to go through puberty again so they'll drop."

"Shut up." I laugh and then stop because that makes me need to go even worse. "I need their respect, not their lust. And I can't have both."

I turn and walk away.

"Where are you going?" Rake shouts after me.

"To pee. I'm about to *explode*." And they do laugh then, but I don't fault them for it given that my walk has turned into a waddle with the urgency of my mission. "If anyone comes within fifty feet of that stream, shoot them."

"You have my word . . . *Duckie*," Rake shouts, but he's laughing so hard he almost chokes on the last word.

Nancy Grace Augusta Wake

NANCY'S FLAT, RUE SAINTE-ANNE, PARIS

January 1937

"Well," Stephanie says, drawing on her cigarette, "I hope you haven't been sending him love letters. Women do stupid things like that after sex."

I fold a black pencil skirt and set it carefully into my suitcase. "How many times do I have to tell you that I did not sleep with Henri Fiocca?"

She rolls her eyes. "Oh, I am *certain* there was no sleeping involved."

"Let me be as clear as I can. We. Are. Not. Having. Sex."

"But you've been seeing him for months."

"Yes. So?"

"Isn't that the way of things?" she asks. Stephanie sits curled up in the small wingback chair in my bedroom. The velvet is faded and it's threadbare, but I'm certain there is no more comfortable seat in all of Paris than right there at my window with the sun shining through the frosted panes.

"Often, yes."

My favorite green cashmere sweater goes into the suitcase next and I smooth out the creases so it will arrive unwrinkled. The color sets off my eyes and the wide neckline flatters my jaw. But it's the softness of the thing—like a rabbit's underbelly—that I'm certain will have Henri Fiocca purring in my ear when I see him tomorrow.

Stephanie blows smoke out her nose, looking for all the world like the concept of not bedding a man has set her brain on fire. "*Ma petite,* say what you like to him, especially on the pillow, but never put it in writing. He will hold you to it forever otherwise."

She's the one who brought up pillows, so I grab one from my bed and throw it at her head, but she ducks it easily, laughing.

"I've had many conversations with Henri Fiocca, but none of them have involved pillows."

"That's how the Count got me, you know," she continues, ignoring me completely. "He swept me off my feet. Bought me flowers and wine and perfume. He sent me letters. Took me to Italy. Of course, I responded. Declared my love in return. And now, whenever I behave badly he waves those letters in my face. How am I supposed to take a lover like a proper Frenchwoman when he's constantly reminding me of my oaths of undying fidelity?"

Stephanie loves Count Gonzales; I know she does. And she remains staunchly faithful to him. But I am now uncertain whether that's by choice.

"I have sent exactly zero love letters to Henri Fiocca," I say in complete honesty. However, I do not mention that we speak at great length on the phone several times per week.

Stephanie is unimpressed. "And yet, here you are, packing your suitcase to travel south yet again. How many times is this in the last four months?"

"Four."

She looks at me with those unnerving blue eyes. "And you will no doubt be staying—"

"At the Hôtel du Louvre et Paix. Like I always do—"

"—with a guest, no doubt."

"Unless you mean Picon, no. Fiocca has his own flat. Somewhere. I've never been there."

Stephanie tosses her cigarette onto the floor and grinds it out with the toe of her shoe. "And why not?" she demands. "What is wrong with you?"

"Well, for starters, he's never invited me." She opens her mouth to interrupt again but I stop her. "Nor has he invited himself up to my room. And, yes, I bloody well know that I could do the inviting on both counts, but I just"—here I struggle to explain myself—"feel like there's nothing wrong with being . . ."

"Ridiculous?"

"Hard to get." I continue packing my suitcase. "That man could have any woman in Marseille."

"Have you *looked* at him? He could have any woman in France." She shakes her head. "I despair of you ever becoming a proper *Parisienne*."

I stab a finger at her. "That's my point *exactly*. Don't you see? In this one instance I'd like to be *different*. If he wants me, he has to work for it. I won't make it easy for him."

"He could be seeing ten different women while he's waiting on you," she says.

"If so, I'll find out. And that will be the end."

I suppose this is possible. Henri Fiocca doesn't lack for opportunity. But something tells me he isn't running around on me. Or maybe I am deluded. Regardless, I have a train to catch, a city to visit, and a story to find—the Hearst Newspaper Group will be expecting an article of some sort next week, and, given the calm political climate in Marseille at the moment, I will have to get creative to find one. For months I've been taking any opportunity that presents itself to travel south. It couldn't be more obvious to Stephanie, or anyone else halfway paying attention for that matter, that I am practically hurling myself toward Marseille—and Henri—every chance I get. To be fair, however, he's doing the same. Paris is landlocked, but you'd think it was the center of the shipping universe the way he makes excuses to travel north for work. Thankfully, he has no one to answer to but his father.

Stephanie stretches, then picks a piece of tobacco from her tongue. "Trust me, *ma petite*, whisper your promises. Don't mail them."

"Fine words from the woman who got me into this mess in the first place," I say, slamming the lid of my suitcase a little harder than necessary.

She grins now, and I see how delighted she really is about my growing love affair. "You're welcome."

VERDUN'S RESTAURANT, MARSEILLE

"Please don't be angry with me," Henri says the next night as he pulls out my chair. He sets his hands on my shoulders, thumbs caressing the soft green sweater. He drops a kiss to one cheek.

I straighten my spine but don't shake off his hands. "Why should I be angry?"

"I've invited someone to join us for dinner."

"Who?"

A whisper in my ear. "My father."

"Your—"

"I didn't tell you because I didn't want you to be nervous." Henri chooses the chair to my left instead of the one across from me.

"I thought you didn't want me to be *angry*?"

"That either."

"Then you can't spring something like this on me."

"To be fair, this is a first. Besides, I was afraid you wouldn't come if you knew he'd be here."

"You were correct." Honestly, if he'd told me we were having dinner with Satan himself I would have come. We're eating at Verdun's tonight. It's my favorite restaurant in Marseille—or at least the ones we've been to so far. It is warm and elegant—white linens and candlelight—and the food is nothing short of a religious experience. I won't admit this, however. I'd rather Henri think I'm upset. Who brings a girl to meet his father and doesn't warn her first?

Henri takes a quick, deep breath and huffs it out. "Listen, he wants to meet you. He's been asking. I go to Paris a lot. He knows it's for a woman. And I'd like you to meet him as well."

"Why?"

"Because we're… This is… not like the other relationships I've had."

I won't smile. I. Will. Not. Smile. Henri Fiocca cannot have the satisfaction of knowing how pleased I am by those words. He can't know how desperately I want to be *special.* To be the one he chooses. So I scowl at him instead. It's the only way to mask the pure elation that I feel.

"*Merde.* There he is," Henri says.

I catch the warning in his eyes—that sudden flash of surprise—just before he stands. Henri's father is not alone.

I follow his gaze and take in the couple who have just stepped inside the front door of Verdun's. The man is clearly Henri's father. They are identical. Same height. Same build. Same handsome face—though Henri's is a good thirty years younger. His father's hair is salt-and-pepper to Henri's black. His laugh lines are deeper. His body softer. But they are one and the same. Cut from the same expensive cloth. The woman at his side, however, cannot be Henri's mother.

"That is..." I search for the name of the woman I met here five months ago.

"Marceline," Henri says. I've never heard him use this cold voice before, and it has my full attention. I return my gaze to him and note the clenched jaw. The single, furious twitch of his upper lip.

"Why—"

"I don't know," he hisses. "But I am sorry. I didn't know, and she wasn't invited."

"By you?"

"Certainly not."

"Okay. I can live with that."

And I'll have to because Joseph, the maître d', is leading them toward our table. They are twenty feet away. Ten. Five. We are standing, and I have summoned a half-hearted smile for the occasion. All teeth but no sincerity. I don't think of myself as the sort of woman who gets nervous, but here I am, heart pounding as Henri introduces me to his father.

"This is Nancy," he says, setting my hand gently into his father's.

"Pleased to meet you." My voice sounds hollow. Insincere. And I can see his eyes narrow.

"Ranier Fiocca," he says, but my brain records him simply as Old Man Fiocca. It's the only way to distinguish him from Henri. They are too similar. He drops my hand without shaking it in return or pressing a customary kiss to the knuckles. I feel as though I have been measured and found wanting.

"And Marceline," Henri adds, the frost heavy in his voice as he looks at his father. "Though I must admit I was not expecting a fourth party."

"I invited her," he says.

"I see."

They glower at each other and I extend my hand to Marceline as father and son engage in a silent battle of wills.

"We've met," she says, glancing at my hand but not taking it.

"Have you?" Old Man Fiocca looks from his son to Marceline, then to me. "Where exactly was that?"

I take my seat and Henri joins me. He moves close enough that the entire lengths of our thighs touch. His hand is on my knee—a comfort, a warning. I don't give Henri a chance to answer his father. I am too angry—too blisteringly angry at him for putting me in this situation—to give him the opportunity to smooth this over.

"Well, the last time we saw one another, she was in the company of your son."

Of all the things I expect Old Man Fiocca to do, laugh is not one of them. But he does. Loud and startling. "Was she? I am glad to hear it! It's been too long since they spent time together."

"I agree." Marceline's voice is a purr. But not a lioness. Hers is the voice of a jackal, one who takes her blood straight from the jugular. And her eyes are on me, looking for weakness. "Henri and I have a long history."

Our waiter arrives to take our drink order and we all, in unison, request brandy. No water. No wine. We're going straight to the liquor. If our waiter is nervous, if he feels the boiling tension surrounding our small corner table, he doesn't let on.

But then Old Man Fiocca looks at me with a calculating glint. "Bring a bottle of Bollinger Cuvée Brut as well."

"Oui, monsieur," our waiter says, then retreats at a fast clip toward the kitchen.

The scent of baking bread and seared steak fills the restaurant, along with the rich aroma of bouillabaisse. Normally this would make my mouth water. But my stomach is a bag of knots instead, coiled and tight.

Marceline has chosen the seat directly across from Henri, putting herself on display. She shimmies out of her fur coat, revealing a brown satin blouse, unbuttoned to a deep—almost immoral—V. I can see her clavicles and sternum clearly, along with the inner curve of each breast. It's cold. It's *January* for Pete's sake. But there she is, no brassiere, nipples evident against the thin fabric. A delicate gold necklace rests along her collarbones, a pendant—in the form of the letter *H*—sits gently in the hollow, and she touches it lightly with one finger.

Oh. Now I see what's happening. *H.* Henri. She has staked her claim and Old Man Fiocca approves. To him, *I* am the unwanted guest. The interloper. And what better way to drive me off than to bring one of Henri's old flames to our first meeting?

Marceline situates her coat over the back of her chair. Smiles gently at Old Man Fiocca. Smiles seductively at Henri. But it's the smile she gives me that is vindictive. She remembers what happened at our last meeting and is out for blood. Is desperate for it, in fact. Given the look on her face, I can see how clearly she has imagined this moment. *Planned* for it—which means she is likely behind this entire fiasco. So I give her a single nod. *I see you,* it says, *and I will not be driven off.*

I am not the sort of woman who waits for the attack, so I'm drawing a breath, about to speak, when Old Man Fiocca asks, "Where exactly are you from, *Mademoiselle* . . . ?"

"Wake," I say, taking a second to recalibrate. "I was born in New Zealand but raised in Australia."

"Not *Français.*" He gives Henri a disapproving glance as though beginning a list of my faults. "And what is it that you do?"

"I am a journalist."

"Is that so?"

I nod.

"And what do you cover?"

"Politics, mostly. But also current affairs. And sports, occasionally. I covered the Olympics last year in Berlin." If this were a different conversation and he a different sort of man, I would tell him what it felt like to stand in that stadium and watch Jesse Owens beat Adolf Hitler's best runners to win the gold medal. And then, what it felt like, afterward, to interview the son of black sharecroppers from Alabama knowing that he had just changed the world. I would tell him about standing in the shadow of the *Hindenburg* as it passed over the field. An engineering marvel desecrated by the black swastika painted on its sides. If he had come to meet me instead of to chase me away, I would tell him any number of things, not the least of which is how enamored I am of his son.

As expected, he is unimpressed. "And which French newspaper do you work for?"

"Not a single one," I say.

"Pardon?"

"I'm a freelancer. I work for the European bureau of the Hearst Newspaper Group."

"Hearst?" he says, as though he's really saying *maggot* or *feces.* "They are American?"

"Yes."

"I am familiar with that tabloid."

The one thing I can tolerate about Marceline—the single feature on her entire, beautifully smug face—is the fact that she does not have a perfect smile. There is an overlap in her two front teeth. Just a small imperfection. So, when she flashes her triumphant grin, it is slightly warped.

I do not need Henri to defend me, and the fact that he doesn't makes me love him all the more. Yes. I love him. I cannot help it. I realized this at the train station today. He found me and kissed me on the platform, in full view of every person there. And then he dug around in my handbag for Picon and kissed him too, right on the nose. Picon returned his affection with a lick right on the chin and I thought my poor battered heart might explode from the joy of it all. My little dog is asleep in my hotel room, on a cushion that Henri Fiocca bought for him. It is purple velvet with black piping and Picon looks like a monarch perched right there in the center. Like the bloody king of England. So Old Man Fiocca and Marceline can say or do what they please, because I have everything I've ever wanted.

I turn to Marceline. Change the subject. "And what do you do?"

"She's a secretary," Old Man Fiocca answers for her.

"For who?"

"Albert Paquet," she says, as though I ought to know who this is.

"Police Commissioner Paquet," Old Man Fiocca clarifies.

I ignore him and continue looking at her. "It must not pay well."

"Why do you say that?" she asks.

I nod at her décolletage. "Apparently you can't even afford a brassiere."

Marceline goes perfectly still, lips parted slightly, as though surprised. And I suppose she is. Most Frenchwomen employ subtlety in their battles, death by a thousand paper cuts. Whereas I prefer a direct attack. Piss or get off the pot. It takes her a moment to rally, and I can see her eyes hardening, her thoughts gathering, when Old Man Fiocca laughs. The sound is one of *delight.* He believes my barb to be the opening bell in a boxing match and he leans forward, eager to see what will happen next.

Once, when I was a very young teen, in Sydney, one of my older brothers took me to a seedy part of town. It was a dare—just a way to pass the time on a boring Saturday afternoon—but we went to an establishment where women wrestled one another, barely clothed, while covered in oil like greased pigs. We didn't stay long, and, in truth, I didn't understand the point of the entire situation at the time. It took many years of puzzled contemplation to figure out that some men enjoy watching women fight. If they expose themselves in the process, even better. Looking at him now, at the pure, fiendish pleasure in his eyes, I am certain that Old Man Fiocca would have very much enjoyed that wrestling match. Hell, he's tried to set one up tonight.

Our waiter returns with brandy and champagne on ice. He pops the cork and evenly pours the golden, bubbling liquid in four separate flutes, but I reach for my brandy and don't even wait to see if Old Man Fiocca will offer a toast before I take my first sip. Henri's hand settles onto my knee again and I think it might be a warning, but this is a war I am determined to win.

Henri leans to his left and I hear him whisper, "May I have a word with you outside, Papa?"

Old Man Fiocca nods. *"Oui."*

Henri stands, then kisses me lightly on my forehead. "If you will excuse us for a moment."

I watch them weave their way through the tables toward the front door, marveling that a man's gait is something that can be inherited, for the two men *walk* exactly the same. Once they are out of earshot I turn back to Marceline.

"Whose idea was this? Yours? Or his?"

She looks at me down the straight line of her nose. "I don't know what you're talking about."

"How about we make a pact? No lies. And no feigned stupidity?"

Her mouth curls into a feral smile. "I do not make pacts with *foreigners*."

"So, your idea, then? Okay. Seems risky. Why bother?"

Marceline takes a moment to reassess the situation. I'm not going to play by the typical rules, and once she makes peace with this fact she leans across the table, her expression that of a jilted lover. "Because Henri is *mine*."

I can't help but laugh. "Not anymore."

She dismisses me with a flick of her wrist. "You're nothing but a distraction. A fling. Henri will come back to me. He always does. Unlike you, he knows his place."

I would like to toss the rest of my brandy in her face, but I take a sip instead. "His place? I take it you mean with a Frenchwoman?"

"With *this* Frenchwoman."

"And he gets no say in this?"

She snorts. "Henri will do what his father tells him."

"I suspect you are quite wrong about that. Otherwise he wouldn't be standing out in the cold scolding his father for bringing you tonight."

If I were ice, Marceline would melt me. If I were fire, she would squelch me. As it stands, I am flesh and bone and she is powerless to do a thing about my presence—in this restaurant or in Henri's life.

We are throwing daggers at each other with our eyes when Henri and his father return to the table. Henri settles into his seat and slides his hand up my thigh until he finds my slip, then plays with the lace edge. "Forgive our rudeness," he says. "Just a bit of *business* that needed to be addressed."

Old Man Fiocca looks at Henri, then at me. "I've not yet heard how you met my son."

"Here in Marseille, at Le Bar de la Marine. A mutual friend introduced us."

"What friend?" he asks.

"A very private one." I will not bring Stephanie into this. I think Henri's father would like her very much. But she wouldn't like being hounded by him. Nor would Count Gonzales.

"Funny. He never mentioned this."

Henri takes a sip of his brandy. "You can ask Marceline. She was there. I suspect the entire evening made quite an *impression* on her."

For all their apparent similarities, Henri is made of sterner stuff than his father. He stares at Old Man Fiocca, daring him to continue. And we all sit there in that silence, waiting to see who will speak first, when the waiter arrives, once more, to take our orders for dinner.

"Coq au vin," I say without even looking at the menu.

This must have been what Marceline wanted, because she looks at me as though I am a physical manifestation of the black plague. *"Ratatouille,"* she snaps.

Old Man Fiocca tersely gives his order. *"Boeuf bourguignon."*

The waiter looks at Henri. "And you, *monsieur*?"

"Sole meunière."

I like to think that Henri will stab his father with the bones of that fish.

"I am curious about one more thing," Old Man Fiocca says.

"What is that?" I ask.

"What exactly do you see in my son?"

"Oh, that is quite simple." There is only a finger of brandy left in my glass and I swallow it in one smooth gulp. I haven't even touched my champagne but I'll break the fingers of anyone who tries to stop me from drinking that next. "Your son is a gentleman and a gentle *man*. Whereas you, sir, are an arse."

* * *

Henri

"Come, *ma chère*," Henri says. "I think it is time you learned to drink."

"I'm not thirsty," she snaps, yanking her arm away.

"That's not what I meant."

They stand on the sidewalk outside Verdun's and she has her back to the window. Little clouds of frozen air drift from her nostrils in angry puffs. But the streetlamps are on and they bathe her face in golden light, making even her fury look angelic. Henri can see his father and Marceline inside the restaurant, at the table where they left them, glaring. He returns the hostile stare until they turn back to their dessert. The January air has an edge tonight—unseasonably cold—and Nancy belts her coat tighter around her waist. Her hands are shaking in anger and he can't blame her. He brought this disaster on himself.

"What did you mean, then?" she asks.

"You've got thimble guts."

"What?"

"You're a lightweight, love. One drink and you go under. It will never do. My father did it on purpose."

"Why?"

"To get you talking. To make you angry."

"Well, it worked."

"Perhaps. But it didn't have the intended effect. You're still here." He watches her sway slightly on her feet. "I'd hate to see it happen again, though. By him or anyone else."

"How long has it been since you and Marceline were lovers?"

"Ah. I see the two of you had a talk as well." He traces her jaw with the tip of one finger. "Many years. I ended it."

"But you were with her the night we met."

He nods. "I was bored and lonely and she wore me down. But I don't regret being there. I wouldn't have met you otherwise."

"Good answer. But you're going to have to work harder than that to smooth this over."

He laughs. "I'm *trying*. Now will you come with me? Please?"

Henri offers his arm, and, after a moment, Nancy accepts, tucking her fingers inside the bend of his elbow.

"Where are we going?" she asks.

"To my favorite bar. First, I will sober you up. And then I will try to get you astonishingly drunk. Your job is to thwart me."

"Sounds like a boxing match with my liver."

"It's a game, actually."

"And if I succeed?"

He winks. "Then I will take you straight up to your room and let you have your way with me."

"Up?"

Henri gives her a mischievous grin. "Ah, *ma chère,* this bar is located quite conveniently inside your hotel."

Marseille is a city offended by the mere suggestion of winter. She was built to be enjoyed at dusk during the height of summer, wineglass in hand, freckles bright from a day in the sun; not hustled through on a cold January night. And yet, there is still an irrefutable charm clinging to her cobblestones and dormant vines. She is an Old World city, boasting good bones and expensive taste. Age has refined her, Henri thinks, and her stately buildings do not crack or crumble. Below them is the harbor, ships tucked in for the night, and above them the Basilica of Notre-Dame de la Garde, lit up like a beacon on the hill. Streetlamps and shop windows bathe the city in amber light. It bounces off the water and the old stone walls. Everything is blue and gold. Regal. The night air stings his eyes as they walk toward the Vieux Port, huddled close for warmth, but Henri turns his face to the sky and sees that it, too, is magnificent. Black velvet and white diamonds. His mind drifts toward the landscape of Nancy's body and he almost misses his turn onto the Canebière, distracted by thoughts of black velvet and white diamonds lying across her collarbone.

Soon the four grand caryatids at the entrance of the Hôtel du Louvre et Paix are before them and he guides her across the street and toward the doors. As he does every time he steps inside the hotel, Henri marvels at the intricacy of the sculptures. Each holds an animal in her marble hands—a sphinx, an elephant, a dromedary, and a fish. He's always thought they are a portent of something—good or evil—but he doesn't know what. Tonight, he's hoping for good.

Henri situates them at the bar instead of the more popular and brightly lit lobby. There are stumpy candles set at intervals along its length, giving the room a warmth the lobby chandeliers cannot rival. He inches his stool closer to Nancy so that their thighs touch and he drops his hand to her knee, squeezing it once with affection.

"First rule of drinking," Henri says, "is mind your temperature."

Nancy tilts her chin to the side in question. He wants to run his finger along her jaw but resists, focusing on the task at hand instead.

"It's a bad combination, drinking too much and being too warm. You'll go right to sleep. Open a window or take off your coat, but mind your temperature at all times."

"I'm beginning to suspect you're just trying to get my clothes off, Fiocca," she says, but shrugs out of her coat and drapes it across the back of the chair anyway.

"That comes later, *ma chère*"—he winks—"assuming you win this little game of ours."

After a moment, the barman comes to take their order. "Antoine," Henri says, "this is *Noncee.*"

Antoine is too handsome for his own good. Trouble is, he knows it. Thankfully he is also short. And at least three decades older than Nancy. He takes her offered hand and turns it over gently, kissing her palm. "Any friend of Henri's is a friend of mine. You are most welcome to anything in this establishment."

The way he says the word *anything* makes it clear that he includes himself in the offer.

"As you can see," Henri continues with a scowl, "Antoine is Corsican and therefore a complete reprobate."

"You insult me!" he says, still stroking Nancy's hand seductively.

"I tell the truth." Henri shakes his head. *Corsicans.*

"I see that you two are well acquainted." Nancy glances between them with suspicion. "I assume Henri brings all his women here?"

"You are the first that I've met, mademoiselle."

She laughs. "You have your barman well trained, Fiocca."

He's affronted by her use of his last name. The second time

tonight. At least she's dropped the *Mister*. She uses it only when trying to put emotional distance between them.

"You persist in your poor opinion of me. I have brought no other women here."

Antoine releases her hand with a sigh of faux reluctance. "And what will you be drinking tonight?"

"First, ice water," Henri says, "and then two fingers of cognac each. We'll take . . ." He thinks for moment. "Gautier. Leave us the bottle."

Antoine limps away and begins to scoop hard nuggets of ice into two tumblers. He once told Henri that there is still shrapnel in his left thigh from the Great War. But he also told him that it was an injury sustained while vigorously exercising in a Milanese brothel. Henri has made peace with the fact that the story of Antoine's limp may never be known. But he sees Nancy eyeing the barman curiously and wouldn't be surprised if she wrestles the truth out of him one day.

He expects her to say something about the limp, but instead she asks, "An entire bottle of brandy?"

"Don't worry. I doubt we'll get through the whole thing."

"So why ask for it?"

"We'll be here awhile and there's no need to make him shuffle back and forth."

She smiles at him. "You do surprise me sometimes, Fiocca. Here I thought you were jealous of the man."

"Jealous?"

"Well, your barman is quite handsome. And you got that pinched look around your eyes when he kissed my hand—"

"He practically *licked* your hand—"

"—the one you get sometimes. It's charming, really." She brushes one warm finger against his lower lip.

Henri is surprised to find heat creeping into his cheeks. It's been years—decades, maybe—since a woman made him blush. He is pleased that she is pleased. So he shrugs. "I like the old *salaud*."

As if summoned, Antoine sets the water in front of them and is off again to locate the Gautier in his vast brandy collection.

Henri leans close to give Nancy instructions on this game they'll be playing. "Drink the water steadily, in several long gulps. It will cool you down and shake the cobwebs from your brain. Once you stop slurring we'll move on to the brandy."

"I am not slurring!"

He winks. "*Au contraire,* your tongue has been moving quite slow for the last hour." She sticks her tongue out at this and he laughs. "Get your mind on the game, *ma chère,* not the victory."

"You have no idea where my mind is."

"Quite happily frolicking about the gutter, I'd say."

Nancy doesn't even attempt to deny it. She's been staring at his mouth since they left the restaurant.

"Drink up," he orders, and for once, she complies. After a moment he adds, "The second rule of drinking is don't cross streams. I know we've already had a bit of champagne, but we'll be sticking with brandy for the rest of the night."

"And the third rule?" she asks.

"How do you know there's a third?"

"You always do things in threes."

"A very astute observation, for a tipsy woman."

"I'm not tipsy."

"Not anymore. The water is working, isn't it?"

Nancy nods.

"Told you so. And that brings us to our third rule—"

"I knew it—"

"Stay hydrated. For every glass of brandy, drink a tumbler of water. Water will dilute the alcohol in your bloodstream. And it will send you to the bathroom frequently. Both are vital when you're learning to build up your tolerance. There are other rules, but we'll stick with those three for now."

"Just out of curiosity, why go with brandy?"

"Apart from wine, it's the most commonly imbibed liquid in France. And it's mostly what you drank at dinner. Besides, you're more likely to be offered brandy than anything else."

"So?"

"*So*... no man trying to take advantage of you is going to pour wine down your throat. Brandy is cheaper and works faster."

"And what if a woman wants to take advantage of you, Fiocca?"

"Oh, that's easy."

Nancy leans close enough to brush her cheek against his as she whispers in his ear, "Tell me how."

He swallows, hard. "You're doing it right now."

Henri grabs Nancy's hand when she moves it to his thigh and sets it back on her lap. He pats her fingers to lessen the sting. "Focus, *ma chère.* This is important."

One of the things Henri loves most about this woman is that she is not naturally inclined to do as she's told. But she must sense his determination, so she applies herself to the task. Henri wonders if this is how she approached the world at sixteen, alone and hungry for adventure, because she goes from shameless flirting to intense focus faster than he can register. Then, they begin to drink.

*

Two hours later Henri pays Antoine and helps Nancy to her feet. "That's enough for one night, *ma fille qui rit.*"

Nancy looks up at him with glassy, adoring eyes. It's the same look she gave him the night he left her alone in bed, and it's quickly becoming one of his favorite expressions. It is both innocent and imploring.

"Did I lose?" she asks.

"*Non.* It was a draw."

"Liar. You're perfectly upright and I can barely stand."

He laughs and nuzzles the top of her head with his chin. "Patience, *ma chère,* it takes time. I've been punishing my liver for years."

The truth is she did quite well. Purposeful drinking and social drinking are different, and she applied herself with verve.

They consumed half the bottle of Gautier between them, taking it neat and in steady intervals. She's wobbling a bit as they head to the elevator and her tongue is heavy on the vowels, but she would be on the floor already without his rules. To be fair,

Henri isn't faring much better. His vision is fuzzy around the edges and he feels as though the room is spinning.

"Does this mean I won't be able to have my way with you tonight?" she asks.

Henri laughs long and hard as the elevator rises to the top floor. He pulls her against him and rests his chin on top of her head. "I doubt you'll be awake long enough to get to the fun part."

"Try me," she says.

* * *

MARSEILLE

Hôtel du Louvre et Paix

I can feel Henri begin to haul himself in, like he always does, pausing just short of any serious sexual advance. He doesn't pull away or stop touching me, it's simply a palpable restraint. A force of will shimmering in the air between us.

"*Mon Dieu,* I love this sweater," Henri says, rubbing his nose along the ridge of my collarbone. His hands slide up my rib cage, thumbs stopping just below the swell of my breasts. He buries his face in my neck. Nuzzles. Inhales. "And your perfume."

"I'm not wearing perfume. But I did think you might like the sweater."

"Tell me where you bought it and I will get you five more. One in every color." His voice is a rumble against my skin, his tongue a whisper in the dip of my clavicle.

We are on the couch in the sitting room of my suite, addled from brandy and exhaustion, and I think it wouldn't be hard to tear down these defenses of his. An invitation, perhaps. A strategic shift in my body below his. But Henri prefers me direct and to the point.

"Will you stay the night?" I ask.

He stretches out on his side and pulls me close so that we are facing each other. I can feel his eyelashes against my face. He kisses me, gentle at first and then deep. His left hand trails down my side. Over my ribs, into the dip of my waist, across the swell of my backside, and down the back of my thigh. He crooks his hand behind my knee and brings my stocking-covered leg over the top of his. He plays with my slip. My garter. For one delicious moment I think that I've gotten my way.

And then he says, *"Non, ma chère."*

"But—"

"Soon." His breath is warm in my ear. His hand dipping beneath the hem of my sweater. His fingers trailing across my spine, up and down, up and down. Gentle. Methodic. He is lulling me to sleep.

"But," I argue, again, "I won the drinking game."

"It was a tie."

"Let's both get what we want, then." I wriggle closer and he laughs. Wraps both arms tight across my shoulders.

Henri Fiocca is a big man. Tall and broad, with a deep, commanding voice. And though my pride stings—am I not desirable enough?—I don't stand a chance. I am so perfectly warm and safe and happy in this moment. So groggy from a long, emotional evening—from hating Old Man Fiocca while falling madly for his son—that I simply drift away right here and I know that sometime tomorrow, when the sun is high in the sky, I will wake alone.

Madame Andrée

CHAUDES-AIGUES PLATEAU, CANTAL, FRANCE

March 21, 1944

Once again, I wake up in the backseat of Denis Rake's little Renault. It is hard, grueling work that we've gotten ourselves into and I am exhausted—what with keeping our radios on hand at all hours to listen for transmissions on the BBC French Service—and being up all night waiting for the drops at various airfields, then cleaning the weapons of grease and packing materials. We've been doing this for three weeks now and my muscles ache. My fingers are dirty and numb. I'd exchange one of my lesser organs—say, an ovary—for a jar of cold cream and a hot bath. There is a natural hot springs near Chaudes-Aigues where we can bathe, but it requires use of a vehicle to get there and several spare hours, so we go only once a week. Most of the Maquis just rinse off in the creek as necessary. Which means I have to go upstream each morning to perform my necessary ablutions. Sleep, when I'm able to get it, is like falling into a deep, dark cavern that swallows me whole. Denden's Renault is a better option than the ground beside the fire. I stay a bit drier this way, and it allows me enough privacy to sleep in one of the two nightgowns I've brought with me. But it's hard to stretch out in the backseat, and all the little muscles along my spine, and down the back of my legs, seize up during the night. They complain at any sudden movement. Each day I wake missing my bed with its proper mattress. I miss Picon. I miss Henri most of all.

But there is work to do and I must get after it. No time to sit around feeling maudlin. So I pull on my clothing beneath the mangy blanket I've acquired from one of the maquisards, cursing, once again, all the various contraptions required to function as a woman. This tiny, inadequate space is the only privacy I have and I am determined to find a better solution.

"Madame Andrée, we have a problem," Fournier says, finding me a short time later at the creek. I am brushing my teeth and tucking the craziest strands of my untrimmed hair beneath my beret.

I sigh and spit toothpaste into a gorse bush. "Of course we do."

"Come with me," he says.

Fournier leads me back up the hill, to the clearing, where a young Frenchman stands beside the fire. He is tall and thin, with a nice jaw, but his pretty eyes are pinched in exquisite pain. A dirty bandage is wrapped around his left hand and blood seeps through the cloth.

I nod at the young man but do not smile. These poor boys take even a half-hearted grin as an invitation to flirt. And given that my left hand is bare, none of them know that I am married. Not that it would do much good anyway.

"This is Louis," Fournier tells me. "He blew three fingers off his hand with a grenade yesterday."

Louis holds up the bandaged knob as proof.

"Why the bloody hell did you do that?" I ask him.

Louis looks so mortified you'd think that I had caught him in the act of pleasuring himself.

Fournier digs the toe of his boot into a patch of charred ground near the fire. "Most of my men do not know *how* to use the weapons. They are tradesmen. Factory workers, mostly. Men who fled our cities during the *relève* so they wouldn't be drafted into working for the Germans. These men, our maquisards, are not traditional soldiers."

"Thus, our problem," I guess.

Fournier nods. This is his most frequent form of communication, and I have learned to read each little bob of his head for subtleties. "We need someone to train the groups in weapons use," he says. "We have to be prepared if the Germans attack."

"When," I correct him. "It's likely to happen sooner rather than later. Unless we strike first."

There are twenty-two thousand Germans garrisoned throughout the Auvergne and Cantal and they know that something has changed within the Maquis structure, not the least of which is that the Resistance is acquiring weapons from an unknown source. So they have increased the number and range of their daily patrols. They are harassing the local villages more often, sometimes to the point of unspeakable violence. Our scouts indicate that the Germans are suspicious and looking for Resistance leaders, they are looking for a fight. And we can't have our men blowing themselves up before the fight even arrives.

I turn to Louis and study him closely. He can't be more than twenty-three years old. "Are you married?" I ask.

The stupid boy cannot help himself. Who knows how long he's been out here in these woods. Even his pain cannot overrule his biology. He looks me over, head to toe and then back again. He smirks. "For now."

Gah! *Frenchmen.* I roll my eyes.

"I would think a married man would be more careful with his hands," I say. "Now go find someone to take you to Chaudes-Aigues so you can see a doctor before the rest of it rots off."

I motion for Fournier to follow me and we leave Louis standing there, bandages pressed against his chest, looking for all the world like he's just been chastised by an irascible schoolmarm.

Fournier chuckles as we turn into the woods and onto a path that has been beaten down by countless footsteps. "Do you have children?" he asks.

"No."

He gives me one of his nods. There is no pity in it. Nor sympathy. Just understanding. "Neither do I."

This surprises me, and I tell him as much.

"My wife and I are unable to. I have come to think of these young men as the children I did not get." He gives me a sideways look followed by a crooked grin. "They like you."

I snort. "A bit too much, perhaps."

He shrugs. "They have been out here for a long while, but they are not dead. So that part is inevitable. What I mean is that they are willing to be *led* by you. It took me nearly a year to gain their trust. But you have done it in weeks."

"You're the one who leads them. I only boss them around occasionally."

"And yet they do what you tell them."

"Only because I threatened to shoot their balls off if they didn't."

"Well, they are not entirely stupid." Fournier stomps through the undergrowth after me.

Though I could easily debate him on that point, I change the subject. "Tell me what you know about the man they call Soutine."

"Gabriel Soutine?" He scratches his chin for a moment as we work our way around a fallen log. "He is a local partisan leader. He lives in the village of Termes."

"Is it true that he monitors the German troop movements throughout the region?"

Fournier looks at me curiously. "Where did you hear this?"

I point to the sky, from whence comes most of our information. "London."

"Ah. Well, yes. If anyone knows where the Germans are and how many, it would be Soutine."

"Will he talk to us, do you think? Hubert and me?"

"I am sure he would be willing to barter information for supplies." At this I get one of Fournier's rare smiles. "You are a very powerful woman, Madame Andrée. Word has gotten out."

"Let's just hope word doesn't get to the wrong ears." The last thing I need is anyone associating the White Mouse with Madame Andrée. Hellfire will rain down on us the moment that connection is made by the Germans. "We will pay Soutine a visit later today."

"I will send word," he says. "But where are we going now?"

"To find Denden."

Fournier looks at the sky. The sun has barely risen. "I imagine he's still sleeping."

"Oh, I'm certain he is."

Denis Rake is up half the night operating his transmitter and listening to the radio. And then of course there are the airdrops. None of us are exempt when those are scheduled. So he has created his own quiet space in the woods to retreat from Fournier's rowdy Frenchmen, and the Maquis generally let him be. They understand that if he's not alert enough to work the transmitter, no one gets their supplies. Denis has erected a small lean-to for himself beneath a giant pine tree in the woods. He has quite cleverly used shipment crates and parachutes to build the small, waterproof dwelling. It's so clever, in fact, that many of Fournier's men have begun doing the same and I am often put upon to settle quarrels about who can abscond with the packing materials once the weapons have been cleaned and distributed.

A low rumble drifts from the lean-to as we approach.

"Denden," I say, louder than necessary, and then, as Fournier steps forward to shove aside the tent flaps, add, "I wouldn't do that if I were you."

"Why?"

"He sleeps naked."

Fournier jumps back as though the tent flaps were vipers ready to strike. "How—"

"Long story that takes place in Scotland and involves myself, Denden, and a rubber duckie."

His eyes narrow. "Do you mean to say that the two of you are—"

"Absolutely not!" I am tempted to add that I am married and Denis Rake is a homosexual, but that is personal information that could be used against us should it ever fall into the wrong hands. I pick up a small rock and toss it toward the tent. "Denden!"

A snort. A groan. And then a thump as Rake tries to sit up and whacks his head against one of the wooden slats. "What?" A pause. "Dammit. That hurt."

"Get up."

"I'd rather not just yet, if it's all the same to you."

"I need you to take notes."

"I am not your secretary, Duckie. Find someone else."

"Ah, but you are my radioman. And I need to make additions to the list of supplies you'll request tonight."

He yawns. "Run out of toothpaste, have you?"

"No. But I could use some face cream. So that will go on your list. Along with a bit of tea." That was my deal with Buckmaster. I get into France and get situated with the Maquis, and I will be allowed to request personal items. "But the real reason I need you to get your skinny arse out of bed is because Fournier's men are out there blowing off bits of themselves in the woods—"

"Bully for them—"

"—so it's time we put in a request for Anselm."

The lean-to goes very quiet at this. Then, after a few seconds, Rake shoves aside the tent flaps and sticks his head out. The man looks as though he's been electrocuted in his sleep, hair going everywhere, and I want to crack a joke about newborns and birth canals. But he's grinning like a madman and I don't want to disrupt his sudden good humor.

"Why didn't you just say so?"

In the end, Hubert and I decide to visit Soutine alone. It takes over an hour as we pick our way north through back roads, near Montluçon. We thought about taking Fournier, but we do not know when the Germans will strike, and it would be unwise to leave the Maquis without their leader. We are on the outskirts of Termes when we see the blockade. Stretched across the road is a Nazi Wehrmacht bus, one of the transport vehicles used to bring soldiers into France. It is parked at such an angle that no traffic can get through from either direction. On the other side of the blockade is the village of Termes, where, according to Fournier, we will find Gabriel Soutine.

The village is set on a low hill overlooking vast pastureland. It is as lovely and picturesque as any French town I've ever seen. But today there is something desperately wrong.

"Pull off the road. Now," I tell Hubert, and he swerves onto the shoulder beside a low fence meant to keep sheep and goats off the road. I can feel him stiffen in the seat beside me and I know he's reaching for his gun.

"Do you see anyone?" I ask.

"No." Hubert rolls down the driver's-side window and listens. He shakes his head. Nothing.

"I'll go check."

"Are you crazy?" he asks.

"Many people think so," I say, digging around in my purse. I fish out my red lipstick, apply a fresh coat, then flash him a disarming smile. "I'll be right back."

The thing I like most about Hubert is that he doesn't argue with me. No doubt he finds me endlessly *trying*. But he lets me do what I think is best. I tuck my revolver into my waistband at the small of my back and cover it with the edge of my blouse, and I'm out of the car, creeping toward the bus.

"Bonjour?" I ask. "Anyone there? We're just needing to get through."

No answer. The bus is parked several hundred feet from our Renault, stretched across the road at a forty-five-degree angle, with its nose pointing in the opposite direction.

"Anyone there?" I call again and lift my hands, palms out, to show I mean no harm. But once again I am greeted by silence.

Closer now, I peer under but see no one. I knock on the door and push it open. Completely empty. The bus has four rows of seats and then, at the back, two long benches that face each other. I assume that this is where the Brownshirts store their machinery. But a quick glance under the benches shows nothing. Whatever they brought with them, they have taken into the village. If packed to capacity, the bus can hold about thirty people. I step outside and move toward the rear, just to be safe. No one.

"We just want to get home," I call, giving Hubert a look over my shoulder. I shake my head.

It's obvious the bus has been parked here but it's strange that no one has been left to guard it. I am walking back to convene with Hubert and see if he has any ideas what we should do, when the sharp, metallic sound of a whistle cuts through the air. It is followed by three more, then a single gunshot. A cascade of horrified screams drifts up from the village on the hill, followed by coarse, guttural shouting. Another shot and all is silent except for a single indecipherable German voice that seems to be giving orders.

I hurl myself toward the car as Hubert puts it in reverse. The road is narrow and he has to make a five-point turn before he's able to get the little Renault pointed in the other direction.

Neither of us speaks for a good ten seconds, but I know we're both thinking the same thing.

"We have to help them," I say.

"Yes," Hubert answers.

He has spoken a grand total of ten words since we left the encampment but he offers an eleventh now. "Soutine."

"I hope not."

"Why else would the Germans be in this little village?"

Hubert drives a short distance in the opposite direction—far enough to round a sharp bend before he pulls the Renault to the side once again. There's a bit more shoulder on this stretch of road, along with patches of gorse brush, so we hide the car and formulate our plan.

"Do you have your binoculars?" he asks.

"In my pack."

"Grab them. We can approach Termes from here but we'll have to go through the pasture."

Hubert's revolver is strapped to his leg, so his hands are free as we scramble through the waist-high grass. There's a flush to his cheeks, and I am reminded that my partner is first and foremost a soldier.

Somewhere, in the village, a small child begins to scream. It's the kind of sound that can make your knees go out from under you. It can twist your stomach into a boiling mass of bile. It can stop your heart. It is the sound of soul-ripping terror.

A German solider shouts.

A lone woman is wailing. Grief and fear penetrating every note of her voice.

And we are running, as quietly and quickly as we can, toward Termes. Like something from a fairy tale, the entire village is surrounded by a low, stacked-stone wall covered in budding vines. It is roughly three feet tall and looks as though it will be buried in honeysuckle blooms within days. But the continuing, traumatized shrieks of that child indicate that what's happening within resembles something from a nightmare. We push through the last section of pasture and come to an abrupt stop behind the wall. We ready ourselves, then peer over the edge, between two stucco buildings, into the center of the village. Like many old French hamlets, it is a cluster of shops and homes built around an open central area—something like a town square, only much smaller. It appears as though the entire village is gathered there, watching something.

Hubert goes over the wall first and I follow close behind, then we ease between the two buildings until we reach the edge of the crowd where an old man leans hard against the wall. Hubert sets his hand on the man's shoulder and he physically recoils. He must be nearing the age of ninety. His spine is bent. His hair is gone. And his eyes have the milky look of one going blind.

"What is going on here?" Hubert whispers, gently, in French.

The old man hangs his head. "You are too late."

"Too late for what?"

"To save her."

"Who?"

"Olivia Soutine," he says.

The crowd sways back and forth, and only then do I realize that they are weeping, silently. Grasping one another for strength. Most of them look at their feet or at the sky, anywhere but the village center. It takes a moment to find the woman chained to the light post. Her arms are stretched taut above her. Her head hangs to her chest at an unnatural angle. And her entire torso is split open from throat to groin. At her feet, in a ghastly pool of blood and entrails, lies her unborn child—a full-size infant, ready to be born. To her left stands a little girl—her daughter—no more than two years old, shrieking and crying like a tiny wounded animal. Eyes red. Nose running. Chest heaving. Her arms are raised to the mother who will never hold her again. And, to Olivia Soutine's left, is the Brownshirt who slaughtered her, dripping bayonet raised above his head.

"Jesus God in heaven," Hubert whispers, his voice stretched thin by the agony of prayer. "Help."

After a moment the toddler looks around and sees an old woman with silver hair and a face creased like worn linen. The little girl stumbles toward her, arms outstretched, desperate, begging to be held against that ample bosom. But the old woman turns her away, visibly shaken, as she denies the deepest instinct of any woman, much less one her age.

The soldiers pace, waiting. Ready. Almost *eager.*

"They will not let anyone help the child," the old man whispers. "They threaten to shoot anyone who does. Twenty-four hours we must leave Olivia there before she can be buried. The child can be taken in at sunset. If we touch them before that, they will shoot all the children in the village and throw their bodies in the well so we can never retrieve them."

I rise up on my tiptoes to peer over the crowd. Only then do I see that the old man is telling the truth. All the village children have been brought to the front, where desperate parents cling to them and cover their eyes.

"Why did they do this?" I ask, but I do not recognize my own voice. It is hollow and tremulous.

He tries to explain. "The garrison commander at Montluçon came looking for her husband, Gabriel. His men blockaded the road on both sides of the village, then went house to house searching for him. But all they could find were his wife and daughter." He nods toward the light post and I feel a wave of nausea rising in my belly. "Once they had her chained they forced everyone out of their homes to watch. The German officer in charge asked her three times where her husband was but she refused him each time. And all the while her daughter stood there, eyes wide, sucking her thumb. I could see, even from here, that Olivia tried to be brave. She kept her voice steady so as not to scare the child. The officer gave her a fourth chance, but when she refused once more, he *screamed*. I have never heard a grown man make such a noise. And then he gave the order for her to be . . ." He gulps. "For his man to do *that*."

Rage is an odd thing, not so different from grief in the way it catches you unaware and then explodes in your chest. It crashes against you like a wave and all I can think in this moment is that we are sitting here, watching this happen. Doing nothing.

"We have to stop them!" I hiss.

"No." The old man looks at me and I am ashamed, suddenly, because his eyes reflect pity. "You need to leave. While you still can."

Hubert sets his hand between my shoulder blades and leans close to whisper, "There are nearly thirty soldiers in this village, all of them heavily armed with rifles and bayonets. The villagers number little more than one hundred and they have nothing. If we move, if we act at all, they will open fire on those children." He points toward Olivia Soutine's child. "And they will start with that little girl."

"So we do *nothing*?"

"They came for Soutine. They came to make a point. They do not want anyone else," the old man says.

There are some things that little eyes can never unsee, some moments that no mind, no matter how young or resilient, can ever forget. For the little girl beside the light post, this will be one. She has gone into shock now. Her tears have ceased, and she drops to the ground beside her dead mother, stupefied.

I lift my binoculars from where they hang on the cord around my neck and inspect the village. Hubert is right. There is one soldier for every three villagers and they all carry rifles affixed with bayonets. I know that I am a coward, but I keep my gaze away from the light post. I cannot bear to see that woman again. I cannot bear to see the face of her child up close. I do not want to know the color of her eyes, because it will henceforth be associated with slaughter. So I scan the crowd instead and I bear witness to the shock and horror on their tear-streaked faces. Hands over mouths. Eyes squeezed shut. Chests that heave with silent tears. Unmitigated fury and despair beyond words. Some are frozen. Others are shaking. More than one young woman and old man has fainted. The old woman who turned the child away has collapsed into the arms of a man beside her.

And then I see the face.

His face. That face made of spare parts and pure hatred. So unique and ghoulish it cannot be mistaken.

Obersturmführer Wolff.

He has stepped from the shadows of a building to oversee his handiwork, walking a lazy circle around the light post as he nods. Wolff speaks in a low voice, so I cannot hear what he says to the officer holding the bayonet, but he is clearly pleased with the work that has been done.

I associate Wolff with that waterwheel in Vienna and my mind struggles to make sense of his presence here. But there is no mistaking him. The cruelty. The hatred. The whip. I don't even realize that I'm lunging forward, trying to push my way through the crowd, until Hubert's arms are around me. He slams me against the nearest building, hard enough to knock the wind out of me.

My grunt, mingled with stinging breath, comes out in an inaudible puff.

"What are you doing? You're going to get us all killed," Hubert hisses.

I am gasping for air like a dying fish and my head throbs from where it's hit the wall. All I can manage to spit out is a strangled whisper. "I've seen that man before."

"I don't care," Hubert says, and there is no small amount of regret in his voice when he adds, "There is nothing we can do for these people."

No. I shake my head because speaking the word feels impossible. It feels like failure.

"We need to leave," Hubert says. His voice is a low, steady thrum in my ear. *"Now."*

How can we walk away without doing anything? I ask myself that over and over, even as we retreat. I feel like a failure. A *traitor*. But the tiny, rational voice at the back of my skull insists that Hubert is right. We accomplish nothing if we get these people killed. If we die ourselves. I let Hubert steady me as we crawl back over the wall and through the pasture toward the road, sick and shaken. He looks as though all the blood has been drained from his body. When we reach the car, we stand there for a moment, feeling helpless and guilty and disgusted with ourselves. Both of us are considering the odds and whether we could have killed the Brownshirts without unleashing more hell on that poor village.

Oh God, that tiny child. I can't help it: I drop to my hands and knees and vomit. Everything I had for breakfast. Weak tea. Some biscuit. And then, bile. When there is nothing left in my stomach I dry-heave while hot, furious tears flood my face. My throat burns. My face feels warm and my hands are cold, shaking. I feel betrayed by my own body, as though I have become the weakest version of myself.

"Nance," Hubert says, so overwhelmed with emotion that he's unaware he has used my real name. "We have to go."

I lift one hand and he helps me to my feet. I suck air in through my nose. I spit, then drag my hands down my face. I stand there, eyes watering, long enough to calm my stomach. My fear is gone now. My nausea fading. All I have left is rage. This impotence is an all-consuming fury. I cannot do anything to help. I am useless. But I want revenge. I want . . . I . . .

I look at the bus parked farther up the road.

I have an idea.

"Where the hell are you going now?" Hubert hisses after me as I march toward the blockade.

I turn, looking at him over my shoulder, cheeks damp and voice raw. "I'm going to take that bus."

Nancy Grace Augusta Wake

VERDUN'S RESTAURANT, MARSEILLE

January 7, 1939

Henri brings me to this restaurant every time I'm in Marseille. I think it is partly to banish the memory of meeting his father, but also because this place was ours first and he does not want to relinquish its meaning to a man who persists in trying to separate us. So, in a way, every meal that we enjoy within these warm, paneled walls is a way of thumbing our noses at Old Man Fiocca. However, he is the last thing on my mind at this particular moment.

"Do you remember that night in Paris when you walked with me along the Seine?" he asks.

"Yes."

"There's something I didn't tell you that night." There is a slight tremble of emotion in his voice and I am intrigued. I have never heard him speak with anything but charm and authority. "Do you remember how I found you at Luigi's with your colleagues?"

"Of course. I *told* you I'd be there, remember? I practically dared you to come."

Henri nods, then covers my hand lightly with his. He brushes his thumb across my knuckles. "I was *so* jealous," he says, as though confessing to murder or burglary or some especially egregious fetish.

"Of who?"

"Them. Your friends." He waves his free hand in the air. "That Frank fellow in particular."

I try not to laugh but I cannot help myself. "Frank Gilmore? Whatever for?"

"Because it was obvious that you were *their* Nancy. I envied the way they made you laugh, their easy acquaintanceship. The fact that you'd chosen them over me—that night, at least. I watched you for several minutes before sending that drink and I found myself consumed with the reality that I wanted you all to myself."

"Is that such a bad thing?"

He averts his eyes for a moment, those dark lashes brushing his cheeks, and when he returns his gaze there is an intensity I have never seen in them before. "I *still* want you all to myself. But the wanting isn't the half of it. I love you. With the entirety of my heart."

"I—"

"Which is why I would like to know if you will be my wife."

Henri pulls a small, red velvet box from his suit pocket and sets it on the white tablecloth. It stands out like a blood drop on snow and I cannot look away.

I stare at him, helpless.

Our relationship has always been strange. The way we came together and the way we have stayed together, long distance, for over two years, scraping out pockets of time to travel back and forth from Marseille to Paris. Despite having me meet his father soon after we began dating, he has never pressed me for anything or set an expectation. We discovered almost immediately how much we enjoy each other's company, which is quite separate from being in love. Love is a choice. It is the active choosing of good for another person. But *like*? It is a gift and it cannot be forced. The degree to which we like each other cannot be overstated. Though I won't deny that we fell fast and hard into love as well. We laugh at the same things and he pretends to be long-suffering about my outspokenness, but I know it delights him. He is my match and I am his and we are both well aware of this. I am stunned that he has offered me a ring only because we have never once spoken of marriage and I have always assumed that such conversations precede a proposal. But here I am, staring at a velvet box, clenching his hand so hard that our knuckles have turned white.

"I..." Once again I try to find the words but they drift away before I can grab hold of them.

He wants me all to himself.

He wants me to be his wife.

I have never thought of myself as the marrying type. The type to settle down. Or *commit.* I don't even own *furniture* for Pete's sake.

"If you need more time—"

"Yes," I say, and then, when I see the hopeful look on his face, hasten to add, "I need time. Just a little bit. I did not expect this. I—" Damn words. Now they choose to tumble out, an unruly mess, and I am in danger of breaking his heart. "I'm so sorry. It's only that—"

"You do not have to apologize. Or explain," Henri says. It is a great testament to his character that he does not get angry. Or defensive. He doesn't backtrack or pretend that what he's asked isn't important. He simply lowers his head in a gentle bow and then lifts my hand from the table and kisses my knuckles. "There is no hurry. I am not going anywhere. I would be happy to marry you first thing in the morning. But if you ask that I wait until we are bent of spine and silver of head, I will."

Then he calls for the waiter and orders a shockingly expensive bottle of champagne, as though we are celebrating. And perhaps we are. Commitment comes in many forms other than matrimony. But it isn't until he has paid the check and is helping me into my jacket that I notice the little red velvet box is no longer sitting on the table.

MARSEILLE

Le Parc Valmer, January 14, 1939

"Come with me," Henri says, pulling off the road and stopping his shiny new Renault beside a low, crumbling stone wall. "I want you to meet someone."

"Not another one of your *relatives,* I hope?" I give him a warning frown but it's all for show.

"No." Henri laughs. "Someone else."

The hillside drops away sharply on the other side of the road, falling swiftly toward the Mediterranean—currently a bright and startling blue—and I stare at the water while he crosses around to my side of the car. I will never get over the staggering beauty of Marseille—even in January, the worst month known to man. Henri opens my door, helps me into my new red wool peacoat, and takes my hand. He leads me through the gate and down a long, winding gravel path.

"Where are we?"

"Le Parc Valmer," he says.

"It looks like a cemetery." I take in the old, bare trees with tangled roots and long, dark branches. The stone benches. The whispered hush that has settled about the place like a wool blanket.

"*Non, ma chère.* It's a park. One of the oldest and smallest in Marseille. But it's the prettiest, I think. You cannot match the view."

He's right. Even if it hadn't been framed by the sea, the little park would be bursting with charm and dignity. The stone wall curves around the perimeter like a stream, offering visitors endless places to sit beneath the latent willows or stretch out in the sun. There are duck ponds, rosebushes—long gone dormant for winter—and footpaths meandering this way and that. Thankfully, there's not a gravestone in sight.

It has been a week since Henri proposed and he has not mentioned it again. He has, however, kept me busy. Every day we go on an excursion. We visit museums and art galleries. We take the train into the nearby countryside and eat at small, family-owned restaurants that do not offer menus. He has taken me shopping and sailing and picnicking and all the while I have thought about his proposal. I know Henri can see that I am growing more comfortable with the idea of marriage. Sometimes I catch him smiling as he watches me.

"This way," Henri says. The path before us forks in half and we go left, then down, and around a sharp curve, only to find a man sitting on a bench to the side of the path with a little dog in his lap. Henri leads me toward him.

"And who is this?" I ask, bending down to scratch the small dog, a wire-haired terrier just like Picon. I look up at the owner—expecting to discover a kindred spirit—and see that he's a short, broad man with a kind face and extraordinary, odd eyes. One is brown and the other gray. Not blue or green like you'd expect with a mismatched pair. But gray. Like one of the pebbles on the path beneath our feet. I feel at once as though he is measuring my soul for quality and a chill runs up the back of my neck.

"It's not my job to name her," the man says.

"It's yours," Henri adds, and when he sees the confusion on my face, he laughs. It's a booming, raucous sound and a puffy bluebird startles from the branch above his head. "She belongs to you now."

The little dog barks as if to confirm this and then she wags her tail, her entire body shivering with anticipation.

"Mine?" I look back and forth between Henri and this man, delighted, and scoop her up to pull her close beneath my chin.

"A wife for Picon," Henry says. "Every gentleman should be so lucky as to marry the woman he loves."

His voice is thick with meaning, and the little Frenchman turns away, suddenly fascinated by something on the horizon. The tip of my nose is nearly frozen in this January air, but my ears grow warm. My face flushes. I clear my throat. "Picon hasn't even met her yet."

Henri shrugs as if this fact is unimportant. "No matter. He will love her. How could he not?"

It's true. She is a lovely little thing. White, with large brown patches, like puddles of chocolate. Eyes as big and round and dark as the buttons on my coat.

I turn to the little Frenchman. "Thank you, *monsieur*!"

He tips his chin toward Henri. "Thank *him*. He's the one who arranged the sale."

"But you had to part with her and that must be terrible. She is perfect. I've only known her for a few moments, but I could never let her go."

This pleases him. I hadn't thought of him as stiff, but his shoulders relax and those startling eyes soften. Whatever measuring he began earlier seems to be complete now, and he gives me a warm smile. "My daughters will be pleased to hear that. They raise the dogs and cry whenever I have to find them homes. But I do not think they will cry tonight."

I offer my hand. "I am so very pleased to meet you, *Monsieur*...?"

"Ficetole," he says.

"Nancy Wake."

He kisses the back of my hand. *"Mademoiselle."*

"Ficetole is the tram conductor here in Marseille. We have known one another for... how many years is it now?" Henri says.

"Fifteen."

"His wife is the best cook in the city. And his daughters the prettiest."

I have no idea whether Henri is telling the truth, but it is clear from the way that Ficetole is beaming that *he* certainly believes this to be true. It makes me love him all the more. He smiles as though his daughters have just been declared the most beautiful in the entire world. I wonder whether they got his eyes, and if so, which color? Perhaps both? And would that be alarming or enchanting in the face of a little girl? I hope to find out one day.

"Thank you as well," I tell Henri, reaching up on my tiptoes to plant a kiss firmly on his lips. "What should I name her?"

"I'm sure you'll think of something," he says, then offers me a sheepish grin. "Keeping her a secret was unbearable. I could hardly wait for you to arrive last week. That train takes fifty forevers to get here. You should probably just move here and put me out of my misery."

He is looking at me pointedly and I suspect he's trying to determine whether I noticed that last comment. I ignore him. There is a name I thought of once and I lift her up and turn her about to determine if it fits. It does.

"Her name is Grenadine," I say.

Ficetole slides off the bench and looks up at me. I am startled, once again, to realize how short he is. Just over five feet. But he gives me a grin and a nod. "I must be getting back to work," he says. He sets a gentle kiss right on the end of her nose. "You be good for your new mistress... Grenadine."

We say our good-byes, then watch Ficetole meander down the path, whistling as he goes.

"What a delightfully strange little man," I say.

"He likes you."

"How on earth could you tell?"

"He let you have her. He does not hand over his daughters' dogs to people he does not like. I've known the man for fifteen years and I still had to convince him to sell me one. He *interviewed* me. Asked about my intentions and how I planned to provide for her. Where she would live and what she would eat. Felt as though I was asking for his blessing to marry one of his daughters. I damned near broke into a sweat."

I drop to the bench and curl Grenadine into the crook of my arm. I hope Picon loves his new friend—wife? lover?—as much as I do already. And I'm not stupid. I know what Henri's doing. How he's trying to win me over. But I don't mind. All is fair in love and war after all.

"Thank you," I say, again, but this time it's a whisper and I'm rather overcome.

Henri settles onto the bench beside me. Drapes one arm over my shoulder. Leans close and whispers, "I would buy you this entire city if only to see the look you have in your eyes right now."

"I don't need the city, Henri. I have you. And Picon."

"And Grenadine," he adds. "You have her now as well."

I excel at stopping errant thoughts. I can trap them and discard them as though disposing of a spider that has wandered onto my pillow. Errant thoughts are *dangerous.* They can give way to hope. And hope can upheave your entire life if it's left alone long enough to put down roots. Errant thoughts can make you unreasonable and sappy. But for one startling moment it occurs to me that *this* is what it must feel like to have a real family. My father left us when I was two. All five of my siblings are many years older than I am. My mother did well just to keep us all alive. And I left home while still a child. So, *family* has always been an odd and loose term for me. But this feels right. It feels good. And the thought is so pleasant—I am so hungry for it in fact—that I cannot discard it.

"Yes," I tell Henri.

He knows what I mean. I'm certain of that because his eyes flash bright. But he is cautious. "Yes . . . *what*?"

"I love you as well. And I will marry you." I wait several long seconds to let him absorb my acceptance before adding, "On one condition."

Henri pulls away. I make him nervous when I say things like this. "Which is?"

"That you let me choose my own wedding present."

His lip twitches into an amused grin. "Do I get any hints as to what you might want?"

"Not yet."

He looks as though I've told him that I require a feather, or a bit of eggshell, in order to be his bride. This clearly makes no sense to him but he doesn't care. Henri Fiocca heaves a great sigh of relief and reaches into his coat pocket to pull out the red velvet box.

"You've been carrying that around all week?"

He gives me a mischievous grin. "I never knew when you might accept. I wanted to be ready." He taps the box. "May I?"

And then I am undone, blinking furiously. I clear my throat. "Yes."

Henri opens the box and lifts an exquisite ring from the padding. It has a simple gold band and the center diamond looks to be almost three carats. It couldn't be more elegant or perfect and my hand trembles as he slides it onto my finger.

"Yes?" he asks, once more, just to make sure.

A firm nod. "Yes."

He takes a deep breath. "You have your condition. Which I accept. But I have another request."

"Oh dear. I'm not sure I can take anything else."

Henri lifts my newly decorated hand to his lips and kisses the ring gently. He closes his eyes. "I hate being apart from you. Will you *please* move to Marseille?"

PARIS

Rue Sainte-Anne, 2nd Arrondissement

"Are you moving in with Henri Fiocca?" Stephanie asks the moment I open the door to my flat. "I didn't think you were the type."

I have been trying to contact her since I returned from Marseille, a week ago, but she and Count Gonzales have been in Spain, on holiday. I finally got through this morning and told her that I'd be taking Le Train Bleu to Marseilles today and would like to say good-bye before leaving Paris once and for all.

"No." I step back so she can enter. "I am not moving in with him. But I *am* moving to Marseille."

We hug. Exchange kisses on each cheek.

"Where will you live, then?" she demands.

"At the Hôtel du Louvre et Paix. Until I find us a flat."

"Us?"

"Me," I say, then grudgingly add, "and Henri."

"To live in *together*?"

"Once we are *married,* yes." I hold up my left hand and show her the ring that Henri placed there last week. I'd wanted to tell her in person. No letters. No phone calls.

Stephanie grabs my hand and brings it close to her face to inspect the ring. She is smiling and crying at the same time. She is the only woman I've ever met who could make such conflicting emotions look beautiful.

"Aren't you happy for me?" I ask.

She nods. "I am."

"But?"

"I am sad for myself. You are leaving me." She looks at me with those huge blue eyes and I see genuine sorrow in them. "You are the only friend I have."

"The Count—"

"Is a man," she interrupts. "It is not the same."

I cannot argue. The friendships of women are strange and wonderful. Fraught and irreplaceable. And yet I can't apologize for moving away to marry the man I love. So instead I ask, "Will you come visit me?"

"Of course."

"And I will return to Paris, often," I promise.

She thinks about this for a moment, weighing the likelihood of either happening, and tries a different tack. "What about your job?"

"The one where I work hard, am paid little, and get no credit?"

It takes an effort but she manages to hide her smile. Even she knows this was a poor argument. "*Oui.* That one."

"I've submitted my final article and my resignation to Milo. I no longer have a job."

"Doesn't that bother you?" Stephanie asks.

"If I'm being honest, it's a relief. At this particular moment I don't give a rat's ass about independence or careers. I just want to be with Henri."

Of everything I've said, this makes the most sense to Stephanie. She wraps her arms around my neck, then kisses each of my cheeks again. "I did warn you about him."

We move to the small table beside the window and sit. The sun is out today, and it comes through the glass panes in bright, warm squares. Stephanie looks around my small kitchen and I know she sees only a handful of boxes packed and ready to ship to Marseille. My transient life has allowed me to collect so few possessions and I am ready to put down roots.

After a moment Stephanie tips her head to the side and asks, "What will you do about your name?"

"My name?"

"Wake. You will keep it, yes?"

She always has been a stickler about this, so I wade in carefully. "No. I plan to take his."

"You will give up your own identity?" Her mouth tightens into a straight line. "Not even Henri Fiocca is worth such a sacrifice."

"You are wrong. He is worth it. But honestly, it has *nothing* to do with identity. Or sacrifice. But it does have everything to do with loyalty." Her eyes narrow, daring me to defend my position. "Why should I keep my father's name? He abandoned my family when I was two. I've never seen him since and I owe him no loyalty."

She sniffs. "Then take your mother's maiden name. Anything but a man's."

I do laugh then. I can't help it. "My mother's maiden name was given to her by *her* father. All surnames are male names—"

"Patriarchal—"

"Fine. But if I have to pick a patriarch, I'll pick the one I actually *like*."

"I do not agree with your decision. Or your logic," she says, "but I do not wish to fight." Stephanie rises from the chair beside my window and walks into the kitchen. She returns with two glasses and a bottle of Rémy Martin. "Once more, for old times?"

"And for new beginnings." I reach for the bottle and she surrenders it to me. Her eyes widen when she sees how much I pour into each glass.

"Oh," she says, proudly placing a hand over her heart. "She finally becomes a *Parisienne,* only to leave Paris."

* * *

Henri

July 1939

"What do you mean you 'took care of it'?" Nancy demands.

She has her bare feet up on the balcony rail outside her suite in the Hôtel du Louvre et Paix—where she's been living since he finally convinced her to move to Marseille. A half-smoked Gitane is in one hand and their marriage license, properly completed and legalized, sits in her lap. It's clear that she's been pulling at her hair for a good part of the day because it's gone wild and she looks as though she's been run over by a trolly. Her green eyes are blazing, her mouth set in defiance. But it's the fact that her skirt has slid down her thigh, revealing her slip, that has captured Henri's attention. If she notices, she doesn't care. Nancy takes another angry puff of her cigarette and waits for him to answer.

"What I mean," Henri says, calmly, refilling her wineglass and turning his gaze back to her face, "is that I went to Town Hall and spoke with him. I *took care of it.*"

"Why bother? He's . . . he's . . ." She drifts off, unable to find an appropriately horrible profanity. Nancy taps the ash from her cigarette in frustration.

"I believe the insult you're looking for is *fils de pute,* and that's exactly what I called him, quite loudly in fact, when I told him off in the middle of Town Hall. More than one person stopped to stare." Henri plucks Nancy's cigarette from her pinched fingers and takes a draw. He grimaces. Smoking is the one filthy habit he never took to. It looks quite sexy on her, however, so he hands it back. He's happy to watch. "Besides, *ma chère*, you'd just called off our engagement. It's not like you left me any choice."

She pouts. "You know I wasn't *serious*."

"You sounded serious on the phone."

"I was angry."

"As you had a right to be. That *enculé*"—he spits out the word as though it's gristle from an overcooked steak—"was toying with you. He hates anyone not from Marseille."

"Why?"

"Because this city is small and insular. Fiercely proud of its inhabitants. Suspicious of strangers. Besides, he's a friend of Marceline's. Has been in love with her for years, though I can't imagine why. I'm certain that entire fiasco was a personal favor to her."

The look on Nancy's face is akin to wonder. "What does that mean? That word you just used."

Henri clears his throat. "It's very bad."

"Clearly. But also effective. That and the other one . . . *fils* . . ." She snaps her fingers, trying to remember. "*Fils* something or other."

He looks at his shoes. Studies the scuff marks on the toes. "*Fils de pute.*"

"You're embarrassed! Whatever for?"

"It's one thing to say these things to a man in the heat of an argument. It's quite another to say them to my fiancée."

She grins wickedly. "Perhaps you should teach me to say them myself, so you don't have to. That way the next time I apply for a marriage license I can deal with that man on my own."

He snorts. "There won't be a next time! I intend to keep you all to myself until the very end of my life."

Nancy turns her face to the sun. "Have you read the papers today? The end of everything—not just our lives—might be coming. They're saying war with Germany is inevitable."

Like most people in France, Henri and Nancy have shut their

eyes to the inevitable. Every day the radios crackle with reports of German atrocities. The newspapers declare, in bold print, that peace talks are falling apart. Meanwhile, France sits at the edge of Europe, like a shiny, unclaimed prize. The sense of claustrophobia grows each day as Germany looms ever closer in the north, to the east Mussolini makes threats, to the west they are hemmed in by the Atlantic Ocean, and in the south the formidable Pyrenees separate France from Spain. The entire nation has nowhere to go. So they wait. They live and dance and kiss with the unspoken fear looming around them that this might not just be the last summer before the war, it could also be their last summer altogether.

And yet, Nancy has moved to Marseille to be with him. She is here, and she is safe. They will be married soon. Henri clings to this. And he clings to her every chance that he gets. Henri thinks for a moment. He does not like how easily she was thwarted by the official at Town Hall. She is a foreigner living in Marseille. He loves his city but . . . it can be hard on outsiders. Nancy will be miserable if she's always having to wait on him to rescue her. A vicious vocabulary could give her bargaining tools she wouldn't have otherwise.

"Okay," he says, finally, "I'll teach you to curse like a Frenchwoman."

"No." She shakes the cigarette in his face. "Teach me to curse like a *Frenchman*."

"My own mother couldn't do that!"

"Do I look like your mother, Henri Fiocca?"

The corner of his mouth lifts in a wanton grin. "Not in the least."

"Just as I thought." She stubs out her Gitane. "Where do we start?"

Henri checks his watch. "I have to be back at the office in twenty minutes. So, we'll start with three—"

"I want the bad ones," she says. "The ones you just used to describe that man at Town Hall."

"Okay. Two bad ones. And one mild. Just to ease my conscience."

"Poor Henri. The awful things your fiancée makes you do."

His gaze returns to her exposed slip and the length of thigh beyond it. He has to suppress the hungry moan that rises in his throat.

"We'll start with the most common word. *Merde.* It can be a noun or an exclamation. It just means 'shit.'"

"Merde," she says. Nancy practices it a few times, getting used to the way the consonants roll off her tongue.

Henri nods once she's got the pronunciation right. "Now use it in a sentence."

She thinks for a moment. "That filthy piece of *merde* stole my car."

"Not bad. But it can also be used in other contexts besides an insult. As a consolation, for example. If I told you my father had just died, you would say . . . ?"

"Thank God."

He laughs. "Okay. Bad example. We'll go with my mother. And that's true. She died before I was twenty."

Nancy is appropriately appalled. "Oh *merde.* I'm sorry, Henri."

"Well done! But in that context you draw it out. Make it two syllables. *MAIR-duh.*"

She mimics him perfectly and then, after a moment, when she's certain he isn't in fact upset about his mother, asks, "Next? What did you call that man—*fils* something or other?"

"*Fils de pute.* It's the equivalent of your 'son of a bitch' but more insulting. It literally means 'son of a whore' and is terribly vulgar. And therefore very effective. It's the sort of thing men say when flinging the finger or grabbing their crotch. It's an insult reserved specifically for *people,* not as a statement of irritation."

"So not the sort of thing you say unless you mean it?"

"Exactly. Try it."

"That *fils de pute* at Town Hall was purposefully making my life miserable."

He beams. "Perfect!"

She's warming to this lesson. "Next!"

Henri runs the pad of his thumb across her lips. "I don't want to taint that pretty mouth of yours."

She snaps at his thumb with her teeth. "A bit late, I'm afraid."

He makes a show of sighing, but really, he's enjoying this. She's taken to the lesson and—filthy as the habit is—it's no less sexy than watching her smoke. *"Enculé,"* he says. "It's really the worst word that I know."

Nancy sets her feet on the floor and scoots forward on her chair. "What does it mean?"

Sometimes it's harder to say the meaning than the actual word. "Ah . . ." He clears his throat. "It means 'one who has been . . .' Ah . . . I believe the English word is 'buggered.' "

"Oh. I say that all the time."

"Non." He shakes his head. "It's different in French. In English it's flippant. But in this language, you mean it literally. *Enculé!* It's something you say to the person you hate most."

Nancy doesn't miss a beat. She offers Henri a waspish smile. "Marceline *'la' enculée.*"

The fact that her voice is so pleasant and sweet as she speaks that particular sentence makes the insult spectacular. Henri leans back in his chair and shakes his head a bit in appreciation. "You're a natural."

Nancy rises from her chair and straddles his lap. She places one gentle kiss on his lips. "I have an excellent teacher."

As always, when she kisses him, Henri is consumed. He glances at his watch. He has only five minutes. It's more than enough time to make sure she gets a proper kiss.

* * *

MARSEILLE

Hôtel du Louvre et Paix, September 3, 1939

Henri set a wedding date of November 30. I think he did this so as not to alarm me. To give me time. Allow me to ease into the idea of being a *wife.* He insisted there was no rush, but I know this is a statement made only for my benefit. He would most certainly love to rush. He would swan-dive into matrimony given the chance. As it stands, however, we take our time. In the interim I have taken up residence at the Hôtel du Louvre et Paix, until our new flat becomes available on the first of December. We spent all spring and summer having light, frivolous fun, as though living at the very top of a soap bubble. But now we have settled into a regular routine filled with wedding plans and the daily chores needed to build a life together.

Henri works his usual, long hours, starting at five in the morning, and ending, promptly, twelve hours later. He does, however, meet me in the hotel bar for *pastis* at eleven—our favorite prelunch pastime—before we wander into the city to find a bistro. And then, once we're stuffed to the gills, he heads back to the office and I to my room upstairs, for a nap. My job, once I wake in the early afternoon, is to begin the process of furnishing our flat. I go into the city and meet with retailers. I look at lavish fabric for draperies and upholstery for chairs. I order Persian rugs and a bar for the drawing room. I pick out china patterns, crystal glasses, and flatware, making my orders, and instructing everything to be delivered to our new flat the second week of December. I've never set up a home before and I find the process both maddening and therapeutic.

I look up from my table in the corner when Henri walks into the bar—smiling, as always—to see him. He's fifteen minutes late today and there is a sense of urgency to his movements.

"Turn on the radio!" he orders Antoine, and I jump at the sound of his voice—booming and authoritative.

Antoine flips it to the BBC French Service and Henri settles into the chair beside me. I look at him but do not ask any questions. His head is bent to the side, listening, as the static gives way to a familiar voice. Neville Chamberlain.

"This morning the British ambassador in Berlin handed the German government a final note stating that, unless we heard from them by eleven o'clock that they were prepared at once to withdraw their troops from Poland, a state of war would exist between us. I have to tell you now that no such undertaking has been received, and that consequently this country is at war with Germany."

There are only a handful of people in the bar but each of us draws a long, somber breath. It's not like we didn't know this was coming. *Of course* we knew. Germany invaded Poland two days ago and Chamberlain delivered his ultimatum for withdrawal. The threat of war has been crackling in the air for several years. But hearing it announced is not a thing you are ever prepared for.

Henri reaches for my hand. Squeezes it. Antoine glances at my face and hands me a napkin. He expects me to cry. And I might. We listen as Chamberlain expresses his dismay with these circumstances, with England's failed efforts to arrange a "peaceful and honorable settlement between Germany and Poland." How Hitler has categorically refused these efforts. Chamberlain tells us how Hitler can be stopped only by force. I remember Berlin. I think of him standing there beneath the *Blutfahne,* the blood banner, and I know that Chamberlain is right. The spilling of blood is the true legacy of Adolf Hitler.

"We and France are today, in fulfillment of our obligations, going to the aid of Poland, who is so bravely resisting this wicked and unprovoked attack on her people. We have a clear conscience. We have done all that any country could do to establish peace. The situation in which no word given by Germany's ruler could be trusted and no people or country could feel themselves safe has become intolerable. And now that we have resolved to finish it, I know that you will all play your part with calmness and courage."

Antoine returns to his place behind the bar and shifts from one foot to another. Every time his weight goes to his left leg he winces slightly. Like Henri, he fought in the Great War, and I wonder if he is thinking of fighting again.

For the next few moments, Neville Chamberlain gives instructions to those who have joined the Civil Defense. He encourages his countrymen to carry on with their jobs.

"Now may God bless you all. May He defend the right. It is the evil things that we shall be fighting against—brute force, bad faith, injustice, oppression and persecution—and against them I am certain that the right will prevail."

We forget about lunch. About work and shopping, and all the small business that usually fills our days. Henri and I sit in Antoine's bar and listen to the radio as more and more people file in. Antoine hands us each a glass of brandy and we sip, slowly, listening to the

British, and then the French, read their declarations of war. Sometime later, King George takes to the airwaves.

"In this grave hour, perhaps the most fateful in our history, I send to every household of my peoples, both at home and overseas, this message, spoken with the same depth of feeling for each one of you as if I were able to cross your threshold and speak to you myself. For the second time in the lives of most of us we are at war. Over and over again we have tried to find a peaceful way out of the differences between ourselves and those who are now our enemies. But it has been in vain."

I am Australian to the bone. And yes, I have taken on a second life as a *Parisienne.* France is my home now. But there are the moments when a woman returns to her roots, and the voice of my monarch reminds me that I am, and always will be, a member of the British Empire. I sit up straighter and swallow the emotion that builds in my throat. Henri drapes his arm across my shoulders.

"This is the ultimate issue which confronts us. For the sake of all that we ourselves hold dear, and of the world's order and peace, it is unthinkable that we should refuse to meet the challenge. It is to this high purpose that I now call my people at home and my peoples across the Seas, who will make our cause their own. I ask them to stand calm, firm and united in this time of trial. The task will be hard. There may be dark days ahead, and war can no longer be confined to the battlefield. But we can only do the right as we see the right, and reverently commit our cause to God. If one and all we keep resolutely faithful to it, ready for whatever service or sacrifice it may demand, then, with God's help, we shall prevail. May He bless and keep us all."

In a moment, just like that, every person in Antoine's bar is struck with the sense that our laughter and our joy will soon turn to tears.

"What does this mean?" I ask Henri.

His gaze goes soft as he stares at the table. "It means, *ma chère,* that one day we will remember our friends and count the dead."

Madame Andrée

MONT MOUCHET, CANTAL, FRANCE

March 21, 1944

Fournier is waiting for us when we return to the encampment. I am driving the stolen Nazi bus and Hubert follows behind in the Renault. It makes me chuckle to see him behind the wheel. He's a big man and it looks like he's been crammed into a tin can. Getting through the checkpoints was a bit tricky, given my new vehicle, but the Maquis guards recognized me and I had all the passwords, so they let me pass. I pull the bus into the clearing and park halfway to the fire pit. Hubert is at the door and up the steps before I can even get out of my seat and stretch.

"Have you ever actually driven a bus before?" he asks.

"No. Have you ever hot-wired one before?"

He laughs. It's a surprising sound, deep and filled with humor. I don't hear it often enough. "Many times."

"Well, thank you."

He scratches his chin with two fingers. It's been over a week since Hubert had a proper shave and he's gone a bit woolly as a result. "What do you intend to do with this anyway? You can't just go riding around in a German transport vehicle."

"I mean to live in it. If I'm going to be stuck in the woods indefinitely, I'd like a bit of privacy and space."

Hubert looks at me as if I've just declared that I'm going to set up residence in the Louvre. "You are going to live in *this*?" He sniffs. "It smells like Nazi crotch."

This makes me laugh and I am grateful, after the horrors of the day. "I don't even want to know how you can identify that scent. Besides, I can open the windows. Air the thing out. And honestly, I think you're just jealous you didn't think of it first."

He looks around the bus, considering the possibilities. "Actually, yes, I am a bit jealous. I think I've got a permanent bend in my spine from weeks spent sleeping on the ground."

"Well, if you're nice I'll let you in occasionally." I waggle a finger in his face. "But only if it's raining."

"I'll take what I can get. Besides. I'm just glad you won't be motoring around in this thing. You're an *awful* driver."

"I am not! I just like to take my half out of the middle."

Hubert looks over his shoulder. "Come on, then. Fournier is out there, pacing. We'd best see what he wants."

"You have a visitor," Fournier says, the moment we step out of the bus.

"Who?"

"Henri Tardivat."

We've not seen the suave little Frenchman since he delivered us to Gaspard's château the night we flew in. It was unclear to me at first what role Tardivat plays in the Resistance, but I have since learned from Fournier that, in addition to collecting counterintelligence—and the occasional parachuter—Tardivat leads his own band of merry men in the forest at Allier. The thing, Fournier insists, that makes Tardivat such a spectacular saboteur is that he has perfected a very specific technique in which he targets German supply convoys, letting most of it pass through his bottleneck before attacking the last two vehicles. By the time the main firepower at the front circles back, they are confronted with torched vehicles, dead soldiers, and vanished Maquis. As Fournier tells me, this ensures ravaged supply lines for the Germans and crushing blows to their morale. I liked Tardivat to begin with, but this knowledge has made me very fond of him indeed. And his timing is excellent because I need to inform him of the target he's been assigned to destroy in the event of an Allied invasion of France. Fournier has his targets already and has been preparing his strike team since we arrived.

Fournier leads us toward his newly acquired tent—thanks to London—where Tardivat sits inside, muddy boots propped up on a stump, arms behind his head.

"*Bonjour!* I don't know how you stand that track," he says, motioning across the clearing to the dirt road he's just driven up. "I nearly bottomed out in a rut a mile back. Thought I'd scraped my transmission clean off."

"We'll make sure to have it paved before your next unexpected arrival," I tell him.

He grins. "Aren't you glad to see me?"

"Depends."

"On?"

"Whether or not you plan to drop me into Gaspard's hairy little paws again."

"Funny you should say that...," he says, looking around the tent, and then at me, as though surprised to see that I've lasted this long under such rough conditions. "Nice place you've got here."

"The tent is Fournier's. That bus"—I hook my thumb over my back—"is mine."

"You're going to sleep in a bus?"

"I will once I find a mattress."

He gnaws at his thumbnail. "I might be able to acquire a mattress. If you're willing to barter."

"For?"

"Sten guns for my men."

"Find me a mattress—a clean one—and I'll request your guns." I laugh. "But that's not why you're here. Get to the point. What's this about Gaspard?"

"He despises you."

"Tell me something I don't know."

"Okay." Tardivat drops both feet to the ground. "Patrice is dead."

Hubert stiffens beside me, and I'm sure the look on my own face is one of dismay. I am one of only three SOE agents in the area who have direct contact with Maurice Buckmaster. The others are

Victor—farther north in the Allier region where Tardivat is based, and Patrice in the Auvergne.

"What happened?"

"He was killed last night by a German agent sent to assassinate Gaspard. But the agent has been captured and Gaspard sent me to ask if you would like to interrogate him. He said it was an olive branch."

"I don't—"

"Listen. If you want to get information from this German agent, you'll have to come with me. Now. Knowing Gaspard, I doubt he'll be alive much longer."

The distance between Fournier's encampment and Gaspard's is little more than fifty kilometers as the crow flies. But they are separated by rugged terrain interlaced with mountains, valleys, and narrow byways. What should be a forty-five-minute drive takes almost two hours as we creep through half a dozen villages and small towns.

There are two ways to get to Mont Mouchet, but we choose to go east, then north in a wide half circle to avoid the German garrison at Montluçon. The last thing we need is to run across an enemy patrol and have to shoot our way through. As we drive I give Tardivat his target: the munitions factory near Montluçon, and he fills us in on what happened to Patrice.

"Early this morning, a German agent was halted by Patrice at a checkpoint four kilometers from Mont Mouchet. He gave the correct password, then requested to be taken to Gaspard so he could join the Maquis. Patrice and one of his maquisards got in the car and guided the agent through that tangled mess of roads that leads to Gaspard's headquarters."

"How could a German so easily fool the Maquis?" Hubert asks.

"Because he wasn't German at all."

"A collaborationist?"

"Yes. His mission was to locate, then assassinate, Gaspard, and he would have likely gotten away with it had Patrice not noticed the key ring that hung from the ignition."

I lift my gaze from the road to look at Tardivat. But I do not interrupt him or ask for clarification. Tardivat fancies himself a storyteller and appreciates a pregnant pause.

"It was engraved with German lettering," he says.

I nod. "Ah. So Patrice would assume that the man he was taking to Gaspard was either a Resistance worker who had commandeered a German vehicle or—"

"—that he was in fact working with the Germans," Tardivat finishes for me. "As the captive tells it—albeit under duress—Patrice and his maquisard began to whisper in the backseat. The agent had his pistol ready beneath his thigh, and the moment he saw Patrice reach inside his coat for his revolver, he turned and fired, hitting Patrice squarely in the throat. Then he shot the maquisard once in the forehead."

"*Merde.*" I wince.

"Unfortunately for the agent, this altercation happened just as they passed into Gaspard's territory. They were surrounded immediately."

"What of Patrice?" Hubert asks from the backseat.

"He died almost immediately. But he did manage to get three shots through the seat and into the agent's back before bleeding out."

This is a terrible blow to the work we're doing, and I feel my shoulders sag. I lean against the passenger-side door, trying to think of what this will mean for communications with London and our own responsibilities with Fournier's group. We are already shorthanded, and Patrice did the work of ten men.

"I take it none of Patrice's shots hit the mark?" I ask.

"They did little damage," Tardivat says. "The agent was wearing a bulletproof vest."

"Of course he was," I mutter, and then something occurs to me. "How do you know all of this?"

Tardivat takes his eyes from the road and turns to me. The look on his face is indecipherable. It could be relief or disgust. Pride or horror. "Gaspard and his men have been torturing him for information."

The first thing we notice when we arrive at the château is the smell of burning flesh. As on our first visit, Tardivat brings his vehicle close to the front door. As soon as we step out of the Renault, the pungent, stomach-churning odor hits us like an invisible cloud. The broad front doors of the château are propped open and guarded by two of Gaspard's men. I don't recognize either of them, but they clearly know who we are, because they step aside and motion us in.

"Good God," I say, clamping a hand over my nose as soon as we cross the threshold.

Tardivat looks at me with pity, clearly knowing what we're about to see. We step into the château and go past the broad staircase, toward the kitchen at the back of the large, square house. The smell grows stronger with each step and I can sense a heavy, gagging feeling claw its way up the back of my throat. Still, I am not prepared for the horrific sight that greets us.

The agent is stripped naked, spread-eagle, and tied by hands and feet to the long, heavy kitchen table where Gaspard and his officers eat their meals. His body is bruised and bloody. He has been whipped and beaten. His face—or what little I can see of it since he's lying on his stomach—has been battered beyond recognition. Two broken teeth lie on the table beside his head in a bloody puddle of spit. But it is the lower half of his body that has me gaping and forcing the bile back down my throat. The unholy stench of burned human hangs so heavily in the air that I have to force my body into stillness. The option of breathing—through nose or mouth—means I must choose between smelling the air or tasting it. I take the smallest possible breaths through my nose that I can. Still, I stare at the table, trying to make sense of the carnage.

By the looks of it, Gaspard's chief lieutenant, Judex, has repeatedly rammed a red-hot poker up the German agent's arse. What remains of his buttocks and thighs is a blackened, bleeding pile of charred flesh. I cannot see his genitals and I dare not ask why. This is beyond the pale of what one human should do to another, regardless of circumstance. Of war. Of information gathering. As for

Judex, he stands beside Gaspard at the far end of the kitchen, resting one hand on the poker—now cooled to its original black—as if it were a cane and he a debonair gentleman. Both men stare at us, assessing our reactions.

The sound that comes from the agent's throat is not human. It is a dialect of suffering known only to those who linger between this life and the next. It is the kind of sound you would not wish upon your worst enemy. Though I suspect Gaspard feels rather differently about that than I do, because he's grinning smugly on a stool fifteen feet away. He smokes a cigarette and nods his approval, as though this is the most fascinating thing he's ever witnessed.

"What are you doing?" I gasp. I can taste the foul, acrid air the moment it enters my mouth and I have to grind my teeth to stop the vomit that now threatens to rise with every breath.

"Interrogating him for information," Gaspard says.

"That," I say, pointing one finger at the table, "goes far beyond interrogation. It is torture. Why didn't you just execute him and get it over with?"

"He had our password. We had to find out where he got it and who he is. What he knows. What he's done."

"Have you?"

"Of course." He taps his ash onto the floor, then takes another draw. "Several hours ago."

"And?"

"His name is Roger le Neveu, a French collaborationist, otherwise known as Gestapo agent number forty-seven."

It takes a monumental effort on my part not to gasp at the name, and I mask my surprise by walking around the table and squatting in front of the man tied there. I grip the table leg to steady myself while mentally berating Gaspard for his barbarism and stupidity. *Quel con, celui-lá!* Roger's eyes are swollen shut and I am grateful because he would no doubt recognize me. And it would be disastrous if Gaspard or anyone in this room noticed. These men cannot know that I have been in France before. That I *lived* here and have a family. Everyone has at least one pressure point, and mine is named Henri.

"Just shoot the poor bastard and get it over with," I say.

Roger's entire body shudders on the table but I do not think it is fear. I think it is relief. He is a man desperate to die.

Gaspard rises from his stool and crosses the floor to where I stand. He moves like a boulder rolling downhill and his men instinctively get out of his way. I stand and face him.

"Why?" he demands once we're almost nose to nose.

It irritates me that I have to look up. "This man can be of no further use to you. Do the right thing and let him die."

"You pity him?"

"I would pity anyone in that condition."

"They do worse to our people," he says. "We got word this afternoon that the Brownshirts slaughtered a woman in Termes. A pregnant wo—"

"—I know what they did," I snap. "I saw it with my own eyes. And this"—I point at Roger again—"isn't justice. It's you, becoming as evil as them."

"Gabriel Soutine is my *friend*," he says.

We should have known that word of what happened in Termes would get out. In many ways the Maquis communication network is more effective than the BBC. The "bush wireless" ensures that what happens in one commune is known in the next within hours.

Gaspard snorts. "You do not think this man should pay for what his friends did to Gabriel's wife?"

"I think he should die for his own crimes."

"Well, there are plenty of those. Take your pick."

Gaspard drops his cigarette to the slate floor and stubs it out with the toe of his boot. Then he pulls a folded sheet of paper from his back pocket. He smooths out the creases and begins to read. "Thanks to a bit of... ah... *creative* questioning by Judex, we know that this man, Roger, is responsible for a series of barbaric tortures and assaults on captured members of the Resistance. They are numerous and transcribed here. I will let you read them at your leisure." Gaspard taps the paper with one clean finger. It is so clean, in contrast to everything and everyone around me, that I realize Gaspard has washed his hands. Scrubbed them of the filth leaking from Roger's body.

He continues. "But there are a few things on this list I think you will be particularly interested in. Seeing as how they concern your precious London. This Roger was directly responsible for the arrest of a man named Patrick O'Leary in Toulouse one year ago."

I shift my weight against the table. I do everything I can to make the movement look relaxed. Not like my knees are about to go out from under me. I force my voice to sound only mildly curious. I know the answer to my next question already, but asking is the only way I can confirm the identity of the man on the table. "And what happened to this O'Leary?"

Gaspard looks at the paper. "He was sent to Dachau."

I can feel my peripheral vision begin to blur. Roger. O'Leary. Toulouse. That particular betrayal has probably cost the life of my friend. I look at the man on the table and fight the anger that snakes through my blood.

"Go on," I say.

"Last night Roger was responsible for the death of Patrice. I believe you are familiar with him?"

"I am."

"Then that leaves just you and Victor to arm my maquisards, doesn't it?"

I ignore the question. I will not talk shop with Gaspard before a tortured, dying man. "Is that all?"

"There is more. If you think the crimes I've stated already don't justify my actions." He taps the paper again, then hands it to me. I read the final line on the sheet. It contains a nickname I am all too familiar with. Gaspard saved this most personal bit of information for last. "In addition to myself, this Roger had a second target. A female British operative who obtains weapons and supplies from England. A woman known to the Germans as *la Souris Blanche* and to the French as Madame Andrée. His mission, once he had killed me, was to locate and then assassinate her." The glint in his eyes is ruthless. "You."

The White Mouse. Roger was after me as well. The Germans have connected the dots.

"Keep his confession," Gaspard says when I try to return the paper. "I'm sure your friends in London will want a copy for their records."

I hand the paper to Hubert, but I say nothing to Gaspard.

"You should thank us, *Madame Andrée.* You were next."

"I can take care of myself." It's true; I've been doing so since I was sixteen. I am not beholden to Gaspard and I will not pretend that I am. "And you are a *fool.* Do you understand what you have done? This man was sent by the Gestapo to find you. When he does not return they will know that he has been either captured or killed. His presence here means they know where you are. They will retaliate in force."

Gaspard does not miss a beat. "Then you will arm my men so we will be better prepared."

Ah. I think this is the reason he sent for me. To Gaspard, this entire war is a game of chess. Moves and countermoves. People fall into strategic categories to be used as he sees fit. Clearly, he thinks of me as little more than a pawn.

I look him squarely in the eyes and ask, "Are you willing to agree to my terms?"

He sneers. "You have . . . *terms*?"

"Two of them, in fact."

Gaspard ponders this. I can see him resist the urge to tell me where I can shove my *terms.* He takes a long breath through his nose, steadying his temper, and his great, broad chest inflates. "I will provide the men. You will provide the weapons. Those are the only *terms* that need discussing."

I see what's happening. His men. He is not willing to lose face in front of them. And I am not willing to give him an inch. What Gaspard has not yet realized is that he cannot give orders to London. He will receive orders, or he will get nothing. There is no give-and-take. No negotiation.

"Good luck with the Germans," I tell him. He opens his mouth to protest but I have already turned to Hubert. "I have no questions for Roger. Please do what Gaspard did not have the courage to do and give him a quick death."

Gaspard closes the space between us and clamps one heavy hand on my left shoulder. "You are making a mistake."

I glance at his hand, then his face. "Do not touch me."

"You are a weak, soft woman. You have no place in this war."

Gaspard expects me to shrink back in fear, so when I shift my weight he only grips me harder. What he doesn't realize is that I've lifted my right boot, stuck my hand inside, and pulled out the knife that I keep strapped to my shin. It's a smooth, clean movement. One I was required to practice for hours and hours on end in SOE training. The sharp, wicked blade is pressed into the skin of his wrist before he realizes what I have done. A thin line of blood seeps into his shirt cuff.

"You will remove your hand from me or I will remove it from your body."

Neither Hubert nor Tardivat has drawn his weapon. They don't need to. I am no damsel in distress. But they do keep a close eye on Gaspard's men.

Gaspard lifts one finger at a time and then his palm. He drops the hand to his side.

"We're done here," I say. Then I nod at Hubert. "Do it."

This is no longer a kitchen. It is no longer a home. To my mind it is, and will always be, a place of cowardice and torture. I walk from the room without another word, Tardivat on my heels. We're almost at the staircase when I hear that single, merciful shot.

"Easy there," Tardivat whispers in my ear as my knees buckle. He places one hand beneath my elbow to steady me.

It is a simple, kind gesture amidst so much horror and I am nearly overcome. I gag, once, and hot tears burn the corners of my eyes. I take one more wobbling step before I straighten and walk out the front doors of the château by his side. Hubert joins us seconds later.

"Gaspard is coming," Hubert whispers in my ear. "Keep it together just a bit longer."

"I'll be fine."

"He's still dangerous, you know. Don't push him too far."

"Don't worry," I say quietly as I turn back to the château doors where Gaspard is barreling toward us. "I'll stop just short of the cliff."

Gaspard steps onto the gravel, filling his lungs, ready for a verbal assault. But he can't inhale and speak at the same time, so I preempt him.

"You have plotted to murder me in my sleep. You have turned

me out of your château when you thought I was useless. You have attempted to steal *my* weapons at *my* drop zone. And you have taken a routine interrogation to the most inhuman, barbaric extreme. Say one rash word and you will never receive so much as a pair of toenail clippers from me. I know you are not stupid. I know you understand me. Make your choice and be quick about it because I have work to do."

He takes two deep breaths through his nose. Unclenches his fists. "What are your *terms*?"

"They are quite simple but nonnegotiable. First, you must divide your men into smaller groups, each with a leader of its own, and disperse them throughout the Auvergne instead of massing them here. And second, you must prepare an escape route for each group in the event of attack." I can see he is itching to respond, his entire body is shuddering with the need to defend himself, but I am not finished. "At the moment you are grossly vulnerable to attack, even more so now, given what you have done to Roger. What you consider to be power in numbers is nothing more than a temptation to the thousands of Germans garrisoned around you. You are poorly armed and unorganized, and it will be a slaughter *when*—not *if*—they advance upon your château. When you have done these two things, and not a moment sooner, I will begin arming your men."

His entire body goes still even as his face turns an alarming shade of purple. His muscles are frozen with rage. After some moments Gaspard unclenches his jaw long enough to say, "It is one thing to accept weaponry and assistance from a *femme*. But I will not take orders from one."

I do not argue or try to change his mind. "Have it your way."

Hubert, Tardivat, and I climb into the car and pull away from the château. From the backseat Hubert gives me that universal male grunt, the one that could mean "well done" or possibly "go bugger your cousin." In this case I prefer to think he's just congratulated me on my leadership skills.

I turn to Tardivat and say, "Take us into the forest, far enough where we won't be seen by Gaspard's men, and then stop."

I close my eyes and take long, deep breaths through my nose. I am sweating. Shaking.

He does as I ask and when we are in the dim, cool shade of the pine forest, parked at the side of the road, I open my car door and vomit onto a bed of dried brown needles. Of all the physiological responses the human body can call upon under duress, this is the one I like the least. Typically, I will go to any lengths *not* to throw up. I can count the number of times, in my adult life, that I have done so. Yet here I am, chucking for the second time today. But I can still smell the stench of Roger's burned carcass. It has seeped into my clothes. I can taste it. So I vomit again. And again. Until the only thing left in my stomach is yellow, stringy bile. And then I spit, forcing the acidic taste from my mouth. I want to bleach my mouth. I want to replace all my teeth.

Hubert and Tardivat wait patiently as I wipe my mouth on my sleeve, push my damp hair back away from my face, and arrange myself in the seat.

"A word of this to anyone and I'll shoot the both of you," I say.

Nancy Fiocca

MARSEILLE

November 30, 1939

Our wedding is small and uneventful. Given that I am not Roman Catholic—nor do I have any intention of converting—I exchange vows, and rings, with Henri Edmond Fiocca at three o'clock in the afternoon, at Town Hall in Marseille. Witnesses are plucked from the hallway and bribed with bottles of Veuve Clicquot champagne. We do engage in one small bit of petty revenge, however, and insist that the useless official who tried to deny us a marriage license perform the ceremony. He stares at me, pop-eyed, as I meet Henri at the altar wearing a low-cut dress of pure black silk. I have painted my lips a scandalous shade of red for the occasion.

Our reception makes up for the simplicity of our wedding ceremony. I am overwhelmed, less than an hour later, when Henri leads me into the ballroom at the Hôtel du Louvre et Paix. It is draped in chiffon and bathed in candlelight. There is a string quartet and four champagne fountains—one in each corner of the room. But even more important, Frank Gilmore and Stephanie Marsic are seated at the head table. The sight of my friends brings tears to my eyes and Henri delivers me to them while he goes to greet his father.

"You came," I say, voice cracking.

Stephanie throws her arms around me. "I would not miss it for the world, *ma petite*."

Frank says nothing, but he does place a big, sloppy kiss right on my mouth—a benign gesture now that I am a married woman—and blinks back tears of his own.

"I'm happy for you, Nance," he says.

I give him a huge hug and a kiss on the cheek. "I'm so glad you're here."

Then Henri is at my side again, and we eat. Oh, do we *eat.* Breads and salads and soups. Sole stuffed with mousseline and sea urchins, then fried until it puffs up like a soufflé. Roasted cutlets of lamb that were bred to graze on fields near the ocean, so the flavor is of both earth and sea, with meat so tender and rich we cut it with spoons and let it melt in our mouths. Whole beef filets with braised vegetables and a spiced wine reduction. Mushrooms stuffed with crab. Grilled artichokes so tender they open like blossoms, and vats of butter to dip them in. Chocolate cake. Chocolate soufflé. Berries and cream. Coffee. Brandy. *Endless* bottles of brandy. My favorite thing, however, and I am only slightly ashamed to admit this, is that we instruct Antoine to spike Old Man Fiocca's drinks with Napoleon brandy and Grand Marnier. We mean him no harm. Truly. But payback is payback. Henri and I laugh as his mood improves throughout the evening and he remarks upon the vintage of the champagne and the sweetness of the orange juice. He is fast asleep in the corner by nine o'clock and we enjoy the rest of our celebration without the slightest provocation.

To feast in the midst of war is no small thing. And to throw such a feast even as we start to feel the effects of rationing is nothing short of a miracle. But this is the only comfort we can give our friends. So we are lavish. And for one night we forget the dangers that are coming for us. And when we can no longer eat or drink another thing, we dance. Frank Gilmore spins Stephanie around the floor in a cumbersome but enthusiastic imitation of the waltz. Ficetole dances with his wife, then each of his daughters, in turn. Henri keeps me all to himself, never allowing me to dance with any of our friends, denying everyone who asks to cut in. I am his and he will not share. His hand stays on the small of my back, long fingers stroking the base of my spine. His face is bent into my neck, warm breath drifting between my breasts. When he speaks it is only to whisper the various ways in which he is about to render me speechless. I am quivering with anticipation, my skin hot and my breath short when the string quartet ends their final song with a flourish.

But there are guests to thank and we are the last to leave the grand ballroom, well after three in the morning.

"What now, love?" I ask as he guides me through the lobby.

"I take you to bed."

But I am confused because he is leading me toward the front door and not the elevators.

I point at the ceiling. "The bed is that way."

"*Non, ma chère.* I have one surprise left." He winks. "And fear not, it has a *very nice* bed."

* * *

Henri

He has thought of everything. Or at least he has *tried* to. During her long residence at the Hôtel du Louvre et Paix Nancy stayed in one of the luxurious junior suites. But he does not want to take her to bed for the first time in the same place she has slept for so many months. He wants something more . . . *personal.* So, he has prepared his own home for the occasion. It took a bit of time and a small crew of helpers but, as of this morning, he was pleased with the result.

For the last twelve years he has lived in a small, one-bedroom flat in the commercial district of Marseille. He chanced upon the space during a tour of a warehouse he was considering buying for the family business. The previous owner built a small apartment on the roof. It would never do for a family but was perfect for a single man who values privacy. Henri bought the building and has lived in the rooftop flat ever since—a mere fifty feet from his office.

Nancy does not ask questions as Henri leads her to a car and gives the address. She curls into his side and he drapes his arm around her. He buries his face in her hair. He lets himself fantasize about the rest of the night.

She is slightly more curious when they pull to the curb in the shipping district and he leads her into the square stone building with *Fiocca Enterprises* emblazoned above the door. There is a single light on at the end of the hall beside the elevator. From there it takes a special key to access the top floor. Henri pulls the key ring from his pocket and they begin the ascent. Neither of them speaks.

His bride watches all this with mute curiosity. And then she watches him, searching his face for clues.

Nancy gasps when he pushes the grate up and leads her into his home.

Henri's flat is the only residence in all of Marseille that offers a three-hundred-and-sixty-degree view of the city but—thanks to its location in the very center of the roof—is entirely hidden from view. There are floor-to-ceiling windows on every wall, but not a single curtain. He and Nancy are surrounded by soft, twinkling lights and a warm glow from the central fireplace. There are candles in the room, and lights on the harbor. Henri thought about music but decided against it, hoping to hear the music of her breath instead. The heavy drumbeat of her heart. That is the song he wants to hear tonight.

Nancy drifts from one small room to another. Living room. Kitchen. Bathroom. Bedroom. She stops, inches from the huge, soft bed, and runs her fingers along the coverlet. She turns to him. Her eyes are quizzical, and she tips her head to the side.

"You look nervous," she says.

"I want you to like it."

"I *love* it. How could I not?"

Henri shakes his head. That's not what he meant. "I want you to like … *me*."

So, yes, he is nervous. Henri has never lacked company, and his company has always been more than willing to offer their bodies for a night in the hopes of securing more. He is no saint. And he feels guilt about this. He does not want to be the sort of man who uses women for his own pleasure and then discards them. Perhaps it would have been different if he had ever felt as though the women who have passed through his life weren't using him as well. Pursuing his fortune instead of him.

Henri Fiocca has in fact never courted a woman before Nancy. And at first, he did not seduce her because he kept getting her drunk. Then he realized there was something exquisitely erotic about the anticipation. It's not that he hasn't wanted her. He has ached from it. But this longing and need have created two things he has never experienced before: intimacy and trust.

Nancy meets his brazen gaze. "I would like you a great deal more if you weren't wearing any clothes."

Henri tries not to smile but cannot help himself. There is a starved look in her eyes and he is the only meal in sight.

Nancy takes a step toward him and rises onto the balls of her feet. She brushes her lips against his. She runs her tongue in the space between them. Slides her warm hands beneath the lapels of his coat, across his chest, and up toward his tie. Nancy loosens the knot with nimble, sure fingers.

"Aren't I supposed to be the one undressing you?" he asks, brushing his lips lightly back and forth against hers.

"Is that a rule?"

He laughs and pulls away in order to see her face. "So I've heard."

She dispatches his tie efficiently. "I *hate* rules."

"How about we take turns? An item for an item?"

"No."

Nancy moves her fingers to his shoulders. She is entirely uninterested in his coat and pushes it off and then down so it drops to the floor at his feet. She moves her fingers to the first button at his throat. Then the next. And the next until his shirt hangs open.

"I hate cuff links," she mutters, fumbling with them.

He pulls them out and decides that he will never wear them again.

Shirt gone.

Undershirt gone.

And there it is, the first hint of music to Henri's ears. Nancy makes a small sound of pleasure at the sight of his bare chest. She sets her palm against his heart, moves her fingers through the light hair, and then she walks around him in a circle—never lowering that hand—and he feels the heat of her skin touching his. Chest. Biceps. Back. She pauses here to explore the dip that runs from shoulder blades to hips. Runs one finger up and down, up and down. He shudders at the featherlight touch. Henri Edmond Fiocca stands in the middle of his bedroom, eyes closed, breath caught in his throat as his wife of twelve hours presses her lips between his shoulder blades. She opens her mouth, running the tip of her tongue all the way to the hollow of his back. He could explode. He could die. He could spin her around and *consume* her.

He doesn't.

Because this, *this,* is the kind of seduction he has always longed for.

Once her circle is complete, Nancy asks, "What are you thinking?"

"Mn . . . gdmeg . . . hrmpt." He doesn't even know what he's trying to say. How would he even explain what is going on inside his mind? His body? Well, that's evident enough, and she has figured it out on her own now that's she's undoing his belt. The button at his trousers. His zipper. Henri had not expected that the groaning would come from him first.

Nancy drops to her knees and lifts one of his feet, then the other, dispatching his shoes and socks efficiently. Given her view from that angle, his feet are the least interesting thing about him. She is grinning, and he is helpless.

Back on her feet, she hooks her thumbs into his waistband and yanks. His trousers fall away easily. His underwear less so, but she is undeterred. After a moment he steps out of them and finds himself completely naked before the only woman he has ever loved.

How vulnerable it is to be disrobed *first.* To be seen *first.* To be touched *first.* To have your body's reactions seen and recorded and enjoyed *first.* He cannot take this any longer.

"Please." Henri is desperate now. His need raw and urgent.

"Lie down," Nancy tells him. She places that warm palm

against his chest and walks him backward, toward the bed. When he bumps up against it, she shoves him lightly. He falls to his back and scoots into position until he's resting on his elbows.

"What are you doing?"

"Ssshhh. Just watch."

One by one she takes the pins from her hair until it falls to her shoulders in waves. She combs her fingers through it. Shakes her head. Lets a section fall across her eyes. She takes out one earring, then another, and tosses them to the carpet. This dress is the most revealing thing Henri has ever seen her in. Like the dress she wore the night they first danced the tango, it is open in the back, all the way to her waist. She commanded the room tonight and he could not even be upset that every man present appreciated the view. Because he knew it belongs to him alone. How he ever earned that right is a mystery he will puzzle over until his dying day.

Henri's entire body is throbbing. His lips burn from where she last kissed him. His ears are ringing as Nancy slides her hand around to the button at the small of her back.

One button.

One three-inch zipper.

Nancy shifts one shoulder, then another, and the black silk flutters to the floor. She steps out of her dress as though dropping a towel.

"Gahrrmmhhh." Henri has always considered himself well-spoken and articulate until now.

She wears nothing underneath her gown and is so beautiful he could weep.

"You could help with the shoes," she says with a wink, "since you were so eager to undress me."

Henri Edmond Fiocca slides off the bed and kneels before his wife. He unbuckles each of her shoes. He bends his forehead to her knees, cradles each calf in his palm, and lifts her feet, sliding the shoes carefully off. Then he drags his nose upward, gratified that it is her turn to breathe heavily.

Ah, music to his ears.

Her arms hang limp at her sides, head thrown back, eyes closed. So he scoops her into his arms, lifts her off the floor, and carries her three steps to his bed. Henri sets her as gently as possible on top of the coverlet. And then he surveys his bride. All the wondrous curves. The rises. The dips and hollows. Smooth skin and pink cheeks. He crawls onto the bed and curls himself against her side. He drops one hand to the indentation of her waist and slides the other beneath her head.

"I love you," Henri whispers. "More than my own life. More than anything at all."

And then he kisses her. It is his turn to be in charge. To explore with his tongue.

But it is her turn to beg. *"Please."*

"Non," he refuses, playing her own game and mastering it on the first try.

Oh, the places he could take that hand. Up? Down? Around? He spins his fingertips in tiny circles, deciding, relishing the goose bumps that rise to greet the pads of his fingers.

Up.

Across her waist, fingers splayed, covering as much skin as possible. Playing with the small gaps between ribs. Listening to her breath come in little gasps as she *waits.* He stops, just below the swell of her breast, allowing his middle finger to brush the soft skin beneath.

"Henri."

"Yes?"

"Henri."

"Yes?"

She pulls away from his kiss. "Please touch me."

He does.

And then he does a great, great deal more. Until they are both sweating and limp and cursing and entirely plundered of emotion and pleasure. Until they curl into each other, arms and legs woven, lips swollen, breath mingling, hearts slowing, as sleep consumes them whole.

* * *

MARSEILLE

January 1940

We honeymooned in Cannes. The day after our wedding, Henri checked us into the Hôtel Martinez and we did not leave for two full weeks. Much of our time was spent in bed, but during the day we also made it to the beach or the marina, and in the evenings to the casinos. We took day trips to Saint-Tropez and Monte Carlo. Sometimes we left the hotel for dinner, but often we ordered room service and ate it in our robes, on the balcony, as Picon and Grenadine scurried around our feet, nipping up the crumbs. We had a corner room that faced the sea and the port, with mountains in the distance. We could see everything happening on the Croisette and we watched the sleek yachts sailing in and out of the bay for hours at a time. It was perfect—fourteen days suspended in time—but, like all things, it had to end. And now we are at home in Marseille, trying to prepare for the inevitable.

"It doesn't feel as though we are actually at war," I say, setting a platter of what used to be pork loin on the table. Henri looks at my pitiful attempt at cooking but doesn't comment. His skeptical glance does not go unnoticed by me, however. "Have I never mentioned that I cannot cook?"

He tries not to laugh. "I don't believe it ever came up."

"It's your fault, really. All that wining and dining. I never had the opportunity to experiment on you."

Henri pokes the charred roast with his fork. "It certainly looks like kitchen chemistry."

"I did try." I push the platter to the edge of the table. "Shall we have cheese and wine instead?"

"Please."

I take the platter to the kitchen and then dig around in one of the cabinet drawers for a pen and notepad.

"What are you doing?" he asks.

"Making a note to schedule cooking lessons."

"That's not necessary. You don't have to cook if you don't want to."

"I know. And I wouldn't. But..."

"What?"

"It's a basic skill and I'll need to have it if we're to make it through what's coming. I can't go around burning our food all the time. It won't be long before there are food shortages throughout the entire country."

"Is that why you've been stockpiling?"

Other society wives in Marseille spend their days making the rounds of dressmakers, hairdressers, and tea salons. They meet for lunch and aperitifs, acting as though if they ignore the thing, it will go away. I've never been good at pretending, however, so I spend my time making friends with the butchers and bakers along the Canebière. I buy more sugar than we need. More coffee. More tea. I buy foodstuffs by the sackful and pack them into every cupboard and closet in our home. I buy cheese by the wheel. I buy canned goods and enough cigarettes to stock a tobacconist's shop. Rice. Beans. Flour. I have turned our spare bedroom into a cellar and it is bursting with every imaginable aperitif and liquor as well as hundreds of bottles of wine. I buy them by the case. Each time I go into the city, I visit a shop and strip a shelf bare, carrying what I can and then having the rest delivered to our new flat. I try not to think what it will cost us each month, but the view—overlooking all of Marseille and the harbor—comes with a high price tag. Henri does not comment on the rent, my acquisitions, or the bills I have sent to his office. But I did catch him standing before a packed wardrobe shaking his head one afternoon as he went to put away his jacket and found the entire thing crammed to the edges with sacks of coffee.

Henri joins me in the kitchen and we compile a rudimentary charcuterie board, which we consume standing up as we lean against the counter and sip our wine, a nice, savory Sangiovese that Antoine recently imported from Italy. I take a moment to savor the wine. It tastes like clove and cherries with a hint of dark chocolate.

I sigh, then open my eyes. "They've been calling this the Phony War."

"Who has?"

"The other women in the building."

His lip twitches. "Your friends don't believe a real war is coming?"

I pluck a piece of cheese out of his fingers and eat it myself. "They are not my *friends*. They are bored old women with more money than sense. But there isn't much happening. It's easy for them to forget."

"Plenty is happening. It's just not happening *here*," Henri says. "The Germans have invaded the Czech lands. They have bombed half of Poland. No point wishing that on us."

"You have forgotten something."

"What?"

"Men are being called up all over the country."

"Yes. They are."

"It's only a matter of time before you'll be called up as well."

The thing about marriage, I am learning, even this early on, is that so much is said without words. The gift of emotional intimacy is that you can read each other's face from a distance. My throat goes dry at the look on his now.

"That time has already passed," Henri says. He offers a half shrug but fails in making it look nonchalant.

"You've gotten your papers?"

He nods, once, sadly. "Yes."

"When?"

"In November. A week before our wedding."

Henri pulls me to his chest and wraps his arms around me, tight, to muffle the insults I am hurling at him. I pound his arms with my fists. The tears that soak into his chest are ones of anger, not fear. The person I trust most has lied to me. As far as betrayals go, it is minor—a mere paper cut. I know this. But still, it stings.

"I should have told you. I know that," he says. "But it would change nothing and I didn't want you to worry."

"You didn't want me to change my mind about the wedding!"

He laughs. We both know nothing would have changed my mind. "No," he says, "my deployment was deferred. I just wanted to give us a short time of normalcy, to be married, before this war changes everything."

As soon as Henri releases me I step back and dry my face with the backs of my hands. I take a deep breath and growl on the exhale. "When do you leave?"

"In March. We still have time. Let's just enjoy it. *Please.*"

I can feel that old, familiar stubbornness wash over me, and it is met with a thought, so intriguing, so *impractical*, that I embrace it immediately. I sniff, stand up straighter. "I know what I want for my wedding gift."

Henri squints. *"What?"*

"A truck."

"And where will I get a truck?"

Silent laughter is rippling across his face, so I glare at him. "You will give me one of the dozens that belong to your shipping company."

He pops a bit of cracker into his mouth. "I will?"

"Yes. And then you will have it converted into an ambulance."

"What for?"

"So that I can drive it to the front and be of some use while you're away."

"You will drive to the front—"

"—and ferry the wounded to field hospitals. Yes."

Poor Henri; he doesn't realize that I am completely serious. He thinks this is a game. So he needles me. "You can better help the war effort here."

"Don't be stupid. Here I help no one."

"I do recall that your first job was as a nurse."

"A nurse's *assistant* for two months over the course of one summer. And I was fifteen. Besides, it's not as though the wounded will be pouring into Marseille."

At least not yet. I can see that both of us are thinking this, but neither of us says it aloud.

"But why would you even want to help? War isn't for women."

I lean very close to him and lower my voice to a dangerous pitch. "And yet we suffer most in them."

Henri sees the flash in my eyes and takes a solid step backward. He throws his hands up in surrender. He tries to laugh off his ignorance. "Haven't I told you how I won the last war for France? Now I will win it again. Have you no confidence in me?"

"Certainly," I say, giving him a saccharine smile. "But I'm sick of hearing how you won the last one. *I* will win this one."

"You and what army?" It's a good thing he's smiling, that a teasing glint is clear in his eyes, otherwise I might swipe at him with a cheese knife.

"I'll build my own army if I have to. Besides, I don't see why I should have to wave you a proud good-bye and then sit at home knitting balaclavas."

Henri thinks for a moment, knowing better than to try to dissuade me. "I will give you your ambulance on one *condition.*"

Ah. That word again. The use of conditions is now one of our favorite bargaining tools. "Which is?"

"That you promise me you won't go unless France is invaded. No running off to Belgium to help on that front just because you're bored."

I stick out my hand and we shake, formally. "Deal."

You might think there was a cactus growing directly between my eyes by the way he is looking at me. He shakes his head. "You are the damnedest woman I've ever met."

Poor Henri. He does not realize that I am serious, or how determined Germany is to spread its cancer across the face of the earth. I saw what they did in Vienna and Berlin, and I know that Hitler has no intentions of stopping at Belgium.

If Henri is going to war, so am I.

PART THREE

Lucienne Carlier

Gentlemen of the human race, I say to hell with the lot of you.

—VICTOR HUGO, *LES MISÉRABLES*

Madame Andrée

CHAUDES-AIGUES PLATEAU, CANTAL, FRANCE

May 15, 1944

I am ripping seats out of the bus when we hear the first explosion. My plan—thanks to a bit of creative engineering and a set of bolt cutters I've borrowed from Fournier—is to create an area at the front of my bus where I can entertain my colleagues out of the elements. I've already turned the back—where the two benches face each other—into something of a bedroom. All I'm waiting for is the mattress that Tardivat promised. At the moment, however, I'm on my hands and knees, head crammed under a seat, trying to pry it loose from the floor, when the distant, unmistakable rumble reaches us. I feel it vibrate up through the ground, across the bus, and into the palms of my hands, like something deep within the earth has torn loose and is charging toward the surface.

I'm on my feet and out the door, bolt cutters still in my hand, before I've even made the conscious decision to move. I run toward the middle of the clearing, where Hubert and Fournier have already planted themselves—like old, weary trees—scowling toward the north. That first explosion is followed by another. Then another. Distant booms that gather momentum in the early-evening air. And then the gunshots begin, scattershot and rapid, echoing through the valleys that lie between us and that far-off ridge.

"What's happening?" I ask Hubert.

"An attack."

"Where?"

He tips his chin toward the north. "Sounds like Mont Mouchet."

"Gaspard."

"It was bound to happen," he says, then looks at me to gauge my reaction. "You did warn him."

"Are we going to help?"

Hubert is quiet. Weighing the possibilities. How long it would take to notify each of Fournier's groups. What it would require of us and whether we could get to Mont Mouchet fast enough on foot—we do not have the vehicles to transport even a tenth of Fournier's troops.

"There are thousands of men under Gaspard's command," I say. "They don't deserve to die for his stupidity."

It is Fournier who answers. He stands behind me and to my left. His voice is quiet but authoritative. "No. But there are mountains between us. Valleys. At least two rivers swollen by spring rains. By the time we can assemble our men, travel, and reach Gaspard, the attack will be over. It may well be headed toward us by then."

"So we do nothing?"

"We wait," Fournier says. "Gaspard has concentrated his forces. They have few weapons and no reserves. They will have to retreat eventually. And when they do, they will come here."

It is a strange thing to hear a battle raging and not engage. I find that my body grows tense and leans forward with each explosion. All that day we listen as the attack, swift and merciless, falls on Gaspard's compound. Fifty kilometers. Technically a short enough distance to walk in half a day. And yet, from where we stand, a treacherous tangle of nearly impassable geography. This is why the maquisards chose to situate themselves in the Auvergne—the Fortress of France—each group claiming a piece of this daunting territory and positioning themselves on high ground amidst the plateaus. But as difficult as it is for the Germans to maneuver through these hills, it is equally difficult for us to reach one another on foot.

And into this complicated mess of guerrilla warfare, Hubert,

Denis, and I have landed, knowing that, busy as we are now, the real work will begin once the Allies arrive in France. Arming and training the Maquis is only half the mission. The fighting and the sabotage that will drive the Germans out of France are yet to come.

We continue with our work, raising our heads occasionally as reverberating strings of gunfire and faint, distant battle cries reach the plateau. From here it sounds like the memory of war, like some strange echo reaching across time to remind us that the Germans were here once before, that we drove them out and we can do it again. But only if we do not waver in our resolve. So we set our minds to the task at hand. I go back to work on my bus, then spend the evening coding messages. Denis radios London and we listen to the BBC French news bulletin until they sign off with their usual phrase letting agents scattered throughout the country know that personal messages are about to be broadcast, *"Et maintenant, quelques messages personnels."*

Hubert, Denis, and I sit beside the radio, listening to the usual endless strings of nonsense. Bits of nursery rhyme. Eighteen surnames. What I can only assume is a grocery list. A recipe for cough syrup. And then, finally, the confirmation that our message has been received and our order approved: "A cricket chirps in Kent." And that settles it. We will receive three airdrops over the next five days.

At nightfall the booms and echoes across the ridge begin to lessen, then stop entirely within two hours. It is almost midnight when Denis pulls his headphones off and yawns. We decide to stretch our legs and go meet Fournier beside the campfire.

"The silence makes me nervous," Hubert says.

"The Germans have retreated." Fournier stands beside the fire. He holds his hands toward the flames, palms out, to warm them. The air smells of damp earth and bright green pine needles. Above us the sky is clear and dotted with a million pinpricks of light. "They will return at dawn. They always do."

As usual, Fournier is right. After a rare night with no shipments to collect, I sleep like a concrete block and wake at six o'clock the next morning, to a tremor and the sound of bus windows rattling. Even in my sleep-drunk state I know that the battle has resumed and we must prepare ourselves for the fallout.

The first of Gaspard's men reach us at midday. A handful of them are wounded and all of them are hungry. Those who are armed have only small weapons, revolvers and rifles, but not a bullet to share among them.

"We retreated when we ran out of ammunition," one of them says, staring at me, curiously, over the bridge of a nose that has been broken at some point in the past. "We went through the Auvergne, but we lost most of our heavy equipment on the way."

"Why did you come to us? Why not Tardivat? He's closer," Hubert asks.

The maquisard tips his chin at me. The look on his face is something akin to wonder. "Because of her. Everyone knows Madame Andrée calls for weapons and they fall from the sky."

Hubert flicks his dark gaze to me, then back to the maquisard. I am startled to realize that he is worried about me. Worried that Madame Andrée's notoriety has spread to the point that even random maquisards know who she is and where to find her.

Fournier, ever the strategist, steps between us and sets his hand on the young man's shoulder. "Tell me," he says, "about the Germans. How many were there? How were they armed? What was their strategy?"

"They outnumbered us almost four to one. So, eleven thousand, we think. But they do not know how treacherous these woods can be. They dislike approaching on foot, so they came with artillery. Tanks. Armored cars. We ambushed the convoys as they entered the forest and then we withdrew before they could gather and return fire. Over and over we did this. Attack. Pull away. Attack again from a different angle." He looks at me, as though seeking approval. "We avoid, as much as possible, a direct battle with the *Boche.* Gaspard taught us to pick them off. To shave off the edges. To grind them down."

It pains me to admit this, but I say, "That is very clever of him."

The maquisard nods, and I see in that single movement how loyal he is to his leader.

"What were your casualties?" I ask.

"About one hundred and fifty. Gaspard did not give the order to scatter until our ammunition was gone."

"And the Germans?"

"They bled like pigs and died by the hundreds," he says, then adds, "Gaspard and his chief lieutenant captured an armored car and two cannons."

"And what do Gaspard and Judex plan to do with these weapons?"

He raises an eyebrow, intrigued that I know this other name. "Bring them here, of course."

Gaspard's men trickle in throughout the evening, into the night, and all the next day. But not just his. More new recruits flock to the Chaudes-Aigues plateau by the dozens. Word of the fighting has spread to small towns and villages throughout the Auvergne. Men, young and old, come to us, eager to join the Maquis, eager to be part of a group known for organization and access to weaponry. I hardly see Hubert or Fournier the entire day. They meet with each man as the scouts bring them in. Asking questions. Gathering information. It is a porous, nerve-racking system we have in place. Any of these men could be Milice—the French auxiliary of the German army tasked with ferreting out members of the Resistance and slaughtering them. Any of them could be German agents. We do the best we can, screening each recruit as though he were volunteering for the British Special Service. Hubert separates the wheat from the chaff by making it clear that traitors won't be jailed or sent away. They will be shot.

By the end of the day Hubert can barely stand. His voice is raw and dark bags hang beneath his eyes. It's been five days since he shaved and three months since his last haircut, and I am amazed at how my buttoned-up partner has turned into a scruffy mountain man in such a short amount of time.

"How many new recruits do we have?" I ask as we sit in my bus. The only seats that remain are four at the front that I have unbolted from the floor and arranged around a broad, flat stump that makes a handy table and the two benches in the back that face each other. Beggars can't be choosers, and besides, the arrangement gives me a semblance of proper living quarters. A place to sleep. And a place to meet with colleagues.

"Almost a thousand. They're coming from every direction. You'd think the sound of all that fighting across the ridge would keep them away. But no," he says. "And that's not even counting the men who've come from Gaspard. Those number at least fifteen hundred already and there are more on the way."

I pass him the bottle of brandy that came through in our last shipment. Occasionally there is a crate marked *Hélène,* and it always contains a small luxury for me. Tea. Chocolates. Toothpaste. A hairbrush or Lizzie Arden lipstick. This last shipment had two bottles of brandy, clean socks, and a jar of face cream.

"What are we going to do with them?" I ask.

"Assign them to groups and ask London to double the shipments."

"No." I shake my head. "We'll have to triple them."

"They need everything, Nance. Food. Boots. Clothes. Money. Weapons. I interviewed a group this morning armed with nothing but rusty pitchforks."

"But they're warm bodies, willing to fight. That's as close to a miracle as we're going to get."

"Fournier's numbers have nearly doubled in recent weeks. Add in those of Gaspard, and do you realize what we've got here?"

I nod. "Enough men to disrupt the German supply lines. To stop their soldiers from reinforcing troops at the battlefront. To destroy every single target that London has given us."

"If we can just put guns in their hands and keep them alive, we have the chance of winning," he says.

Gaspard reaches Chaudes-Aigues two days later. He stomps into Fournier's camp as though he's the bloody prime minister of France.

"Nance . . . ," Denis says, from where he's sitting at the front of my bus, ear tuned to the radio, pen scratching code across a fresh sheet of paper.

"I see him," I say, pulling my pack from underneath one of the benches at the back of the bus. I dig around until I find my lipstick and the compact Buckmaster gave me. Then I carefully apply a coat of blood-red armor. I've not worn my lipstick in weeks. But the sight of Gaspard leaves me feeling as though I could use a bit of reinforcement. I look at Denis and smile.

"You are the strangest woman I've ever met," he says.

"How so?"

"I tell you that Gaspard—the greatest herpes blister in all of France—is walking through our camp, and you put on lipstick."

"Would you go into battle without a bulletproof vest?" I ask.

"No."

"Neither would I." I wink. "You stay here. Finish that transmission. I'll deal with the festering pustule that is our dear friend Gaspard."

He lifts one perfectly arched eyebrow toward his hairline.

"What?" I ask.

"Do we know if the man even has a last name?"

"We do not know. And we do not care."

The thing about lipstick, the reason it's so powerful, is that it is distracting. Men don't see the flashes of anger in your eyes or your clenched fists when you wear it. They see a woman, not a warrior, and that gives me the advantage. I cannot throw a decent punch or carry a grown man across a battlefield, but I can wear red lipstick as though my life depends on it. And the truth is, these days, it often does.

Gaspard blinks twice when he sees me approach. I am wearing army boots, slacks—now quite loose, thanks to months in the forest—and a short-sleeved silk blouse because it is too hot for anything else now that summer has arrived.

I tip my head to the side and take in Gaspard's bedraggled appearance. His beard has gone wild. His hair is greasy. Torn pants. Ratty collar. There is blood and grime smeared over most of his body. He smells like a wet, mangy swamp dog.

I give him my best smile. "Bringing up the rear, I see."

"I have come for my men," he says.

"The men who fled your compound and came to me for arms?"

"You mean to take them?"

"No. I was simply noting a fact. What do you want?"

Gaspard's lip twitches and he turns to look over his shoulder. His lieutenant, Judex, is several yards away, talking to Hubert. "A conference. To discuss your terms."

Oh, it is a *herculean* effort not to smile. Not to act superior. I would lose my advantage, and this war is too important for me to indulge my ego. "Very well. But I'm in the middle of something. You may meet me in my office in two hours."

He snorts. "Your *office?*"

I lift an arm casually toward my bus. "Two hours."

I spend the next one hundred and twenty minutes coding messages for Denis Rake. We need London to increase the amount of supplies they send in each airdrop if we're to outfit our new recruits. I put in another urgent request for the weapons instructor I know only as Anselm. Hubert does his best, but we need a dedicated trainer to turn these farm boys into fighters. Hubert is outnumbered and out of his league and Anselm is our only hope of getting these troops trained in time.

Speaking of the devil, Hubert stomps up the bus steps and drops into one of the four seats I've arranged around my stump. "Gaspard is coming," he says. "This should be fun."

"Define *fun,*" Denis mutters, shuffling papers and stuffing them into his pack. It's unlikely that Gaspard can read his particular brand of Hungarian shorthand, but he won't take chances regardless.

"Watching Nancy go for the jugular."

Gaspard does not come alone. Nor does he knock. He and Judex are through the door and up the steps without a word of greeting. They survey my office with skepticism but say nothing.

"Please, sit down." I motion to the benches at the rear of the bus. Gaspard eyes the empty seat beside me but does as he's told. "You've met Hubert. And this is Denden, our radio operator. As luck would have it, he picked us up a few miles from Mont Mouchet the morning you turned us away."

I know it is unnecessary, and possibly cruel, but I want Gaspard to understand how easily he could have been in a position of power had he not been so rash from the start.

Gaspard looks at Denis Rake and I can see all the calculations flash across his eyes. Whatever he's thinking he keeps to himself, choosing instead to nod, once, in greeting.

I speak to Gaspard in a voice devoid of accusation. "Patrice is dead. Victor has rejected your overtures. There are now seven thousand maquisards in this camp, two-thirds of whom are yours—all of them without arms. And I am the only source of communication between here and London."

He does not dispute this, which is good, given how little he will like what I have to say next.

"Your security is awful. So awful, in fact, that a known German double agent was able to get through your checkpoints, kill Patrice, and arrive at your doorstep before being apprehended. Your lack of emergency planning at Mont Mouchet is unpardonable. I *told you* to break your men into smaller groups and disperse them throughout the area. I *told you* to have escape routes prepared in the event of an attack. Had you done as I instructed, you would have been fully armed and able to drive the Germans back in a decisive victory instead of retreating here.

"But here you are. Under my command." Hubert's eyes widen in surprise and Gaspard opens his mouth to argue, so I cut him off. "I am *chef du parachutage.* You have no other means of getting weapons, explosives, supplies, or finances. It comes from me or it does not come at all. If you want that to be your legacy, you may take your men—those who are willing to go with you—and leave immediately." I lean forward and rest my elbows on my knees. "Otherwise you will consider me your bloody field marshal and you will never argue with me again."

Judex flicks a nervous glance toward Gaspard but says nothing. They are both proud men and I know that abandoning Mont Mouchet to the Germans is more painful to them than receiving a dressing-down from me.

"I will arm you," I say. "But only if you conform to my standards of military preparedness."

I do not ask for permission or agreement. I let them consider my words. And I wait.

After a good thirty seconds Gaspard nods in mute acceptance.

"We have an understanding, then. Leave, now, and begin organizing your men into groups of one hundred. Each of them must have a leader who reports directly to you. And as I have done with Fournier, I will meet with your chosen leaders, individually, to assess their needs. Only then will I begin requesting your arms from London. You have twenty-four hours to begin dispersing your troops."

Gaspard rises from the bench and motions for Judex to follow him. Neither of them looks at me as they move toward the door.

"Wait," I say, and Gaspard turns, eyes narrowed, jaw clenched. He's had all he can take for one day. I pull a set of papers—folded into thirds—from my back pocket and hold them out.

"What is that?" he asks, as though I'm handing over a court summons.

"A list of known underground cables the Germans have installed throughout the countryside as a means of communication. We believe there to be many more, however, and your job is to locate them, so they can be systematically destroyed by you and your men when we give the word," I say. "Prepare accordingly."

Gaspard does not like me. He will probably *never* like me. But in this moment I think he respects me, and that is far more important. "Madame Andrée," he says with curt nod.

I hand him the papers. "Don't make me regret this."

Nancy Fiocca

MARSEILLES

March 1, 1940

I say good-bye to my husband on an unusually cold, rainy morning. The Gare Saint-Charles platform is crowded with travelers rushing to catch their trains and I cling to him as though we are parting for eternity. I want everything to stop. I want everyone to leave. I would pause time if I could, anything for a few more precious moments together. But there is no more sand in the hourglass. Henri's bags are packed, and his train leaves for the Alsace in three minutes.

He will be stationed somewhere along the Maginot Line, defending an *ouvrage*—one of the concrete weapons installations recently built along the French border as a means of resisting German invasion. To our army he is simply a warm body. A former soldier called to duty in time of need. A number. He knows this, and I know this, but to me, Henri is the only number that matters.

He pulls me close against his chest as we stand beneath the overhang, inches from the downpour. He buries his face in my neck. Inhales. Presses one hand to the small of my back and runs the other through my hair. It feels as though he is trying to absorb me right into his body.

"I hate to see you cry," he whispers.

"I hate this fucking *war*." I cannot stop the tears or my ragged breath or the panic that fills my mind and makes it hard to imagine anything but disaster. Already I see a version of my future, the

Widow Fiocca, just another woman who loses her husband to the Nazi scourge. I cannot accept this. I *will* not. "Please come home. Please. *Please,*" I beg.

"I will."

"Promise me."

"I promise you, *ma fille qui rit.* I will come home."

"Alive."

He laughs but I don't think it's funny. "Of course," he says.

"Henri Edmond Fiocca, I will never forgive you if you don't."

"I must. How else will I ever hear your laughter again?" Henri brushes his lips against mine in the barest whisper of a kiss. His warm, brown eyes are filled with determination. Then he takes a step backward into the downpour and the last thing I hear him say is "Back soon."

MARSEILLE

Hôtel du Louvre et Paix, April 25, 1940

Antoine looks at the suitcase I set on the floor, beside my barstool, and raises one eyebrow. "Taking a trip?" he asks.

"Yes," I tell him as I stick out my hand, palm up. "Scissors, please. And a menu."

He slides both across the bar and I cut the tags from my newly purchased case. I've not heard from Henri in almost two months and I've grown restless. I miss him, and I can't seem to stop my mind from imagining one terrible scenario after another. At this rate I'll be certifiably insane by summer. I need a change of scenery. But first, lunch.

"Where are you going?"

"Cannes. For the weekend."

"I like Cannes. Where are you staying?"

"The Hôtel Martinez."

"Really?" Antoine has been polishing the bar with an old rag, but he stops and looks at me with a calculating glint in his eyes. "You might be able to help me, then."

"Yes. *How?*"

"Would you deliver a package to the front desk at the hotel? It would save me a trip."

"For you, of course."

Antoine leans closer and says, "Not for me, technically. For a friend."

I cannot decide whether I am drawn to the intrigue because it runs so counter to what I know of Antoine's personality, or because it provides a much-needed diversion.

"And what sort of *friend* might she be?" I ask with a grin, imagining that the barman has found himself a lover.

"The sort who helps Jews escape Nazi-occupied Europe," he whispers.

"Oh," I say, and then, "So this package—"

"—could get us both in a great deal of trouble."

Four years ago, when Stephanie and Count Gonzales helped me get Janos Lieberman out of France, it took an act of God and Parliament. I can't imagine how difficult the process must be now. But I am glad to know that my friend is doing what he can. And he ought to know by now that I'm not one to run from trouble.

The smile I offer Antoine is all the answer he needs. "I'll have the bouillabaisse," I say.

I leave Antoine's and go directly to see the tram conductor, Ficetole, and arrange for him to care for Picon and Grenadine while I am gone. Then I return to our flat to pack my things. On my way out I am met on the landing by Monsieur Paquet, the local commissioner of police. He lives in the apartment across from us, on the top floor of our building, and has taken a rather unnerving interest in me since Henri left.

"Madame Fiocca." He nods, then glances at my suitcase. "Are you leaving town?"

"Oui." The way he studies my face makes me nervous, so I lie. "I am off to visit Paris with a friend."

"Which friend?" he asks, unable to hide the glint of interest in his eyes.

"An old one. *À bientôt!*" And then I am off, down the stairs, elated at having something useful to do.

CANNES

The Hôtel Martinez

It's only an envelope. That's what I tell myself, repeatedly, on the train. And there is nothing in this envelope but a set of fake identification cards. Four in total. To be delivered to the front desk of the Hôtel Martinez and picked up by a guest named Simón Bolívar. The only reason I know that this is not the real name of the person who will collect the envelope is because I have a very strange memory. I *remember things.* Irrational things. Odd little tidbits that stick in my brain and remain there forever. I think of it as a box, of sorts, that holds information at the ready should I ever need it. Sometimes it even empties itself of random objects and hurls them at me, unbidden. The middle names of half a dozen famous authors. Bawdy limericks. Dates. Locations. Faces. Accents. Because of this I know that Simón Bolívar is in fact, not a real guest at the Hôtel Martinez, but a nineteenth-century military and political leader in Venezuela responsible for freeing six South American states from colonized Spanish rule.

Whoever collects this envelope will distribute the contents to four desperate people within the coming days. The identification cards will allow their owners to travel freely under assumed French names from Cannes to Marseille to Toulouse, where they will be collected by Antoine's friend—a woman he calls Françoise, though I suspect that is not her real name—who will escort them to Perpignan and, finally, across the Pyrenees Mountains to whatever freedom they can find.

The Marseille-Cannes train rattles along its track for two hours and I sit in my seat, hair coiffed, belt neatly cinched, glad to be of use. I am wearing Victory Red lipstick, there are false identification papers tucked inside my purse, and my heart is ticking fast enough to make me sweat.

I check into the Martinez under my own name and the girl behind the counter gives my papers a cursory glance. When she hands me the key to my room, I pull the now-rumpled manila envelope from my purse.

"Can I leave this here for one of your guests?" I ask.

"Oui." She looks at the name printed on the envelope, then checks her guest list, puts it into the appropriate mailbox, and gives me a bright smile.

"Enjoy your stay!" she says, then turns back to her work.

Who knew subversive activity could be so simple? Heart rate restored, I walk through the lobby toward the bank of elevators but something occurs to me as my finger hovers over the button: the hotel bar is across the lobby from the check-in desk, and I am very curious to learn the real identity of one Simón Bolívar.

Whatever his name might actually be, Monsieur Bolívar is not Spanish. Nor is he French. As a matter of fact, if I had to lay money down, I'd say he was British. Or at the very least, from somewhere in the Commonwealth. Because I am sitting beside the window, suitcase tucked under my table, chin tipped toward the sun, drinking my second French 75, when a tall, redheaded man with excellent posture walks through the lobby, speaks with the girl behind the desk, and collects my envelope.

MARSEILLE

May 12, 1940

Word reached Marseille yesterday that the Germans have broken the Maginot Line and crossed into France. Over a million German soldiers and almost two thousand tanks have entered the Ardennes forest—a thing that every single French general said was impossible. They mean to drive the English back to the sea at Dunkirk and cut off the Maginot Line from the rest of France. In the meantime they litter the countryside with wounded civilians. I cannot sit here, waiting to deliver another envelope for Antoine, so I return the dogs to Ficetole and begin the long process of driving north.

Henri made good on his promise a week before deploying to the front and delivered a rickety truck that I had fitted as an ambulance, then parked behind our building. My driving lessons consisted of one literal crash course given by a nerve-racked mechanic who works for Henri's company and was terrified he might kill the boss's wife. Every day since, I have driven it into the hills and now feel as comfortable driving a truck as I do engaging in subversive activity—which is to say, my heart races every time I'm behind the wheel.

There is one rather large complication, however. I did not arrive in Europe until I was well into my twenties. Long enough to become quite settled with the belief that cars should be driven on the *left* side of the road. In France, however, as in the United States, they drive on the *right* side. It's one thing to be a passenger in such circumstances but something else to be behind the wheel. It is a new habit that does not come naturally to my Anglo-Saxon mind. That long first day, driving north, I inevitably drift to the left-hand side, swerving at the last moment to miss oncoming traffic. No wonder Henri was so hesitant to make good on his promise. I am a menace on the road and, more than once, passing cars are forced into a hedge or fence.

On my second day, I take regular breaks and try to stay more alert. I won't be much good to the war effort if I can't even reach the front lines without mangling myself in a car crash.

It takes another day of solid driving to reach the northern front near Belgium, and I arrive without having forced anyone into the hedgerow in a good six hours. Upon arrival I am directed to a voluntary ambulance corps that has set up headquarters in a field hospital in the small town of Marville. It is a near-straight shot north from Marseille, from the bottom of France to the top, but accessible only by a winding network of narrow roads and byways. My entire body is sore and tight when I climb from the truck and face the reality of what is before me.

I have been living in the land of make-believe. Of blue skies and sunshine. Marseille is a naive paradise, hidden from the realities of war. This is the true France, a battered, bleeding outpost filled with wounded soldiers and fleeing refugees.

It smells of fear and unwashed male. Gunshots echo in the distance and military trucks roar through the streets every few moments. Beyond that, there is an eerie silence.

"Who's in charge here?" I ask the first soldier I see. He can't be more than seventeen. Crooked teeth, face pockmarked with acne scars. "Of the ambulances, I mean."

He points in the general direction of an old church with arched windows and a high stone steeple. "Bulgar," he says, and then shuffles off without another word.

Bulgar? Or did he mean *bulgur,* like the wheat? What sort of name is that? These are the things I'm wondering as I mount the steps and walk into the church. The smell stops me short. Marville's place of worship has been converted into a field hospital. The sick and dying are scattered everywhere. Or what's left of them. There are more people with missing limbs and bullet holes than I can count. At least a dozen of them children. The smell of sickness and infection hovers in the air. Like rotten fruit, it cloys at the nostrils. I must look stricken, because a passing nurse approaches me.

"Are you looking for someone?" she asks. "A loved one?"

"No." I blink. Shake my head. "I mean yes. I am looking for someone. But not a patient. I need to find . . . *Bulgur*?" I go with the wheat. It seems the most likely option.

She is young, but her face is worn and tired and it takes a moment for the confusion to pass. "Oh. You mean Petar Konev?"

"Does he run the voluntary ambulance corps?"

"Yes."

"Then that's who I'm looking for."

"Out there." She mercifully points to a cobblestone courtyard outside the church.

I thank her and make a hasty exit from the infirmary. So not bulgur wheat, but *Bulgarian.* I shake my head and take three huge lungfuls of fresh air, only to realize I've not asked her what he looks like. But there's no way I'm going back inside that building unless I am wounded myself. I weave my way through a crowd of soldiers. Almost all of them young. Exhausted. Shell-shocked. Each of them has the hollow-eyed expression of a man who has looked death in the face. I search for Henri everywhere I look. Terrified I will actually find him. These men hardly notice me as I push my way to the side of the church.

It's not that hard to find Konev in the end. He's the one shouting instructions. A tall, willow switch of a man with milky blue eyes, a narrow jaw, and a voice filled with gravel and dust.

"Are you Petar?" I ask.

He looks me over and then says in a heavy accent, "Yes."

"I've come to volunteer."

"Go see Marie. She directs the nurses."

"No. I have an ambulance."

I can see that he wants to laugh but the expression on my face stops him. "We have no women drivers."

"You do now." Honestly, I'm so tired of this bullshit. I can't have a byline because I'm a *woman.* I can't apply for a marriage license on my own because I'm a *woman.* I can't drive an ambulance because I'm a *woman.*

"Tell me where to go and who to collect or I'll just head off on my own and cause everyone more trouble," I say.

Petar gives in more easily than some of the men I've known. He shrugs, as though he's too tired for this nonsense. "Take the road north out of Marville. It won't take you long to see the steady stream of people. But try to avoid stopping for the first group you see. Those are the ones who can walk, who can get here on their own. The ones who really need your help are miles farther on. They'll have pieces blown off."

I don't get a "thank you" or "good luck" or even "what's your name?" Petar Konev turns away and resumes shouting orders to the other, weary ambulance drivers gathered in the courtyard.

"Well, I guess that's that," I mutter as I climb back behind the wheel of my truck and turn on the engine. My lower back and hamstrings begin to protest. I have already been in this truck for far too long. But I turn on the engine, put it in gear, and head north.

Because I can either sit in this seat and do some good or sit at home in Marseille, waiting and worthless.

Every morning I head out in my ambulance, turning onto now-familiar roads, only to find that there are bodies everywhere, more victims caught in gunfire during the night. There are bombed-out vehicles on roads that were clear the day before. Sometimes I have to wait for them to be cleared before I can pass. These days are the worst because I am left to witness the carnage up close. The bodies of children are hardest to see. Scattered beside the road like so much garbage. I want to bury them. I want to weep for them. But I have to force myself onward. I can only shake my head in dismay at the mattresses strapped to the top of many of the vehicles that pass. They will not protect the passengers within from strafing by the Luftwaffe's Stukas. All too often, when I head back, hours later, I see the dead and dying who have been hit by those planes, proof that the mattresses did very little to deter the barrage of German bullets.

In my youth, before I left Australia, I worked as a nurse's assistant in the Mudgee mining hospital. I know how to stitch a wound and how to stanch the flow of blood. At the time there were fewer career paths open to young girls, and I had not yet gone abroad in search of a more interesting life. I'd not yet learned to take shorthand or write an article. My time there had its benefits, however. I can give an immunization and, when necessary, make a tourniquet. But these are basic skills, of little use when an old woman has lost her left hand because she stuck it out the window and caught a stray bullet at the wrist. Or when a bus has taken gunfire and exploded, leaving fifteen people with third-degree burns. I am unprepared for the realities of battle. I have never seen injuries like these. Most days, as I drive along, listening to the cries and moans that drift up from the truck bed behind me, I pray for Henri. Though I could not surrender my Protestant past for his Catholic present, I do remember how to pray, and I know that God is God regardless of which denominational peg I hang my hat upon. I know that Henri is somewhere, nearby, but I hope that he is not in an ambulance such as this, his life slipping away as he bounces over ill-kept roads.

Some days I ignore Petar Konev's instruction and fill the back of my ambulance with refugees too tired to walk any longer. And other days I fill it with the wounded, men, women, and children who have been strafed by German Stukas flying low, shooting at desperate, easy targets. Often, I am too late. Often, there are too many. Always, I sleep in my ambulance, sprawled out across the seat, too tired to care that I can't remember the last time I bathed or properly brushed my hair. I eat my meals at the mess hall in Marville but taste nothing. I focus on doing the next thing.

A little over four weeks into my volunteer assignment the French government decides that Marville must be evacuated. Belgium has fallen, and the Germans have pushed all the way through the Ardennes forest and are now advancing toward our location. If we stay we will be taken prisoner. To make matters worse, a thing they are calling "The Blitz" is raging in England, and, I am ashamed to say, the French military dissolves into disorganization. We are instructed to pick up whomever we can. Wounded soldiers. Civilians, gunned down by Nazi machine guns. Anyone at all, really: walking, limping, or crawling. So, on the morning of June 10, I collect my last load of passengers, drop them at the field hospital, and head south.

Retreat is a dismal thing. It tastes of bile and regret. And as I drive back, toward Marseille, I wonder how the French military could be so grossly unprepared. *I* saw this coming four years ago. Why weren't *they* prepared? The reality of what is headed for us makes me sick to my stomach. It seems as though the air itself reeks with the stink of death and despair.

Three days later my ambulance gives up the ghost. It sputters to a halt twenty kilometers from Nîmes. I tap the gas gauge. It's half-full. But it's an old truck and it was never meant to endure the punishment I've put it through. I'm only two hours from home and I am stranded on the side of the road.

Exhaustion and discouragement have seeped into every fiber of my being. I feel as though the very strands of my hair are limp with it. I am hungry. I am thirsty. And my damn period started this morning. I stand there beside the truck, cramps spreading across my belly, into my back, and down to the tops of my thighs, and I think of every awful curse word Henri has ever taught me. I kick the tire of my poor old ambulance, so hard my toes hurt. I kick it again. *"Merde! Putain de merde! Fils de pute, toi! Va te faire foutre! Tu me fais chier! Putain de bordel de merde! Quel salaud! Quelle conne! Vous tu es connasse! Trou du cul!"* I am breathing hard, practically sweating, by the time I finish my tirade. Yet there is nothing left to be done but grab Henri's suitcase and begin walking.

Near sunset I reach Nîmes and secure a room at a small hotel. It does not serve meals and there is one bathroom per floor, but each room does come equipped with a radio. After a long, cold shower I fall into bed and switch on the BBC French Service, only to hear that the Germans marched into Paris earlier that day and met no resistance. Defeat and humiliation are poor bedfellows, and I lie there wondering where my husband might be. The thought hits me much like a thunderbolt: if he is alive, he will head for Marseille once his unit is disbanded. If Marville has been evacuated, then the rest of northern France has been as well. If Paris has surrendered without a fight, all conscripted soldiers will be sent home. That thought is the only thing that allows me to sleep.

I begin walking again, the next morning, until I get one lift, and then another, piecemealing my way back to Marseille, only to find that in my absence it had been bombed by Benito Mussolini. Parts of the city have been blown to bits. The harbor is in shambles. The causeway destroyed. But our flat, high on the hill, is still standing.

It is a quarter past noon when I walk into our home, only to be greeted by silence. The curtains are drawn. Dust lies heavy on every surface. The dogs are still with Ficetole. My husband is somewhere at the front, whether dead or alive I do not know. And the war has finally found us in Marseille. I slide down the wall and sit on the floor, crying at the great, awful waste of it all.

* * *

Henri

LEMBACH, ALSACE, OUVRAGE FOUR-À-CHAUX,
COMBAT UNIT NUMBER 5

June 28, 1940

France was caught unawares. Although Germany invaded Denmark and Norway in April, no one was prepared for the attacks on Holland, Luxembourg, and Belgium in May. None of the great military strategists could conceive that Germany would violate Belgium's neutral stance and march straight through to the Ardennes forest. When the British retreated from Dunkirk, the exodus began. Paris fell. The Maginot Line was cut off and Henri and his fellow soldiers in Lembach were trapped. Helpless as the Germans marched through the Somme valley and into France. It took only a month for his noble country to fall to its knees.

In theory the Maginot Line was a brilliant idea. Each state-of-the-art installation is connected by an underground railway and can hold over one thousand men. Each embodies the arrogance and power of France. But the Germans do not play by the established rules of warfare. They see. They want. They take. France was the next thing in line.

Three days ago Henri and the others sat in their bunker and listened to the radio as it was announced that Marshal Pétain, the newly assigned prime minister, had signed the Armistice Convention, giving the German army full control of the northern half of France. He listened as his countrymen stated with dull voices where the lines of demarcation have been drawn. Occupied Zone and Free Zone. Northern France, with captured Paris as its capital. Southern France, to be administered, henceforth, from Vichy. Their leaders having promised goodwill and allegiance to the Führer. Papers will be required to pass from one side to another. Rations will go into effect. Movements will be restricted. Freedoms will be taken. Northern France has been rendered an occupied country. It is only a matter of time before the same will be true of the South.

The idea of Nancy trapped in Marseille with leering, violent Germans makes Henri want to beat the walls around him and scream. So he lies in his bunk, taking comfort in the fact that he will be able to return to Marseille now that the French army has surrendered. He can keep his promise to Nancy. He can come home alive. And there are other promises he wants to keep as well, promises he made to himself.

Henri reaches down and grabs a flashlight from his pack, then fishes in his back pocket for his wallet. There, hidden behind a number of francs, is a battered piece of stationery. Henri pulls it out, unfolds it, and lifts it in front of the flashlight. A faded gold *HB* is written at the top in swirling script. It is thin as tissue paper and the ink is smudged in several places. But in perfect, legible—albeit tiny—script, it reads:

Nancy hates:
Beer
Cats
Goat cheese

Nancy cannot:
Sing
Whistle
Clap in time to music
Ride a bike

*Teach her

It is the list he made that first night when she walked with him beside the Seine. She still hates beer, goat cheese, and cats. But he did teach her to whistle on their honeymoon. Despite his best efforts he doubts that she will ever be able to sing a note or clap in time to music, but he can still do something about the bicycle.

Henri stares at this list, his anxious mind racing, when the first bomb lands, two kilometers away. The walls of the ouvrage begin to rattle and groan. Henri stumbles out of his bunk and into complete bedlam as the sirens screech and the lights start to flash. The deep, destructive boom of a second bomb, and then a third, even closer, can be felt through the floors, up his body, and into his teeth. But it isn't until the artillery bombardment begins, moments later, that concrete dust trickles down the walls and cracks start to spread across the ceiling.

* * *

Madame Andrée

CHAUDES-AIGUES PLATEAU, CANTAL, FRANCE

May 1944

In many ways it feels as though I am starting over once Gaspard and his men arrive at Chaudes-Aigues. I have Fournier's men *trained.* They know better than to leer or whistle. It's been months since I looked over my shoulder on my daily trip to the creek. But no sooner do the maquisards from Mont Mouchet arrive than I am set back. It is unacceptable. *Untenable.* And I've put my knife to three different Adam's apples since breakfast.

The particular middle-aged Frenchman whom I have pressed up against a tree finds me much less attractive than he did thirty seconds ago now that I have the pointy end of one knife positioned against his jugular, and the sharp edge of another ready to slice off his testicles. There's nothing like the fear of castration to eliminate a man's sexual ardor.

"Je ne suis pas une pute. Comprenez vous?" The fool is holding his breath and he'll likely pass out before I've had the chance to finish what I am saying. I need him to understand me. It is very important that he and his friends learn this lesson quickly. I can't spend my days defending myself from harassment. "Nod if you understand."

He's afraid to move his head but he shifts it up and down slightly. I drop both knives and step away. "Good. Now go tell your friends exactly what I just told you. But first, repeat it to me."

He clears his throat. "You are not a whore."

"And you will not treat me like one. Go. Now."

He scuttles into the forest and I wait until he's gone before turning to the shadows where Hubert has been standing for the last few moments.

"This is never going to work," I tell him.

"No. It isn't."

"Do you know who that man is?"

"I don't remember his name. But he belongs to Gaspard. He was one of the first to retreat from Mont Mouchet. He arrived three days ago. Smelled of dried piss and cheap brandy," he says.

"He doesn't smell any better now." I roll my neck from left to right. I slept wrong and there's a kink at the base of my skull that's making it painful to look up. "Do you know which group he's been assigned to?"

"Judex's."

"Excellent. I'd planned to start with him anyway."

Hubert is one of those men who can ask questions without speaking. He can simply look at you and tip his chin. Or flare one nostril. On more than one occasion he's made no expression whatsoever and I know exactly what he's asking anyway. Ours is a platonic marriage in which we have learned to read each other like a primer.

"I have to visit each of Gaspard's groups," I say. "And I may as well start at the top. These men reflect their leaders and my best chance of being taken seriously is for word to get out, from the top, that I'm not to be trifled with."

"I think neutering him would have done that nicely," he says.

"Yes, well, I still have to meet with Judex. Better to start off on the right foot."

"Do you mean to say that you are going to meet with him by yourself?"

"Of course not! You're coming with me." I pat Hubert on the chest as I pass him. "Gaspard has his lieutenant and I have mine."

SAINT-MARTIAL, CANTAL, FRANCE

May 20, 1944

The village of Saint-Martial is only five kilometers from our encampment atop the Chaudes-Aigues plateau. Recently abandoned by its inhabitants due to German troop movements in the area, it gives Gaspard a place to reconvene with his troops and has the added benefit of getting them out of my immediate presence.

I sent the middle-aged bugger who accosted me in the forest yesterday on ahead with a message that I will be visiting Gaspard today, to meet with him and Judex. What he does not know is that I had Hubert take me to three of his groups this morning to assess the troops. I asked them what weapons they have, and about those they lost after leaving Mont Mouchet. I asked about uniforms—or the lack thereof—and transportation. What they have eaten all these long months and where they acquire it. I asked what they think of their leaders and their fellow men-in-arms. So, by the time Hubert rounds the last bend on the narrow, pitted lane between Chaudes-Aigues and Saint-Martial, I know a great deal more about Gaspard, his men, and their needs than he imagines I do.

True to form, Gaspard has avoided camping in the woods. As soon as he heard about the availability of housing in Saint-Martial, he directed his lieutenants to take up residence. Neither Hubert nor I bothered to point out that the German Luftwaffe regularly strafes farms and villages. The residents of Saint-Martial would still be in their homes otherwise. The village itself is composed of no more than fifteen small stone buildings scattered across the hilltop above a large reservoir with a single dirt road that leads in and out.

As soon as we pull into the village, Gaspard's men spring from the hedgerow wielding rifles that I know are unloaded. I roll down my window and say, "Madame Andrée. Gaspard is expecting me."

We are directed to the largest building in the village and Gaspard stands in the doorway, arms crossed. I am perversely happy to see that the lack of château makes him appear less intimidating. The house makes the man, I suppose.

Gaspard leads us through the door. "Please," he says, once Hubert and I are inside, "won't you join Judex and me for a drink?"

"Of course."

To the Maquis, the ability to outdrink an opponent is proof of one's manhood. To refuse Gaspard would be to undo all the progress we've made these last few days. Besides, I know what game he's playing, and I intend to win. Henri trained me well.

Once seated around an old, scuffed kitchen table, with a glass of brandy in my hand, I tell Gaspard, "I can offer you and each of your men thirty-five francs a day. That should nicely accommodate your needs for food and basic supplies."

"Non," Gaspard says, shaking a thick finger in my face. "I know for a fact that Fournier and his men receive forty-five."

"What I give to them is none of your concern."

"Come, Madame Andrée! You must be equitable."

I look around the small, tidy kitchen. "Is it equitable that you have lodgings and he does not?"

"This village has been here, empty, for months. He could have taken possession anytime he liked."

I hide my smile with a sip of brandy. "I believe he likes to maintain the high ground. Comfort is less important to Fournier than security."

If that hits the mark, Gaspard does a remarkable job of not letting it show.

However, I can see Judex grip his glass a little tighter. "These men are not the same," he mutters, then swallows a large mouthful of brandy.

"Thirty-five francs a day. Boots. Revolvers. And ammunition. That is where we will begin." Gaspard's brandy isn't the worst I've had. But it clearly hasn't been long in the bottle and there's a trail of heat at the back of my throat. It's strong. Too strong to take as quickly as they are. "But your men are obviously of strong fighting caliber. They'd have to be to fend off the Germans the way they did. You killed ten men for every one you lost. That's impressive."

Big men and small boys are much the same. They need female validation. And I don't regret saying this to Gaspard—it's not an empty compliment. He and his men fought ferociously. I can respect that. And I don't mind tossing him that bone if it will help bring him into line.

Gaspard nods, pleased with the compliment, and pours each of us another finger of brandy. I lift my glass and gaze at the warm, amber liquid. I think of Henri and his drinking rules. Then I take off my jacket and place it on the back of the chair.

I take a sip. Smile. "Thirty-five francs. Boots. Weapons. Ammunition. And tomorrow I will place an order for the explosives you'll need to destroy the railway that services the German garrison near Le Puy." It's what I've planned to give him all along, but Gaspard thinks I've made a concession. He congratulates himself by tipping a bit more brandy into my glass.

"Drink up!" he insists.

I lift my glass and raise it toward Hubert. "Cheers!"

He clinks his glass to mine and squints.

God love Hubert. The man could spot a cue at fifty paces.

Hubert reaches inside his jacket and pulls out the map Fournier has given us. "Now we must discuss our plans for retreat in the event of attack," he says.

"There's no need!" Judex says. "Together our numbers are strong. We can fight off the Germans easily."

"That's what you thought once before," I say. "And our numbers, together, are just over seven thousand. One-third of what the Germans have. We will not take chances. And we will be prepared."

Hubert turns the map and pushes it across the table to face Gaspard and Judex. "Here, here, and here," he says, tapping the map, "are the lines of retreat that we have established."

"But those are rivers." Judex blinks heavily. The brandy is already getting to him. "And you have us going through the deepest sections. That is insanity."

"You might be surprised how passable they can be. Fournier has spent a great deal of time working out this route," Hubert says.

I raise my glass once more and roll the amber liquid over my tongue. I let the heat ground me as it slides down the back of my throat. "You may have been the king of Mont Mouchet, but Fournier knows this area and you will have to trust that the rivers are the safest means of retreat."

"No matter," Judex says, and I detect the faintest slur at the edge of his words. "We won't need to retreat."

There is less than a finger of brandy left in Gaspard's glass and he tips it into his mouth. He holds it there for several seconds and then I see his Adam's apple bob as he swallows. "Now let us discuss the weapons. I want to be there during the airdrop."

"No," I say.

"I have the right—"

"No," I say again. "You do not."

"I could come anyway."

"You tried that once," I say. "I would hope you've not forgotten how that ended."

Judex looks back and forth between us curiously and I realize that he doesn't know what we're talking about. Interesting.

The tip of Gaspard's nose is red, but I can't tell whether it's caused by anger or brandy. He lifts the bottle and tips it toward me in question.

I nod.

He pours me another finger. Then two more for himself. Hubert, I notice, swirls the brandy around his glass and continually lifts it to his mouth, but there is little change in the level of alcohol. He's doing an excellent job of making it look as though he's drinking, however, because Gaspard tips a bit more into his glass without paying attention to how much is there already.

"If you'll excuse me," I say, "I need the loo."

This was Henri's fourth lesson, learned many months after that first dinner with his father. Excuse yourself. Use the bathroom. And, if at all possible, get some fresh air.

"Outhouse," Judex says, pointing toward the kitchen door.

Hubert takes his cue and repositions the map in the middle of the table. He taps six different areas marked in red. "Here are the known German positions," he says.

Gaspard and Judex lean over the map and neither of them notices me take my glass with me. I push through the kitchen door and out into the night air. The outhouse is located several hundred feet away, but I take a moment to assess myself. I can feel the pleasant tingle of a buzz but nothing more. A guard stands on either side of the door and I smile at each of them in turn.

"Follow me to that outhouse and I'll cut your throats."

Once inside the stone privy, I hold my breath, pour the rest of my brandy down the hole, and relieve myself. On the way back to the house I find what I'm looking for. The water pump is almost hidden in a clump of weeds beside the garden gate, but it works. And the water is clean and cold. I drink an entire glass before heading back inside.

The brandy bottle is almost empty now, but Gaspard does not hesitate to offer me more. I accept, noting that Judex can hardly sit upright any longer. My guess is that he will be the first to fall. And I'm not wrong. It's not that he goes out of his chair a few minutes later, but rather that he sinks, slowly, to the table, chin resting on his forearm. His eyes are glassy, the tip of his nose is red, and the corners of his mouth are turned down. His bluster has turned to melancholy and the effect is one of being deflated. I wouldn't have taken him for a sad drunk. Not the thing you'd expect from a man who could ruthlessly torture his enemy with a red-hot poker.

When I finish off my brandy half an hour later, Gaspard concedes defeat. "You are not at all drunk," he tells me.

"No. I am not."

"I did try."

"I knew you would."

"But did you know, Madame Andrée, that you are a brass-plated bitch?" Somehow, coming from Gaspard, in this moment, it does not sound like an insult. In fact, this may be the closest he ever comes to paying me a compliment.

"I do. And I would very much appreciate it if you would communicate that to your men."

"They'll leave you alone from now on."

"Good. I will send word when your shipment has arrived, and I will be present when it's delivered."

"Why?"

"Because you must sign receipts," I say.

He doesn't say good-bye or walk us to the door. He simply watches us leave with a newfound interest. It is after one in the morning, but the stars are so numerous and so bright that Hubert and I can see each other's face plainly as we walk to the car.

Hubert slides behind the wheel of the Renault and gives me the most curious gaze. "How the flaming hell did you do that?" he asks.

"Do what?"

"Drink like that. I've never seen anything like it. You knocked back twice as much brandy as Judex—and he's passed out on the table, while you're as chipper as a bluebird—"

"—more like a pigeon—"

"—my point is you're the last man standing—"

"—woman—"

"Good grief! You know what I mean, Nance. Just shut up for a second. I can't figure out where it all went. Much less how you're even conscious. It's like you have a hollow leg." He throws his hands up, in exasperation, then starts the car and puts it in reverse. "That is one of the most extraordinary things I've ever seen."

"I had a very good teacher." I lean my head back against the seat, pleasantly tired and happy with this part of the night's work. Gaspard got what he wanted—weapons and supplies for his men—and I got what I wanted: dominance. I yawn as Hubert pulls the Renault onto the dirt track to drive us the short distance back to our encampment. "Pity we can't go to sleep."

"Why not?"

"We've got to help Fournier with tonight's shipment."

And this marks the first time I have ever heard Hubert well and properly curse.

CHAUDES-AIGUES PLATEAU, CANTAL, FRANCE

June 5, 1944

Special message for Hélène. Anselm delivered to Montluçon this a.m. Collect immediately.

I take the message from Denis Rake, read it, then shake it in his face. "What the *hell* am I supposed to do with this?"

He sits across from me in the bus. "Well, apparently, Duckie, you are to drive your scrawny arse—"

"—I am *not* scrawny—"

"—you are, actually. You've lost at least a stone since being here. But that's beside the point. You're to go collect Anselm."

"And how am I supposed to know where he is?"

He shakes his head, exasperated. "Can't you read? He's in Montluçon."

"And Montluçon is Maurice Southgate's area. He was supposed to meet us at the drop zone, remember? Oh no, that's right. You were off cavorting in Bourges with your lover."

"I was *not*"—he sticks a finger in my face—"in Bourges."

Despite much prodding, Denis has kept the name and location of his lover a secret. And for good reason: both men would likely be shot on sight if they were discovered together.

"My point is that Maurice Southgate was supposed to give me the address and the password for his contact in Montluçon the night we landed. But I was met by Tardivat instead. Without that information it will be nearly impossible to collect Anselm."

Denis props his feet up on the stump, leans his head against the back of his seat, and thinks for a moment. "Don't you have a name for this contact?"

"Madame Renard, and I know that she was once the housekeeper of an ambassador in Paris. Also, that she makes excellent cakes, but this does me little good when I don't even know where to begin looking for her."

"That's not entirely true. Just head to Mont—" he says, and then ducks out the door quickly to avoid the boot I've thrown at his head.

"—luçon, I know," I say. "To find a woman who might live anywhere, and, having found her, persuade her to give up Anselm without a password. Easy enough. Sure. No matter that I'd shoot anyone who tried to pull a stunt like that on me."

I think of Gaspard and what he did to Roger. And Roger had the correct password. I drop my head to my hands, shake it. I've been given a direct order and I can't very well leave one of Britain's best weapons instructors unattended in the middle of territory thick with Germans. I have no choice.

"Dammit," I say as I dig beneath a seat for my pack. "Time to go find a needle in a haystack."

Fournier gives me his best car and Jacques—one of his lieutenants—to drive. I'd thought of going alone but Hubert rejected the idea out of hand. We know the Brownshirts are looking for the White Mouse. We know that they have connected said mouse to Madame Andrée. He argues they will be less suspicious of a "married couple" than of a woman driving alone through occupied territory. The fact that we are driving at all is problematic. Access to a vehicle immediately identifies us as either Resistance or German and, depending on who controls each checkpoint along the way, could mean the patrols shoot first and ask questions later. I'd take one of Fournier's bicycles but it's a long trip and Anselm won't fit on the back. I have no other choice than to go with Jacques and pretend to be his wife should we be apprehended.

Jacques wisely does not crack a smile at this arrangement. In fact, he does not smile at all. He seems to be the sort of man whose lips were sewn together at birth. He is silent as we load the car with grenades and a Sten gun in case we came across German patrol. Then I strap a bicycle to the roof—it will be less conspicuous to ride around on that once we reach Montluçon. We are about to be off when someone calls for me.

"Madame Andrée!" I turn to see Louis jog across the clearing. He raises his bandaged hand in greeting.

"You look less green around the gills," I tell him. "Did you find a doctor in Chaudes-Aigues?"

"Oui." He clears his throat. "I hear you are going to Montluçon."

"Word travels fast, I see."

"That is where I lived, before the war. My wife is there still. She is pregnant."

I'm not sure whether to congratulate him or offer my condolences. I pity anyone bringing a child into the world right now.

"Would you deliver something to her for me?" He reaches into his pocket and pulls out an envelope stuffed with francs. An address is scribbled across the front. "My wages. I've saved them all for her."

"What are you eating, then?"

He shrugs. "Enough."

Louis's thin frame would suggest otherwise, so I pull a lump of bills from the envelope and hand them back to him. "Yes, I'll take this to your wife. But you must keep yourself fed in the meantime."

"Thank you, Madame Andrée. Her name is Simone Autry."

Jacques has the most curious expression on his face when I climb into the car. "What?" I ask.

"C-c-careful," Jacques says with a slight twitch of his jaw, struggling to control his staggered consonants, "or you'll end up being p-p-postmaster as well."

I look at him, fascinated. He *stutters*. No wonder the man hasn't spoken a single word since our arrival three months ago. He is looking at me now, one eye pinched tight in expectation of ridicule. But he has trusted me with this secret and I refuse to shame him.

"Jacques!" I say. "Did you just crack a joke?"

"C-c-course not." His stoic face belies nothing as he starts the engine and puts the car in drive, but I think I catch the hint of a smile when he turns away.

Before long I am grateful for his presence. The whole area is crawling with Brownshirts. There are patrols and roadblocks everywhere and we are forced to take back roads and send friendly scouts ahead when we can find them. Montluçon is only two hours from Fournier's encampment, but we stop at every farm and village along the way to inquire about German patrols. He stays in the car while I knock at doors and ask about troop movements nearby. I pass along a few francs with each handshake, and explain that we are trying to go north, unmolested by Brownshirts.

"Just down there," one villager says, pointing to a main crossroads. "They've set up an ambush behind the curve."

"Merci beaucoup!" I say, and we're off again, skirting around town through an alley and across a field to avoid being detected.

It goes on and on like this for hours, as we creep toward Montluçon. Sometimes it's not the Germans who give us trouble, however. "They have gone," one woman tells us, "but the Maquis will stop you. I will come with you and tell them that you are of the

Maquis d'Auvergne. I taught half of those boys in school. They will listen to me."

With local chaperones we proceed slowly, never once having to make use of the Sten gun hidden under the floorboard at my feet.

It is early evening when we reach Montluçon and I have Jacques stop the car a quarter of a mile from the address Louis gave me. I take the bike down while he scouts a position to watch the car.

"If the car draws unwanted attention, come and warn me," I say.

Jacques nods, then slips into the hedgerow to keep watch.

I cycle into town and look for the house number. Few people bother to lift their heads as I pass.

The cottage is small and tidy. There are flowers in the window boxes and the front step has been swept. I am always a little startled to find my countrymen maintaining any kind of normalcy in the face of war. I respect it. It is one of a thousand courageous ways of thumbing your nose at the enemy. A quick breath, then I tuck my hair behind my ears, trying to look as presentable as possible. I knock on the door.

It is answered by an older woman who appears to be blind in one eye. This cannot be Louis's wife.

"Madame Autry?" I ask, my voice laced with hesitance.

"Non." Her hair is like silver feathers drifting in the breeze, and I'm momentarily distracted by its ethereal beauty. "Who are you?" she asks.

"A friend of Louis's. I've come with a message for Simone."

"Okay, then," she says, and turns over her shoulder. "Simone! You have a visitor!"

A young, pretty woman, with auburn hair, comes to the door. She looks rather like a toothpick that has swallowed an olive.

"Heavens! You poor dear. I've never seen anyone as pregnant as you." The words are out of my mouth before I can stop them, and I could kick myself. The last thing I need is to offend her.

But much to my relief, the girl laughs. "I feel as though I will be the only woman in the history of the world to be pregnant forever." She wipes one hand on her apron and offers it to me. "Simone."

"Andrée." I shake her hand, then motion to a little bench sitting beside the house. "Come, I have a message from your husband."

"Louis . . . ?"

"Is perfectly fine and unharmed." No point mentioning the fingers. It's only a tiny lie, so I don't even wince. "I saw him this morning."

Simone waddles to the bench and lowers her body onto it. She groans and lifts her swollen feet, rolling her ankles, before setting them back on the ground.

I hand her the envelope. "From your husband. For you and the baby. He sends his love."

Simone peeks into the envelope, gasps, then presses it to her chest. She juts out her chin and blinks hard, trying not to cry.

"We did not think he would be paid."

"He has earned every penny."

I sit for a moment and answer all her questions. How is he? What has he been doing? Does he have enough to eat? Are his spirits up? Finally, I set my hand on her forearm and get to my point.

"Before I go, there is one thing you can help me with," I tell her.

"Anything!"

"I am looking for a Madame Renard. Do you know of her?"

Simone shakes her head and her hair swings at her shoulders. It looks like brass in the fading sun and I am envious of the color, the way it catches the light and tosses it back against her skin. "No. What does she look like?"

I shrug. "I only know that she lives on the outskirts of town, that she makes marvelous cakes, and that she used to work for an ambassador."

"An ambassador! I have a friend who told me once that her neighbor used to work in Paris for the French ambassador to Sweden."

"Where does your friend live?"

Simone gives me the address with instructions to tell her friend that she sent me, and once more I am pedaling off on this most ridiculous goose chase. The house in question is two streets over and twice as well kept as that of Simone and her parents. There isn't a dead leaf or cobweb to be seen anywhere in the yard or on the exterior of the home. But the porch light is on and the door is opened by a woman Simone's exact opposite. Nearly as wide as she is tall and twice as old.

"*Bonjour, madame!* Pardon the intrusion. Simone Autry sent me." I am feeling less inclined to believe this expedition will result in anything at all, so I skip the formalities and get right to the point. "I am looking for a Madame Renard. Simone said you have a friend who once worked for an ambassador in Paris."

The woman—I do not even bother to ask her name at this point—has very small eyes in her very round face. It gives her the most strangely cheerful expression I've ever seen. Like a cookie that smiles back right before you eat it. "Do you mean Alice?"

I wager a guess. "Alice Renard?"

"Yes!"

"Then yes, that is exactly who I'm looking for, and I do not mean to be rude, but time is of the essence."

She points to a larger home at the end of the street. "Tell her that Inès sent you."

For the dozenth time today I am shouting, *"Merci beaucoup!"* over my shoulder. Then I am pedaling, pedaling once again. I catch my breath in this yard, looking back the way I've come, trying to mentally retrace my route. I've been in such a rush to get here that it's possible I might get lost and not be able to find my way back to Jacques. He, meanwhile, has no idea that I've gone on from Louis's wife.

I straighten my hair, dust off my slacks, and wipe a bead of perspiration from my forehead. I knock, three times. There is no answer. But the lights are on and I see the curtains twitch in my peripheral vision. I knock again. Nothing. I am debating whether to call out to her and if that will do any good. I decide against it and lift my hand once more, but the door pulls inward before I can try again.

Before me stands a distinguished-looking woman with thin lips and a red-checkered apron. There is a smudge of flour on the end of her nose.

"Madame Renard?"

She nods but says nothing.

"My name is Andrée. You do not know me, but I know of you." I want to add that Maurice Southgate sent me, but if my suspicions are true and he is dead, she might know this already and I could end up with a bullet between my eyes. So I take a riskier tack. "I believe you have a . . . *packet* . . . for me."

Alice Renard draws herself up straighter, like a measuring tape pulled taut, and I see that she is several inches taller than me. She stands on her doorstep, very still and very quiet. I have come too far and gone to such trouble and the thought of leaving without Anselm when I might be only feet away from him is intolerable. So I break my own rules.

"You do not have to believe me. I wouldn't if I were you, to be honest. But I've just come from the home of your friend Inès. And before that a friend of hers. Both of them pointed me in the direction of the only woman they knew who once worked in the home of an ambassador." I pause long enough to take a breath and that is when I smell it. Baking. The heavy, sweet, unmistakable scent of *baba au rhum.* I lean forward, close my eyes, and inhale. My mouth waters. "I have heard so much about your cakes!"

This is better than any password.

She smiles then, and it transforms her face. She glances over my shoulder, no doubt to make sure I have not been followed. "I have been cooking for a guest. Please, come in."

Madame Renard steps aside, lets me into her home, then shuts the door. She leads me into the kitchen, where the smell of rum cake permeates the air so heavily I can almost taste it.

"You can come out now," Madame Renard says, as though to no one in particular.

It occurs to me, a moment too late, that this is how special operatives die. They wander like idiots into traps. They don't ask enough questions. They follow friendly directions and end up behind closed doors at the mercy of strangers. All these thoughts are colliding as the door of an enormous armoire swings open and a man steps out. His mouth is drawn tight and a .45-caliber revolver is in his hand and pointed directly at my face.

Nancy Fiocca

MARSEILLE

July 18, 1940

I head to the Hôtel du Louvre et Paix but instead of going in the front entrance on the Canebière, I circle to the side and enter through a back door on the cours Belsunce. Within weeks of the armistice, Marseille was flooded by Gestapo thinly disguised as the German Commission. All of them dress in mufti—civilian clothes—but they fool no one. They're just so *damned* German. Blond and blue-eyed, with those clean-shaven, square jaws. The guttural words. They ooze arrogance, not even bothering to speak French, ordering the staff around like servants. They've taken up residence in many of the popular hotels, hogging the bars and scaring the locals. This particular group of German secret police—seven in total—has claimed the elaborate foyer of the Hôtel du Louvre et Paix as their watering hole. I avoid them whenever I come to visit Antoine.

I've not seen my husband in four and a half months. I am worried. I am lonely. But mostly I detest eating dinner by myself. So, most evenings I find my way to Antoine's and enjoy an aperitif or two until dinner, which I eat at the bar. Sometimes I bring a novel to read—mostly Victor Hugo, since I am working my way through Henri's collection—but I am often depressed by the tender romance I find on those pages, so there are many nights that I sit here and talk to Antoine, listen to the radio, or to the conversations of others.

We seem to have developed a new rapport since my trip to Cannes, and his company makes me feel less alone.

"How did you get that limp?" I ask Antoine when he shuffles toward me with a glass of brandy in hand. I've wondered for years and it occurs to me that I may as well ask.

He sets the glass down in front of me, then gives me the most curious glance. "Did you know that you are the only person who has ever asked me that question outright?"

"What about Henri?"

"*Non.* He stares sometimes, so I tell him stories of being wounded during the Great War. Or"—he offers a guilty smile—"other things not fit for a lady's ear. But not because he asks."

"And what answer will you give me?"

"The truth, if that's what you'd like."

"Please."

"I was kicked in the thigh by a mule fifteen years ago. It snapped my femur in half." He touches his leg to show me where. "The doctors tried to set it, but"—he shrugs—"I am not young, and it healed poorly. My options were limited. So I left the family vineyard in Corsica and came here to tend bar. I'm good with people. I know wine. It made sense at the time and now I am too old for a career change."

There is nothing outrageous about the story. Nothing grandiose. I am inclined to believe him. It's the sort of random injury that turns a man's life upside down, and it's not that I am grateful Antoine was injured but I am certainly glad that he is here, in this place, now.

I wink at him. "Your secret is safe with me."

"You are collecting my secrets at an astonishing rate, madame."

Antoine limps off and that is when I see the two men sitting at the other end of the bar. One of them is reading a Joseph Conrad novel and the other is staring at me. Both of them have a general sense of unease about them. I let my gaze float past them, pretending a casual survey of the bar, then focus once more on my brandy. I did not think my trip to Cannes would catch up with me so quickly.

After a few minutes I give Antoine a quick glance. He holds my gaze for a moment to let me know he's seen the request, then polishes several glasses and straightens a few bottles on the shelf before making his way back toward me.

"About that envelope that I delivered to Cannes..."

"Yes?"

"Does anyone know it passed through here?"

"Françoise, my contact in Toulouse. Why?"

"Because that man at the end of the bar, with the red hair, is the one who collected it at the Hôtel Martinez."

Antoine doesn't turn to look but the muscle along his jaw does tense. "Why do I get the impression you won't be satisfied to just sit and wonder what he's doing here?"

"Because they're in my bar—"

"—*my bar,* actually—"

"—and I don't like the idea that I could have been followed. So I may as well get to the bottom of it."

"Henri will kill me if I let you go anywhere near those men," he hisses.

"Henri, as you well know, has run off to be a hero. What he doesn't know won't upset him. Besides, I have no intention of going over there." I flash him a wicked grin. "I mean to make them come to me."

"And what good will that do?"

"It will help me understand what they're doing in Marseille." For the second time in as many weeks, I hold out my hand and ask for a menu.

As always, Antoine's radio is on, tuned to some Big Band playing swing music. We have been speaking in low voices, and in French, so there is little chance the strangers at the end of the bar can follow our conversation. Still, Antoine does as I ask. He reaches under the bar, pulls out a menu, and hands it to me.

"Merci," I say, then pretend to look it over. I've committed to playing this part, so I go all in. After a moment I shake my head, then say, in an exasperated voice, in English, "What I wouldn't give for a plate of bangers and mash."

I am gratified to find that my gut instincts are still in good working order, because both men at the end of the bar sit up straighter and twist their heads to look at me. It takes a great effort not to laugh because the sudden movement makes them appear rather like

American prairie dogs. I can see them confer, out of the corner of my eye. Both nod, and then make their way toward me.

The redhead reaches me first. "Excuse me," he says, also in English. "But we couldn't help overhearing you just now. Are you British?"

Now that he's standing beside me I can see that my guess about him being part of the Commonwealth was spot-on. He's a Scotsman through and through. Tall, broad-shouldered—although thin at the moment—charming, and friendly. Until I met Henri he would have been the embodiment of my very favorite species of man.

"Not quite," I say with a grin. I do love being right. "Australian."

"That counts." He plops down on the stool to my right, relieved.

Antoine does not speak English, so I know he can't follow the conversation, but he is watching me. And once he sees that I'm not alarmed by their arrival, he reaches toward the radio and turns it up another notch to protect us from being overheard by the men in the lobby.

"We thought you were French, at first," says the second man. His accent is harder to place. Lots of French. A hint of German. And something else, something... with a bit of zing to it. He has a high, broad forehead with a receding hairline. Dark, wavy hair. Warm brown eyes. I like his nose as well. It is strong and straight and provides him an excellent profile.

"Only by marriage." I hold up my left hand to show them the thin, gold band on my ring finger. And then I make a decision based on instinct alone. "Please, have a seat. Join me for dinner. It's always nice to meet another subject of the Crown."

"Ian Garrow." The Scottish redhead extends his hand.

"Is *that* your name?" I ask. A pause. A triumphant grin. And then, "I thought you went by Simón Bolívar?"

He is so genuinely startled that I laugh out loud.

"How—"

"I was curious to see who would collect the envelope. So I waited in the bar," I tell him. Then I take the hand that is still outstretched before me. "Nancy Fiocca."

They don't know me, but they know Françoise. I don't know Françoise, but I know Antoine. I trust him and he trusts her, so it is not a huge stretch for any of us to trust one another—at least enough to sit and have dinner. I can tell they are thinking the same thing. These two men look at each other, assessing, and I see them make a silent decision. It's there in the slant of their mouths, the way their shoulders relax, the faint nod. They choose to put their caution aside.

"This is my friend Patrick O'Leary," Garrow says.

I turn to the man on my left. "O'Leary is an Irish name."

"Yes."

"You are not Irish."

"No," he says with a wink.

"What are you, then?"

"Cautious," he says. But he does so with a smile, and I think that I might like him in the end.

"What are you doing in Marseille?" I ask, looking from one to the other.

There is a loud burst of laughter from the lobby where the Germans are gathered. Garrow looks over his shoulder and thinks for a moment. "In order to explain that to you, madame, we will need to go somewhere a great deal more private."

"We run a network of safe houses between here and Spain," Patrick O'Leary says. "We are on our way to Perpignan with four Jewish refugees, and thanks to the papers you delivered to Cannes, they should be able to get into Spain with minimal trouble."

Belgian! It comes to me suddenly. He's Belgian. That zing in O'Leary's accent is a touch of Flemish. And when combined with the French and German, it makes up the typical Belgian accent. He clearly doesn't want me to know this, however, so I keep the revelation to myself.

All I have to go on is my gut. Trust is always an act of faith, and I listen as Garrow and O'Leary explain how they have begun the process of establishing an escape route for captured soldiers and persecuted Jews. They tell me that there are over two hundred British soldiers interred in Marseille's Fort Saint-Jean alone. But none of that convinces me of their trustworthiness. It is the fact that they sit in my living room, drinking my liquor, while my dogs lie curled up in each of their laps, asleep. I have always believed Picon and Grenadine to be excellent judges of character. They would never allow me to fall in with a pack of traitors.

"You work with Françoise?" I ask once they have divulged the basics of their operation.

If he's surprised that I know this name, he doesn't let on. "She is the last stop on our route," O'Leary says.

I have Henri's radio turned up one notch higher than I'd like and set to classical music so that our neighbor, Monsieur Paquet, cannot overhear our conversation. He has long been the commissioner of police, but since the armistice I have learned that he is also loyal to the new government in Vichy, and more than happy to inform on his fellow citizens.

"Why have you trusted me with all of this?" I ask.

Garrow scratches his chin. "My gut says that you are an ally. You delivered those papers to Cannes. You were in the bar where Françoise told us to meet her Marseille contact. At the very least, you're not working against us."

I pull my bare feet under me and lean my head against the wing of my chair. "Four years ago I saw a Brownshirt in Vienna nearly whip an old woman to death. I promised myself that day that if there was anything I could ever do to fight against the Germans, I would. So no, I'm not working against you. And if I'm being perfectly honest, delivering transit papers to a luxury hotel hardly feels like work at all."

Garrow sniffs the glass in his hand. It's a single-malt Scotch whisky that I handed him within minutes of his arrival. He seems to regard it as a priceless object because he's taken only one sip, and his eyes rolled back in pleasure at that, so I have no idea what he'd do if I poured him another finger. He smells the scotch again, closes his eyes, and whistles a few bars of "Auld Lang Syne."

I know they've come for something but neither of them has gotten around to asking yet. Perhaps they feel as though they need to butter me up. Regardless, I won't know until they spit it out.

"I doubt that you reveal the specifics of your Resistance activities to every person you meet. My guess is that you came to me for something very specific?" I ask.

"We need a radio," Patrick O'Leary says, bluntly. I am learning that he is the more practical and direct of the two. "So we can get information straight from the BBC and not have to filter out the lies coming from Vichy. To hear them tell it, we've already lost the war and London is the new Nazi headquarters of Europe."

"Also," Garrow says, voice deadpan, "it wouldn't hurt if we could get our hands on a thousand cigarettes." He doesn't crack a smile as he says this, and I can't tell whether he's serious.

"What on earth do you need with so many cigarettes?"

"Intelligence gathering," Garrow says. "You would be stunned at the way people talk when you hand them a cigarette."

"Do you plan on talking to a thousand people?"

"Eventually. But some people take more bribing than others. It doesn't hurt to be prepared."

"You seem very sure of my ability to help," I say.

"You are clearly a woman of financial means." Garrow looks around the flat. "You're the loyal wife of an upstanding French businessman—where is he anyway?"

"Somewhere in the north of France, defending the Maginot Line. Or what's left of it."

He winces. "I was sorry to hear it fell."

I have to clear my throat so the words will come out properly. "So was I."

Garrow takes another sip of whisky. "I believe you can help because you have papers that let you move easily anywhere in the Free Zone. And by your own admission, you are a Nazi-hating loyal subject of the Crown. Pardon me for being blunt, Madame Fiocca, but you are exactly the kind of person we need to know right now."

"I can get you a radio tomorrow and—"

There is a knock at the door and our heads swivel to the foyer. A second knock, more insistent this time, and I hold up one finger. "Wait here," I tell them.

"Should we hide?" O'Leary asks.

"Absolutely not. This is my home, I can entertain whomever I want."

Picon trots along behind me, a low rumble in his throat. I bend down and pick him up, then whisper, "Easy, boy," in his soft little ear.

Before Henri left for the front he installed two extra locks—a dead bolt and a chain lock—and it takes a moment to undo everything before I can swing the door open. Police Commissioner Monsieur Paquet stands on the mat. His stiff exterior belies a vicious, waspish interior. Clear eyes. Straight nose. Mustache. Hair cropped close to his head. Starched shirt.

"Hello, Commissioner, how can I help you?"

He tries to peer around me, his eyes narrowing into slits. "I heard voices."

"So?"

"It's late in the evening."

"I have company."

"But your husband is gone."

"I am allowed to entertain in his absence."

He clicks his tongue. "People might get the wrong idea."

"What people? You?"

"Henri asked me to look out for you while he is gone."

"He didn't mention that."

"He wouldn't want you to know, of course."

"My husband and I do not keep secrets from each other, Commissioner."

The commissioner's mustache twitches in anger. "Then he will not mind hearing that you have been entertaining strange men in his absence."

"There is nothing strange about the men in my flat. And I am certain that my husband will be delighted to hear that my cousins have come to visit me. He's rather fond of them."

"Cousins?"

"Yes. The sons of my mother's brothers. Have you no cousins of your own?"

"I find it difficult to believe that—"

"Are we really going to stand here and argue about the tangled nature of my family tree while my guests are left unattended?"

Police Commissioner Monsieur Paquet glares at me.

"I didn't think so. Now. Have you any other business than sticking your nose in mine?"

I can see the muscle along his jaw tense. "Your radio is too loud."

"I will make sure to turn it down. Good night, Commissioner," I say, then close the door in his face. I set all three locks, lean my forehead against the door, and whisper, *"Merde."*

"Who was that?"

It is Ian Garrow, behind me, his voice little more than a whisper.

"The Vichy commissioner of police."

"I don't think he likes you very much."

"What he likes," I say, "is my flat. And he will do anything in his power to get me evicted. Even if it means threatening me with noise violations and questioning my fidelity."

Garrow snorts. "I've known you for three hours and I can already tell that you are a lot of things, but unfaithful isn't one of them."

I turn and face him. The time for pleasantries has long passed. "Why are you here? You're after more than a radio and cigarettes. Right?"

Garrow lifts his tumbler up to the light and peers at the last of his scotch. "The thing about you, Nancy, is that no one seems to ask questions."

I hook my thumb toward the door behind me. "Did you just get here? He asked all sorts of questions. And mark my words, he'll be back."

Garrow shakes his head. "That's different. He knows you. He *knows* we shouldn't be here. Everyone else? They seem to be dazzled by you. I watched it happen tonight. That bartender? Smitten. There were seven Nazi officers in the lobby of that hotel and you walked right out the front door. Not a single one stopped you or asked questions. They just stepped aside. Let you go through. Blinked a little bit in your wake."

"Ha-ha."

"What."

"Wake."

"What do you mean?"

"That's my maiden name."

Ian Garrow takes the rest of his whisky in one long swallow. "Of *course* it is. Of course." He laughs.

"Get to the point."

"The point is . . . we need your help."

"With?"

"Supplies. And smuggling—"

"—I've been doing that already—"

"—people," he says. "Not just papers. But real, living, breathing people. Can you do *that*?"

The flat I share with Henri is well over two thousand square feet. The ceilings are twelve feet tall. The windows are floor-to-ceiling. Wood floor. Marble countertops. Brass fixtures. Persian rugs. Fine china. Sterling silver. Crystal goblets. Two bedrooms. Two bathrooms. The best views in all of Marseille. I am privileged on a stupid, irrational, almost immoral level. And still, all the air escapes from these perfect, plastered rooms. It's sucked out as though some minor deity has gasped for air. Ian Garrow wants me to smuggle human beings out of France.

"Where will I take them?"

"To Françoise at the Spanish border."

Ian Garrow balances his empty glass on one finger, the way he might balance a broomstick or a penny. He is letting me consider his request, and there must be something wrong with me. I should be terrified. Hesitant. But instead, the heightened throbbing of my pulse tells me something else. I am *excited.* This feels like a challenge. And much to my surprise I am ready for it.

"Wait here," I tell him, then retreat to the guest bedroom. I emerge a few seconds later with three long rectangular boxes. I toss them to Garrow one at a time and say, "I'll do it."

"What's this?" he asks, fumbling the boxes as he tries to hold them in the crook of his arm.

"You did ask for a thousand cigarettes."

MARSEILLE

August 20, 1940

I return home at two in the afternoon and stand at the threshold of my flat, glaring at the door suspiciously. All my senses are still dialed up to eleven, even though I safely delivered a young Jewish woman and her baby to Toulouse early this morning.

The thing is, I know that I locked the door to our flat when I left yesterday. I remember turning the key counterclockwise and checking the handle. It's an old habit born of being on my own for so long. Single women in the world learn this at an early age—more so when they travel alone and live alone and come home alone, every night, for years and years. So I know I locked the door. But it isn't just unlocked now, it's cracked open a fraction of an inch, the way it does in the summer months when heat swells the doorjamb and you don't quite pull it shut all the way. And that can mean only one of two things:

Someone has been in our flat.

Or someone is there now.

There are four flats on each floor of our apartment building in the cours Julien district. Each occupies one full corner. Henri and I live in the premier flat on the top floor, and we pay for it handsomely. I lived in the Hôtel du Louvre et Paix for six months while we waited for the lease to become available. And it was an open secret that Police Commissioner Paquet tried to bribe the owners to cancel our agreement and lease the flat to him instead. I know this because Henri had to negotiate changes in our agreed rent twice before we moved in. Marseille is stunning and beautiful and picturesque, but it is also a city whose pulse beats to the rhythm of grift. This is nothing new to my husband, however, and the Fiocca name goes a long way in these "negotiations."

I stand right in the middle of the broad landing, glaring at Commissioner Paquet's front door. "He wouldn't *dare*," I hiss, under my breath.

Ficetole is working the tram. It wouldn't be fair to pull him away from his job just because I'm afraid to enter my flat. I could track down Garrow and O'Leary, but I don't dare risk Paquet seeing them here again. We've made arrangements to meet elsewhere from now on.

I listen for the sound of barking or growling but Picon and Grendine are silent. This worries me more than anything else. If something has happened to them...

There are no footsteps. I can't hear the thump of cabinet doors being opened and closed. No scrape of wooden drawers. If I had a gun I would pull it. If I had a knife I would hold it. But I have no weapons and no skill to use them regardless, so I am defenseless as I wrap my fingers around the doorknob and slowly push the door open. I take one soundless step inside the flat, then another. I listen. I wait. And then I hear it.

A single thump. That of something being set down on a flat wooden surface.

My footsteps fall silently, one after another, as I move forward, determined to catch this thief—whoever he is—in the act. I round the corner, fists clenched, ready to scream. But my breath comes out in a whoosh instead.

"Henri," I say, stopping dead in my tracks.

He's sitting in his favorite leather armchair beside the open window. The sheer curtain billows toward him in the breeze. I did not hear the dogs because they are both asleep in his lap, tongues lolling, bellies exposed. Happier than they've been in months. The sun is on his face. His hair is damp from the shower. A glass of brandy is in his right hand. And his left arm is in a sling.

"Who else were you expecting?" he asks.

* * *

Henri

"I have a confession to make," Nancy says, lying naked, facedown, in their bed. It is early evening and the sun falls warm and golden through the window.

Henri trails a finger down her spine, counting each knob—as though they are marbles set in a row—with the tip of one finger. He pauses in the hollow of her back, tracing the S-curve of her spine, back and forth, back and forth, then moves on to the dimples of Venus. Never in his life has he been so obsessed with the indentation created by muscle and ligament. He rests, propped up on his right elbow, marveling at the sight before him.

Nancy is furious with him for getting wounded, but he assured her, countless times, as they made love that it is a single bullet wound and it will heal. Honestly, he feels as though he could lift an entire car with that arm right now. Never, in his life, has he been so elated as when she walked into the apartment.

It finally occurs to Henri that he should respond to her comment. "I hope you mean to confess that you missed me dreadfully while I was gone."

"Well, yes . . ."

"You don't sound very convincing." He drops a kiss to the small of her back.

"Of *course* I missed you!"

"But? I hear it in your voice. There's something else."

She buries her face in the blanket so her voice is muffled. "I didn't sit around the flat and mope while you were gone."

"I didn't think you would. But I'll have to teach you how to sin if that's the only thing you've got to confess." He pokes her, gently, in the ribs.

Nancy grunts. It's the most unladylike sound he's ever heard her make and he has to stifle his laugh. "Oh, I've sinned," she says.

Despite appearances, Henri Fiocca is a cautious man. It's how he's expanded the family fortune and kept himself out of trouble. But at these words from his wife, something at the back of his skull begins to thrum with alarm.

"What do you mean?"

"I think you *know* what I mean, Fiocca."

"I do not in fact. *Madame Fiocca.*" They are one and the same now. She cannot distance herself any longer by using his surname.

Nancy sits up and wraps the sheet around her. She crosses her legs. Juts out her chin. For one terrible moment Henri expects her to say that she has taken a lover in his absence. He suspects half the wives in Marseille have done just that over the last five months. It's a very French thing, the numbing of loneliness with illicit sex. But Nancy? Just the idea makes a hard knot form in the pit of his stomach.

"I have lied," Nancy says. "Straight to the faces of at least two dozen Nazi officers. I have purchased items on the black market. I have transported forbidden materials—mostly fake identification and ration cards—not to mention actual humans from one end of France to the other. I have committed *treason,*" she whispers, "or at least that's what Vichy will say if they ever find out. And I've almost been caught in the act three times. Your wife is a criminal, Henri Fiocca."

All the air rushes from his lungs in a grunt. His wife hasn't been sleeping with other men. "Is that all?"

"I thought you'd be *furious*!"

"And I thought you were about to say you'd taken a lover. By comparison, espionage seems saintly."

Henri has to move quickly in order to duck the pillow she swings at his head.

"Well, I haven't made my confession yet."

"There's more?"

"My confession is that I have no intention of quitting now that you're home."

"Ah."

"I knew you'd be displeased."

"I could ask you to stop."

"And I would say no. We've been able to help so many people."

"We?"

"My friends and I. You'll meet them soon."

"I could *demand* that you stop. It is my right as your husband," Henri says, then holds up a finger the second her mouth opens. "But I wouldn't do that."

"I know. It's why I married you." Nancy looks at him, eyes pleading. "So, what will you do?"

Henri sighs and climbs out of bed. He can feel the shift in her eyes, that focused attention. He is totally naked after all, and it pleases him that, all these months into their marriage, she is still distracted by the sight of him. "I will get dressed."

"Why?" Nancy asks as she lets her sheet fall away.

It's a mercenary move meant to draw him back to bed, but Henri is determined. "Because we're going out."

"Where?"

"To buy you a bicycle."

*

They leave the dogs at home. Nancy is afraid she'll wreck the bike and hurt them in the process. And he can tell that she is nervous as they walk to the nearest park.

"I still don't understand," she says.

He pulls her tight against his side. "In France, a woman on a bicycle is invisible. Think about it. They are *everywhere.* We don't even see them anymore. But you, *ma chère,* are the type of woman who always gets noticed. People see you. They take note. And if I cannot stop you from doing this work—and please know that it is work that I *admire*—then I want you to be safe. I don't *want* anyone to notice you. At least, with this, you can move about the city with anonymity."

She lowers her chin. Gnaws at the corner of her bottom lip. And she doesn't exactly wring her hands, but they are clasped tightly in front of her as he walks the bike along the path. This is a new look for Nancy, something to be filed away in the running catalog Henri keeps of her expressions.

"What's wrong?" he asks.

"I don't know how."

"It's not hard."

"Perhaps for someone who's known how since he was eight."

"Five."

"Exactly my point."

Henri studies her. "How does a woman reach adulthood and not know how to ride a bike? It's a mandatory part of childhood."

She glances away, avoiding his gaze. "Not everyone grew up with wealthy parents. When you're the youngest of six you're lucky to have clean bathwater, much less a bicycle. It didn't exist in my world. And I never knew it should have until many years after I left home."

Henri is abashed. Luxury is an odd thing. You don't know you have it until confronted with someone else's lack. He has always known he was wealthy—his father made sure of that, made sure it was *flaunted.* Every meal of his entire life has been either gourmet or damn near close. He has seen parts of the world most people only dream about. He replaces his wardrobe every two years. He has an expansive wine cellar. He can speak three languages fluently and is passable in two more. He is tall and handsome and has excellent teeth. He *knows* these things. Has always been thankful for them. But a bicycle? It's such a small thing. A signpost of childhood. Never once in his life has it occurred to him that there are people in the world who didn't have one. Until now.

"I am sorry," he says, "I didn't mean—"

"It's not your fault. You couldn't have known. Besides, it's a stupid little thing. Just a bicycle. It's not like a yacht or a topaz or a vacation home."

"No. Don't downplay this. Learning to ride a bike is a rite of passage."

Nancy Wake—no, Henri reminds himself, *Nancy Fiocca*—is the kind of woman who conquers the world. Fearless. Ferocious. Nancy is the sort of woman who bathes in a meteor shower. She is *not* the kind of woman who concedes to anyone. And yet, this time, she surprises him.

"Teach me," she says.

So he does.

*

"I hate it!" Nancy howls an hour later as she wobbles down the empty path. "Who invented this seat?"

"I believe it's called a saddle." Henri chuckles as he jogs along beside her.

"It is a device of torture. An anvil on my bloody pelvic bone. I may as well be sitting on the edge of a sword. I swear—I damn well *swear*"—and she does, throwing out an impressive string of invectives—"that this was invented by a man. The same one who created that damned cotton log known as the menstrual pad. I'll kill him with my bare hands if we ever meet." She teeters, and for one awful moment Henri thinks she's going to end up in the brush. "If I can ever walk again."

If Henri wasn't actually afraid of her in this moment, he would laugh. But his lips twitch, and she glares at him.

"I hate you," she says.

"No, you don't."

"I do, in fact, but we can argue about it later. I'm much too afraid of dying at the moment."

"If it makes you feel any better, bicycle saddles weren't exactly created for comfort when it comes to male anatomy either. As a matter of fact, when I was nine years old—"

She gives him a withering look and Henri decides that story is best left for another day. It's a good story, though. She'll laugh at his expense. "Go on, *ma chère*," he says, giving her another push down the gentle slope. "Let's see you ride this thing."

And she does, for thirty feet, before her front wheel hits a rock and she starts to teeter. Nancy digs the toes of her new leather pumps—highly impractical bike wear; he did try to talk her out of them—into the gravel, ruining them completely. She grinds to a stop and whips her head around to chastise him.

"You didn't fall and you are perfectly fine," he interjects before she can get a word out. "You are allowed to complain only when your knees and elbows are bloody. This is a mandatory life skill. No different than reading or writing."

"I hate you," she says again, but it's with a delighted grin. There's a light in her eyes that he hasn't seen before. Nancy presses hard, on the left pedal, and she's off once more. "And I will consider it entirely your fault if my lady parts are ruined beyond repair!" But this warning is shouted over her shoulder and Henri has to run to catch up with her.

* * *

GRENOBLE, FRANCE

October 1940

I step off the train and onto the platform of the Gare de Grenoble. In all the years I've lived in France, this is my first time visiting the famed medieval city. I am here to deliver one radio—currently disassembled and ensconced in my suitcase—three identification cards, and twelve food ration cards to a woman known only as Vivienne. We are to meet in four hours atop the Bastille and I will know her by the green feather tucked into the band of her red velvet cap.

Every day I think things cannot become more restrictive in the Free Zone, and every day I am proven wrong. A week ago the Vichy government signed into law a decree that declares all foreign-born Jews to be illegal immigrants. They are, without warning or chance of appeal, to be sent directly to Germany and housed in concentration camps. Garrow, O'Leary, and I cannot work fast enough. We cannot procure documents fast enough. When I grow tired and overwhelmed by the amount of travel before me, I remind myself that my feelings are nothing compared to those of the thousands of Jews running for their lives.

There is a nip in the air, but the sky is bright and blue and I look up to take in the perfect, cloudless magnitude of it. I ground myself in the beauty of a perfect fall day. And that is why I collide with someone directly in the middle of the platform. My first instinct is to grip the handle of my suitcase even tighter. My second is to apologize.

"Pardo—" The word catches in my mouth as I stare at the beautiful blonde in front of me. "Stephanie?"

Her hair is mussed. Her clothes are disheveled. She has been crying. And she is gripping the hand of the man beside her as though they are about to be ripped apart for all eternity.

It takes Stephanie a moment longer to recognize me. I can see her pull her thoughts away from whatever problem has so deeply upset her. She focuses on my face. Her mouth forms a gentle O. And then Stephanie Marsic releases the man's hand and throws herself into my arms.

"Ma petite!"

It is difficult to return the hug with one arm, but I must not release my package under any circumstances. I know better. I've heard the stories of men and women caught with contraband. Rumors are spreading that the Vichy police now consider listening to the BBC a treasonous crime punishable by death. This is France under German occupation.

"Nancy," she says, then steps back. She wipes her face with her sleeve and looks at the man she's traveling with. "This is my husband, Paul."

"Count Gonzales! How wonderful to finally meet you!"

I expected a *specimen.* A man of staggering beauty. But the man who stands before me is . . . normal. His hair is peppered with silver, his waist is a bit soft, and he's barely taller than his wife. Two days' worth of stubble covers his jaw. His nose is crooked. And his brow is furrowed in concern. He looks over my head, scanning for something. I don't know what I have said or done wrong, but I take a step back from both of them.

It takes a moment, but the Count finally extends his hand. "Pleased to meet you." The words are French but heavily accented in Spanish.

"Nancy is an old friend of mine," Stephanie says. And there is something in the tone of her voice that makes me wonder if she is telling him I can be trusted.

He looks between us for a moment, then gently kisses her on the forehead. "Why don't you grab a coffee with your friend? I'll get our tickets." He points to a small café across the street. "I'll be back in twenty minutes."

"Sí." Stephanie rises onto her tiptoes and plants a fierce kiss on his mouth. Then she grabs my hand and pulls me to the café.

Stephanie insists on sitting inside, in a far, dim corner. A waitress arrives the moment we take our seats, but we are informed that, due to a coffee shortage, they have only tea and ersatz. I detest the roasted acorn and hickory faux coffee but do not object when Stephanie orders us each a cup.

I have never seen her like this. So rattled. So . . . out of control.

"What are you doing in Grenoble? Of all places," she asks.

I set my suitcase beneath the table and I squeeze it between my knees. I open my mouth to answer, realizing at the last possible second that I cannot tell her the truth. This realization makes me suddenly, staggeringly lonely.

"I have come to meet Henri for the weekend," I say instead. If she were halfway paying attention she would know that I am lying. Stephanie knows me too well. But she hasn't paid attention to my answer. Her eyes are already on the door, looking for her husband.

I set my hand on hers. "Stephanie, what's wrong?"

Her fragile composure crumbles. She begins to sob, and I can barely hear the answer to my question. "We have to leave France. We have to escape."

"Why?"

"The Germans are after Paul. We are trying to get across the border into Switzerland."

This makes no sense. I shake my head. "Why not Spain? Surely—"

Her voice drops to a whisper. "No. We can't. Not ever again. If Paul sets foot in Spain, he will be arrested for treason."

I suppose that I've always had strong instincts. I wouldn't have made it in the world as long as I did on my own if I hadn't. But since I have been working with Garrow and O'Leary those instincts have become heightened. I can feel when a situation is *wrong*. Or dangerous. I clamp the suitcase tighter, then reach across the table and circle her wrist with the fingers of my right hand.

"What did he do, Steph?"

I don't know what to do with this new, weeping version of my friend. It's a struggle not to shake her by the shoulders as I wait for answers. I am growing impatient.

"He sold weapons," she says, finally, between sobs.

"To who?"

Stephanie Marsic looks up at me. Her eyes are red. Her lashes are wet. Her mouth is trembling. "Everyone. Anyone who would buy them. The Spanish at first. But then the French. The Germans too. He had an entire network built around smuggling them into Europe and selling them to the highest bidder. That's where his money came from. Every bit of it."

I can feel my fingers tighten on her wrist. I don't want to hurt her. I *force* myself not to hurt her. "Did you know?" I whisper.

"No." She shakes her head. "Not until last week. Not until we had to leave Paris."

"Why are the Germans after him?"

"He took payment for a weapons shipment two weeks ago but never delivered it to the Germans."

"What happened to it?"

"He sold the shipment to some Frenchman in the Auvergne instead."

I force myself to loosen my grip on her hand. I release my fingers one by one and set my hand on the table beside hers. "What Frenchman?"

"I don't know his name. Paul calls him a maquisard. Says he's gathering soldiers near Mont Mouchet to fight back against the Germans." She shrugs, and when her shoulders drop I can see every last scrap of hope she has left fall away. Her words tumble out uncontrollably. "Paul isn't a bad man. And I didn't know. He had a change of heart, at the end. He didn't care about the money anymore. And he didn't want to help the Germans."

Too bloody late, I think. If I said the words aloud they might kill her. If it were anyone else I would delight in the assassination. I would enjoy watching them writhe. But I cannot do that to her. Not to Stephanie. Keeping silent is the only mercy I can offer.

"Stephanie," Paul says from the doorway fifteen feet away. "Time to go."

I cannot look at him again. I refuse. I look at my dearest friend instead. "You don't have to."

She grabs my hand and squeezes it hard. Silent tears run down her face. She shrugs again but I'm not sure whom she's apologizing to. "I love him," she says, then kisses me good-bye on the forehead.

I don't look around until I hear the little bell chime above the café door. I catch a final glimpse of her bright blond hair in the October sun. It glints in the light, like a final wink, and then they are lost in the crowd. But I remain at that table, in the corner, breath caught in my throat because I am certain—as certain as I have been of anything in my life—that I will never see her again.

Madame Andrée

CHAUDES-AIGUES PLATEAU, CANTAL, FRANCE

June 5, 1944

The man in the armoire blinks three times, then says, "Oh. Hello, Nancy."

Madame Renard glances between us, then offers a short, approving nod, satisfied that I have not arrived for a nefarious purpose. She returns to her baking.

René Dusacq is an SOE operative by way of an American mother and a French father. I met him in London during my SOE training and he is not only a good friend, but one of the last people to see me off before I was flown back to France. Hell, he was the one who talked me into that third bottle of wine and was responsible for my wretched hangover on the plane. He kissed me good-bye, for Pete's sake.

"*You* are Anselm?"

He tucks his revolver into the holster strapped to his thigh and gives me a little bow. "In the flesh. You're not the only one who got a code name, you know."

I laugh. I can't help it. There is so much that London chooses *not* to tell us. Code names. Personal histories. Details of our fellow agents' assignments. All these things can be used by the Germans if we're captured. So, in many respects, we fly in wearing blinders, focused only on the task we have been given. None of that matters now, however. I throw my arms around his neck and give him a sloppy kiss on the cheek.

"I'm so glad you're here," I tell him. "We need your help."

Anselm has just arrived in country and has yet to make peace with the fact that half of the instructions London gave him prior to departure are useless. He sits in the backseat of Jacques's car, revolver in one hand, a thick slice of rum cake in the other, listening as I prattle on for a good ten minutes about how he needs to forget everything he thinks he knows about being embedded with the Resistance.

"I was told we'd be taking bicycles," he says in English.

"Everyone was. But they're practically useless unless you're a woman or in an urban area." I twist around and look at him in the backseat. "Did you keep your parachute?"

"No. I buried it. As instructed."

"Damn. I could really use one about now. The bugs are getting awful at night."

"Who's this?" he asks, motioning toward our driver.

"Jacques," I say. "And no, he never smiles."

"Does he speak?"

"Not often."

Anselm peers out the window. It is dark and Montluçon is going to sleep. We sit in the car, watching lights go off around the city.

"Why aren't we leaving?" he asks.

"It's safer to drive at night, without headlights. The fewer people who see or hear us, the better."

"I'm sorry? We'll be driving without lights?"

"You'll get used to it."

Jacques starts the Renault a little after midnight. He has a remarkable memory when it comes to back roads and byways and navigates the car with skill through the countryside. But, given our limited speed and vision, the drive back to Fournier's encampment takes twice as long as the one to Montluçon did. I've got the Sten gun in my lap and Jacques has half a dozen grenades beside him just in case we run into an unfriendly patrol. Anselm remains wide-awake, uncertain, and stiff as a board in the seat behind us.

We reach Fournier's encampment just after nine in the morning and I step out of the car, feeling twice as old as my thirty-two years. Various joints pop. My knees. My shoulders. My mouth feels as though I've brushed my teeth with sardines. I refuse to calculate how long it has been since I've washed my hair, but my scalp itches and that's never a good sign.

I look to my bus, eager for sleep, but notice that the camp is buzzing with activity. Soldiers are running hither and yon. People are shouting. Cheering. Hugging.

"What the hell?" I say, mostly to myself, as I make a beeline for Fournier's tent.

He's gone. So is Hubert.

I grab Louis by the sleeve as he trots by. "What's happened—" I ask, and then add, before he changes the subject, "Yes, I found your wife. Yes, she's fine. It looks like she'll have the baby in a week or two. Now tell me what the *hell* has happened."

"*It* has happened!"

"What has?"

"D-Day! The Allies have landed at Normandy."

"You can sleep in the car," I tell Anselm. "I've done it often enough myself. We'll find you a tent tomorrow."

I shuffle toward my bus and see that there is a note stuck in the door. I slide the paper out and unfold it, expecting to read a short missive from Hubert. What I find instead is a note from Henri Tardivat.

You're welcome. Also, I'd like my Sten guns now.

The sheet is on the house. It was yours to start with.

Besides, I did tell you to keep it.

—H.T.

"Surely not," I mutter, and push the door open.

I hurry to the back of the bus and there it is. My mattress, just as Tardivat promised. The two rear benches face each other, and the mattress sits nicely on top of them, supported in the middle by a wooden crate. Lying, neatly folded, on top, is my old parachute. Beside it are my wool blanket and my red satin pillow.

I've never been all that good at being a *girl.* A woman, yes. I've developed that skill in spades. But *girlishness* is a luxury I was never afforded as a child or a young woman. I had to grow up quickly. I had to adapt. But the older I get, the more I am brought up short by simple luxuries and basic acts of kindness. Especially here, in this place. I crawl onto the mattress, wrap myself in my old parachute—it does feel like a sheet—and lay my head on the little pillow.

It's happened. D-Day. Though in reality, we had no way of knowing if it ever would. So much depends on the winds of war and the SOE gives us very little information. No details of the broader military strategy. Dates, times, and locations that do not pertain to our mission are all kept top secret. And I understand why. If we are captured and interrogated, we could cost the Allies a victory. We know only the specifics of our own assignment: train, arm, and organize the Maquis for battle. Everything beyond that was a contingency based on the *hope* of an Allied invasion. But now that it has happened, the second phase of our mission has gone into effect and I wasn't here to see it. Overcome by exhaustion, disappointment, and the sense that I have missed the most important night of the war, I cry myself to sleep.

I wake to pounding on the door. The sun is high in the sky and hangs somewhere over the bus. Warm yellow light drifts in through the windows. I am still in the clothes I was wearing yesterday. My boots are still on. It takes a moment to realize that no, I have not gone blind in one eye—my beret has fallen over my face.

"Wake up, Duckie!" Denis Rake shouts.

"Bastard. Go away. This is a terrible time for payback," I mutter.

The door creaks open. "What's that? I can't hear you." And then, "What the *jolly hell* is that? Where did you get a *mattress*?"

What I try to say is "I stole and bartered for it," but what comes out sounds something more like "I farted in public."

"Are you drunk?" Denis asks.

"Oh, bugger off." That comes out clear enough.

"Listen, while you've been in here wasting the day, we've been getting news about the invasion. You're going to want to hear this. Get up."

We spend the rest of the day glued to the radios. News trickles in slowly but consistently.

"It came in last night, about four in the morning," Denis says. "It was just gibberish at first. A good hour of it. You know, the typical nonsense. 'The crocodile is thirsty' or 'You may now shake the trees and gather the pears' or 'Is Mrs. Munchkin ready to play a game of *boules* in the yonder dark forest?' Just all that garbage they spout every night as misinformation. But then it came. That one phrase. 'I wish I was by the seaside at sunrise.' And everyone *knew*."

I am so horribly sad to have missed it. Three and a half months we've been waiting for that very phrase. Gathering weapons. Organizing troops. Waiting to strike. The moment it went out over the airwaves, hundreds of Resistance leaders and Allied operatives, scattered from Marseille to Dunkirk, knew that the time had come to destroy whatever targets they had been assigned. Bridges. Towers. Tunnels. Trains or railways or ships. We have never been given exact numbers—that information is classified—but Hubert believes it to be hundreds of German-held targets.

Throughout the Auvergne, Gaspard, Tardivat, and Fournier, along with Hubert, are crippling the German military. Gaspard is cutting a series of underground cables the Germans use to communicate. Fournier is blowing up a munitions factory at Clermont-Ferrand while Tardivat does the same with one near Montluçon. Even Hubert has gotten in on the action and taken a dozen Maquis to Moulins, where sometime in the next few hours they will destroy a railway junction the Nazis use to transport troops and supplies throughout the countryside.

It is terrible of me, but I am jealous of my colleagues. I so badly wanted to participate in these acts of sabotage. I wanted to light fuses and throw grenades, to watch buildings, bridges, and tunnels crumble. I wanted the pure satisfaction of seeing our plan unfold. Because the next phase of our mission will go into effect the moment they are done.

Along with the weapons we use to arm our maquisards, London has also been dropping explosives into France. Collected and held, not just for today, but for a second influx of Allied troops in the coming weeks. I brought the lengthy target lists myself. Rolled up on tissue paper and tucked into the lining of my purse. Or, for the top secret ones, stored within the folds of my own brain. I personally assigned them to Fournier, Tardivat, and Gaspard.

I've missed so much tonight. It's as though a month of Christmases has come in a single night and I wasn't there to unwrap a single present. These are things I cannot say out loud, of course. It is selfish and stupid and vain of me to even think them. We've all been given a job to do and it is ridiculous to be jealous of anyone else's. I've done mine. For three months straight, I've done my job. Last night I collected Anselm and now our forces can be properly trained. My colleagues are all celebrating. They pass bottles of brandy. They cheer. And we all hover beside our radios, tuned to the BBC French Service. We hear about Normandy and the ships that crossed through unforgiving waters—well over five thousand, they are saying—gunwales brimming with Allied soldiers that have landed on the northern coast of France. Aeroplanes—hundreds and hundreds of aeroplanes—from the United States and the British Royal Air Force, dropping paratroopers inland at Normandy. And other planes behind them, bombers, roaring in to destroy the German coastal defenses. We hear of the ghastly blood-filled waves at Normandy. The countless bodies lying on the beach. And the tens of thousands of men who are even now pushing inland. Who are fighting back. Who are resisting the great evil that Hitler has unleashed upon the continent.

And now the real work begins. This is why we have come to France. Because the Maquis d'Auvergne is the only thing standing between the Hermann Göring Division—an armored mass of troops, almost twenty thousand strong and supported by the Luftwaffe, that, having ravaged Italy, is even now moving north from the Côte d'Azur—and the Allied soldiers at Normandy.

CHAUDES-AIGUES PLATEAU, CANTAL, FRANCE

June 10, 1944

"We have to get out of here, Nance," Hubert says, stretching out with an exhausted groan on top of my mattress. I'm tempted to tell him to go find his own bed but that would be cruel. He's been sleeping on the ground since March. "There are too many Maquis."

"The sky rains guns and the forest bleeds new recruits yet my partner complains?"

He cracks one eye and scowls at me. "With Fournier's troops, and now Gaspard's, plus all these volunteers, there are seven thousand men massed in these hills. That's twice as bad as what Gaspard did at Mont Mouchet. Mark my words, the Germans have noticed. We're practically begging for an ambush. We need to take Anselm, Denden, and our team and move west. Just far enough to where we won't get the full brunt of the next attack. We're no good to London if we go and get ourselves blown up."

"You're right. But we have an airdrop tonight at Strawberry. And another one tomorrow as well at Pineapple. And the day after that will be the daytime airdrop."

I have Hubert's full attention at this. He pushes up onto his elbows and looks at me. "London agreed?"

"Denis got word less than an hour ago. Two days from now we're getting one hundred and fifty planes, fifteen crates each. Everything we've asked for. In triplicate. It will take five fields and every man we've got to collect the shipment. The coordinates are in and we can't change them now. This one delivery will arm us to the teeth and ensure we can stop the *Boche* from marching toward Normandy. We can move west, but not for at least three days."

"Okay," Hubert says, and I can hear the drone of looming sleep in his voice. "But as soon as everything is collected and distributed we relocate."

"Agreed."

"Nance?"

"Yeah?"

"I have another group of recruits to interview and assign tonight."

"I figured."

"But I don't have to meet Fournier for another hour—"

"—and you want to nap where you are?" I try not to laugh.

"It's not that—I mean, yes, this bed is damned comfortable—it's just that I can't actually get up."

It's true. He looks like some enormous Great Dane stretched out on the mattress, limbs akimbo, already starting to drool from one corner of his mouth.

"Just don't get used to it," I say. Then I grab my coat and my pack and I'm out the door to collect tonight's shipment.

I pry open a crate the size of a small Volkswagen to find it crammed to the lid with no fewer than two hundred pairs of British army boots. It is five in the morning, I am freezing cold and exhausted all the way into my bones, but at least there is still a bright moon and we don't need torches to unpack this latest airdrop.

"About damn time," I mutter, tossing the crowbar to my feet and pulling out a brand-new pair of size elevens, fitted with laces, each boot stuffed with a pair of heavy wool socks. It's not much as far as uniforms go, but a quarter of our new recruits are arriving barefoot, so beggars can't be choosers. Besides, I've been requesting footwear for six weeks now, and it feels like nothing short of victory to have received exactly what I've asked for. I suppose London didn't consider them a priority until now, given that guns kill *Boche* but boots do not. Or at least not easily. One would have to have a German skull directly under one's foot and, in my experience, they don't willingly lie down in your path.

"Jacques! Come look at this!" I shout, drawing the attention of Fournier's favorite—and my newly commandeered—lieutenant. "Our volunteers will be British to their bootstraps!"

Jacques looks up from his position across the clearing and holds up one finger, indicating he'll be over in a moment. He's unloading a crate of his own filled with what appear to be four or five dozen Sten guns, and has begun the long, arduous process of degreasing them. Even from here I can see the thick, oily gunk on his hands. Tonight's shipment came in two hours late but was average in size. Fifteen planes with fifteen crates each. Each crate the size of a small vehicle, except for the last, labeled *Personal for Hélène.* It is no bigger than a hatbox, and I'll open it later, in the privacy of my bus.

The clearing is about the size of a rugby field and there are eighty men scattered about, working like fiends to unload the crates, clean and catalog their contents, and load everything on flatbed trucks. These are men whom Hubert, Denis, and I plucked out from Fournier's groups, chosen for their intellect, loyalty, bravery, and work ethic. Their one job is to accompany us to drop sites and prepare the fields. They light bonfires, gather crates and parachutes, unpack and clean the weapons, and distribute the supplies to each group as we have determined. Then, together, we do it all again the next night. Sleep has become a thing that happens in snatches—often only an hour at a time—stolen, most days, directly after lunch when the chaos is at a minimum.

Volunteers have been arriving by the dozens, every day, for the last month. Word of the Allied landing has spread to every crack and cranny in France, and able-bodied men stream from the woods like termites ahead of fire, wanting to be part of the famed Maquis d'Auvergne.

"They smell of m-m-mothballs," Jacques told me two nights ago as we carefully lifted mortars from a long, narrow crate and set them into racks on one of the trucks. As usual, the plateau was a good thirty degrees colder than the valley below. So we chewed on sugar loaf soaked in *eau de vie* to give us the illusion of warmth, and tried not to snap at each other. That's the hard part, not taking your misery out on your colleagues. In truth, the plum brandy does little to keep us warm, but it helps with morale.

"They've been hiding in closets the last four years," I said. "Trying to wait out the war. But now that victory is at hand they want to say they fought for their country."

Jacques may suspect the motives of these fair-weather friends, but I am happy to see them. Every new recruit must be interviewed, though, to ensure he's not a German double agent or part of the Milice, and then assigned to a group. This job falls to Hubert and has prevented him from joining me at the airdrops for several weeks. It's gotten so bad that Fournier has been assisting him. Only once the men have been approved and placed within an existing group do they come to me for weapons and ammunition. Then I pass them on to Anselm for training, both in their new service gear but also in the larger artillery and explosives we've begun receiving. The Maquis have affectionately begun referring to Anselm as "Bazooka," given his tendency to wax eloquent about that particular stovepipe-shaped weapon. The fact that he's been begging for, but has not yet received, any is no small source of irritation for him.

I look around the clearing, at the number of crates remaining and the exhaustion of our men, and know there's no way we'll finish by dawn, not with the late delivery and the low temperatures. We're all limp and battered.

"Jacques!" I call again, and this time he leaves his crate and jogs over to me.

"Oui?"

His bloodshot eyes are evident even by moonlight. "How many crates do we have left?"

"One hundred. M-m-maybe more."

I look at the horizon and squint. Sunrise will be on us soon. "Tell the men to finish the crates they're working on now and then I want you to send all but ten back to camp for some rest. Leave the others to guard the clearing. They can relieve the guards and resume work after a bit of sleep and some breakfast." I smack the crate beside me, twice, with the flat of my hand. "I want these boots, along with a crate each of cleaned rifles and revolvers, delivered outside my bus. Hubert has an entire group of one hundred new recruits for me to outfit."

"Oui."

He doesn't go so far as to salute me, but he looks as though he'd like to. He reminds me of Picon in his absolute loyalty and confidence in my abilities.

I stand and stretch, listening to all the various parts of my body pop and crackle like so much packing material. My hamstrings and the muscles that run along my spine are so tight and sore, I can barely straighten myself to my full height. My fingernails are black with gun grease. My hair is limp and filthy and smells like that of a teenage boy. And I am alarmed to realize that there is an odor wafting from my own person. Something has to be done.

"I will meet you back at the encampment," I say.

"W-w-here . . . ?"

He doesn't finish the question, but I know what he means. Jacques isn't being overprotective. He knows that Hubert is going to ask, and he wants to have an answer.

"To the hot springs in Chaudes-Aigues, and then for a quick sleep. I can't go on like this. I've not bathed in three weeks and I've hardly slept the last three days."

Chaudes-Aigues is a city of red-tiled roofs and old stone buildings set close together in a large valley accessible by the surrounding plateaus. It has narrow, sloping streets. One cathedral. A ruined castle. And, most important, hot springs. The renowned public baths are set into the side of a natural rock formation on the west end of town, and by the time I reach them I can barely stand, much less walk toward the women's side, pay an admission fee of three francs, and stumble to the dressing room. I am too filthy to go straight to the pools, so I set my pack to the side and strip naked, tossing my clothing beneath one of the many metal spouts protruding from the limestone wall like curled metal tongues, and pull the lever above it. Within seconds a stream of hot water is pouring onto my clothing, creating a dirty puddle and an unfortunate smell. I stand there, breathing the steam, until the puddle turns clear and runs off in one of the countless little gutters that have been carved into the floor. Then I take my turn beneath the spout and stand, head down, watching the grime run down my body.

It is worth noting that I am not one for public nudity—my own, or that of others. But these are special circumstances and there is a very large, severe-looking woman at the gate to the women's side of the baths. I doubt there is a Frenchman for one hundred kilometers in any direction who would dare to cross her. God forbid a German tried. The men's section is on the other side of the rock formation, and while there is a mixed area between the two, I have no intention of venturing anywhere near it.

Once I've stood under the spout for five minutes, I dig around in my pack for one of my most prized possessions: the bar of rose-scented soap that Buckmaster sent. I build up a lather and coat every inch of my skin, along with my hair. I repeat this three times until I'm sure there is no residue left on my body. Then I collect my pack and my pile of drenched clothing and walk into the spa itself. It's a large cave, open on two sides. Directly in front of me is a twenty-foot-wide bowl, carved out of the floor and filled with gently steaming water. Beyond that, through one of the openings, is a courtyard with another, larger pool. I choose the one in front of me for no other reason than it is closest and the thought of walking fifty extra steps makes me want to cry. Besides, there are fewer women in the bowl and therefore less chance someone will want to talk.

I set my pack and clothes on the lip of the bowl, then sit with a groan, and slide the rest of my body into the water. It is almost too hot but not quite, and I've adjusted in a few seconds. It smells of mineral and rock with the faintest tinge of sulfur. Somewhere in a corner there is incense burning and the floral scent of lavender covers up the more pungent smells of water heated by subterranean volcanoes. I make a mental note not to think of volcanoes. Lava. Explosions. Or the idea of myself getting boiled like so much raw chicken.

There are two other women in the bowl. An elderly woman whose breasts float on the surface like empty hot water bottles. They drift off in different directions, as though irritated with each other and needing a bit of time apart. The other woman looks like a younger version of the first and I decide they are sisters separated by at least a decade. The younger one has no breasts to speak of whatsoever. Or if she does, she's not comfortable flaunting them to family or strangers, because she's tucked herself into the water so far that it comes almost to her nostrils.

I let go altogether and slide under the surface. My hair floats around me in a dark cloud and I consider, for one terrible moment, that this wouldn't be a bad way to go if it came to that. At least I'm warm. And clean. Who cares if a volcano chose this moment to rumble to life?

This is what exhaustion does to me. I become maudlin. Bah! Get a grip on yourself, Nancy. What you need is a nap, not an early exit from what has been a perfectly exciting life.

I push to the surface and grab a bit of pumice stone from a pile beside the bowl, and I go to work on my skin. First my hands and fingernails. All those places stained by gun grease and dirt. Elbows. Knees. The calluses along the outside of my big toes. Five more minutes, that's all I give myself as I put the stone away and sit, eyes closed, feeling the water swirl around me, and then away as it moves on to wherever its natural course takes it.

Both women watch me as I climb out of the bowl and begin wrestling wet, and now cold, items of clothing onto my body. I imagine I must look rather like a drowned rat. But I'm more tired now than I was when I arrived, and I know there is no chance whatsoever that I'll be able to drive all the way back to Fournier's encampment before I pass out. So I stumble out of the bathhouse and into the street.

Two blocks down is a small inn with a vacancy sign dangling above the door. A couple hours of sleep, that's all I need and I'll feel better. It's close enough that I don't bother driving. Nor do I ask details about the rooms, other than which is available. The innkeeper takes my money, hands me a key, and points me to a room down the hall.

The only thing I do before throwing myself at the bed is open the curtains, peel off my clothes once more, and set them in a patch of early-morning sun to dry. Then I pull a soft, pink nightgown from my pack and crawl into bed, thankful once more that at least I can sleep like a lady.

I wake to the sound of gunfire. Rifles. My brain registers this before my eyes have opened. It sounds like a horde of irresponsible children have let off a bevy of fireworks. The air pops and crackles with the sound of it. And I think I'm getting out of bed. Or at least I'm trying to, willing my mind to move. But it isn't until I hear the first artillery shell that I'm actually moving.

Rip off the nightgown.

Scramble for my clothes. They are no longer dripping, but they are still damp, so I've been asleep only a short while. Underwear. Bra. Camisole. Pants. Belt. Shirt. All of it clings to my skin and takes five times longer to situate than normal. Have you ever tried pulling on wet socks? Well, you may as well crawl back in the birth canal for all the good it does. I give up after a couple seconds and pull my boots on without them. Then I grab my pack and double-check that it still holds my money, carbine, and revolver. Cram my nightgown and socks inside and I'm out the door, down the hall, and hurtling into the street and toward my car two blocks away.

As I run, I check the hills for signs of activity and am relieved to see that the smoke is coming from the direction opposite Fournier's encampment. But the Germans are headed that way and I have to get there before they do.

Lucienne Carlier

MARSEILLE

July 1942

"I hate the *Boche*," I tell Henri early one morning.

"Who doesn't?"

"They've ruined everything!" I throw back the covers and take a deep breath of humid summer air.

We sleep with the windows open now because we often wake to find that the ceiling fans have gone still in the night. The entire infrastructure of Marseille has collapsed in just two years. Unreliable electricity. Empty markets. Rationed gas. All the transport services have been run into the ground. The trams are broken. The taxis have been confiscated. The only thing that works are the trains, and they're never on time.

Henri pulls me closer beneath the blankets and drapes his leg over mine. I lie there for a moment longer, sweltering beneath him, until the dogs start whining to be let out.

"I'll get them," Henri says, planting a kiss on my forehead. He slides out from under the covers, and I watch him move across the room. I have always loved his back. The muscles that run along his spine. The way he walks, hips low-slung and steady.

"You're staring again," Henri says.

"Can't help myself."

"I'd be sad if you could." He covers his naked body with his robe, then leads Picon and Grenadine out of our room and to the front door of the flat.

The clever little things have long since learned how to go down the stairs, to the lobby, and out the mail slot in the side entrance. None of the other tenants seem to mind, and the arrangement saves us from having to walk them early in the day.

Henri returns to bed several minutes later and curls around me once more. "Where will you be today?" he asks.

I crane my head to look at his face. I search for a furrowed brow or pursed mouth and see neither. His expression is deceptively passive. "Toulouse."

"And *who* will you be today?"

There is no hint of worry in his voice, but I know it's there, regardless. For the last year and a half, I have been burrowing myself ever deeper in Resistance activities as he maintains the persona of an upstanding, impartial businessman. I have smuggled documents, radios, contraband, ration cards, and human beings from one end of the Free Zone to the other. I own three different identification cards. The real one, listing me as one Mme. Fiocca of Marseille; a second card—obtained from a loyal police official—also identifying me as Mme. Fiocca of Marseille, but conveniently omitting the fact that I am also a British subject, because nothing gets me stopped and questioned at a checkpoint more quickly than that bit of information; and a third, acquired with the help of Patrick O'Leary, that lists my name as Mlle. Lucienne Suzanne Carlier, the secretary to a French doctor.

"Lucienne," I say, and notice the briefest flicker of dismay in his eyes. This is the identity card I use when the work is particularly dangerous, when I need to keep Henri's identity safe should I be arrested and interrogated. "I only hope Monsieur Carlier will not be too worried while I'm away."

Henri answers carefully, "Monsieur Carlier has long since realized that worry does him no good. It will not stop his wife from leaving, nor will it guarantee her safe return."

We do not often talk of my work, so this bit of honesty cuts deep. *"Henri—"*

He sets one finger against my lips. "Monsieur Carlier prays instead. Constantly. For her safety."

I drop my cheek to his chest, relishing the feel of his silk robe against my skin. I listen to the strong thump of his heart beneath my ear and breathe in the scent so unique to him. He smells of clean sheets left to dry in the sun. Of brandy and citrus and pine. But something deeper as well, like he's walked through a room filled with pipe smoke.

He prays for me. What am I supposed to say to that? I have no idea. But I open my mouth and try to find something anyway.

"Don't," Henri says. "I never wanted a tame wife."

"But did you want a reckless one?"

"Are you being reckless?"

I answer honestly. "No."

"I didn't think so." Henri cups my face with his free hand and turns it upward so that we are looking each other in the eye. "I want you exactly as you are. Brave and bawdy."

I laugh. "I think you like the bawdy part best."

He begins the process of showing me exactly how much he likes my bawdiness, but there is a scratch at the front door followed by Picon's whine.

"We've got to do something about their timing," he mutters, sliding out from beneath the covers once more. "Don't move. I'll be right back."

I roll onto my back and stare at the ceiling as I listen to his bare feet pad across the wood floors. I have to be at the train station in two hours, so we have plenty of time to say a proper good-bye. I listen to the jiggle of the door handle and think of Henri's large, wonderfully shaped hands. I think of what they are about to do.

"Oh," he says. "Hello."

Henri's greeting is followed by a male voice speaking so low I can't hear the words. I push onto my elbows.

"She's in bed," Henri says.

I catch only three words of the response: "...get her...important..."

And then there is silence and I know Henri is standing at our door, arms crossed, face set in an expression of displeasure. It's something he rarely shows me, but I'm not out there right now.

After a moment of deliberation he says, "Come in. She'll be out in a moment."

I'm already out of bed, getting dressed in yesterday's clothes, by the time Henri walks back into our bedroom. He leans against the door frame and looks at me. "Watching you put those on is not nearly as fun as it was watching you take them off last night."

How do you tell your husband that you are sorry? That you'll make it up to him? That you wish this war hadn't swooped in and inhaled what should be the best years of your marriage? That you love him more than any other person alive and the only thing you really want to do is get back in bed and make love until you're both so spent that you fall asleep again? That you want this more than anything but you are still going to answer the door when trouble comes calling? I certainly don't know. I think Henri sees me struggle to find the words because he crosses the bedroom, moves my hair out of my face, and kisses me gently.

"Patrick O'Leary needs you," he says.

"And you?" I ask, finally.

"I am willing to share. For today."

O'Leary stands at our living room window, looking out over the harbor. His back is to us and he's tugging at his ear. For a moment he looks like a small, lost boy and I find this both endearing and frightening. I've never seen him look scared.

"O'Leary?"

He turns, watching Henri cross the living room and switch on the radio. This is our routine, long established, whenever I have company. O'Leary does not comment on Henri's robe or my disheveled appearance. Picon begins to whine again. He rises up on his hind feet and paws at Henri's leg.

"What's wrong?" I ask.

"Ian Garrow has been arrested by the Gestapo."

O'Leary walks me to the train station. Our heads are bent toward each other as we whisper. Anyone watching us would think we are friends, not lovers. And it is well known that Madame Fiocca has many friends.

"Where is he?" I ask.

"In Marseille. They are holding him at Fort Saint-Nicolas. For now." O'Leary has the most unnerving gaze of anyone I've ever met. He never seems to blink when he looks at you.

"For now?"

"They are moving him to the Mauzac concentration camp in the Dordogne after he serves ninety days in solitary confinement."

"How do you know this?"

"I know a man at Fort Saint-Nicolas."

"A guard?" I ask, hopefully.

"A cook."

"Any chance this cook owes you a favor?"

"I'm afraid it's the other way around."

"Hhhmm." I think for a moment but come up with no easy solutions. I'll have to figure out a way to contact Garrow once I'm done with this trip. "Where did they catch him?"

He hesitates before saying, "At the checkpoint a block from the train station."

The very checkpoint that I'm headed toward now. The one I must go through, with my fake identification card, before traveling on to Nice to collect the Jewish wife of an Italian lawyer and their three young daughters, to whom I will provide identification cards stating they are Spanish citizens living in Gibraltar. I am not so much worried about the woman and her daughters as I am the five downed British pilots who will also be traveling with us back to Marseille and then on to Toulouse, where I will pass them all off to Françoise, who will get them to the Pyrenees and into Spain. In my experience, British soldiers always look like British soldiers no matter where they are in the world. It's the mustaches, for one thing. But also the height and posture and the . . . the . . . *straightness* of them.

"On what grounds did they arrest him?"

"I think there is a double agent somewhere in our organization who tipped off the Gestapo and gave them a physical description of Garrow. So when he got off the train last night he was picked up immediately as a 'person of interest.' "

I take a quick breath through my nose and regret it immediately. The city has begun to smell like rotten fish in recent weeks. Most city services, including the formerly meticulous groundskeeping, have been halted. "Well, let's hope they find me less interesting than Ian Garrow."

"Not likely."

He says this so matter-of-factly that I give him a curious glance. "What is that supposed to mean?"

"It means," he says, "that my friend at Fort Saint-Nicolas says the Gestapo is also looking for a woman."

The train station is only three blocks away and the checkpoint only two. "What kind of woman?"

"One known as *la Souris Blanche.*"

"The White Mouse?"

He smiles sadly. "A woman known for smuggling contraband and people through the country."

"Why the nickname?" I ask.

"They know she exists but they cannot find her."

"And what else do they know about this white mouse?"

O'Leary leans closer and his voice is a whisper in my ear. "That she laughs often, is a British subject, and is known in the city as *l'Australienne de Marseille.*"

"Well, that's unnerving."

"Yes, but it's not all bad news right now."

"How so?"

"Have you heard about the *relève*?" he asks.

I nod. Last summer the Germans announced that they required three hundred and fifty thousand French workers to help man their industries. They want *us* to build the damn tanks and bombs they intend to kill us with.

"And your president—"

"—Pétain." I spit the word.

"Yes. Pétain. He has agreed to this."

"Traitor." I shake my head. "He tried to soften the blow by arranging for one French prisoner of war to be released by the Nazis for every three workers who go to Germany voluntarily."

"But your countrymen are not responding to the call," O'Leary says. "They are disappearing by the thousands. Slipping into the woods—the Auvergne, mostly—to live in small groups. They are forming an anti-Nazi outlaw group known as the Maquis. They intend to fight back."

"With what weapons? What leaders?"

His shoulders twitch. "Whatever they can find, I suppose."

I think of Stephanie, her husband, and their desperate escape toward Switzerland. I think of Count Gonzales giving his final shipment of weapons to a Resistance group instead of the Nazis. I think . . . I *hope* . . . that maybe, perhaps, all is not lost.

"We need to find out more about these groups. We need to help them if we can."

"Well, first we need to figure out what to do about Garrow," he says.

Patrick O'Leary drapes his arm across my shoulders and squeezes me to his side, once, firmly, before saying, "Be careful. Don't trust anyone. I am told that one of the people searching for *la Souris Blanche* is a woman." Then he falls out of step with me and turns a corner so quickly I don't have time to tell him good-bye.

I can see the checkpoint up ahead and I slow my breathing. I try to slow my heart rate as well but there's nothing to be done about that. The trouble, I think, is that I don't know how to not be me. I have never been quiet or temperate or demure. But thanks to O'Leary, I now understand that being *seen* could be a very dangerous thing.

I join the group of travelers moving through the checkpoint and do my best to keep my chin tipped down and my eyes focused on the middle distance. When my turn comes at the gate I hand my papers to the guard.

He flips open the cover, looks at my name, and asks in passable French, "Mademoiselle Carlier?"

"Oui."

"Where are you headed?"

"Nice."

"For?"

"Work."

He turns another page and runs his thumbs over the stamps. They are numerous. His eyes move on to me. My face. My chest. My waist. My shoes. "It says here you are a doctor's secretary."

"Oui."

He extends his hand. "Your purse. It must be checked."

This is new, but I hand it over regardless. "Of course."

I watch as he rifles through my personal belongings. Lipstick. Sanitary pads. Coin purse. Hairbrush. Finding nothing, he hands it back as I take a small breath, letting my ribs expand against the four identification cards I carry between corset and skin.

"I do wonder," he says, "how it is that a secretary, one who no doubt makes a low wage, is able to travel as often as you do, mademoiselle?" His eyes return to my leather purse, the gold bracelet at my wrist, and then to the hem of my dress. "Not to mention that your clothing is quite fine for a woman of such modest means. What kind of secretary are you, *exactly?*"

Merde. Putain. Merde. I'd say those words to him, and more as well, if I didn't think it would land me in prison right beside Ian Garrow. I throw a quick glance behind me, then take a small step toward the guard, doing my best to manufacture a blush.

"The, ah, very . . . *private* . . . kind," I say, adding a quick glance at him, up through my eyelashes, for effect. "I am on my way to meet my employer now."

He grins the base male smile I would expect of a Nazi guard. Then he stamps my card and steps aside. "Far be it from me to get in the way of another man's pleasure," he says, and it takes everything within me not to turn around and punch him when he smacks me on the ass as I walk by.

I call Henri at work from a café once I've arrived in Nice.

He exhales audibly at the sound of my voice. *"Ma fille qui rit,"* he says. "You are safe."

My laughing girl.

Oh, how devastated Henri would be if he knew that the laughter he loves so much now puts my life at risk. Is an omission the same thing as a lie? Have I crossed some Rubicon in which I keep things from my husband for his own protection? The thought makes me ill.

"I miss you," I tell him. I miss us. I miss the life we had before, the one we'll never have again because this war stole it from us.

"Noncee," he says, pausing, "there's something..."

I grip the receiver. "What?"

"This morning, when we let the dogs out..."

"Yes?"

"Did you see Grenadine come home?"

I lean my head against the wall and close my eyes. I rewind my memory to that moment lying in bed, hearing Picon scratch against the door and whine to be let back in. I sift through every memory after that, as though they are slides in a box and I am looking for one specific frame. Picon pawing at Henri's leg. Picon... just Picon.

"Oh no."

"Merde." Henri sighs. "I didn't even notice, not with O'Leary there. I should have noticed. I should have gone to look for her."

I gnaw at the inside of my lip. "It's not your fault. I was there too. Picon tried to tell me but I was too distracted."

"I didn't notice until I left for work," he says. "But I thought she must be asleep under a bed somewhere. So I went home again at lunch and Picon was frantic by then. I called Ficetole and we spent an hour looking for her. But nothing. I'm so sorry, *ma chère.* What do you want me to do?"

"Wait. Maybe she's just lost. Maybe she'll find her way back. But don't let Picon out on his own anymore." I know, even as I say these words, that it is wishful thinking. My cheeks are wet and I dry them with the back of my hand. I breathe through my nose. I clear my throat. "Meat is in short supply right now and the sausage makers are shameless. So don't buy sausages from any of the butchers this month."

MARSEILLE

September 1942

One of the realities of this new life I lead is that, whenever the entrance bell to our flat rings, I hide. If Henri is home, he answers it. If Henri is at work, I look through the peephole and swing the door open only if I know the person on the other side very well. This is one of the many small promises I have made to my husband in order to continue working with the Resistance. It is important to me that my husband be able to go about his life and work without worrying that I have been arrested and sent off to prison in the middle of the day.

Today, however, Henri is home, and he answers the door. Our bedroom door is propped open and I stand behind it, looking through the crack as Henri sets one eye against the peephole.

"Who is it?" I ask in a stage whisper.

"I don't know," he replies. And that is my cue to retreat farther into the room. I hear the front door creak open and Henri say, *"Bonjour. Comment suis-je t'aider?"* in a normal, friendly voice.

"Monsieur Fiocca?" the stranger asks.

"Oui."

"I have a message for your wife."

"From?"

"Ian Garrow."

Two trains of thought diverge in my mind. One: Garrow would never, under any circumstances, send a dangerous person to my home. Two: Garrow has been tortured for information and given me up to the Gestapo. I waver between these two possibilities, tottering back and forth between them like a woman on a high wire having to decide which side to fall from. I choose the first. Garrow is a lot of things, but he's not a coward and he wouldn't have offered my name to save himself.

Henri, knowing that I can hear, stands there and says nothing. He is giving me a few seconds to assess.

"How do you know Garrow?" I ask, stepping out from behind the bedroom door.

Seeing this, Henri moves aside and motions for the man to enter. Then he closes the door behind him. This is not a conversation to have within earshot of our neighbors. I motion for him to follow me into the living room as Henri goes to turn on the radio.

"My name is Arnal," he says, "and we were prisoners together in Fort Saint-Nicolas."

"Were?"

He sees the flash of fear in my face, rightly assuming that I believe he's come to tell me that Garrow is dead. Arnal takes a step forward to comfort me, but Henri stops him from moving closer by setting his palm against Arnal's chest.

Realizing his mistake, he raises both hands in a show of surrender. "Garrow is fine. As well as he can be under the circumstances. I served my time and was released this morning."

"Why were you in Fort Saint-Nicolas?"

"I own a chemist's shop in Toulon and the Gestapo caught me selling medicine to a Jewish woman with a sick child."

"How long were you there?"

"Six weeks of solitary confinement, in the cell beside Garrow's."

"What is his message?" I ask.

"There are two, actually." Arnal looks down at Henri's hand, where it still rests against his chest, then back at his face. "May I?"

Henri drops his hand and Arnal walks toward me. Then he wraps his arms around me in a rib-bruising hug followed by a sloppy kiss to each cheek. I don't dare look at my husband for fear of what I might see on his face.

"Thank you," Arnal says. "For the food and the whisky."

Henri snorts. Even he can't help but find this funny. "You sent Ian Garrow whisky? In prison?"

"Well, he *is* Scottish. Besides, I put it in a half-full bottle of cough syrup. I'm sure that ruined the whisky but I figured Garrow would get use out of it."

"Those packages you send every week are keeping him alive. He wanted you to know that. And I thank you as well because he shared what he could with me through cracks in the wall. It's a hard way to get a full meal but it works if that's all you have."

Hearing this is such an enormous relief. I've had no other way of knowing whether my packages are being delivered.

"What is Garrow's other message?"

Arnal's face turns somber. "He is being transferred to Mauzac next month."

"I know. I've been trying to find a lawyer who will file an appeal."

We are behind closed doors but Arnal leans in anyway and whispers, "If that fails there is a prison guard at Mauzac—a French national—who is open to bribery."

I grab the lapels of his shirt. "What is his name?"

"I don't know. I've only heard rumors. Hopefully it won't come to bribery. Mauzac is a hellhole that I would not wish upon my worst enemy."

BERGERAC

November 11, 1942

Taking a page from the Nazi playbook, the officials in Vichy decided to create a concentration camp of their own. They named it Mauzac and built it on the banks of the Dordogne River, twenty-four kilometers from the nearest train station in Bergerac. Getting there from Marseille requires a strong motive and an entire day of my life. I take the Bordeaux express from Marseille to Toulouse, but transfer at Agen to the Périgueux train, then I connect, a short way down the tracks, to the Sarlat-Bergerac line. From Bergerac it will be tricky to get to the miserable camp housing my friend.

Arnal was able to tell me nothing about this guard I might be able to bribe. Word has gotten out and the man takes great pains to keep his identity a secret—not that I can blame him, it's the firing squad if he's discovered—so I arrive in Bergerac with little in the way of a plan. I rent a bicycle for the weekend and ask around for the recommendation of quiet lodgings with a good view and privacy so I might spend a leisurely weekend painting. I pat the shoulder bag I carry to indicate that I've brought my supplies with me. I am told there is a wonderful old inn several kilometers north of Bergerac that sits on a cliff overlooking the Dordogne River but that it is too close to the new Vichyiste concentration camp. It is recommended that I secure lodgings in town instead. I agree that this is the wiser course of action and, as soon as I part ways with this stranger, get on my bicycle and go straight to the inn he mentioned.

Mauzac is only five kilometers from the inn, so I make the trip on foot, enjoying the chance to stretch my legs after such a laborious train ride. The camp itself is little more than a series of hastily constructed wooden buildings surrounded by a tall barbed-wire fence and protected by four dozen armed guards. There are groups of prisoners huddled together on the other side of the fence talking to one another, and I have to walk right by them to get to the camp entrance. I can feel their gazes on the back of my neck as I pass. I can hear the whispers increase and then, several minutes later, the unmistakable sound of someone whistling "Auld Lang Syne."

I do hum a bit under my breath, delighted that my clever friend has been on the lookout for me. "Should auld acquaintance be forgot…"

I reach the entrance to the gate and hand over the card identifying me as Mademoiselle Carlier. Because this particular camp is operated by the French and houses mainly French citizens—who at least maintain the semblance of legal rights—the rules are slightly different than in camps operated by the Germans. Security is less strict and visitors are allowed during certain hours.

"Who are you here to see?" the gendarme at the gate asks.

"My cousin."

"And what is his name?"

"Ian Garrow."

The man looks me over and shakes his head. I purposely dressed the part of Marseille socialite. I need to look pretty and clueless and very wealthy because there is one guard, somewhere in this camp, who needs to believe he can get money from me.

"You have thirty minutes," the gendarme says, letting me into the central courtyard.

There are only three other people visiting prisoners today, all of them old women weeping against the fence as they talk to younger men I assume to be their sons. The courtyard is the size of a small parking lot and there are two guard towers that overlook the happenings below. Three other guards patrol the courtyard, rifles up and resting against their shoulders. None of them are much to look at. All of them have the shifty look of men who know they've thrown their lot in with the wrong side. One of them has a harelip that was mended badly at some point in childhood, leaving him with a permanent snarl. Two of them can't be over twenty.

Based on the whistle I heard earlier, I assume that Garrow will find me, so I drift to the nearest fence and wait. He is there, five minutes later, out of breath but grinning like a fool.

He presses his face against the wire and I say, "Hello, cousin!" then do my best to kiss each of his cheeks through the wire.

"I knew you'd come," he whispers. "I knew it."

"Well, being here and being able to do anything for you are two very different things, but I will certainly try." I tell him quickly—and as quietly as I can without attracting suspicions—what I learned from Arnal.

"I've heard nothing about a friendly guard," he says, tapping a fading bruise beneath one dark and sunken eye. "And I certainly haven't met any."

"Well, if I can't find him then I'll make sure he finds me."

"Is that why you're dressed up like that?"

I grin. "Excessive, isn't it?"

"You look ridiculous," he says, returning my grin. "But I'd say you've announced your presence."

"It's a terrible plan but it's all I've got. We'll just have to trust that Arnal heard correctly."

Garrow asks me about Marseille and our friends in couched language and I answer him in turn, careful to say nothing that would incriminate either of us. As the minutes tick away his face gets the pinched look of a man racing the buzzer and I realize that he is scared to be left alone in the camp again.

A short time later the long, metallic shriek of a whistle sounds from one of the towers overhead and Garrow pulls away from the fence.

"Changing of the guard. Visiting hours are up."

"How do the guards come and go?" I ask.

"Lots of ways," he says, nodding at a string of vehicles making their way down the dirt road I've just traveled. We watch as they pull up to the prison and park outside the fence. "Most of them walk or ride bicycles. But some have vehicles."

"I'll keep an eye out then. I leave on the first train Monday morning, but I'll be back tomorrow. In the meantime, I'll see what I can learn about our friend."

I follow the three older women out of the courtyard and watch them pedal away on their bicycles while I linger beside the fence, adjusting the strap on my shoe. Garrow and the other prisoners fall back to the buildings during the changing of the guard. I have stayed a bit longer than is safe, but I want to be seen by all the guards, those leaving and those arriving. I've done all I can for now, however, so I move to the shoulder of the road and begin the short walk back to my inn as vehicles begin to leave the camp, stirring up dust in their wake. When the final vehicle passes me, something hits my shoulder and I think, for a moment, that one of the tires has kicked up a bit of gravel. But then the thing drops on my foot and I look down to see a stone about the size of an egg with a note wrapped around it. I pick it up and slide it into the pocket of my skirt.

Only once I am back at the inn and safely locked inside my room do I read the note.

Lalinde bridge. Midnight.

On one hand I am elated. Arnal was right! On the other I want to throttle the bastard who tossed this note at me. Curfew is eight o'clock, Lalinde is twenty-five kilometers east of here, and I will have to make the entire trip in the dark, on bicycle.

The bridge at Lalinde is a broad, stout, stone structure spanning the Dordogne River. There are four arches and a low rail but it's not much to look at overall. The main problem, however, is that I am standing here, in the open, beneath a full moon. Anyone on the road at either end, or in the buildings that frame the river, can see me clearly. Me in my fur coat, nice dress, and Italian leather pumps. Me looking every bit the sort of woman who *could* bribe a prison guard if she *wanted* to.

It is cold, but not freezing, and my breath turns into little tendrils of fog as it leaves my nostrils. The water rolls steadily along beneath me, untroubled by motor or paddle.

I check my watch: 12:15.

Perhaps it was a trick? Or maybe a trap? But no, my gut says our friendly guard is testing his prospects. Lalinde is quiet tonight, her citizens having obediently tucked themselves in behind closed doors at eight. A few lights are on in the windows but there are no vehicles rumbling through the streets. No voices. This unnatural silence makes it easier for me to hear the footsteps at the end of the bridge.

Bumps rise along the surface of my arms but not from the cold. I can feel myself being watched as I turn toward the village, and see the silhouette of a man at the end of the bridge. He wears a trench coat and a hat. A lit cigarette is pinched between two fingers and he stands there, watching me.

He could be anyone. An average citizen like myself. Gendarme on patrol. The guard I've come to find. I say nothing and neither does he. But after several seconds he lifts the cigarette, takes a long draw, then flicks it to the ground and crushes it with the toe of his shoe. The man exhales and the smoke flows from his nostrils in two perfect streams before clouding together, then dissipating.

He nods once, turns on his heel, and walks away.

Well, fuck you too, I think. *Bastard. You made me come all this way for nothing.*

My train leaves for Marseille in three hours and I sit in a small café near the station sipping weak tea and wondering how I will explain this to my husband. I went to visit Garrow again this afternoon. He was waiting for me at the fence and I told him about the note and the mysterious figure on the bridge.

"It was a waste of time," I said. "I'm sorry."

"No. It's part of the process. He can't afford to get caught either."

"So he strings me along?"

"He makes sure you're serious."

"I am *seriously* angry for being dragged out in the middle of the night and having nothing to show for it," I hissed.

"Try again when you come back," Garrow said, then dropped his eyes to the ground. He stared at his feet for a moment. When he looked at me again his cheeks were burning. "You *are* coming back, aren't you?"

There was nothing I could do to comfort my friend other than slide my fingers through the fence and set them over his hand. "Of course."

Henri won't like it. He didn't want me coming here in the first place. He *begged* me not to leave. But what was I supposed to do? Leave Garrow to die in this godforsaken outpost? No. I can't. If I were the one who'd been arrested, I would want my friends to do everything within their power to secure my freedom.

"Merde," I mutter now as I poke my tea bag with one finger. The cup is chipped and stained, and the water is lukewarm. Tea is just another pleasantry that I seem to have lost the taste for.

"Such an ugly word for such a pretty mouth," a man says, dropping into the seat across from me. He's got a cigarette pinched between two fingers and he takes a puff, blowing the smoke into the air between us. His harelip is even more distinctive close up and I am mesmerized by his twisted mouth.

"You," I say.

"Expecting someone else?"

"I didn't know what to expect." This isn't entirely true, of course. If I'd had to put money on it I would have bet on the gendarme at the gate. I make a note to pay more attention in the future.

Harelip looks me over, assessing. There is nothing lewd in his glance. He's trying to determine what I'm worth. Finally, he makes a guess.

"Five hundred thousand francs for the Scotsman," he says.

"I don't understand."

"Sure you do. And don't bother saying you don't have the money. You're practically *dripping* money."

"I only have ten thousand francs on me."

We stare at each other for a moment in silence.

"That's a pity," he says, "because I require a deposit of fifty thousand."

"You make a lot of demands for a man who hasn't assured me of anything."

"I can assure you, madame, that if you want your friend out of Mauzac, I am the only person who will do it. But my price isn't negotiable. You have five hours to meet me back here with my deposit or we will never speak again. And what's more," he says, "should you ever visit the Scotsman again, I will tell the prison authorities that you tried to bribe me."

"That's not enough time. My train leaves in three hours," I say.

"Then you have two and a half."

I watch Harelip leave the café as I swallow the remainder of my cold tea.

Damn. Damn. Dammit. I have no choice but to call my husband.

* * *

Henri

There is a clicking noise when Henri picks up the phone, like someone is flicking a fingernail in his ear. He taps the receiver three times on the heel of his hand and then says, *"Henri Fiocca a l'appareil."*

"Hello, love," Nancy says.

"Noncee." His voice is a purr. He can't help himself. "How has your weekend gone? Done any brilliant painting?"

Again with the clicking, only longer this time. Henri holds the receiver away from his face and looks at it, his jaw clenched.

"What's that?" he asks after a moment. "I didn't catch what you said."

"It's been perfect. I got exactly the landscape I came for."

"Wonderful! When will you be home?"

"Tonight. But…"

"What?"

"Well—" She laughs, but it sounds forced, and even from this distance, on a clicking line, he knows something is wrong. "It seems I've gone over budget at my hotel and I need you to wire some money so I can pay my tab."

"Of course. How much?"

He hears her take a deep breath, then hesitate. "Forty thousand francs."

"*How* much?" Henri asks.

She repeats the sum. "I only brought ten with me."

"I..." His voice trails off. He grunts twice, editing out the questions he would like to ask. What has she gotten herself into? What the hell is going on? What has gone wrong?

"I have never asked you for anything," Nancy says.

"Have you forgotten the ambulance?"

"That was for a good cause. But I see your point. I have never asked you for *money.*"

"It's *our* money. You don't have to ask me for it."

"And yet here we are," she says, and Henri winces. She has always been touchy about this.

Henri leans back in his chair and looks out over the harbor. Yachts bob in the water, their sails furled tight against their masts five stories below him.

"Henri? Are you there? Are you angry?"

"*Non, ma chère.* Of course not." *I am terrified for your safety,* he thinks but does not say aloud, because the clicking has begun again and Henri Fiocca now understands what is happening. His phone line has been bugged. "I will wire it to the post office immediately. It should be there in an hour. I am delighted you've enjoyed your stay. And I cannot wait to see what you've painted. I love you."

"I love you too! Thank you, Henri. Thank you!"

He sets the receiver into its cradle and leans away from the phone, as though it might bite him.

"Merde," he says, then adds in English, on behalf of his wife, "Bloody hell."

Henri lowers his face to his hands and shakes it back and forth.

"Something wrong?"

The female voice startles him and he looks up to find Marceline standing in the door of his office. She is wearing a gray dress and a bright smile.

"What are you doing here?" he asks.

Marceline takes this as an invitation. She steps into his office and closes the door. Wanders through the room, looking at things, touching things. Finally, she sits on the edge of his desk, crosses her legs, and picks up his pen.

"I just stopped in to say hello," she says.

It's a lie and he knows it, but he does not want to argue with her. "Why?"

"We're friends, aren't we? Friends are allowed to do such things."

Henri doesn't want to debate the definition of friendship with this woman, so he says, "I'm working."

"It sounded like you were arguing with your wife."

"I wasn't. But it doesn't matter. Because you shouldn't have been listening to my conversation."

"It's not my fault you were shouting."

"I wasn't—" Henri takes a deep breath and glares at her pointedly, about to order her out of his office, but then he sees the gold necklace hanging around her neck. "I wish you wouldn't wear that."

She pinches the *H* between two fingers. "Why not? You gave it to me."

"A long time ago. When we were—"

"Lovers?"

"Young." He is exhausted. "What do you want?"

"To see if you're hungry."

"I'm not."

She scoots closer, dislodging a pile of papers. "Thirsty?"

"No."

Marceline reaches for his tie and loosens the knot. She looks at him through lashes heavy with mascara. "Lonely?"

Henri knocks her hand away and stands up. He pushes his chair back and steps around his desk.

"I don't understand what happened to you. There was a time you loved going to bed with me," she says, and her mouth twists into a jealous pout. "She isn't even French. Don't you miss our lovemaking?"

"No," Henri says. He doesn't have the time or interest to play Marceline's games. "Unlike you, my *wife* has curves *and* a heart."

He grabs his coat and walks to the door.

"Where are you going?" she demands.

"None of your business."

* * *

BERGERAC

I buy a newspaper and apply a fresh coat of lipstick before walking to the post office. It's a small building with a counter running the length of the lobby and a man standing behind it. The postmaster is entirely bald and has the arrogant look of a former military officer.

"I've come to collect a wire transfer," I say, approaching the counter. "For a Madame Fiocca."

"You have papers?"

I hand them over, and he takes longer than necessary to inspect them.

"Forty thousand francs is a large sum of money for a Marseille housewife visiting Bergerac."

"What business is it of yours?"

"Vichy business. I am under orders to report all large money transfers."

I lean against the counter, allowing him a good glance at my face and the absolute lack of concern I feel regarding his suspicions. "Well, I suppose that forty thousand francs would seem like a great deal of money for a man on your salary, but it is nothing to me. I've had bigger bar tabs than this."

The postmaster reaches behind him and pulls an envelope from one of the slots. I make a show of spreading it out and counting it. Then I tap the bills together, slide them back into the envelope, and say, "I will be making a formal complaint about your actions to the main post office in Bergerac. How dare you harass an innocent Frenchwoman for the crime of going about her business?"

He flinches and I take the win. A guilty woman would scuttle from his presence, whereas an innocent woman, wrongly accused, would be indignant, so that's what I let him see. I believe that the only way I can convince him of this part I'm playing is to believe it myself.

Nose up, hips swinging, I walk out the door, slamming it as I go. I pause in the street, taking note of my heart rate and my breathing. Only slightly elevated. I'm getting better at this. A glance at my watch shows that I have less than fifteen minutes to get to the café and complete this deal with Harelip or I lose the chance to rescue Garrow.

I make a quick trip to the ladies' room so I can count the money and tuck the envelope inside the newspaper I bought. Then I freshen up. My eyes are bright and my cheeks are flushed, but neither looks out of order for a society lady about to make a shady business deal. I return to my earlier table and wait.

As he was on the bridge last night, Harelip is late. But not quite so late that I'll miss my train. He slides into his chair and looks at me.

"Well?"

"Only bad news, as usual." I slide the newspaper across the table and tap a headline declaring food shortages across the country.

"I thought that was the case." Harelip tucks the rolled newspaper into an inside pocket of his coat. "Meet me back here in four weeks—"

"That's a long time—"

"—not if you want people to forget the pretty lady from Marseille who collected a lot of money at the post office." He glares at me. "Like I said, four weeks. Bring the rest of the money and a prison guard's uniform."

Harelip walks out of the café and I count to one hundred before following him and turning toward the train station. I arrive just as it begins boarding and I go through the hassle of showing my papers and ticket. The Sarlat-Bergerac line does not have a first-class carriage, so I board with all the other passengers and we step onto the train, only to find that it is already half-filled with German officers. I hesitate only one half step before finding a seat next to an elderly man with a book on his lap.

"What's going on?" I whisper.

The old man closes his eyes and leans his head back against the seat as though going to sleep. His lips barely move as he answers, "The Allied forces have arrived in North Africa. So the Germans are tightening security throughout the Free Zone."

Madame Andrée

CHAUDES-AIGUES PLATEAU, CANTAL, FRANCE

June 10, 1944

"Where the hell have you been?" Hubert shouts the moment I throw open the door to my bus.

"Bathing. And be glad for it, otherwise I'd be far less pleasant to deal with right now." I point back out the door. "Where is everyone?"

"At their battle stations. They left the moment we heard the first shots." He takes in my wet clothing and damp hair and shakes his head.

"Who's taking fire?" I ask.

"Several of Fournier's groups to the east. He went to back them up."

Denis Rake seems to have taken up permanent residence in my bus. His radio is set right in the middle of my stump and he's got the receiver to one ear, listening intently. Every few seconds he lifts his right hand and taps out a frantic message, then bends his ear to the receiver again.

"So?" I ask. "What have we got?"

"Armageddon," Hubert says. "Our scouts are reporting roughly twenty-two thousand *Boche.* They say all the paths and roads are crowded with Germans and that they're supported by almost a thousand vehicles, including tanks and armored cars, all of them armed with artillery and mortars. They've also got ten aircraft circling the southeastern rim of the plateau and heading toward us."

"When did they approach? And why didn't we see them coming?"

"They came in during the night, infantry first, and picked off some of our scouts. By the time we heard the vehicles it was too late." Hubert shakes his head, furious. "I told you it was only a matter of time."

Denis hasn't said a word through all of this. He's kept his eyes down and is tapping furiously at his radio. "What's he doing?" I ask.

"Trying to get through to London. We have to cancel the airdrops. There's no way we can receive them while under attack."

Hubert stands up, straps his revolver to his thigh, and walks toward the door. "Where are you going?" I ask.

"To confer with Gaspard. Based on what I'm hearing, Fournier is already losing ground and I want us all to be on the same page if we have to retreat."

I didn't get enough sleep. Not anywhere close to enough, in fact, and I can feel the exhaustion claw its way back into my bones.

"How long before we can expect word from the others?" I ask.

"A couple of hours," Denis says.

"Okay. I'll be back."

"Good grief, where are you off to now, Duckie?"

"Strawberry Field. I've got containers to unload and deliver. I can't just leave them sitting around for the Germans to confiscate in case they take the plateau. And besides, that might be the last shipment we get for a while and we're going to need every bullet. You keep trying to get through to London."

It takes twenty minutes to reach Strawberry Field and the sight that greets me almost brings tears to my eyes. Jacques and his men are hard at work emptying the crates. I don't know whether they left when I told them to or they stayed, and I don't ask.

"I could kiss you!" I say as I find Jacques beside a crate of cleaned and stacked Sten guns.

"Your h-h-husband would n-n-not like that," he says without looking up.

"He'd understand, given the circumstances."

Smiles are few and hard-won where Jacques is concerned, but he graces me with one now. "My wife w-w-wouldn't."

Then there's nothing for it but to get to work. We finish unpacking the remaining crates and put the weapons in working order. It takes three hours but soon there's nothing left in Strawberry Field except a pile of crates, and those are promptly burned. All the weapons are loaded onto flatbed trucks and each man is given instructions on where to take them. Jacques takes five men and drives the heaviest artillery to Fournier and his men at the front. I take the position closest to the encampment and drive to where I can see a group of men, led by the fingerless Louis and Anselm.

Once they've helped me unload all the arms and ammunition, Anselm gives me a sloppy, unapologetic kiss on the forehead and thanks me. He's like a little boy let loose to play in the mud.

Louis's group has an oncoming section of Germans pinned down in the valley below. They're taking heavy casualties amidst the volcanic rocks as Louis and Anselm rain down on them with Sten guns and mortars. The entire valley booms and rattles as though some small boy has been left to destroy a set of drums.

I'm just about to congratulate them on their work when a boulder, five yards away from us, explodes. I stumble backward and shield my eyes from the bits of rock flying in every direction.

"Keep your eye on their fire!" I shout. "That was too close."

Anselm looks around, eyebrows pinched together. "Did you come alone?"

"Yes. Why?"

"Where's Jacques? Why isn't he with you?"

"Because he's taking a load to Fournier, off that way," I say, pointing down the valley to the left of the Germans below us. "Besides, I can take care of myself."

"I know! I know. I just . . . shit . . . Nance. London will murder me if you're killed. Please get back to camp. I'm assigning someone to look after you."

The thought makes me laugh. Like I need a babysitter! "Oh, Bazooka," I say, using the nickname that I know irritates him, "I didn't know you cared!"

"Whatever. Just scram!"

As I drive away I notice that the shelling becomes heavier, and I worry that Louis will end up with some new body part blown off and I won't know how to explain that to his wife.

Denis is still glued to his radio when I arrive back at the bus.

"Got through to London yet, Den?"

"Yes. I've canceled the airdrops for tonight and tomorrow. And they've given me a time to radio back if we need another transmission. But there's more."

"What?"

"Hubert came back. He met with Gaspard and was told that it doesn't matter what we decide, he has no intention of withdrawing."

"Where's Hubert now?"

"Gone back to try and talk some sense into him again. Fournier has agreed to pull out at nightfall. We're meeting in Fridefont and then heading out in individual groups. Our rendezvous point is Saint-Santin, a hundred kilometers away."

"Merde," I hiss. *"Gaspard l'enculé!"*

"I'm afraid to ask what that means."

"It means Gaspard can shove the next red-hot poker he finds up his own arse," I say. "It's not our job to fight to the death. Fight, yes. But fight to live another day. This war could last years. If Gaspard and his men die stupidly on this hill, we'll be crippled."

I didn't even have the chance to comb my hair after bathing and it has dried in clumps against my skull. I rake my fingers through them now, thinking. "Den?"

"Yeah?"

"When you get through to London next, I want you to request that they order Gaspard to withdraw. Ask that they apply leverage through de Gaulle's Free French forces. That's the only authority he feels answerable to."

"Think that will work, Duckie?"

"It better. If Gaspard won't take direct orders from de Gaulle, he won't take them from anyone."

By now I am so exhausted that I can't take another step. I throw myself onto the bed at the back of the bus and groan. It feels as though all my muscles are separating themselves from the bones, like they're peeling away in revolt. I try to count how many hours of actual sleep I've gotten in the last seventy-two hours and come up with five, but that seems wrong. It seems impossible. How can anyone survive on so little sleep?

"Really?" Denis asks. "You're sleeping in this ruckus?"

"At this point I could sleep anywhere. I just need a kip, or I won't be able to function at all. Wake me when you get through to London."

Denis doesn't argue with me again, so I take off my boots and both revolvers. I loosen the belt on my trousers. The only thing that could keep me awake right now would be an armed German soldier right in front of me. Even then it might take Obersturmführer Wolff. I am asleep before I can even begin fantasizing about putting my knife against his throat.

I'm woken sometime later by a gentle nudge from Denis.

"We've got it, Duckie!" he says, and I don't miss the triumphant note in his voice. "London has given the order for Gaspard to evacuate!"

I'm up, then. Boots on. Belt tightened. Revolvers strapped in. "Let me see it."

He hands me the message and I read it carefully. "Will you do something for me?" I ask.

"What?"

"Type it again and this time sign it Koenig."

Denis blinks at me a few times. "As in Marie-Pierre Koenig? De Gaulle's second in command? *Why?*"

"Because if we sign it de Gaulle, Gaspard will know we're bluffing. But he respects titles and authority—at least French titles and authority—and an order from Koenig should do the trick."

Denis bends over his machine and begins typing. "And I suppose you're going to deliver this to him?"

"I wouldn't miss the chance to see Gaspard back down for anything."

I am a bit sad to abandon my bus, particularly my mattress, but time is of the essence. I grab my pack and the little crate that came through in last night's shipment and I say good-bye to Denis, who is leaving to meet up with Jacques, then head to our rendezvous point at Fridefont. I watch him load his Renault with radio equipment and speed away from the encampment. And then I'm off in the truck to put Gaspard in his place.

It's even more satisfying than I expected. Gaspard is a mile away, atop the plateau, and it takes only a few minutes to reach his group. I march past a visibly frustrated Hubert and offer him one sly wink before handing Gaspard the message with all the pomp and circumstance due such an official communiqué. He reads it, slowly.

"Koenig," he whispers, in awe. Then he looks at me and I don't see even the hint of suspicion in his eyes. "When did you receive this?"

"Less than fifteen minutes ago."

Gaspard turns to the horizon and squints at the sun. "We don't have much time."

And that is all it takes for the most stubborn man in all of France to begin giving the word for his men to retreat.

"We will see you in Fridefont tonight! Fournier will be waiting for us there," I say as I jog toward my truck.

"How the *hell* did you do that?" Hubert hisses as he trots along beside me.

"Just a bit of lying and forgery. All's fair in love and war, you know."

"Where's Denis?"

"With Jacques, on the way to Fridefont."

"Excellent! I'll see you there."

Hubert turns to his car and I turn to the truck I've been using all day, and before long we're both speeding through two separate clouds of dust along the ridge toward Fridefont. But Hubert has the advantage of a lead foot and the little Renault, so before long I've lost sight of him.

I make it no farther than the outskirts of Saint-Martial before I'm spotted by the German Henschels. I've been driving for several kilometers along the winding, exposed mountaintop road when I hear the incessant buzzing of a plane engine. Five aeroplanes zoom above the forest in front of me, skimming the treetops, headed for Gaspard's group. Then they pass over me with a roar and I gun the engine, trying to get as much distance between myself and them as possible.

A nervous glance in the rearview mirror proves that it was indeed too much to hope that they would consider me a worthless target. One of the aeroplanes peels out of formation and circles back. It swoops around in a wide arc until it's parallel with my truck and then accelerates. I watch the plane, knowing exactly what it's going to do. And there's nothing I can do to stop it. I have no one to fire on the plane and no good place to pull off the road. No cover to speak of whatsoever. The best I can hope for is to get farther into the valley, where it will be difficult for the Henschel to maneuver.

But it's too late. The plane is in front of me once again, barreling toward me, lower now. There is a ferocious roar and then machine-gun fire on the road fifty yards in front of me. I can see the sand pop up in the little puffs as it absorbs each bullet.

"Merde. Merde. Merde."

Terror is a strong thing. It comes upon you instantly and consumes all thought and reason. I cannot speed up or I will meet the gunfire sooner. I cannot veer off the road or I will find myself tumbling, ass over teakettle, down the cliff into the valley below. And I cannot slam on the brakes or I will give the Henschel a sitting target. Conscious mind paralyzed, I lift my foot from the pedal, and the truck slows down. Miraculously this does the trick.

The Henschel barrels toward me, firing, and the last spray of bullets stops just feet from the front of my truck as he roars overhead once more. And then I am gunning the engine, flying down the mountain road and into the valley. I have bought myself only a bit of time, however, because the Henschel has turned and is coming at me again. Only this time it's decided to make short work of me and is approaching from behind.

I can hear the screeching whine of the plane in a sharp descent. It levels out, lining my truck in its sights for a merciless strafing. I have thirty seconds at most and my overwhelmed, exhausted brain will not tell me what to do.

And that is when I see the young maquisard standing in the middle of the road in front of me, waving his arms.

"Louis?"

I slam on the brakes, spitting sand all over him.

"Get out!" he shouts. "Bazooka sent me."

One quick glance in the rearview mirror, and I've thrown the car door open. Louis grabs my arms and pulls me toward the ditch before I remember something.

"No! Wait!" I yank my arm out of his and run back to the truck, where my pack, Sten gun, and the package I received from London are sitting on the seat.

I hear the wicked popping of machine-gun fire. I smell exhaust and the harsh scent of gasoline settling into the air. I grab my things and throw myself toward Louis just as the clatter of bullets hitting metal explodes around us.

I am thrown none too gently into the ditch and then all the air is knocked out of my lungs as Louis lands on top of me. His hands cover my ears and his face is buried in my shoulder. My belongings are scattered on the ground in front of us. "What the ever-loving hell did you do that for?" he screams. "What is so important that you would risk your life to get it?"

I would like to explain myself, but he is heavier than he looks and my mouth flaps open and closed like a dying fish as my lungs struggle to expand. As soon as he rolls off of me the truck explodes and I am silenced, not by lack of oxygen, but by the giant fireball that roars a few measly feet above us. The heat is immoral, something straight from the first circle of hell, and I fear it will descend on us and burn us alive. But it's gone as quickly as it came, leaving nothing behind but the faint smell of burned hair. Louis won't need a haircut anytime soon.

"Quick," he says, yanking me to my feet. "We need to get to the woods. He's circling back around."

FRIDEFONT

By the time Louis and I reach Fridefont, our rendezvous spot has been abandoned. Given that my truck is now a burned-out shell on the side of the road, we had to make the trip on foot. And what should have taken two hours has taken fifteen instead.

"They left without us." I look around a clearing filled with nothing but crushed grass and cigarette butts.

"Not everyone." I turn to find Anselm emerging from the tree line. "Denden left with Fournier's group and Hubert with Gaspard's. Young Louis here was charged with making sure you arrived safely—though I daresay the two of you could have been a bit quicker about it."

"There was a bit of an incident," I tell him.

"I figured you were out there, courting trouble."

"It was the other way around, in fact. Trouble takes great delight in courting me. But we made it." I am pleased to see my old friend. "You stayed behind?"

He grins, and the effect is quite comical given that his hair is wild and his face so dirty it looks like he's been rolling around a coal bucket. "I did say I would make sure you were looked after."

I throw myself at Anselm and give him the tightest hug I'm capable of in my exhausted condition. "Thank you," I whisper.

I pull away when I hear Louis laughing.

"What?"

He's got his back turned to us, his face lifted toward the plateau we've just fled. "Think about it," he says. "The damn *Boche* are up there, wondering where the hell we are. They thought we were putting up such a bloody fight because they had us surrounded. And now they're wandering around the top of that hill, scratching their heads, baffled that a group of French farmers and factory workers evaporated into thin air."

"There'll be time for patting ourselves on the back later," Anselm says, picking at a scab on his chin. "We have to get to Saint-Santin and reconvene with the others. They've got a day's head start and a far better idea of where they're going than we do."

Louis shakes his head. "Not entirely true. I helped Fournier set up the river crossings. I know where to go."

Anselm squints at him. "River crossings?"

"The Germans patrol all the bridges along the River Truyère, along with any sections of the river that can be crossed on foot. For the most part it's deep and treacherous, with rapids and rocks at every turn," Louis says.

Anselm does not look encouraged. "Then how are we supposed to cross?"

"Fournier surveyed miles and miles of river along the plateaus, looking for the most dangerous crossing points, places the Germans would never think we'd be stupid enough to try. Then we installed layers of heavy stone slabs across the river at ten different points. They are buried eleven inches beneath the water's surface, so you can't see them from above. All we have to do is remove our boots, roll up our pants, balance ourselves with a walking stick—which we've kept in bundles at all the crossing points—and walk to the other side."

"I'll be damned," Anselm says. Then he motions to Louis. "Lead the way."

The river crossing is not quite as simple as Louis made it sound. Moss has grown across the rock slabs and, in our bare feet, they are slippery as greased ball bearings. But with only a few minor wobbles, the three of us make it across without falling in the drink. And a good thing too, because with all the spring rains and snowmelt higher in the mountains, the Truyère is moving at such a ferocious clip they'd likely find our corpses bobbing in the Garabit Viaduct two months from now.

"How far from here to Saint-Santin on foot?" I ask Louis once we're safely on the other side of the river.

"About four days," he says. "But only because we have to go south first, cross another mountain range, then loop our way north to avoid the German patrols. The Maquis have been separated into groups of fifty and are each taking different routes to avoid capture."

"Excellent idea," I mutter. "I wonder who thought of that."

We take a moment to put our shoes back on and arrange our clothing. I dig around my pack, looking for a bit of food, and find a half-eaten package of biscuits and three squares of chocolate that I share with Louis and Anselm. Sadly, after having risked my life to save that package from Buckmaster, it contained only tea, toothpaste, and two cans of sardines. Louis and I ate the sardines last night for dinner. Everything else is crammed into my pack.

"Ready?" Anselm asks.

"I suppose lying right here and sleeping for two days isn't an option?"

"Sadly, no."

"Then help me up."

SAINT-SANTIN

The German Luftwaffe crisscrosses the entire area during our four-day march. Sometimes they drop bombs, hoping to hit random groups of Maquis, and sometimes they scream low over the treetops trying to flush us out. I imagine it's harder for the larger groups to avoid detection, but we just stop and rest beneath a tree until they're gone.

We sleep beneath the stars, drink from streams, and eat what roots and herbs we can find this early in the summer. In desperation one evening I eat a handful of green strawberries that I find beside a creek, then spend the rest of the evening with a bellyache. The nights are chilly, and we huddle together for warmth. Finally, just after noon on the fourth day, mud-splattered and bug-bitten, we stumble into the Maquis encampment outside Saint-Santin. The entire area is thick with trees and the Maquis remain hidden from the German bombers beneath the sprawling canopy.

Gaspard is the first to spot us. I would have liked a bit of warning before facing him. I would have liked the chance to wash my face, brush my hair, and put on lipstick. However, I root myself to the ground, straighten my back, and stare him down as he stomps toward me.

"Salut, Andrée!" he shouts across the clearing. I see a flash of teeth and think, for a moment, that he's ready to bite. But then I realize he is smiling. In all the months that I have dealt with Gaspard, I have never once seen him smile. The effect is rather disconcerting. I take a step back.

He stands before me, nodding. "You were right," he says.

Then, before I can protest, he drops one heavy arm across my shoulders and guides me into camp. Gaspard says nothing else, but I think this is his way of communicating that he respects me, that we are comrades-in-arms. I'd shake him off if I didn't fear it would break this fragile truce. I need him to cooperate now more than ever.

Gaspard leads me to where Hubert is lying on his back, arms behind his head, fast asleep.

I kick Hubert's boots. "Wake up! This is no time for a nap."

He startles awake, takes one look at me, and leaps to his feet. Hubert is not an emotive man. He's not affectionate either. But he pulls me away from Gaspard and tight into his chest. "We thought you were dead."

"Ha! It will take more than a Henschel, a blown-up truck, and a bit of machine-gun fire to kill me. I'm made of sterner stuff than that, you know."

"I don't even want to know," Hubert says, throwing his hands up.

"Good. Because I'm too starving and exhausted to explain. What do you have in the way of food around this place?"

"Absolutely nothing."

"Haven't you radioed for provisions?"

"About that, Duckie," Denis Rake says. I turn to find him, hands stuffed in pockets, looking rather abashed. "I had to bury my radio and transmitter before we left Fridefont."

"Why the bloody hell would you do a thing like that?"

He greets me with a friendly kiss on the cheek. "Protocol, darling."

"What about the codes?"

"Chewed them into paste and swallowed them."

"Are you saying that we are a four-day hike from where London believes us to be, with no means of communication and no way to feed or continue to arm seven thousand French Resistance soldiers?"

"What I'm saying, Duckie, is that we are absolutely, catastrophically *buggered* without a radio."

Lucienne Carlier

GARE DE MARSEILLE-BLANCARDE

December 7, 1942

As the occupation has worsened, the daughters of France begin fighting back in their own way. For every ten German men who have poured into the Côte d'Azur, three German women have followed. Wives. Girlfriends. Lovers. All of them eager to escape the shambles of their own country and take advantage of the beauty and luxury of Marseille. The French hate these impostors, of course, and do everything possible to make their lives a living hell. Observing that most Frenchwomen go without hats, the officers' wives stop wearing them as well. Within days the women of Marseille rally and begin wearing hats again, but, determined to thumb their noses at the Hausfraus, they all stick green feathers—nicknamed *les haricots verts,* our rude term for the Germans—in the bands and walk, head high, knowing their rivals will not follow suit because, now, simply wearing a hat is to spit at the Third Reich.

However, the daughters of France save their deepest ferocity for fellow countrymen who choose to collaborate with the Germans. The men are categorically ignored—on the street and in the bedroom—which is considered to be a fate worse than death to a Frenchman. But it is the women who are found to be in league with the Germans who are treated ruthlessly. They are shaved bald and thrown into the streets with a swastika painted on their foreheads in red lipstick. It marks them as traitors on sight. A shameful excommunication.

I, for one, am delighted to see green feathers sprouting from every hat on the train station this morning. Sometimes we need to see that we are not alone.

"Why do I let you do this?" Henri mutters into my neck as we stand on the platform. I can feel the warmth of his breath against my clavicle as he curses, *"Tu me fais chier!"*

"You could tell me to stay."

"Would you?"

"No."

"Which is why I've made it a point to *never* tell you anything, *ma chère.*" He snorts, and I feel his whiskers scrape my skin. "You are determined to do this?"

"Yes."

"Then I won't try to stop you. Just come home. Or I'll never forgive you," he says, repeating what I told him not that long ago when he left for Alsace.

"Two days from now this will all be over, and I will be home again. I promise."

Henri tucks my hair behind my ears. He kisses the tip of my nose and hands me my train ticket. "Here. I've reserved you a return seat on the Bordeaux train. Be on it. *Please.* I don't know what I'll do if you don't step off that train on Sunday."

I set the return ticket in my purse and throw my arms around his neck. "Thank you. I love you. Kiss Picon for me. I know how lonely he is without Grenadine."

"Not half as lonely as I am without you."

This is what our farewells have become of late. Desperate attempts to say everything in case we never have the chance again. It's like heaving my own heart into an open volcano. I am doing this to *myself.* To him. I am choosing a life that has me teetering on the edge of disaster.

The whistle blows, and I step back. I blow Henri a kiss and leave him standing at the ticket booth, looking at me as though he has opened a vein right there on the platform and his very lifeblood is draining away. I try not to feel guilty. I *cannot* feel guilty. The life of my friend depends upon me. So I turn away. Shake my head. Clear my throat. And I step onto the train.

Patrick O'Leary boards the train several hours later at Toulouse. I offer him a glance and a polite nod when he sits down across from me, but we do not speak or give any indication that we know each other. He's carrying a leather satchel, which he tucks beneath his seat. Then he leans his head against the window and pretends to go to sleep. There are a handful of German officers sprinkled throughout the carriage, and they keep a watchful eye on the passengers but harass no one.

O'Leary leaves the train first at Agen while I leisurely rearrange the contents of my purse. By the time I transfer trains and take my seat in the main carriage of the Périgueux train, O'Leary is sitting in the last row, back to the wall, his satchel on the floor beneath the seat next to him. I take that empty spot, but we don't speak until we've determined that none of the people in this carriage were on the last.

"Thank you for coming," I whisper in English.

"Wouldn't miss it for anything."

"Have you arranged a vehicle?"

"Yes," he says. "My radioman has borrowed one. He'll pick me up at the station in Bergerac and we'll be waiting half a mile from the camp tomorrow after the changing of the guard. If all goes well, Garrow will be in Spain this time next week."

"I don't think so."

"You don't think it's going to work?"

"Frankly," I say, "I hope he's still alive. He was all ribs the last time I saw him. He won't be able to make that trip over the mountains for weeks. He'll need to recuperate. He needs *food.* And a lot of it. He's lost three stone. At least."

"I'll get him to Françoise. She'll fatten him up," O'Leary says. "You have the money?"

"Of course."

"Your husband . . . ?"

It's not exactly a question. More of a concern. And there are fifty different ways I could answer it, but none of them are O'Leary's business. So I say, "He is waiting for me at home."

"Well, thank God for that. I'd hate for him to come after me if this operation turns into a big Belgian backhander."

I've never heard this expression before. I turn to him, mouth open, about to ask, when he interrupts.

"You don't want to know—"

"—but—"

"—just trust me."

"I'll figure it out eventually."

"I'm sure you will. But I'd rather not be around when you do."

For the second time today, O'Leary exits the train first. But his satchel is still under my seat and I collect it before leaving the train and walking to the café where I am to meet Harelip. As I did a month ago, I visit the ladies' room first. And, as O'Leary promised, a gently used guard's uniform is folded at the bottom of the satchel, along with a pair of socks and worn, brown leather shoes. It occurs to me that I don't remember whether Garrow was wearing shoes when I last saw him. I was too concerned about his face—the hollows and bruises—to notice his feet.

The reflection that greets me in the mirror betrays nothing of my inward state. Namely, fear and excitement and steely resolve. God have mercy on Harelip if he is trying to deceive or betray me. Because I certainly won't.

I pull nine envelopes—the remaining four hundred and fifty thousand francs—from my purse and place them beneath the uniform. I splash a little cold water on my face to revive it from hours of travel. I brush my hair until it crackles and shines, then pull a brand-new tube of lipstick from my purse. I take my time coloring my lips, paying special attention to the Cupid's bow and the curve of my lower lip. I treat these seconds as a benediction.

Once seated at a corner table farthest from the door, I pull Henri's old, worn copy of *Les Misérables* from my purse and try to read. Speaking French and reading French are different skills to start with. Reading road signs is one thing and Victor Hugo something else. But I am making progress, and I am sympathizing with Jean Valjean and the discomfort caused by his yellow passport, when the chair across from me is pulled away from the table.

Harelip is alone, and this is a small mercy because Henri made me bring a knife and I don't know how to use it. I spent most of the train ride aware of its presence at the bottom of my handbag, worried that I'd just end up with it turned back on me. My imagination wreaks havoc when let loose. What does a stabbing feel like? Could I defend myself? How quickly would it take for me to die? These are the thoughts that consumed me during many of the long hours between Marseille and Bergerac.

"You came," Harelip says, and I see that he is genuinely surprised. This makes me wonder how many takers he's had on this extortion ploy.

"Of course. The man you're holding in Mauzac is important to me."

"Your husband?"

"My cousin."

"Not likely."

I don't bother trying to convince Harelip of anything. But I do stare at him so long he grows uncomfortable and turns away to look out the window. From this angle the scar on his lip is even more exaggerated, as though someone took a box cutter to his upper lip and stitched it back together with a safety pin. I am alarmed at the sudden wave of pity that I feel. What is it like to go through life as a disfigured man? As the sort of person others turn away from? Does he know friendship or love or intimacy or the safe embrace of a woman's arms?

Merde. This is not what you are here for. Get a grip, Nancy, I scold myself. *This man holds Ian Garrow's life in his hands. You cannot pity him.*

I'd like to shake my head, to center myself, but I don't. Control. That's what I must maintain. I sit still and I wait. Everything that happens going forward will be on his terms.

"Did you bring the items we agreed on?" he asks.

As an answer I slide the satchel under the table until it rests between his feet.

"If I find anything out of order—to a single franc—our deal is off."

"I always keep my word, monsieur. You'd best do the same." It occurs to me that I have never asked his real name.

"I will find your cousin tomorrow and tell him that the uniform will be left in the bathroom of barracks number one, in the first stall, behind the toilet, one hour before the changing of the guard. One. One. One. I hope he is smart enough to remember that, because everything else is up to him."

Harelip does not look in the satchel to make sure our terms have been met. He grabs the bag and walks out the door without another word. I remain in my seat, staring at a chip in the tabletop, unwilling to drink my tea. I'm not sure what exactly the café brewed but it tastes of old leaves and disappointment. I shove it aside and open my book once more.

Patrick O'Leary pulls out the seat opposite me, an hour later.

"Did you follow him?" I ask.

"Across the bridge to an old neighborhood. I lost him once he reached the statue of Cyrano de Bergerac at the Place de la Myrpe. He met no one. Talked to no one. It looked as though he was headed home."

"Are we buggered?" I ask. "Do you think he's going to take the money and run?"

"One way to find out. Where are you staying?"

I give him the name of the cliff-side inn where I stayed last time.

"Did you give him the address?"

"No. He didn't ask, and I didn't volunteer the information."

"Then all we can do is wait and see. Go back to your inn and I'll call you there tomorrow, one way or another." O'Leary shrugs. "If you don't hear from me by five o'clock, run."

BERGERAC

December 8, 1942

I sit in the drawing room on the first floor of the inn and wait. Changing of the guard at Mauzac happens at four o'clock in the afternoon. I pick my nails. I cross my legs and swing my foot. I read *Les Misérables,* turning the pages for over an hour, absorbing not a single word. I know the words before me are epic, part of the canon of great literature. And yet, nothing. Jean Valjean. Candlesticks. Fantine. Diseases. Cosette. Paris. Gangs. Murders. Robbers. Revolts. I see the lines that Henri thought particularly beautiful, underlined in pencil. But none of it means anything. I may as well be reading about the history of mushrooms. Or cumulonimbus clouds. *Les Misérables. I* am miserable with all this *waiting.* What is taking so long? What is happening with Garrow? Did he get caught? Get shot? Is he even alive right now while I sit in this inn with a book in my lap? Are they coming for me? Will they send me to Mauzac right along with Garrow? Does it even hold women? Or will I be sent to Ravensbrück, where no friend will be able to rescue me? Oh, the morbid places my mind can travel when fed a steady diet of fear for an afternoon.

4:00
4:13
4:47
5:05
5:15
5:18

I'm not stupid. It's time to go. I've left my rented bicycle leaning against the garden fence behind the inn. I won't return to Bergerac. That's where they will be looking for me. I'll go east, toward Lalinde, and catch the train there. I think about ways to disguise my appearance. I did not give Harelip my name, but we've met twice, and he can pass on a good description. It's the hair and the eyes that give me away. I didn't bring a change of clothes, so I'll do what I can. I should probably purchase a wig if I'm able to make it back to Marseille alive.

I stand, collect my purse, and take three steps toward the door of the inn, when the phone at the front desk rings. The innkeeper's daughter is pretty and silly and fifteen years old. She answers the phone.

"Allô." A pause and then her eyes lift to mine. *"Mademoiselle Carlier? Oui."*

It's odd, the way you can hear your own heart beating in a moment like this. I count four loud thumps, the blood pumping through my ears, before she holds the receiver toward me.

"For you," she says.

I lean across the counter and set the receiver against my ear. There is only the slightest tremble in my voice as I say, "Lucienne Carlier."

"Nancy." It is Ian Garrow's voice, choked with emotion, staticky, and from a distance. But unmistakably his. "Thank you."

The innkeeper's daughter is looking at me, curiosity blooming in her light brown eyes.

"Of course," I say. "Get home safely." I set the receiver down, adjust the shoulder strap on my purse, and bid the girl farewell.

I am sweaty and panicked by the time I reach the train station in Lalinde but I arrive just as the whistle blows. I produce my papers and my ticket and take the first empty seat I can find.

"Running late, mademoiselle?"

I look up to see a middle-aged German officer staring at the bare ring finger of my left hand. His right earlobe is missing, as though it has been chewed off by some small, toothy animal. I try not to smile at the sight. And I force myself not to hide my bare hand. I left my wedding ring with Henri because this is one of those trips where he cannot, under any circumstances, be implicated should I get caught.

I brush a damp lock of hair off my forehead and give the Brownshirt an embarrassed smile. "I am always running late."

"Such a pretty girl," he says with a tsk, "traveling alone. Where are you headed?"

"Cannes," I lie.

His thin lips twist into a smile. "Pity. I'm only going so far as Marseille."

"Why is that a pity?"

"I would have taken you to dinner."

Anyone who knows me would say the laugh I offer him is fake, but he doesn't seem to notice. "Do I not have a say?"

"About?"

"Whether or not we have dinner?"

"Haven't you heard?" the officer asks.

"What?"

"We have taken Vichy. All of France is occupied now. You have no say in anything whatsoever."

MARSEILLE

December 12, 1942

I am *tired* of shopping. It's a sport I've never much cared for in the first place but a necessary one since returning to Marseille four days ago. I have gotten word from O'Leary that Ian Garrow was delivered to our safe house roughly the same time as my train arrived in Marseille. And I was careful to ensure that no one saw me anywhere near the camp in Mauzac while in Bergerac. Yes, it can be argued that I was traveling on the same day that Garrow escaped, but I travel often, so that detail is not incriminating in and of itself. Still, I have made a deliberate effort to be seen out and about in Marseille a great deal the last few days. I have socialized. I have lunched. I have flitted about from one boutique to another, buying skirts and trousers and new underthings. Henri and I had dinner with friends once and we have eaten out twice. It's all for show of course. Harmless socialite is just one of the many personas I maintain these days.

Knowing I have covered my tracks well does not stop me from jumping when someone pounds on the door of our flat. I look at Picon and his ears lie flat against his head. He growls. I go to the door and look through the peephole. Police Commissioner Paquet stands on the mat, glaring. He pounds again. He is alone, so I open the door.

"Monsieur Paquet!" I lean on the door frame and greet him with false enthusiasm.

"May I come in?"

"My husband is not at home."

"I've actually got a bit of news for you, madame."

"Good or bad?" I ask.

"That depends."

"On?"

"Where your loyalties lie."

Intrigued, I step away from the door and motion for him to enter. I lead him to the living room. He sits in Henri's favorite chair and I pour us each a brandy.

He takes his glass and sniffs with appreciation. *"Merci."*

"What is this news you speak of, Commissioner?"

"Your cousin, Captain Garrow, has escaped from prison," he says, watching me over the rim of his glass as he sips his brandy.

"Has he?"

Paquet's eyes narrow. "You seem to be quite pleased."

"Of course I am!" I don't even bother hiding my elation—it would only make me appear guilty. "Wouldn't *you* be pleased if *your* cousin had been arrested for no reason, sent to prison, and then escaped?"

His mouth tightens. The effect is not complimentary toward his mustache. "I suppose I would."

I take a large swallow of brandy, then lean forward and tap my glass against his. "Cheers to this bit of excellent news you've brought me, Commissioner."

Paquet offers a rather unenthusiastic smile, finishes his brandy a bit more quickly than the vintage deserves, and excuses himself from my flat. The moment I hear his door close across the landing I try to ring Henri at work, but there is a strange clicking noise and then the line goes dead. I set the phone gently back in its cradle.

I turn to Picon and say, "Well, I'll be buggered. They've tapped our home lines too."

* * *

Henri

March 1, 1943

Henri steps onto the balcony as soon as Nancy leaves to run errands. She isn't traveling today. She's simply making her usual round of friends and shops. But two things happened yesterday that have him on edge.

He hadn't meant to watch her leave the day before, but he noticed they'd left wineglasses on the balcony and he went out to collect them. Then he paused to watch her cross the street because—God help him—the sight of her swaying hips still makes his mouth go dry. He'd intended to admire his wife for only a few seconds. And he's glad he did, or he wouldn't have noticed that man begin to follow her. He was nondescript. Henri can't remember a single thing about him. Not face or hair or clothing. But he does remember that the moment his wife passed him at the bistro, he looked up—Henri couldn't blame him at first, not with that figure of hers—but then he finished his coffee in one gulp, stood, and followed her down the street. Then she turned a corner and they were both out of sight within moments.

He might have written the entire thing off as paranoia if he hadn't found someone going through their letter box five minutes later. Henri usually leaves for work before sunrise. But they'd made love after breakfast and he allowed himself the joy of holding her as the sun rose. He was late and she left before him, and by the time he made it to the lobby it was almost nine o'clock. The man at their letter box wore a hat and his face was turned away but there was something about him that seemed *very* German. Very *square.*

Henri is proud of the fact that he did not skip a step or call out to the man or show any signs of concern. He kept walking through the lobby and out the door. But the little hairs along the back of his neck stood up straight and remained that way until he was seated at his desk fifteen minutes later.

His wife is being followed.

He might be as well, for all he knows—he never turned around to look yesterday.

Their phones are tapped.

Their mail is being intercepted.

The Vichy commissioner of police is watching them.

He stands on the balcony now, just inside the shadow cast by the overhang, and watches Nancy cross the street again. There are no men lingering on the corners or sitting outside the café as she strolls by. And he almost breathes a sigh of relief. Almost. But this time it is a woman. He can see her reflection in the shop window, where she appears to be looking at a green, feathered hat. And he can see her chin tilt to the right as Nancy passes.

Henri counts to himself. "One . . . two . . . three . . . four . . . five."

The woman turns and follows Nancy down the street.

"Fils de pute," he hisses.

She is so far away that he can see nothing of her face. Only that her hair has been shorn close to her head and she does not wear a hat. A collaborationist. *Salope.* Henri grinds his teeth. The woman is thin, but he cannot tell her age or height or whether she is attractive. He knows nothing other than the fact that she—and the man who came before her—is hunting his wife.

They have run out of time.

Henri has spent his entire adult life coordinating the logistics of a complicated shipping empire. He knows how to piece details together quickly. How to make arrangements.

He calls Ficetole at home. Now that the tram service is broken, his old friend has little to do other than be home with his wife, daughters, and dogs. Henri does his best to provide him with small jobs. Anything, really, to give the man a source of income so he can feed his family.

"Henri!" he says, delighted. "How can I help you?"

The clicking in Henri's ear reminds him to be careful with his words.

"I need a piece of furniture moved to my office. Can you bring your cart to my flat in an hour?"

"*Oui! Oui!* I'll be there."

Buried under twenty-seven sacks of flour in their spare room is the trunk that Henri and Nancy took on their honeymoon. He drags it into their bedroom and opens Nancy's closet.

She has to leave. This is the thought that first began growing in his mind yesterday morning when his wife was followed. He tried to squash it at first, but it took root when he passed that man rifling through their mail. And it burst into full bloom the moment he saw that woman at the window turn after Nancy.

She has to leave.

Immediately.

He packs her trunk because she will not have time to do this herself. Henri is careful. He pulls her favorite items from their hangers, folding them neatly and setting them into the trunk. Skirts, blouses, and slacks. A handful of dresses. A blue wool day dress with black buttons down the front because he knows she likes it. A dressing gown. A winter coat. Hats. Gloves. Scarves. Underclothes—but not her prettiest lingerie. That he keeps here with him because he has to believe she will return and he will have the chance to see it on her again. Stockings. Shoes—high heels mostly, but also one pair of hiking boots. Socks. He does put two satin nightgowns—one blue and one pink—into the trunk because he knows that his wife believes in going to bed in the most feminine way possible. He'd rather she slept naked but he can't argue the appeal of satin rubbing against his own bare skin. They never stay on her long, but Henri knows she would want to have them.

He pulls the green cashmere sweater from the closet and begins to fold it, then hesitates and presses it against his face. He inhales that seductive scent so unique to his wife. Juniper berries and jasmine and vanilla. It smells bright and warm and clean. He loves this sweater. He loves his wife *in* this sweater. Her body was made for cashmere. He tosses it onto his pillow instead of setting it in the trunk. He will ask forgiveness later.

None of these things can travel with her, however. They will have to be shipped. So he grabs her second-best handbag from the closet and turns toward her jewelry case. Her engagement ring goes in first, zipped snugly inside an interior pocket. Then the diamond eternity ring he gave her on their first anniversary. A watch with diamonds that circle the face. He never cared about diamonds until he met Nancy. But he likes the way they sparkle against her skin and he'd bathe her in them if she'd let him. Her favorite little brooch, also diamonds, in the shape of a wire-haired terrier—he gave it to her the week after they lost Grenadine. Three gold bracelets. Two dinner rings. But no necklaces. Nancy rarely wears them, arguing that a good set of clavicles is far better adornment. He won't fight her on that point. And besides, he suspects her aversion has something to do with Marceline and that damn letter *H*.

The majority of their cash is kept in his safe-deposit box in Marseille. He does not have time to get there, however. Nancy will be home for lunch soon and then he must send her away. But there are twenty thousand francs at the bottom of his armoire and he adds half of it to the contents of her purse—along with the set of papers declaring her to be Madame Fiocca, without the pesky details of her British heritage—and the other half he hides through the trunk in her clothing, waistbands and pockets mostly. He shoves a set of spare keys—apartment, his office, and safe-deposit boxes—to the bottom of the trunk in case she comes home.

For one reckless moment he considers stuffing Picon into the bag as well but then he laughs. If he were to send *everything* she loves, he'd have to find a way to pack himself as well. He wants to go with her. He would give anything to go with her. But if the two of them were to approach the train station together, they would no doubt arouse the suspicion of every Gestapo officer in the city. No. He will send her first and then he will follow later. Besides, there are other things he must arrange. Other loose ends to tie.

But for now, there is nothing left to pack. He drags the trunk into the living room. Pours himself a double brandy, sits down, collects Picon into his lap, and waits.

* * *

MARSEILLE

March 1, 1943

I come home for lunch. This is the agreement we have made in recent weeks. If I am not traveling, we eat lunch together at home. There is this need to see and touch each other. To know the other is safe. There is nothing to be done about this fear while I am traveling for the Resistance, but when I am home neither of us can wait an entire workday. So I return to the flat at noon, breezing through the door, a greeting on the tip of my tongue, when I notice Henri in the middle of the living room, sitting on a large trunk. Picon is on his lap, and the look on his face tells me everything.

"What's wrong?" I whisper.

He shrugs, then says in a voice I can barely hear, "They know. I don't know how, but they do. And you have to leave. Right now. Yesterday I thought someone was following you. But today I'm sure. Yesterday it was a man. Today it was a woman."

This stuns me. "I didn't see anyone."

"I did. Our phones have been tapped—"

"I know. We talked about that. We have a system—"

"And yesterday I caught someone going through our mail."

Henri stands, takes five long strides across the floor, and pulls me into a crushing hug. He bends his mouth low to my ear. "I will send your trunk with Ficetole and he will ship it to Barcelona."

"Henri—" I try to plead with him, but he cuts me off.

"We have run out of time, *ma chère*." His voice cracks. "This is the only way. Let me know when you get across the mountains. Promise me."

"I promise."

"Where is your purse?" he asks.

I hold it up, only to see that my hand is shaking.

Henri takes it and then returns to the trunk, where my other purse sits on the floor. He empties the contents of the one I've just handed him into the other. "I will join you in London as soon as it's safe."

Through all this, Picon has been standing at our feet, his little head swiveling back and forth, his body shaking. I pick him up and press my face into his neck. I scratch him between the ears. But he knows. And he begins to whine.

"Ssshhh," I tell him.

His whine becomes a series of loud, panicked barks, and Henri pulls him away from me.

"You have to go now," he says. Then adds, "If anything happens to me, you can go to the bank, the Société Marseillaise de Crédit. I have a safe-deposit box set up in your name and you will be well cared for."

I didn't realize I was crying until he said this. I wipe my face on my sleeve. "No."

"There is cash, gold, and bonds inside," he says, ignoring me. "Roughly sixty thousand pounds in British currency. It's yours. And I will not touch it no matter what happens. Promise me you will collect it."

"Henri."

"Promise me!" he hisses.

I am choking back sobs now. "I promise."

"Ssshhh." It is his turn to quiet me. Then he whispers, "Call O'Leary from the train station. Tell him what's happened."

And now he has me by the elbow and is steering me toward the door. Henri hands me my second-best purse, packed with who knows what. He kisses me firmly on the lips. There is nothing sensual about it. This is not the sort of kiss he would use to seduce me. This is an emotional kiss. Urgent and terrified. The sort of kiss a man gives his wife when he's going off to war. But I am the one leaving. How, *how,* am I supposed to leave?

Picon is losing his mind now, howling and snapping at Henri to be let down. He tucks my sweet little dog into the crook of his arm so that neither of them will be hurt. Then Henri swings open our front door.

"Have fun at lunch!" he says, his eyes flooded and his mouth trembling.

I stare at him, stricken. I don't know what to do. I don't know what to say. The words, when they come, are not enough.

"Back soon!"

PART FOUR

Hélène

It is one thing to study war and another to live the warrior's life.

—TELAMON OF ARCADIA,
MERCENARY OF THE FIFTH CENTURY B.C.

Madame Andrée

FRIDEFONT, CANTAL, FRANCE

June 1944

"Where, where, where in the name of Winston Churchill are we going to find a radio and transmitter?" I demand.

It is now sunset and while my mood has not improved, my clarity of thought has, thanks to a long nap.

Denis scratches the stubble on his chin. "I think I might know."

"Do tell. Because I'm out of ideas."

Fifteen different emotions chase one another across his face and I cannot name a single one of them. Finally, after some intense, silent deliberation, he says, "There is an SOE radio operator in Châteauroux. His name is Alex. He will help you if you tell him that I have sent you."

Oh.

His lover.

"Does this Alex have a last name?"

He clears his throat. "I never asked. That was our arrangement. First names only. You know. In case…"

"I know."

In case they get captured. Interrogated. We've all made these little arrangements with those we care about. Ways of keeping each other safe.

"How will I convince him that I'm not some German spy?" I ask.

"His group uses a bit of nursery rhyme as their password."

Denis tells it to me and I commit it to memory.

Hubert consults the Michelin map that he keeps folded and tucked inside his boot. Denis and I both watch as he finds our current location with one finger. He taps that spot, then searches the map for Châteauroux. I see the fingers of his left hand pop up one by one as he does the arithmetic.

After a few seconds, he looks at us, stricken. "That is two hundred and fifty kilometers away."

As we have been pondering our predicament, we are joined by Anselm, Jacques, then Gaspard, and finally Fournier, who sweeps me into a giant hug.

"What is two hundred and fifty kilometers away?" he asks.

"The closest radio and transmitter," Hubert answers. "Since ours was disposed of at Fridefont."

Denis, tired of defending himself, shouts, "Protocol!"

"Then there's only one thing to be done," I say.

"And what is that?" Hubert asks.

"I will go to Châteauroux and speak with this radio operator. I will ask him to message London on our behalf and request new equipment."

"And how are you going to get there?"

I point at Fournier. "I will take his Renault. I can be back before lunch tomorrow."

Fournier was one of two dozen group leaders who drove, first from the Chaudes-Aigues plateau to Fridefont, and then to Saint-Santin.

Fournier shakes his head. "*Non.* You cannot drive. It is too dangerous. The Germans have installed roadblocks across the entire region. You will never make it through."

"You made it here safely enough."

"I was driving on dirt tracks in a heavily wooded area, beneath a canopy. There is little but national highway between here and Châteauroux. It is entirely different. Besides"—he looks right at me—"where was your identity card issued?"

"The Cantal."

"Then it is useless. All cards issued in the Cantal have been invalidated. The Germans have ordered them all to be exchanged at local police stations under supervision of the Gestapo. You cannot show your face in a police station and you cannot make that drive without papers. Anyone caught without proper identification is sent to the Nazi garrison in Montluçon for interrogation."

"Be that as it may, without a radio we cannot stop the Germans from advancing north. All our work will have been for nothing." I shake my head, unwilling to accept defeat. "I am going to Châteauroux one way or another."

Fournier snorts. "Do you intend to walk? It would take you a week just to get there."

He's right. It's been five days since we were last in communication with London. We don't have another five to spare. I cannot walk. I cannot drive. But there is one other option.

"I will bicycle."

This brings a rousing chorus of laughter from my companions.

"I suppose one of you has a better idea?"

That shuts them up.

"None of you can go," I say. "You're so bloody *male* . . . so bloody . . . *obvious.* One look at you and the *Boche* would know you're Resistance. I can get through without much attention. No one in this country ever seems to notice a woman on a bicycle. I could ride across your upper lip and you'd never look twice."

"Your bicycle was left on the plateau," Hubert reminds me.

"Then I'll have to buy another one in Saint-Santin."

Gaspard nods his great shaggy head beside me. "It's a good plan if not for one small flaw."

"Which is?"

"You look like shit. You're dressed in filthy trousers and British army boots. No German patrol would mistake you for an innocent French housewife."

He's right. Over the last six days I have been through a battle, shot at by an aeroplane, watched my truck get blown to bits, crossed a river, and have slept in the woods five nights straight. It pains me to admit that Gaspard has a point.

"Then what do you propose?"

"If you're going to do this you'll need new clothes." He sniffs. "A bath. And a bicycle. Who is going to acquire all of that for you?"

Jacques steps forward, shoulders back, and says, "I w-w-will."

SAINT-SANTIN

"Is there no way I can talk you out of this?" Fournier asks the next morning as we sit beside a small campfire.

"None whatsoever."

"Then how can I help?"

I am ready for my trip, thanks to Jacques, who purchased my bicycle, clothing, and a small amount of food in Saint-Santin last night. What I do not have is any idea what I've gotten myself into.

"I need a route," I tell him. "Along with a sense of where the German troop movements will be. There's no point going to all this trouble if I'm just going to end up arrested and shot."

Fournier nods. "I will send a few men ahead of you into the Cantal and the Puy de Dôme to tell the villagers to look out for you and warn you of any trouble. But you'll be on your own in the Allier. You'll have to trust luck."

All that's left for me to do is bathe. I'd like a tub and a hot water spout but that is out of the question—even if I thought it was safe to waltz into town on my own. The fact is that we've run out of time. I have to find that radio, sooner rather than later. We are massed in Saint-Santin and it's only a matter of time before the Germans realize it. Only this time we won't be able to defend ourselves because we have only small weapons and limited ammunition. If they discover us we will be slaughtered.

So, it's a cold dunk in the stream for me.

"Denis," I say, "come with me."

"Why?"

"I need you to stand guard."

He may have lost his radio but he's still in possession of his service revolver. And given the fact that he abhors using the thing, I know he hasn't fired a shot. Denis has all his bullets.

"Over what?"

"Me."

"Have to piss again, do you, Duckie?"

"No. I need a bath."

"Well, why the blooming hell do you want me to come along?"

"Because I don't have to worry that you're going to peek."

As I suspected, Denis Rake stands still as a stump, back turned to me, as I strip naked and wade into a shallow pool in the closest stream. I gasp the second my toe hits the water.

He laughs.

"Shut up," I tell him.

"For as little as I care to see you naked, Duckie, I would love to catch a glimpse of the expression on your face right now."

"Turn around and it will be the last thing you see."

Denis Rake never turns, but he does chuckle the entire time I bathe. Every gasp, gurgle, curse, and mutter brings another round of cackling.

"You're enjoying this a bit too much," I tell him, teeth chattering.

"Serves you right."

"What's that supposed to mean?"

"Payback is a bitch," he says.

I scoop up a handful of frigid water and toss it at the back of his head. He gasps and swats at his hair but never turns around.

"How was I supposed to know you sleep naked?" I ask.

"You weren't. That's the point," he says, then adds, "How's that water feel, Duckie? Cold enough for you?"

"Ha-ha. Feeling avenged, are you?"

"Indeed. I do believe there is a God in heaven after all."

I've got a bar of soap in my pack and I put it to good use, scrubbing every inch of my skin, hair, and fingernails. I watch brown suds slip away in the gentle current, revealing pink, raw skin underneath. A few more full-body dunks and I'm done.

It is June and the sun is shining. The air is warm. And since I don't have anything close to a towel, I sit on a rock beside the stream, chin tilted, hair dripping down my back, until I'm somewhat dry.

I grab my pack from beside the stream, comb my hair, pull on new underclothes—I forgo the stockings—then get dressed in the skirt, blouse, and walking shoes that have been purchased for me. Not what I would have gotten for myself, but they're clean and they fit well enough. It's been so long since I've worn anything other than boots and trousers that I feel strangely vulnerable. I feel more like a woman and less like a warrior. But perhaps that is a good thing given the task ahead of me.

ROUTE NATIONALE

I am very careful about what I place in my string bag. Money. My toiletries. The last bottle of brandy that Buckmaster sent me. A small loaf of bread and a little wheel of Brie that Jacques purchased for me in Saint-Santin. That's it. I can't pack for a long journey. I am simply a French housewife out for the day. So I fold my Michelin map, tuck it inside the waistband of my skirt, and push off toward the Route Nationale.

The nearest stretch of road is also the most trafficked. But there is no way to get from Saint-Santin to Châteauroux without first taking the two-lane highway that runs north. I walk my bike the first ten kilometers instead of riding in case I am approached by any German patrols. It will be easier to ditch the bike, dive into a ditch, and wait until they pass if I have that extra few seconds' warning. At Saint-Gérons I consult my map, then switch to a smaller, country road and begin cycling. The first five hours aren't all that bad. I'm rested, I'm fed, and the sun is warm. Once I've gotten up to speed, it's easy to maintain. I conserve my energy for the hills and coast down the other side, stopping to drink from streams when I'm thirsty. I nibble on cheese and bread before starting again to keep my growling stomach at bay.

I ride all morning and into the early afternoon, determined to get as many kilometers behind me as possible. Twenty. Fifty. Seventy-five. By the time the sun has passed its zenith, my legs are growing tired. I am sweating. My hair is damp along the nape of my neck. My tailbone throbs and I can feel the dull ache of chafing along my inner thighs. And, not for the first time, I am cursing whatever sadistic man designed the bicycle seat.

By four o'clock I am exhausted. There is not a cloud in the sky. I can feel the hot breath of the sun blaze a path through the part in my hair. My scalp is hot. I stop for a drink but the idea of eating anything makes me nauseated. I allow myself five minutes to rest and stretch my legs, then I plunge my hands into the stream, leaving them there until my fingers are so cold they tingle. I lift my skirt and set my palms against the irritated patches on my thighs. I dare not look to see how badly they are blistered.

"Buckmaster." I spit his name as though it's a curse word. "Bury the radio, my ass. I'll tell you what I think of your stupid protocols the next time we meet."

I shift routes again in the early evening to bypass Montluçon and its Nazi garrison. Roger le Neveu was stationed there. I have not forgotten him or what he did to Patrick O'Leary. And I suspect that, given its proximity to Termes, Obersturmführer Wolff might be stationed there now. I do not want to come across him, or his infamous whip, without my service revolver. Hubert and I deliberated long and hard about whether I should bring it with me. If captured, I could not explain my way out of having a British-issued military piece. And yet, I will likely need it. Round and round the mulberry bush we went. The simple fact, however, is that French housewives don't carry them. And if I am to succeed in this mission, I must be convincing.

So I left it in Hubert's care, along with my pack.

And now I am defenseless.

By sunset I can no longer sit on my bicycle seat. I stand up to ride and my energy fades with the light. Each push of the pedal grows harder than the last. The soreness radiates from the front of my legs to the back. The muscles in my arse begin to burn and spasm.

"Let someone else volunteer next time," I mutter to myself. "Keep your damn mouth shut, Nancy."

I make a deal with myself that I will continue riding until the light is gone. It keeps me going another thirty minutes. And then I come to a long, sloping hill. My lungs ache at the sight of it. I get off and push my bike to the top. My legs do not consider this a break, however. They tremble and quake with every step. I've been gripping the handlebars for so long, there are blisters bubbling up on my palms and my knuckles ache from the pressure. My hands are swollen. My feet are swollen. I…

…am at the top of the hill.

Below me stretches a broad valley, and at the far side, the lights of Saint-Armand. I have biked over two hundred kilometers in one day. My knees buckle with relief. But I remind myself that the most dangerous part of my journey is ahead.

The valley is littered with little farms and I search for a barn that is not close to any house. There is only one, and it appears to store seed, not animals. I stash my bicycle between a roll of hay and the barn and go inspect the interior. It so dark inside that I can barely see. A mound of old hay is piled into one corner, but I glare at it.

"Not this time," I say. I will not suffer scabies along with blisters, bruises, and total body failure.

Once more I demand an excruciating feat from my body.

I climb a rickety ladder into the loft. I would be delighted to find bare floorboards but what greets me is even better. The loft is filled with sacks of alfalfa seed. It smells sweet and musty. I kick off my shoes. Unbutton my blouse. Push my skirt off my hips. I stand there, wearing nothing but my underclothes, letting the cool night air-dry the sweat along my skin, then I hang my clothes over the rail to dry.

I crawl onto the sacks, wedging them around my body to support thighs, back, and neck. I do not think. I do not worry. I do not pray. I simply disappear into that great void of consciousness known as sleep.

I am woken by air raid sirens. Thin silver light drifts through the rafters, so I know the sun hasn't risen yet. Every muscle in my body throbs. But I have to get up. It takes one mighty push and I time my scream to coincide with the siren. Just one. That is all I allow myself. And then I am shoving myself onto all fours. Sit. Stand. Slowly, very slowly twist and turn my body. Lift my knees. Crane my neck. Get the blood flowing again so I don't pass out and tumble over the railing.

I take stock of my physical situation. There are blisters on my feet, thighs, and palms. My tailbone is bruised. The skin on my thighs is raw, chafed, and angry. My scalp is sunburned. My lips are cracked. And there is no actual word in the English language to explain the state of my muscles. I am surprised by how difficult it is to get my clothing on. How hard it is to zip my skirt and button my blouse. To pull on my walking shoes.

The bread and cheese is all I have for breakfast, so I nibble it, standing in the hayloft as I listen for the whine of falling bombs. Nothing. After five minutes the sirens die down. I listen for the distant drone of airplanes. But the skies are silent. A false alarm.

I know that the brandy won't do anything to numb the pain in my body, but I decide it will help me feel better about the situation. I allow myself a single, long swallow, then stretch again before climbing down from the loft. I retrieve my bicycle, brush my hair, gather my string bag, and hang it over the handlebars. Now I look like any other woman headed into market early on a Saturday morning.

By the time I hit the outskirts of Saint-Armand I am hidden in a crowd of twenty different women cycling into town. I look for a good place to gather information about what's ahead of me. I choose a café populated by old men and park my bicycle beside a table on the patio.

I offer my best smile to a group playing cards at a nearby table. *"Bonjour!"*

They tip their hats. Offer toothless grins. Mutter quietly among themselves. I hear one of them say he wishes he was fifty years younger and this pleases me, not because I want the attention, but because the ruse is working.

I don't sit gracefully—it is more of an exhausted plop—but at least I don't burst into tears, and that is the main goal.

When the waiter comes I order coffee and am delighted to discover that they have it. So I request two cups. They have no cream or sugar, but I am happy to drink it black. After my first sip, I ask the old men what news there is today.

"Bourges was raided yesterday," one of them tells me. I think he must be the leader of the group, because he possesses the greatest number of teeth. "The Germans took five men from a bistro and beat them in the street. Then they shot the hostages when they had nothing useful to tell."

It is not hard to appear shocked. I will never *not* be shocked by this kind of brutality. "Are the Germans still in Bourges?"

"I do not think so. They rumbled through town on their way back to Montluçon, cracking their whips in the air."

I have to clear my throat before I ask, "Whips?"

"Just the one," another old man says. "Only one of them had a whip."

"The garrison commander. Ugly *fils de pute*."

None of them argue this fact.

"Do you know his name?" I ask. "The garrison commander?" While the designation of a whip isn't all that common in Hitler's military, there are many *Obersturmführers* and I need to be sure.

"Non," the man says, and several others shake their heads.

Then the group leader picks a bit of coffee ground from between his two front teeth with the end of his tongue and says, "My son lives near the garrison in Montluçon and has told me about this man. He is cruel and evil. His name is Wolff."

I finish my coffee before it turns cold, then wish the men good day. When I cycle through Bourges an hour later, the town is silent. Businesses are closed. Shades are drawn. Mourning hangs thick in the air. I do not know which street the men were killed on, so I keep my eyes off the ground and get through town as fast as I can. I have seen enough bloody cobblestones to last a lifetime.

I make Issoudun by lunchtime and I am badly in need of another break. So I make my way into the town square and walk my bicycle through the local market, hoping no one notices how I must lean on it for balance or how I wince with each step. I move slowly, perusing the stalls, buying as much produce as I can fit in the basket at the front of my bicycle—squash, zucchini, peaches. A loaf of bread. Another small wheel of cheese. I arrange them carefully and hope that I pass for a housewife doing her weekend shopping.

There is a German checkpoint at the far end of Issoudun, so I duck into an alley between two houses and run the brush through my hair. I coat my lips in Victory Red. I set my jaw and square my shoulders, then press on, determined not to look as though I am avoiding the checkpoint.

When I draw close I can *feel* the Germans staring at me. I climb off the bike and join the queue. I force myself not to limp. When my turn comes to pass between the gates, I look at the guard in charge.

"Halt!" he shouts.

My heart stutters. I think about the price on my head. The description of me that has been passed from one Gestapo headquarters to another. My nickname, the White Mouse. He motions me forward, then yanks my string bag out of the basket. I watch him as he rifles through my belongings.

"What is this?" he demands, waving the brandy bottle in my face.

"Lunch."

This gets a laugh from his colleagues and the tip of the guard's nose turns pink. "For me," he says, then waves me on without replacing the bottle.

The road to Châteauroux curves to the south and is littered with German vehicles, so I cycle west to Brion, then southwest to Villedieu-sur-Indre, and enter Châteauroux at its northern end. I was lucky that the guard did not ask for my papers, but I might not be so lucky again.

I cross the main bridge into town, cycle through the roundabout, and take the second exit onto the main street. The house at the edge of town looks exactly as Denden described it, but I am far less graceful with my approach down the paved walkway than I would like. I drop my bike at the gate and limp, bowlegged, toward the door so my thighs won't rub together. It swings open before I can knock.

"Who are you?" a middle-aged gentleman with muddy eyes and a widow's peak asks. His French is terrible.

"A friend," I say, in English, then give the bit of nursery rhyme Denis instructed me to use. "Silver bells and cockleshells."

He opens the door wider and I step in.

The little house is almost bare of furniture but for a kitchen table, two chairs, and one long bench where a couch ought to be. I assume there are beds in the bedrooms but the doors are closed and I cannot see. I have so many questions and no time to ask them.

"How can I help you?" the man asks.

"I am Andrée," I tell him, "and I have a message for Alex."

"I'm Bernard." He extends his hand. "And I'm afraid that's not possible."

"Why not?"

He winces. "Alex is not here."

"When will he be back?"

"Never."

Unease settles heavily onto my shoulders. "What has happened?"

"He was shot by the Germans yesterday in Bourges."

My unease turns to despair. "Why was he in Bourges?"

Bernard shrugs. "He goes the first Saturday of every month. I do not know why."

I drop into one of the kitchen chairs, then drop my forehead to the rough wood and begin to cry. I cannot help myself. "You mean to tell me that you have no radio operator?"

I have failed. My chest heaves with sobs. The man is speaking to me, but I cannot hear him over the sound of my own self-pity.

Finally, he shakes me by the shoulder.

"Madame! Did you hear me?" he asks.

"No."

"I said I can work the radio. But it won't do you any good."

"Why not?"

"Because I can't code the messages."

My tears stop as quickly as they came.

"I can."

The message is short.

> Hélène to London. Position abandoned. Protocol enacted. Request new radio and transmitter. Send to four four point six four eight nine degrees north, two point two one eight two degrees east. Urgent.

I double-check the coordinates for the small clearing outside Saint-Santin three times before handing Bernard the message. He is not quite so efficient in typing it out as Denden but it gets through nonetheless. Ten minutes later his machine begins to chirp.

"London confirmed your message," he says. "They will deliver your radio at one o'clock in the morning, tomorrow."

"Thank you," I tell him. "You just saved seven thousand lives." And then I shuffle toward the doorway.

"Where are you going?" he asks.

"Back to my camp."

"Right now? It's after midnight."

"Yes. And about this time tomorrow I have to be in Saint-Santin to collect an airdrop from London because my friends don't know it's coming."

I do not have scabies. I feared that my night spent in the barn would have infected me even though I didn't sleep in the hay. This is the only thing I can find to be grateful for when I climb back onto my bicycle. Otherwise I might just lie down in a ditch and die. Because whatever pain I felt yesterday is nothing compared to what descends upon me during the night as I pedal south. I could not handle this agony and the crawling, oozing, unrelenting itch of scabies as well.

I do not care about Germans or checkpoints or danger. I must get back to Saint-Santin. My only goal is to find the quickest route home and I stop only to consult the map, peering at it in the moonlight. Every kilometer is pure agony. By three o'clock in the morning I am certain that if I get off this bicycle I will never get on again. I no longer stop or look at the map. I rely on memory and instinct and the base desire to no longer be in pain. I have rubbed all the skin from my inner thighs. Blood oozes down my legs, soaking into the hem of my skirt. I can no longer sit on the seat. I can no longer stand on the pedals. I have to do these things anyway. I sit until my thighs are screaming. I stand until my hamstrings are screaming. Then I do it again, alternating back and forth between the two. My breath is fire. My blood is lava. My jaw is clenched. My throat is parched. The kilometers fall away as I press forward in a trance.

By the time I push my bicycle into the French Resistance camp at Saint-Santin, I have pedaled five hundred kilometers round trip.

My friends stare at me, speechless, as I take the last excruciating steps toward the campfire. The edges of my vision grow dark, shrinking like a pair of binoculars facing the wrong direction. I see nothing but tunnels with pricks of light at the end.

I let my bicycle fall to the ground beside me as I teeter on my feet, unable to maintain my balance. "London is sending a new radio and transmitter at one o'clock in the morning," I say.

All goes black and I can feel myself falling through the air, but I have no idea whether anyone moves to catch me.

Lucienne Carlier

MARSEILLE

March 1, 1943

I don't let myself cry until I am across the street, around the corner, and one block away from our flat. Even then I have to stand tall and walk straight as the tears drip down my chin. With every step I take toward the train station a single thought is berating me: my last words to Henri should have been "I love you." If I could go back fifteen minutes—just *fifteen minutes*—that is what I would tell him before turning away with a flippant farewell and going down the stairs. And Picon. Oh God. I can't even think about that terrified howling of his. He knew I was leaving, possibly forever, and he was trying to call me back.

The train station is ten blocks from our flat and I walk there in a daze. I check the boards and see that the next train for Toulouse doesn't leave for another thirty minutes, so I find a public restroom, lock myself in the stall, and sit on the toilet, blowing my nose and wiping mascara from my cheeks. My breath comes in hard little hiccups that hurt my back. There is a cut on the inside of my lower lip and I'm stunned to realize it was caused by my own teeth—gnawing—as I walked.

My hands are shaking.

My heart is pounding in my chest.

I am sweating.

It's done. It's over. I've left. And I have to pull myself together or the last three years of my life and all that Henri has sacrificed will be for nothing. I check the contents of my purse and find my wallet, toiletries, brush, makeup, and papers—Henri has sent me away as Madame Fiocca, though not the British subject of the same name—as well as a good amount of money and all my favorite jewelry. I find my engagement ring in an inside pocket and slide it onto my hand. My fingers are slimmer than they were when we married—everything is slimmer thanks to rationing—and it moves easily over the second knuckle. I spin the ring around on my finger three times—reciting his full name, Henri Edmond Fiocca—as I breathe through my nose. The money I separate into two different stacks and tuck inside the cups of my brassiere, leaving out only enough to buy my ticket and whatever meal they are serving on the train.

I am overwhelmed. Angry. Utterly in love with my husband. I feel everything all at once. But I am no longer crying. Once I am certain I won't scare anyone, I leave the stall and inspect my reflection in the mirror. I look atrocious. So bad, in fact, that I will draw attention to myself. I brush my hair. Apply a fresh coat of lipstick. Pinch my cheeks until they are so pink no one will notice my bloodshot eyes. Lift my chin. Then I go buy my train ticket.

Fifteen minutes. That's all I have to let O'Leary know what's happened. But the Marseille station does not yet have public telephones. I have to charm my way into the ticket office and convince the station manager to let me use the phone.

"I need to speak with my husband," I tell him. "It's an emergency."

He is unconvinced. "What kind of emergency?"

Thank goodness for my pinched cheeks. They give the illusion of a blush. "I am about to make a five-hour journey—"

"—as are most of the other people on that platform—"

"—and my monthly cycle has started." I look at the floor for effect, gnaw the corner of my lip. "But I've forgotten the, ah, necessary . . . *supplies* at home . . . if you take my meaning." A glance upward, and then back at the toe of my shoe. "And I am afraid that unless my husband brings them to me I will . . . er . . . bleed all over the—"

"Fine! But make it quick," he interrupts, unwilling to hear any more about my imaginary affliction.

He ushers me into the back room and I close the door behind him and snort. Men. I have known them to sit and discuss hemorrhoids, ejaculation, diarrhea, vomit, and countless other bodily fluids without so much as a hint of discomfort. But menstruation? Perish the thought!

I dial the number for the safe house in Toulouse, hoping to get O'Leary, but there is no answer on the other end. I hang up after ten rings.

Then I try again, letting it ring fifteen times.

And again. Twenty this time.

Nothing.

There is a pounding on the office door. A rumble on the tracks as the train chugs to life. The staticky announcement over the loudspeakers that the train to Toulouse will be departing in three minutes.

I have counted another twenty-five rings when someone finally picks up the phone.

"Allô." A woman's voice, breathless, as though she has just run up several flights of stairs.

Dammit. "May I speak with Patrick O'Leary?"

"*Non.* He is not here."

"Is this Françoise?"

A pause, and then, *"Oui."*

The train whistle blows loud and clear.

"Please tell him that Lucienne Carlier called and that I am sorry to have missed him."

"Should he return your call?"

"No. I won't be here to receive it."

I hang up the phone, throw the door open, speed-walk through the ticket office and onto the platform. I step into the train carriage right before the door closes and I stand there, forehead pressed to the glass, hoping that O'Leary will correctly interpret my message.

TOULOUSE

The weather is atrocious. Wet and cold and windy. There is frost forming at the corners of my window and I think that it is about to start snowing at any moment. The damn Pyrenees. It feels as though the mountain range that forms the border between France and Spain has its own climate—different from either neighbor—and pushes all its cold air down into the surrounding countryside. We are less than a mile from Toulouse when I feel the train begin to slow. Then we are all thrown forward as it stops abruptly on the tracks.

I'm not expecting the whistle and, like everyone else in our carriage, I startle at the sound. Then the doors are thrown back and we are boarded by a dozen armed Vichy police officers.

"Merde," I hiss under my breath. Even if the window were open, I couldn't make it out in time.

"What's going on?" one of the passengers behind me asks. There is a tremor of fear in his voice that makes me wince. Fear is an impossible luxury. *Get ahold of yourself, man.*

"You are all coming with us," one of them says, and I take him to be in charge because he is wearing a round black helmet. It's shiny, like a beetle, as are the buttons on his coat.

"Where?" the man behind me asks, and I want to slap him. The tremor is louder now, and Beetle Cap is looking at him with far too much curiosity.

"To the police station." He waves an arm and the other officers move forward, guns drawn. "Off the train. Now."

I was right. It's snowing. I step off the train into the early-evening air to find the first light flakes beginning to fall. One lands on the tip of my nose and I watch it melt with crossed eyes. Then there is little time for further observations about the weather because we are all loaded onto a series of waiting trucks and driven to the police station.

If O'Leary received my message he will be waiting for me at the Hôtel Paris, which is neither a hotel nor Parisian, but rather the safe house operated by Françoise. It's where we sent Ian Garrow and hundreds of other displaced, abandoned, and persecuted refugees, prisoners, and Jews. If he did not receive my message, he will not be waiting for me at all and I am on my own.

I'd like to kick something, but the only things near enough are the bars of my cell and that would do no good. The Vichy police put me in two hours ago, along with the other women from my carriage, but they have all been released, so it's only me now. I sit and bide my time. Because I know what's coming next.

As it turns out, I don't have to wait long.

My stomach has just announced that dinner is late when one of the younger police officers approaches the cell, unlocks it, and points at me.

"You," he says. "Come with me."

I am taken to a small interrogation room down the hall. It is empty except for a scuffed table and two wooden chairs. Beetle Cap is sitting in one and I am directed to the other.

"Name?" he asks, and his voice echoes off the bare cinder-block walls.

I sit, open my purse, remove my papers, and hand them over.

"Madame Fiocca?"

"Oui."

"Where were you born?"

Welling-bloody-fucking-ton, New Zealand, you traitorous bag of shit, I think, but do not say, of course. And I am pleased that my voice sounds only tired, and not enraged, when I answer, "In France."

"Where?"

"Nice."

"So it says here."

"Then why ask?"

"Just being thorough." He taps my papers against his chin. "What are you doing in Toulouse?"

"Getting away from my husband for the weekend."

"And why would you want to do that?"

"Because he's being a proper ass at the moment and I wanted a few days to myself."

"Just a few days?"

"Yes."

"Why Toulouse?"

"It was the first train leaving when I reached the station."

"Then where is your suitcase?"

"On the train. With all the others," I lie.

"What color is it?"

"Brown."

He snorts. "Half the bags in France are brown."

"Then it will probably take you a while to find the right one if you intend to search it."

Beetle Cap shifts in his chair. He studies my papers again. Looks at me over the top of them. "Where are you coming from?"

"Marseille."

"Interesting," he mutters. Then he stands and moves to the door. "Wait here. I need to make a phone call."

Not like I have any choice in the matter, since he locks the door behind him.

Beetle Cap is back in less than two minutes. Far too quickly for him to have called anyone. I notice that my papers are now tucked into his shirt pocket and it is a struggle to keep my hands wrapped around the handles of my purse instead of reaching across the table and yanking them away.

"You are lying," he says once he's seated again.

"Non."

"I called my associates in Marseille. There is no one by the name of Fiocca in that city."

Ah. Okay. So *this* is the game we're playing. I loop my purse over the crook of my arm, get up, walk to the door, then turn to him with the most pompous look of expectation I can muster.

"What are you doing?" he asks.

"Going back to my cell. You don't believe me. And I have nothing of interest to tell you."

He stands and takes three steps toward me. "You could start with the truth."

"I've told you the truth."

"*Non.* The truth, mademoiselle, is that you match the description of a known prostitute from Lourdes." His mouth twists into a lascivious grin as he looks at my chest. "Black hair. Blue eyes. Excellent figure."

My eyes are green. It's a common mistake that people make—particularly from a distance—and while it irritates me, it does not offend me. The insinuation that I trade sex for money, however, well... it takes a moment to gather a full head of steam, but my voice is properly outraged when I say, "I am no—"

The slap is so quick that I never see it coming. It knocks me to the side and I stumble into the door. Stars explode across my field of vision and I taste blood in my mouth—the cut from this morning, no doubt. My teeth are throbbing. The skin on my left cheek is on fire. My eyes begin to water.

Beetle Cap lifts the whistle from around his neck and blows it, hard, as though I'm some pickpocket trying to get away. It sounds like hell and damnation inside my already ringing skull. The door is thrown back a moment later and two officers wearing vice squad arm patches step in and grab me. Clearly they've been waiting outside the door this entire time.

"Take her back to her cell," Beetle Cap says.

After thirty minutes of begging, I am finally allowed to use the toilet. And even then, one of the vice officers follows me into the tiny water closet. I am exhausted. I am hungry. And my bladder is so full and heavy one sneeze could leave me drenched. But having an audience is just too much.

"Get out."

"I was told to watch you. Whether you piss or not is none of my concern."

I would very much like a gun right now. I would like to shoot him in the crotch so he has to pee sitting down for the rest of his life.

"You could at least turn around."

"I could. But I won't."

My only alternative is wetting myself. And since I have no idea how long I'll be here or if I'll ever get a change of clothes, I do the thing that has to be done. A contortionist would be proud of the maneuvers I take to keep myself covered—as much as possible at least. The humiliation of it, however, leaves me red in the face and shaking, and I think that perhaps I've never heard anything so loud as the prolonged trickling that fills the toilet bowl. I am so aware of how vulnerable I am in this moment, how easily I could be overpowered and assaulted, that I swear that I will never be put in this situation again. Not by anyone. Ever.

The cleanup required is every bit as demeaning as the act itself, and I make quick use of the toilet paper and drop my skirt, choosing to arrange my undergarments the best I can from the outside, never once breaking eye contact.

"Happy?" I ask.

He throws open the door. "Wait in the hallway. They want to question you again."

I have done nothing but think of all the things that could go wrong. Hundreds. Absolutely hundreds of things could go wrong. No doubt O'Leary would qualify my current predicament as a big Belgian backhander. I have been forced to leave my home, arrested, interrogated, slapped, and subjected to gross voyeurism. But things could be worse. The Gestapo could have me in custody instead of the Vichy police.

I lean my head against the wall and turn it to the side, so my bruised cheekbone is against the cool plaster. My eyelids weigh a hundred pounds and I have to drag them open after a particularly long blink.

At first I think I've imagined him since he's just been running around my thoughts, but no, Patrick O'Leary really is there, and he's standing a few feet away between two Vichy police officers. He says something to one of them, then smiles at me. It's an expression I've never seen on his face before, and it makes a pit open at the bottom of my stomach.

* * *

Henri

Henri is surprised at the number of people crowded into Antoine's tonight. He came here to escape the deadening silence in their apartment, only to find the bar filled to capacity. It's the kind of evening Nancy would love. No doubt she would be holding court, regaling this group of strangers with some funny story and he would be next to her, both marveling and keeping an eye on her admirers. For once, he is not cheered at the thought of his wife.

"Another," Henri says, raising his glass and motioning to Antoine.

The barkeeper limps over to him, bottle of Rémy Martin in hand. He pours two fingers into Henri's glass but says nothing. Antoine has always had a good sense of when he doesn't want to talk. Henri isn't feeling kindly toward him at the moment anyway. Antoine is the one who got Nancy into this in the first place. Not that it matters much. She would have found her way into Resistance work regardless. That's just the kind of woman she is.

As promised, Ficetole came by the apartment an hour after Nancy left and took her trunk to the train station. If all goes according to plan, it will arrive in Barcelona shortly after she does.

"Keep the spare key," Henri told Ficetole. "I'll need you to come back a week from today for another trunk. But I won't be here to let you in."

There are business affairs he must attend to in Marseille, but Henri plans to wait no longer than necessary before joining his wife in England. Tonight, however, he doesn't have the stomach to be alone. He lifts the glass to his lips and lets the rich, amber liquid slide across his tongue. He could live to be one thousand years old and the joy of good brandy would never be lost on him.

The barstool next to Henri has remained empty for much of the night—he clearly doesn't look like pleasant company—but someone slides onto it now. He turns his head to the right. The face before him is familiar but he struggles to place it.

"*Bonjour,* Henri," she says.

The voice brings everything together. He did not recognize her because her head has been shaved and without her long, blond hair, each of her features looks strange and out of place.

"Marceline."

She leans in for *la bise*—the customary double kiss favored by his countrymen—but he turns his face away.

Marceline pouts. "What's wrong? Don't you like me anymore, Henri?"

"I never liked you."

"You liked me just fine from what I remember. No need to lie. It isn't very nice."

"Neither are you." He watches as she sets a self-conscious hand against her head, fingering the uneven locks. "You are working with the Germans?"

"*Non.* I am loyal to Vichy. It's not the same thing."

"You're right. It's *worse.*"

"That wife of yours has infected you with stupid ideas. France belongs to the French. I couldn't care less if the Germans purge the foreigners."

"By which you mean Jews?"

The corner of her mouth curls upward. Most men would be enchanted by Marceline's smile. Her bright teeth and the sharp point of her Cupid's bow. But he has always found it threatening and calculated. As though she wants to bite him. "And Australians."

Henri is rarely unkind to women. But he doesn't have the patience for Marceline tonight. As usual, she is wearing far less than the weather requires. He recognizes the brown satin blouse as the same one she wore to dinner several years back with Nancy and his father, but like everyone in Marseille, she has lost weight, and it hangs looser on her now.

"I know your wife is away. And she won't know we've spent the evening together. Unless you tell her."

"We are not spending the evening together."

"Why shouldn't we? We're both adults. The night is young—"

"Good night." Henri sets his glass down and leans away from her. He no longer wants his brandy. He no longer wants to be here at all.

"Wait." Marceline sets her hand on his knee and runs it up his thigh. "You have needs. I can meet them."

He knocks her hand away and stands up. "Leave me alone."

Henri digs through his wallet and pulls out enough to cover his tab and tip Antoine as well.

"Walking away from me would be a mistake, Henri."

He shakes his head in disgust and leaves the bar, cursing quietly as Marceline follows him. But he stops at the door, inches before colliding with Police Commissioner Paquet.

"This would have been so much easier if you'd just taken me home. I did give you the chance," Marceline says. "Now it would be best if you didn't make a scene."

"Best for who?" He turns, slowly, to look her in the eye, because something has just occurred to him. He takes one menacing step toward her. "How did you know my wife is away?"

She closes the gap between them and sets one palm against his cheek. He tries to shake it off, but she returns that hand to his skin with a sharp little slap. Once again, her voice is so low that only he can hear it.

"Who do you think has been following her all these weeks? Your wife bought a ticket to Toulouse this afternoon and took nothing but her purse. This trip is quite different than the others, I think. As a matter of fact, I doubt she'll be coming back at all. I've already phoned the Vichy police to let them know which carriage she's riding in."

Enough. He turns from Marceline and moves toward the door again, but Paquet steps forward.

"What are you doing here?" Henri asks.

"You can come with us willingly," Paquet says, "or I can arrest you in front of everyone."

"On what charge?"

"I don't need one. Vichy has given me the authority to perform preventative arrests anytime I see fit. I can imprison you on the mere *suspicion* of being an enemy of the state."

Henri has just enough time to glance at Antoine before getting shoved into the lobby. The barkeeper, helpless to do anything else, nods once in acknowledgment.

As usual, the lobby is filled with Brownshirts, and each of them watches, curious, as Henri, Marceline, and Paquet pass through. Once outside the hotel and down the broad steps, Paquet leads him toward a black vehicle flanked by two more Vichy police officers with pistols in their hands. The back door is open and Marceline saunters past him and climbs inside. She pats the seat beside her.

"Do get in," she says. "I didn't like it the last time you sent me off alone."

* * *

TOULOUSE

My thoughts collide like marbles being shaken around in a bucket. I left that message for O'Leary. My train was boarded outside Toulouse. I was arrested. Interrogated. Knocked around. And now O'Leary is here, standing between Beetle Cap and one of the vice officers, looking for all the world like the cat that ate the canary?

Those marbles start shattering now, sharp little splinters spinning off inside my mind, vicious in their destructive possibilities. I *trusted* O'Leary. He knows *everything* about our Resistance operation. He knows everything about my *husband.* Has he betrayed me? Am I capable of killing a man with my bare hands? Because that's what I'd like to do right now as I look at him.

O'Leary whispers something else to Beetle Cap and begins to walk toward me. I curl my fists and open my mouth to hurl the best insults I know. Before I can speak, however, he hisses, "Smile, you fool, you're supposed to be my mistress."

And then he gives me the most aggressive, ridiculous kiss right in the middle of the hallway. It's like something from a silent movie. Exaggerated. Pantomimed. What the ever-loving hell?

"Come on, then," he says, loud enough for everyone to hear as he smacks my rear end, "let's get you out of here, darling."

I am not the sort of woman who is often rendered speechless, but I stare at him, pop-eyed.

"I have a few questions first, if you don't mind. In my office," Beetle Cap says.

By this point O'Leary has grabbed my hand and is squeezing so hard I'm certain he's cut off my blood supply. But I get the message: *Don't say a word, Nance. Let me do the talking.*

"Why did you lie to me?" Beetle Cap demands once we're standing before his desk. He looks at me as though I've murdered a puppy.

O'Leary clears his throat. "As you can imagine... my *friend* here has a very... ah... *jealous* husband. He's an important man. Wealthy. Likes maintaining control of his own property, if you know what I mean. So we prefer to keep our rendezvous a secret."

"That's all she had to say."

"It was none of your—" O'Leary squeezes my hand again, so I snap my mouth closed.

"Get out," he says, disgusted. "Both of you."

O'Leary wastes no time thanking Beetle Cap and steering me into the hallway.

"Is that it?" I whisper.

"You want more? Because I don't. Let's get out of here while we can."

O'Leary has one hand and my purse dangles from the other. "But he still has my papers."

"Your pick, Nance. Your life or your papers."

Fair enough.

Once we're outside on the street and have walked several blocks, I laugh and throw my arms around O'Leary. "Thank you," I say. "But if you ever put your dirty Belgian tongue in my mouth again, I will strangle you with it."

"How on earth did you find me?" I ask O'Leary.

We have been walking through the streets of Toulouse for an hour. Our safe house is less than a mile away, but he wants to make sure we're not being followed. So we take a winding route through several wealthy neighborhoods and I lean against him, freezing.

"I got your message," he says. "So I guessed you left Marseilles and would be coming to Toulouse. And when you never showed up at the safe house, I knew that something had happened during the trip. I was just relieved to hear, from our whisper network, that the arrest had happened here instead of somewhere else along the tracks. I might have never found you, had that been the case."

"But you walked right into Vichy headquarters. Do you even understand how risky that was?"

Patrick O'Leary stops then, right in the middle of the street. He sticks a finger in my face and shakes it. "And you walked right into Mauzac to free Ian Garrow. Did you think I would do any less for you?"

My face burns bright and I hope he interprets it as gratitude and not the shame I feel for believing that he had betrayed me.

"But how?" I ask. "How on earth did you ever convince them to let me go?"

He shrugs. "You aren't the only one with fake names and documents. I keep a set stating I'm a member of the Milice."

I raise one eyebrow.

He laughs. "I may have also insinuated that I am a close associate of Pierre Laval."

"The Vichy vice president?"

"I would have gone for Marshal Pétain himself. But claiming to be friends with the president seemed a bit like overkill. Besides, I happen to know that Laval is in Berlin right now. So they had to take my word for it. And rejecting me was the greater risk since they had nothing on you."

I shake my head. There are a few streetlamps in this part of town and the shadows stretch long between the buildings. The snow has stopped but there is a fine dusting of powder still on the ground and the stars have been swallowed by low-hanging clouds. I shiver. And then I am overcome with the urge to cry. I shove the heels of my hands into my eyes to stem the flow.

"What's wrong?"

"I'm just glad it worked," I say.

"Well, you're not in the clear yet, Nance. There's still a mountain between you and freedom."

Patrick O'Leary delivers me into the capable arms of Françoise thirty minutes later. She is the ugliest woman I have ever met. Her face is a perfect square and she has the strangest owl eyes—enormous, unblinking, and so light brown they are almost yellow—but there doesn't seem to be a single eyelash on either top or bottom lids. Her brown hair is parted down the middle and pulled into two tight plaits that fall to her waist. It is impossible to tell her age because she doesn't do a single thing to improve her looks. And then of course there's the fact that she is an incurable chain-smoker. Inside. Outside. It doesn't matter. She is never without a cigarette holder in one hand and a drink in the other. Françoise has never volunteered her last name and, as far as I know, no one in the Resistance network has ever asked. The less we know, the better. She cuts an intimidating figure and I doubt the information could be wrestled out of her, regardless.

Much like Marseille, Toulouse is an old city constructed around the whims of long-gone farmers and merchants. But without the seaport, it has less charm and feels claustrophobic to me. Once we are situated in her flat, Françoise is quick to tell me that she owns and operates the bakery three floors below us. The floors between are her personal residence. The attic, where I now find myself, is where she hides and feeds the refugees whom we send to her. It feels strange to be in need of her services myself.

Once we are alone she turns to me, cheeks pink, and asks, "How is Antoine?"

"I haven't seen him in a few days, but I believe he's well."

She sighs, wistful. "Handsomest man I've ever met. Have fancied him for years. Even though my mother once made me promise I'd never bed a Corsican. Said they're all devils."

My mouth falls open. I snap it shut. I cannot imagine Françoise and Antoine in the same room together—much less the same bed—so I nod and say, "He's a good man."

"Pity about that wife of his."

"He's *married*?" I gasp.

"She won't leave Corsica and he won't leave her."

"I've known the man for seven years and he's never mentioned a wife."

"Love is strange," she tells me, and then, "Sleep. We have much to arrange tomorrow."

I wake to sunlight and a gentle shake from Patrick O'Leary. "Get up," he says.

"I'd rather not if it's all the same to you."

"Listen. I'm heading out and I need to give you instructions. I can't do that while you're drooling on the furniture."

"I do not *drool,*" I argue, wiping my chin, even as I glare at O'Leary. "I am a deep sleeper, that's all."

"Well, all that *sleep* of yours is messing up the throw pillows."

I hurl one of said pillows at his head and he ducks just in time.

"I'm off to meet with a new volunteer. He was brought on by a colleague in Paris and has made his way south to help move people through the escape route."

I sit up. Stretch. Yawn. "If you give me a few minutes to clean up I can come with you."

"No. I can't take you along."

"Why?"

"Because something seems off about him. When we made contact a few days ago by phone he asked if I would bring along 'that amusing girl from Marseille that he's heard so much about in Paris.' "

"How has he heard about me?"

"That is the very thing I aim to discover."

"Then why the hell are you going? This could be a trap."

"Yes. It could be. And I'll find out soon enough since I told him that I would bring you along."

"Have you lost your damn mind?" I ask. "What the hell do you plan to do if he corners you?"

He smiles then. "I mean to kill him. Because if he is who I suspect him to be, then it means we have a traitor in our organization. If I am not back by noon, you are to leave here immediately and head for the Pyrenees. Do you understand?"

"Yes. But—"

"There are no buts, Nance." He taps my forehead with his finger, hard, three times. "They had you at the train station and I won't let that happen again. You know too much. You are too important to this organization. I cannot let you be captured."

"So you're going to throw yourself into a trap?"

"No. I'm going to figure out who betrayed Garrow. And who got you arrested." O'Leary steps back and walks toward the door. "Remember, if I'm not back by noon, you run. Promise?"

Everything about this feels wrong to me. "*O'Leary,* who is this man you're meeting?"

His jaw is clenched so hard his teeth are grinding together. *"Say it."*

"I promise! Okay? I *swear.* But who is this man?"

"They call him the Légionnaire. But his name is Roger le Neveu."

I don't wait until noon because Françoise delivers the news with my breakfast. She bustles into the attic carrying a tray laden with freshly baked bread, soft butter, and cold milk.

"I will never be able to eat all this. You've brought too much," I tell her.

"I know," she says. "Some is for breakfast. The rest is for your journey."

Just like that, I am no longer hungry. "What happened to him?"

"The daughter of a friend works at the bistro where O'Leary met this man Roger. She's a mousy little thing, quite unattractive if I'm being honest. It's her greatest gift. No one pays her any mind. She snuck away and came straight to me."

"And what did she tell you?"

Françoise looks at me with her curious owl eyes and they are filled with genuine grief. "That the moment O'Leary sat down at the table he was surrounded by Gestapo agents. They arrested him on the spot. As they dragged him through the door she heard Roger giving instructions that he was to be taken directly to the train station."

"We have to help him!"

"*Non.* You promised him, *remember*?"

Her words sting, like lemon juice in a cut. I knew I shouldn't have let him force me into that promise. But I nod because Françoise strikes me as the sort of woman who does not tolerate broken promises.

"Besides," she says, "my little friend says his train has already departed. He is to be interrogated en route. They are sending him to Dachau."

Madame Andrée

SAINT-SANTIN, FRANCE

July 1, 1944

"Who is that man?" I ask Hubert. I don't know how long I slept at first, or who dressed my wounds, but I can move again—not without pain, but at least it isn't excruciating. At some point I woke to find myself in a canvas tent and had to assume that Denis, having received his new radio, requested it for me.

The man in question is walking toward my tent. He's in his mid-fifties, wearing a French military uniform, and possessed of uncommon swagger. He reminds me of Gaspard and I dislike him already.

Hubert helps me to my feet, then gives me a look that makes me wish I was still bedridden. "He is . . . *unwelcome*."

"Colonel Pierre Segal," the man says the moment he's in front of me. He looks me over and is clearly unimpressed. "And you must be the infamous Madame Andrée."

"I am."

"Excellent. I have come to take over this group and run it on correct military terms. Every person in this camp now reports to me."

I swallow my first response, take one breath through my nose, and ask, "On whose orders?"

"Charles de Gaulle."

The uniform looks right. Khaki pants and jacket. Knee-high boots. Belt. Narrow cap. He has all the right bars, medals, and insignia. But this story is doubtful. The commander of the French military is in London right now, separated from the front by hundreds of kilometers and a large body of water, and I know for a fact that the SOE does not share details of their covert operations with de Gaulle's Free French forces. Besides, this man couldn't have angered me more if he said he was sent to take command directly by Satan himself. I am still furious with de Gaulle's men for turning me away in London.

"I do not answer to Charles de Gaulle," I tell him, then turn to Hubert with a question in my eyes.

"He arrived while you were gone," he says.

"This man has been in our camp for four days and no one thought to tell me?"

"You were in no condition."

Colonel Segal steps between us and sticks a finger in my face. "I am in charge. You will address all questions to me."

I am distracted by Hubert, who curses, violently, under his breath, then mutters something about a death wish.

"Get your finger out of my face."

He doesn't.

I hear the click of a hammer being drawn back. Just like that Hubert has leveled his service revolver against Segal's temple. "Madame Andrée gave you an order. And in this camp, her orders are followed without hesitation."

Slowly, that hand falls away. The expression on his face is one of undiluted rage. Hubert pulls his gun away but does not put it into his holster.

"Now," I say, palm out. "Let me see your papers."

Segal hands them to me and I thumb through them, indifferent. "This tells me nothing."

"It tells you I am a colonel in the French army!"

"Perhaps you are. I neither know nor care. These could be fake."

"They most certainly are not!"

"Well, mine are." I point to Hubert. "So are his. And everyone else's for that matter. There isn't a soul within one hundred kilometers who has authentic papers. I could shit a *pile* of papers onto your boot and not a damn one of them would mean anything."

The man is horrified. "You have no idea—"

"Here is what I know. A blind man could tell that victory is within sight. We have the Germans trapped at Normandy. And now every blowhard in France wants to jump on the bandwagon and play politics. To be the hero. To lead the final charge. I am not impressed by your speech, *Colonel.* I will not fund you or provide arms to you or anyone in your command. I answer to London only. Not de Gaulle. And certainly not you. Now get out of my camp."

What Buckmaster cannot understand, from his high command on Baker Street, is that, very quickly, the ground war in France has turned political. The Resistance itself has splintered into factions. Those on the right and those on the left. Devoted Communists. Politicians. Ousted government officials looking to make a comeback. Those disillusioned with Vichy. Those who oppose the Milice. Former army. Current army. The thing is, we will never accomplish what we've come here to do if we get drawn into that nonsense. I leave Colonel Segal—if that's who he really is—slack-jawed beside my tent.

Hubert walks after me as I limp away but doesn't speak until we are out of earshot. "Gaspard has already sworn him allegiance. Has already fallen in line."

"Then it will be Gaspard's responsibility to remove him. Besides, we've both seen how easily he can be fooled. A forged message did the trick last time." Now that my indignation is dying down, my energy is going with it. Hubert has to catch me as I stumble. "Segal's arrival does give us an opportunity, however."

"To do what?"

"The very thing you suggested before we left the plateau. To get away from this camp. There's no telling who will show up next, trying to take credit or order us around. No telling when the Germans will strike again."

Our exit plan is simple. Hubert and I convene with Denis Rake, Anselm, Jacques, and Fournier to explain that I will code a message for London asking for the massive weapons shipment we were supposed to receive before our retreat from Chaudes-Aigues. Once delivered, Fournier will be responsible for distributing all arms, supplies, and payments. Gaspard and his men are not to receive a single bullet or franc while Colonel Segal remains in camp. Once Segal has been dismissed, and the weapons distributed, the two groups are to separate and spread their men into smaller groups.

"Jacques and Louis will come with us," I tell him. "Along with the other eighty men we have trained."

"And where will you go?" Fournier asks. I can tell that he is both proud of this new responsibility and sad to see us leave.

I glance at Hubert and he nods. "North, near Montluçon, to join Tardivat and his men."

It does not escape my attention that Denis perks up at this bit of information, and I feel a pang of guilt for knowing about Alex but not having told him yet. Now is not the time.

Everything I tell these men is true. But I leave out the fact that I have a secondary motivation in wanting to move north. The Nazi garrison at Montluçon has long gone unchecked. Wolff has unleashed hell around the garrison without consequence. And of all the Resistance groups that I have met, Tardivat's is the one most eager to go on the offensive. Ever since I cycled through Bourges, a plan has been germinating in my mind. And I will need Tardivat's help to pull it off.

Anselm clears his throat. "It was hard enough to get you to Châteauroux by bicycle all by yourself. How do you mean to move eighty men north without detection?"

"I never said it would be easy," I tell him. "And we have one advantage now that we did not have then."

"Which is?"

"Time."

Fournier is the first to realize my mind is set. "When will you leave?"

"Once we've received your shipment."

We are discussing the specifics of that shipment—adding only the heavy machinery we were forced to leave behind—when Louis jogs toward us, waving his hands.

He comes to where I am sitting on a log and drops to one knee to give his report. "We have a problem, Madame Andrée."

Great. "What is it?"

"We have found three women being hidden in one of Gaspard's groups." He blushes, and I don't have to ask what they are being used for.

"That *is* a problem."

"No. It's worse than that, actually. I've been told they are all German spies."

Everyone is looking at me, gauging my response. I was never violent before the war—had never harmed so much as a spider. Something has shifted in me, however. It is deep and primal and fearful. I am no longer afraid to use my own hands to render justice. I am no longer *afraid.* My capacity for hate has also grown. It is deep and virulent toward the Germans and all who serve them. I am no longer a nice person. But I do not lose sleep over it. So my decision is simple.

"Bring them to me."

The women are gaunt. Filthy. Bruised. Two of them can't be older than twenty and they have the haunted look of women who have been broken by sexual violation. I can tell little about the third because she will not meet my eyes.

"Where did you find them?" I ask Louis.

"With Judex's group. I went to find Gaspard as you instructed. He wasn't there so I went to Judex. He was gone as well but that's when I heard one of the women crying. No one will admit to capturing them."

"How long have they been in camp?"

"Two days. Maybe three. They won't say much."

I look at the poor girls; two are huddling on the ground, crying. They're cold. Faces buried in their knees. Who can blame them? The third sits apart, head down, perfectly still. She says nothing. Looks at no one.

"I will speak to them privately," I tell Louis.

The first girl is nineteen. Her name is Cécile and she sits on the floor of my tent, folded in on herself. She was captured in a field near Aurillac. She had gone out to scavenge for strawberries as some of Judex's men surveilled the area. Her father is dead, her mother ill, and she helps care for her younger brother. She does not know a word of German and cannot find Berlin on a map. Cécile throws herself on my neck, weeping with gratitude when I tell her she can go home.

"If you will wait a moment," I say, "Louis will take you to your mother."

The second girl is older than she looks. Her name is Floria and she is twenty-five. They captured her the same day as the first, on the road as she walked home from market. They took what she'd bought—a loaf of bread, four apples, and a dozen eggs—and ate it before they raped her. She speaks calmly, unafraid of me, and my entire body seizes with rage as I hear her story. I am not foolish enough to think that I will be treated any differently if the Germans capture me. Never would I receive the same courtesy that I am offering these women. But I will not condone torture or brutality from anyone who serves under me.

"How many men were involved in this? How many did this to you and the others?"

She lifts one hand and wiggles her fingers. Five.

"Louis!" She jumps when I shout his name.

He sticks his head through the tent flaps a moment later. *"Oui, Madame Andrée?"*

"Is Hubert still here?"

"Oui."

"Good. I need him."

I lead Floria from the tent and return her to Cécile's side. They huddle together again, shaking, but no longer crying. The third woman has turned her back to my tent. I circle around to study her profile. The set of her jaw. An uncomfortable suspicion begins to bloom in my mind.

"Five men in Judex's group did this," I tell Hubert as he approaches my tent. "I need you to take them back to his camp so they can identify their assailants. The girls you will send home with Louis. The men you will bring to me."

His face is set like stone. "What will you do with them?"

"Have them shot."

"Good." He tips his head to the third woman. "And what of that one?"

I look at the back of her head, the chin-length blond hair. Her neck is long and her shoulders thin. My suspicion grows stronger but there is only one way to know for sure.

"Marceline?" I ask.

She turns.

Gaspard and Judex are livid when they reach my tent.

"Where are my men?" Judex demands.

"Hubert is bringing them here."

"You will release them immediately," he says.

"No. I will not. Your men have committed war crimes. And they will pay with their lives."

Gaspard pushes between us and I have to breathe through my mouth so as not to smell the odor drifting from his body. If he's bathed at any point in the last month, I certainly can't tell.

"You mean to shoot French patriots in their own camp!"

"I mean to execute men who have kidnapped and raped innocent women in the name of patriotism."

"The Nazis would do worse to you," Gaspard spits.

"Yes. They would. And we must not become like the Nazis. A firing squad is far more merciful than getting sodomized with a red-hot poker, don't you think?"

I do not believe Gaspard or Judex is sorry for what they did to Roger le Neveu, but at least they do not try to defend themselves.

"Judex answers to you," I tell Gaspard. "And the men who did this answer to him. So Judex will participate in the firing squad or I will no longer arm you or any of the men who report to you. It is as simple as that. I could not stop your barbarism at Mont Mouchet. But I can stop it here. An example must be set."

"Three of them deserted," Hubert tells me. "They ran the moment Louis discovered the girls. But the other two were drunk. They'd shared a bottle of brandy . . . *afterward* . . . and fell asleep."

"Where are they?"

He points to a copse of trees not far away, where two French soldiers sit, bound at the hands and feet. The degree of their trouble has only just now dawned on them and they are sobering quickly. Good. I would like them well and truly terrified before they face justice.

"How do you know they are the ones?" I ask.

"They didn't deny it. Said the girls were lying German prostitutes and they deserved what they'd gotten."

"They'd have to believe that to justify what they did. And the girls? Did they accuse anyone else?"

He shakes his head. "I sent them on with Louis. But he asked that you wait until he gets back. He wants to see justice done."

War is a calamity. It brings sorrow and loss of life. It hardens the human soul. When else does one rejoice in an execution? I am sorry for Louis, that this is who he has become. And I am sorry for myself that I have lived to see such a good young man lose a part of his soul to vengeance.

"We can wait," I say. "And besides, we'll need him. If we're to do this according to the book, we'll need seven for the firing squad."

Hubert looks at me and I think that he's aged a decade in six months. I don't remember all those lines on his face or the gray at his temples. Is that what I'll see when I finally see a mirror again? A middle-aged woman who has seen too much? After a moment Hubert's gaze drifts to Marceline and where she sits outside my tent, hands and feet tied together. She stares at us. Cold and stubborn. Hateful.

"Are you going to tell me how you know that woman?" he asks.

"We were acquainted in Marseille." Hubert knows little of my personal history, so this is new information to him. "She loved my husband once, I think. If she's capable of love. But she has always hated me."

"So that's why she's glaring at you. How on earth did she come to be here?"

"I don't know."

"You haven't questioned her yet?"

"I was waiting until you got back."

"What on earth for?" he asks.

"If my suspicions are correct, I want to have a witness."

"Why?"

I look at him and I wonder what he sees on my face when I say, "So that I can never be accused of war crimes myself."

I squat beside Marceline and point at the copse of trees where Judex's men await execution. "Did either of those men bring you to camp?"

"Non." There is no less acid in her voice than there was the last time we spoke.

"How did you get here, then?"

"On foot."

"You can make this difficult if you like. But sooner or later I *will* find out why you are here."

She looks up at me. Twists her mouth in a viper's grin. "I came here to find *you*."

"And why would you want to do that?"

There is no joy in her laughter. "Everyone wants to find *la Souris Blanche*. There is a five-million-franc price on your head, after all."

Hubert shifts his weight. Only I know that is a sign of discomfort. All talk of the White Mouse makes him uneasy.

"How did you find me?"

"A group of Maquis led by a woman matching your description retreats from Chaudes-Aigues? Then days later thousands of Maquis begin to mass near Fridefont?" She shakes her head. "You really should be more careful. We have eyes and ears everywhere."

"You are working with the Germans?" I ask.

"Vichy." Her spine is straight, and her jaw jutted as she says this. Marceline is *proud*.

"And Vichy is loyal to Germany."

She shrugs, indifferent. "They are a means to an end. A way to purge this country of those who don't belong. If I can help them find the vermin at the top of their most-wanted list, then so be it."

"Who sent you here?"

"My boss."

I look at her, so proud and defiant. I am baffled as to why this woman would be in this place. Why an irritant from my past would show up in a Maquis camp hundreds of kilometers from Marseille. I rock back on my heels and study her, trying to remember anything I may have missed from our past interactions. Some clue. A line that would connect these dots.

Marceline is dirty and haggard, wearing a plain dress and loafers with no socks. The top button on her dress is missing and the collar lies askew against her prominent clavicles. The last time I saw her she was wearing a delicate gold necklace with an *H* pendant, but her throat is bare now. Something in my mind starts to whir, like a gear trying to slide into place. I close my eyes and summon the details of that awful night with Marceline and Henri's father. She was brazen and arrogant. Intentionally provocative. Possessive of Henri. Friends with his father. A secretary of some sort. A secretary . . .

The pieces click into place. Marceline told me she worked for a man named Albert Paquet. Then Henri's father boasted that he was the commissioner of police. And in my fury, I did not give it a second thought. I had other concerns that night, and I have not seen her since. Paquet never once mentioned Marceline in our conversations, so this detail was lost to a dusty pocket of my memory. Until now.

I flash her a triumphant smile. "Paquet sent you? Why?"

"Because he recently learned that Nancy Fiocca is *la Souris Blanche*. And *la Souris Blanche* is the most wanted person, not just in France but in all of Germany as well. My job is to find you. Then kill you."

It is Hubert's turn to speak now. "I won't let you do that."

Marceline looks up at him as though looking at a gargoyle. Her eyes are filled with disgust. She turns away without a word.

"So you came here and offered your body to those men in the hope that they would lead you to me?" I am as disgusted by this as I am by what they did to Floria and Cécile.

"Men are *stupid*. They are *weak*. They will tell you anything if you crawl into bed with them."

"Clearly you don't know the right sort of men." I pity her, and she sees it on my face.

"My conscience is clear," she hisses, unwilling to accept even that from me.

"I doubt you will feel quite so confident when you stand before your Maker. You will pay for what you have done."

"What I have done?" The smile she gives me turns my stomach sour. It makes a warning bell ring at the back of my skull. It makes me feel as though I'm being watched, as though there are bugs beneath my skin. "You have *no idea* what *I* have done."

Lucienne Carlier

TOULOUSE, FRANCE

March 4, 1943

I have two choices: get arrested, *again*—only this time by the Gestapo—or jump from a moving train. Madame Françoise has arranged for me to take the train to Perpignan along with three men who are also looking to escape through the Pyrenees: two Frenchmen, a radio operator for the Resistance and a police officer unwilling to submit to Vichy orders; and one New Zealand airman who was shot down along the coast and is making his way home. Our little group of four is to stay close despite giving the appearances of traveling separately. We all assembled in the same compartment but haven't spoken more than the usual pleasantries. Pleased with how well the journey seemed to be going, I'd just lit a cigarette when a railway official—no doubt under the employ of Françoise—stuck his head into our compartment and hissed that Germans were about to stop and search the train.

"Good grief, not again," I mutter.

A quick glance at my traveling companions confirms that we are all of the same mind.

"Jump!" the airman screams.

Since the train has already begun to slow, there is no time for discussion. He pulls the window down, steps onto the seat, grabs the window frame, and jumps out feetfirst. There is a thump and the spray of gravel and the train slows even more. My turn. It's a small space and an awkward leap, but I do my best. But the second I am clear of the train I hear the *rat-tat-tat-tat* of machine-gun fire. By the time my feet—now clad in sturdy boots, thanks to Françoise—hit the ground, the bullets are cutting through the air all around me. Whizzing past my ears. Burning through my hair as it flops around my head. I run like a starving jackal through the ditch and into an adjacent field. There is a vineyard on top of the hill and I shout to my companions to head in that direction, hoping the Germans can't hear my orders over the sound of gunfire. The airman is ahead of me and to the right, but I'm uncertain whether the radioman or policeman made it off the train. I can hear shouting and the grinding of wheels against the tracks. The steam engine behind me pants like an old man who has just climbed the stairs.

There is nothing like machine-gun fire being pelted at your arse to prove that your gym teacher was correct. You *can* run faster than you think. Head down, shoulders curved, I haul through the grass and around the shrubbery without looking back. Nostrils flared. Lungs burning. A stitch forms in my side. My breath wheezes. My heart thumps and crashes inside my chest. But I run anyway, arms pumping at my sides, always one stumble away from careening out of control. I don't turn to see if I'm being followed. I don't look for my companions.

Five, ten minutes? I'm not sure how long it takes to reach the top of the hill, but I collapse into a heap when I do. The others aren't there, so I pull myself into a ball at the base of a trellised vine and wait, trying to control my breathing as I suck air in through my nose.

It's a bright, clear, cold afternoon and I'm sweating profusely. I reach for my hand out of habit to turn my engagement ring around on my finger three times. My good-luck charm. My mantra. Henri. Edmond. Fiocca.

My finger is bare.

I lift my hand before my face, appalled to find that my ring is gone. A frantic search on the ground beneath the vine proves useless. I think of the jumping and running, and I know that I have lost Henri's precious gift. My breath, already shallow, comes hard and painful now as I weep into the crook of my arm, determined not to be heard in case the Germans are somewhere near, searching for us. And they must be, because my companions have not arrived.

It takes longer to realize that my purse is gone as well. Left on the train in my haste, most likely. I've lost everything but the money I keep tucked into my brassiere. I am alive. *I am alive.* That is all that matters. I know it is all that would matter to Henri. He would care nothing about the jewelry. But it is a grievous loss to me. A piece of him that I no longer have.

* * *

Henri

"I have always liked your hands," Marceline says as she tries Henri's wedding ring on each of her fingers. "They're so big."

He sits on the floor of his cell, right arm manacled to the wall, wondering how hard it would be to snap her thin, little fingers in half. *Probably like pencils,* he thinks. *It wouldn't be hard at all.* Two of the fingers on his left hand are broken thanks to his own efforts to stop her from removing his ring. He'd clenched his hand into a fist until Paquet struck it with a baton, thirty minutes earlier, effectively shattering the knuckles on his pinkie and ring finger. Nancy will be furious when she finds out. She too has always loved his hands and his left will never be the same. It is pulled against his chest now. Swollen, bruised, and filled with an unholy sort of pain that makes dark spots float across his eyes.

There are no windows in his cell. It is in the basement of Marseille's Fort Saint-Nicolas and is lit by a single bare lightbulb. The stone walls are thick, and they absorb the sound of screaming. He is grateful for this. Because there are a dozen cells in this basement and all the men within are receiving similar treatment to him, most at the hands of the Gestapo, but some, like Henri, are here courtesy of the Vichy police.

Marceline has traded in her brown blouse for one that is white, and is wearing a pair of navy slacks. Plain clothes don't suit her. Her hair is gone, and she wears no makeup. Without the trappings of glamour, she has lost even a vestige of beauty.

Henri's clothes are in a pile on the other side of the room. Cold. He has never been so cold as he is now, sitting naked on the floor of this cell. His jaw aches from chattering and clenching. Well, that and the punch he took outside the Hôtel du Louvre et Paix after refusing to get into the car with Marceline.

His ring is far too big for any of her fingers, but Marceline jams it onto the thumb of her right hand anyway. Then she squats to pick his trousers off the floor.

"Would you like these back?" she asks. "You must be uncomfortable."

He glares at her.

She sighs. "It never had to be this hard, you know. All you had to do was fall in love with me." She rolls one finger across her bottom lip. "I would have even settled for lust."

There are fifteen adequate insults he could lob at her. But that's what she wants. Marceline thrives on reaction. He drowns her in apathy instead.

Henri leans his head back and closes his eyes, silent.

He can hear the jangling of his belt. The rustling of the fine wool of his trousers. The jingling of his keys. The scrape of her fingernail against leather—his wallet most likely. But it is the crinkling of thin paper that forces his eyes open.

Marceline unfolds the list he has kept in his wallet for the last seven years. A growl rumbles through his chest. It sounds blistered. As though coming from a raw throat. Which it is, of course. He'd tried not to scream when Paquet broke his fingers, but there's only so much a man can do under such circumstances.

"Oh, that gets a response," she says, looking up at him curiously. "So, what exactly do we have here?" He watches the confusion roll across her face as she reads his faded handwriting. "Nancy hates beer, cats, and goat cheese. Nancy cannot sing, whistle, clap in time to music, or ride a bike. Teach her."

She could have no more violated him had she read his most intimate thoughts. He would like to stand. To rush her. To hurt her. But he doesn't. Henri forces himself to remain sitting.

"I do not understand what you see in her," Marceline says as she tears his list into tiny pieces and drops them to the floor. She crosses the room and squats in front of him.

"My associates are after a woman called the White Mouse. There is a five-million-franc price on her head. Did you know that?"

He doesn't answer.

"This *woman* has developed quite a reputation. And I've suspected for some time that your wife is the little vermin they're searching for. I'm certain of it now. Have been for several weeks, actually. But I've kept this information to myself in the hopes that you and I might reach an understanding."

"What understanding?" The words sound strange coming from his ravaged throat.

She is not a kind or gentle woman but, when she speaks, it is the most vulnerable he has ever seen her. "I want you to *want* me."

Marceline leans forward and kisses Henri. Her lips are warm, her tongue is slick, and he remains still as she sets about her work. She rocks back on her heels several seconds later, searching his face for any hint of reciprocation.

"It doesn't have to be this way. I can help you. I can get you out of here," she says. "All you have to do is choose *me*."

Henri rolls his chin to the side and wipes off her kiss on his shoulder. "I love my wife."

The expression on her face shifts between disappointment and disgust. "You've made your choice, then?"

"I made it a long time ago."

"You will regret it," she says.

Marceline rises to her feet and dusts off her slacks, then crosses the floor and bangs hard on the cell door. A moment later Paquet steps into the room.

"You've learned something?" he asks.

She smiles at him. "The name of your White Mouse is Nancy Fiocca."

* * *

PERPIGNAN

I wait half an hour for my companions, but they don't arrive. When I creep to the edge of the vineyard and look into the valley below, I see that the train has gone and, as far as I can tell, so have the Germans.

The trousers Françoise provided me with are torn from the jump. My blouse and wool jacket are filthy. There are twigs in my hair, dirt on my face, and scratches along my cheekbones and the palms of my hands. I am hungry. I suspect I pulled several muscles on my sprint up the hill. The sun will be down in an hour and it is getting colder by the moment. And according to my best estimate, Perpignan is still twenty kilometers away and the Gestapo knows I'm coming.

Damn Roger le Neveu. I hope that, before this war is over, he gets exactly what he deserves.

There is nothing for it but to walk.

It is dawn when I reach the outskirts of Perpignan and I don't know where to find my next contact. Like many of the Resistance operatives working throughout France, Patrick O'Leary kept his secrets close to the vest. Unfortunately for me, that means I don't know the name of the man in Perpignan who arranges the guides for our organization. Without these guides, it is impossible to safely cross the Pyrenees into Spain. All O'Leary would tell me when I asked him, weeks ago, is that he lives on the rue Jean Racine and that we have been instructed to pound the lion's-head door knocker seven times when we arrive. Irritated, I reminded O'Leary that I kept no such secrets from him. He knew everything about me. He'd been in my *home*. He'd met my *husband*.

"Yes," he said at the time, "and I also know that you have a hefty price on your head. Lots of people are looking for you. There are some things it's safer for you *not* to know."

"You think I'd betray our organization!"

"The opposite, in fact. I think you'd die trying to protect us. I'm just giving you one less reason to martyr yourself."

Asking directions—particularly in my state of disarray—is risky, so I part with a few precious francs and buy a map at a small newsstand along the Têt River. After splurging on a croissant at a nearby bakery, I locate a park bench, and then rue Jean Racine on my map. Thankfully it is a short residential street, only two blocks long, and less than a mile from my current location.

It is impossible in my condition to look clean, but I can appear confident. I straighten my back and lift my chin and make it to Perpignan's residential area without incident. A quick stroll up and down rue Jean Racine finds three houses with lion's-head door knockers. I am stuck with the process of elimination.

The first door is yanked open after the fourth knock by an angry old woman, who takes one look at my disreputable self and slams the door shut in my face.

"I don't want any!" she shouts from within.

I move on to the second. No one answers. I wait a moment and try again but am greeted by stony silence. I can't risk looking desperate or confused to any passerby—Perpignan is *crawling* with Gestapo thanks to its proximity to the border. I turn away from that house as well.

The third door is covered with chipping green paint and the knocker is the size of a dinner plate. I stop after seven knocks, take a step backward, and wait. It is opened ten seconds later by a man of medium height and medium attractiveness who considers my person without the slightest bit of alarm.

"Bonjour," he says. "How may I help you?"

My options are limited, so I am blunt. "My name is Nancy Fiocca. I work with Patrick O'Leary and I know that you do as well. You're in charge of our guides. I need to get over the mountains and into Spain and I cannot do that without your help."

I stop to take a breath and he says, "What is the password?"

"Listen. I've had the worst few days of my life. I have been forced to flee my home, I have been separated from my husband. I have been thrown into prison, interrogated, slapped around, and accused of prostitution. I have jumped from a moving train and been shot at in the process. Sprinted to the top of a damn *mountain,* lost my belongings, and have walked all night while on the lookout for traps and roadblocks. I've had enough trouble getting here and finding your house, so I'm not going to take any crap about a *password*!"

To my complete surprise he laughs.

"Come in," he says. "You look like you could use a drink."

I have never turned down a drink in my life—not from friend or foe—and I have no intention of doing so now. I follow him into the little row house, through the first-floor sitting room, and into the kitchen.

"I am Bastian, and you are in luck. My guides are taking the next group at midnight tonight. There are five others, but they are all asleep upstairs." He pulls a bottle of brandy from the back of his cupboard and pours me a finger's worth. I swallow it in a single gulp. Bastian sets a hand on my shoulder. "There's a bath upstairs if you'd like to freshen up. I can't replace your trousers, but I can offer needle and thread so you can mend them," he tells me.

"That would be lovely."

I follow him upstairs and thank him as he shows me the bathroom and hands me a clean towel.

"Enjoy your bath and your rest," he says. "This will likely be the last time you are warm or clean for some time."

We are all given an extra pair of socks, a string bag, and a loaf of bread. Bastian leads the little group out the back door of his row house at nine o'clock sharp. The wind cuts through the alley like a freshly sharpened razor and I gasp at its bite. At least I have trousers. The two Frenchwomen are traveling in dresses with little more than stockings to cover their legs.

"This way," Bastian whispers. "Keep to the shadows near the wall. Night patrols have been tripled along the border."

Like the rest of France, Perpignan is under strict curfew. The streets are empty, and the lights are off in most of the homes. We walk for two hours, first through the dark, winding streets of the ancient Majorcan city, and then, by moonlight, through the exposed flatland beyond until Bastian motions us into a dry creek bed at the side of the road. Smooth pebbles line the bottom and a metal culvert runs under the road. It is wide enough to hide several full-grown men if necessary. Never a fan of enclosed spaces, I decide that, if necessary, I'll make a run for it instead.

"We'll wait here for the coal lorry that will take you through the military zone," Bastian says.

Now that we are no longer moving, the cold begins to gnaw at us once more and steam rises from our nostrils. None of us speak, and in the silence, I hear chattering teeth.

"We're inside the forbidden zone now," Bastian explains after a moment. "It is twenty kilometers deep on this side of the Pyrenees and fifty kilometers deep on the Spanish side. Anyone living within is required to hold a residential permit. Anyone found without a permit is shot on sight." He pauses for effect. "Please do not get caught."

With the dark and the cold and that dire warning, it feels as though the lorry takes hours to arrive. In reality it's less than half an hour before we hear the distant sputter of an engine. Bastian motions for us to lie flat in the ditch. The lorry arrives moments later, headlights off, and stops above the culvert.

The driver whistles one bar of the French anthem.

Bastian whistles the next.

"Vive la France!" the driver responds.

"Get up," Bastian tells us. "This is your ride."

"Aren't you coming?" one of the Frenchwomen asks.

"*Non.* I've done my part. Raoul will take you to the guides."

The six of us climb onto the back of the lorry while Bastian and Raoul cover us with empty sacks and loose coal.

"No matter what happens, be quiet and be still," Raoul says when we're situated. "Sometimes the Germans stop me, but my cargo has never been checked. They don't like getting their precious uniforms grubby."

Bastian and Raoul say their good-byes and then the lorry shifts into gear once more and we are on our way. The sacks smell of old cigar smoke and I can feel the grit of coal powder settle into my hair and my clothes with every bump in the road.

True to his word, we are stopped twice, and we listen, breathless, as Raoul presents his papers at the different checkpoints. Once we hear someone walk around the back of the vehicle and one of the bags near the tailgate is poked with a rifle—to ensure it is in fact coal he's carrying, I suppose—but we're released without further inspection.

The remainder of the trip takes less than an hour and Raoul finally turns off the engine just after one o'clock in the morning. He bangs on the side of the lorry with his fist. "We're here," he says. "You can get out."

"Where are we?" I ask, looking at the abandoned barn beside his truck.

"At the foothills of the great Pyrenees Mountains. You'll stay here for the rest of the night. There is hay inside. It won't keep you warm, but it will stop you from freezing. Your guides will be here at dawn. Sleep while you can. The trek across the mountains takes about two days and once your guides have started, they won't stop."

He gets into the lorry and drives off without further comment.

I find an unclaimed corner of the hayloft but do not sleep. I think and I shiver and I worry. The coal dust itches. The hay itches. And I imagine little things crawling over my body. I burrow deeper into the pile and curl into a ball, trying to stay warm.

Our guides arrive just as the sky turns from ink to pewter. I never hear them approach. One moment the barn is silent, except for the scurrying of mice and the hiss of wind, and the next someone is clapping their hands.

"Wake up!" a man commands. He isn't shouting but his voice sounds loud and authoritative.

Six exhausted, bedraggled, sooty travelers emerge from the hay. Two people stand before us: an older gentleman—easily in his late sixties—and a very pretty young woman.

"I am Jean," the man says, "and this is my granddaughter Pilar. We will be your guides."

Pilar is carrying a small mongrel terrier, and she has the longest, thickest hair I've ever seen. It is pulled tight, into a single braid that is easily two inches thick, and it falls past her bottom. Her face betrays nothing as she takes stock of us.

"You were given socks, correct?" Jean asks.

"Yes," I say.

"Good. Keep them dry. You're going to need them."

Jean wastes no time getting on our way.

"We will keep to the higher peaks. It's harder for walking but safer from the Germans. They patrol the lower routes with police dogs," he tells us thirty minutes later as we begin our ascent into the foothills.

The sky has turned the most astonishing color of lilac and I force myself not to look upward. The path before us is uneven and it is hard to tell what is shadow and what is root in the dim light.

We walk in single file behind Jean, with Pilar bringing up the rear. Jean charges forward at a fast clip, his polished walking stick leaving pockmarks on the path behind him. "We will walk for two hours, then stop and rest for ten minutes," he says. "When we stop you will remove your shoes, take off your wet socks, and put your dry ones on. You will put your wet socks back on before we begin walking again. Do not fail to do this or your feet will blister and bleed at best. At worst you will get frostbite."

O'Leary told me that these guides once ushered a prince across the mountains but paid him no special attention. On this journey the guide is king, and his word is law.

The itching begins at noon. We have been walking for a little over six hours and at first I think my clothes have begun to chafe against my skin and the fine layer of sweat that runs across my entire body. But when we stop for our next break and I remove my socks, I see the red blisters on my ankles. A quick inspection finds that they are on my legs, arms, neck, back, and torso as well.

Scabies.

I wasn't imagining that crawling feeling in the dark last night after all. The hay was infested with mites and they feasted on us while we slept. It takes only a few moments for the others to discover our situation as well. The women cry. The men curse. I grit my teeth so hard my jaw aches. I replace my socks with grim determination, realizing that a grueling journey just became a great deal more difficult.

"Time to go," Jean says as he pops to his feet once more.

We hike through the night and it seems that with every step the temperature drops. Still, we move forward, except for our ten-minute breaks. Jean was right. Our socks are soaked with sweat and the skin of our feet is clammy and white. We blister anyway, but our brief time in the dry socks every couple of hours saves us from further agony.

The higher we climb into the mountains, the more snow we face. Soon it covers the path, soaking our shoes and the first few inches of our trousers. The sky is obscured by heavy, black-bottomed clouds that block the light and predict a day more miserable than the last.

Our bodies have resorted to the rote sort of movements that befall those simply trying to survive. Heads down. Aching joints. Burning muscles. One foot in front of the other.

I have managed not to scratch the sores along my body but that does not stop them from oozing. The thick, sticky liquid begins to seep from my skin at roughly the same time that the blizzard falls upon us. The howling wind and biting shards of ice are the only things that divert my attention from the all-consuming itch that crawls across my body. We cannot stop and shelter because there is no shelter. So we carry on, heads down, tears freezing to our cheeks, teeth chattering, fingernails digging into our palms, forging headfirst into another long, sleepless night.

We follow the pockmarks left by Jean's walking stick. We follow the footsteps left in the snow ahead of us, warping them with our own. We walk and we walk and we don't stop until Jean tells us to change our socks. Those of us who have bread left eat it. Those of us who don't remain hungry. Seconds, minutes, hours. Days or years perhaps. I lose all track of time. This is my life and it feels as though I have always lived along the ragged, hateful cliffs of the Pyrenees Mountains. I am not in Europe, but in purgatory.

I think that Jean does not tell us we are climbing the last mountain because relief would come too soon. We might stop altogether, miles from the end. But as light fills the sky on the morning of our third day we begin the steep descent into a Spanish valley. The snow stops. The wind lessens. Patches of green replace the blanket of white.

Jean stops along a bluff and waits for our eyes to clear, for our minds to register what we are seeing. "Look," he says. "To the horizon. Do you see the river?"

Yes. We nod, trying to focus on the ribbon of water winding through the valley.

"That is the Riu Rippol. Everything between us and it is the forbidden zone of Spain. But once we cross, we will be out of German-controlled Europe."

PART FIVE

The White Mouse

You who suffer because you love, love still more.

To die of love, is to live by it.

—VICTOR HUGO, *LES MISÉRABLES*

Madame Andrée

SAINT-SANTIN

July 1, 1944

There are seven members of the firing squad. Judex. Gaspard. Hubert. Louis. Anselm. Jacques. And myself. I have exempted Denis from participating, in part because he despises firearms, but also because the only gun he *will* use—and only when absolutely necessary—is a Welrod pistol with a whopping twelve-inch barrel and a silencer. He's chosen it because it is quiet, and therefore, in his estimation, civilized. But for this task, the use of rifles is required.

Each of us holds an Enfield rifle with one bullet in the chamber, but because there are two men tied to the trees, five of us have blanks. It is to ease the conscience, to create doubt. Killing an enemy in the heat of battle is one thing. But rendering a death sentence on a fellow soldier who has betrayed his own conscience is not a weight any man should carry alone.

"Do you know their names?" I ask Judex.

He stands beside me, quiet and uneasy, staring at the men blindfolded and tied to the trees. We are only ten feet away. Close enough to see the snot dripping from their noses as they cry. Close enough to ensure that we will not miss.

Judex shakes his head. "Only their faces."

"Do you want to ask?"

"Non."

"God knows their names. Pray for them anyway," I say, then raise the rifle to my shoulder.

Hubert stands to my left and gives the orders. "On my count. Aim for the heart."

I hear seven people inhale deeply and prepare themselves.

"Ready!" Hubert shouts. "Aim!" And then, a breath later, "Fire!"

One-two.

Three-four-five.

Six.

Seven.

I wonder who hesitated. I wonder who was fast on the trigger. I was somewhere in the middle, though I don't know where. We stand there for a moment, looking at the two soldiers with hanging heads and spreading red splotches on their chests. With each second that ticks by their skin grows paler, their lips blue. No one moves.

When the echoes have fully gone silent Hubert goes to check their throats for a pulse.

"They're dead. Take the bodies down," he says, then looks at me. "There is one more."

Seven heads turn to look at Marceline. We had agreed she should not die with two flawed, wicked French soldiers. She will meet death alone. Jacques and Anselm set their rifles down and go to her. Each takes an elbow and lifts her to her feet. She doesn't fight them. Marceline walks to the tree on her own. She presses her back against it. Gives me the glare I have grown to hate. As though everything is my fault. As though I should have left Henri to her and none of this would have happened. Anselm places the blindfold as Jacques secures her to the tree. They return to the line and pick up their rifles.

"Madame Andrée," Louis says, "I don't think I can… It seems wrong to kill a woman."

"It would be. If she were innocent."

Only two and a half fingers remain on his left hand. Thumb. Ring finger. Half of his pinkie. He cradles the barrel of his rifle in that damaged gap and I feel responsible for all that has happened to him. Everything he has become. He should be holding his wife and baby now, not standing in a field aiming a rifle at a heartless woman.

"I am sorry," I tell him.

"For what?"

"For everything." I step out of line and turn to this group of men that I have assembled to be executioners. "I will do it."

There is another way. No less lethal but perhaps more civilized. I finger the second button on the cuff of my left sleeve. In it lies the cyanide pill I brought from London. They gave it to us so we would have the option of a quick death. A way out when no other way presents itself. I take a step toward her, then hesitate. No. She doesn't deserve such mercy.

"Get back in line," Hubert commands. "We do this together."

It is the first time I can remember Hubert giving me an order. We stare at each other for three long seconds before I resume my place in line.

"Do you have any final words?" I ask Marceline.

She smiles in my direction, then draws her head back, pulling every ounce of spit and phlegm into her mouth. Then she hurls it at me. I do not flinch or step away. It lands three feet from my boot, dripping off the curled leaves of a small fern.

I lift my rifle and look through the sight.

Hubert's voice rings steady in my ears. "Ready! Aim! Fire!"

YGRANDE

August 10, 1944

"Alex is dead."

I watch Denis's face for a response. It is remarkably blank for a man normally possessed of great emotional articulation.

"How?" His voice cracks. He swallows. Shakes his head. And tries again. "How did he die?"

There is no good time to deliver such news. So I waited until Fournier's group was properly supplied and we had arrived at Tardivat's encampment near Ygrande.

"The Germans shot him in Bourges," I say. He stares at me, stricken, as I explain. "He was in a bistro. I was told that he went there the first Saturday of every month. I learned of it when I went to Châteauroux. I'm so sorry. I should have told you sooner."

Denis is silent for a long time. He nods, then moves as though to get out of the car, and I fear he hates me for delivering this news. For having kept it from him for so long. But then he crumples back into his seat and the look he gives me is one of utter bereavement.

"He was waiting for me," Denis explains. He shrugs, wipes his eyes on the back of his sleeve, then growls, like he's trying to dislodge a boulder from his throat. "It's my fault."

"No. It's not," I tell him. "And I promise you I will kill the man who did this."

Denis pushes open the car door and gets out. "Don't make promises you can't keep, Duckie."

"But I *can* keep this one."

He turns. Looks at me. "How?"

"Because I know who he is, and where to find him."

Our work with the Maquis is never finished. Hubert, Denis, Anselm, and I have been accompanied by the eighty men we conscripted from Fournier's group. As far as we are concerned, they are an official part of the Allied team. I know them each by name, but what's more, I *like* them. And I am satisfied that, rather than having political aspirations like Colonel Segal, they simply want to see France rid of foreign occupation.

Tardivat, like Fournier, has been flooded with volunteers escaping the *relève.* Two years ago Germany began pulling French workers to man their unrelenting war factories. But they did not get the necessary numbers needed, so Vichy has complied with their demands and able-bodied men are now required to join the German workforce. Thus, able-bodied men are vanishing by the thousands and showing up at the doorsteps of every Resistance group in France, this one included. And since we do not want to find ourselves in the same position we were in with Gaspard—surrounded by untrained Maquis and massed in a concentrated area—we determine that the first order of business will be to tighten our security and create a workable escape route. And this can be done only if our small group remains separate from Tardivat's larger one.

We establish rules. Never remain in one spot for more than a week at a time, no matter how favorable the location. All members of our group will know the next established rendezvous spot should our camp need to be abandoned. In the event of attack, Denis's radio, transmitter, and wireless equipment will be distributed among various members of the group and brought with us. If Maurice Buckmaster has an issue with that, he can take it up with me directly *after* the war.

These security measures are put to the test within forty-eight hours of our arrival in Ygrande when three of our scouts, led by Louis, creep back to the farmhouse in the dead of night to warn us that a large patrol of German soldiers is approaching.

"How large?" I ask

He hesitates, but only for a moment. "Three hundred. At least."

"That doesn't sound like a patrol. That sounds like a search party. What are they looking for?"

"You, I think," Louis says. "They've come from Montluçon. Do we fight? Or retreat?"

Almost four-to-one. Not my favorite odds. We're armed to the teeth but it's still not worth the risk. I look at Hubert and he shakes his head.

"Retreat," he says, and I watch in great delight as each man in the farmhouse slips away to inform his own small group.

Thirty minutes later we watch from a neighboring hill as three hundred Germans waste an ungodly amount of ammunition firing on an empty farmhouse. We've lost our shelter for the night, but Denis is still in possession of his equipment, Anselm has confirmed that all our weapons are secure, and Hubert is looking as close to being pleased as I've ever seen him.

His expression darkens when he meets my gaze, however. "They'll be back. You know that, right?"

"Yes."

"And there will be a hell of a lot more than three hundred next time."

YGRANDE

August 15, 1944

"Do you know," I tell Hubert five days later as we stand beneath the overhang of an old barn, "that the Germans have taken to calling us forest terrorists?"

We are studying a map of the Allier in order to find new drop zones for the ever-increasing shipments from London. Like everything else, these have to be moved continually so as not to risk being discovered by the roaming Nazi patrols.

"There are worse things to be called," he says, without looking up.

I have decided that that phrase offends me and that I will stay offended regardless of differing opinions. "*We're* the forest terrorists? They're the ones who have spread their sickness across Europe."

Hubert lifts his head and surveys our current campsite. "Not much forest here."

We've taken up residence in an open stretch of farmland in the Ygrande river valley with a dozen empty barns that housed dairy cows before the Nazis swept through and confiscated them. Though Hubert hasn't said so out loud, I'm certain the landscape makes him nervous. There's nowhere to hide.

After a moment of amiable silence Hubert tells me, "Go on, say it."

"What?"

"I don't know. But you've been picking your fingernails for the last five minutes and I can practically hear the wheels grinding in your mind. You ought to grease them more often." He winks at me then and I am stunned. I didn't know Hubert *could* wink. "Whatever it is, spit it out."

It's not exactly mind reading, but it's pretty damn close and we've both gotten good at it over the last six months. There is no easy way to approach the subject, so I tell him, matter-of-factly, "I want to strike the Nazi headquarters at Montluçon."

Now I've got his full attention. "Why?"

"Because cutting the head off the snake will do more damage than blowing up the occasional convoy."

"That snake has a lot of heads, Nance."

"About four dozen," I tell him. "But there is one in particular that needs to be severed."

Hubert straightens. He crosses his arms over his chest. "What are you up to?"

"Just a bit of long-awaited revenge."

"On whose behalf?"

"Do you remember that man in Mont Mouchet? The one Gaspard and Judex—"

"Yes." He shudders. "Not a thing I'll ever forget."

"His name was Roger le Neveu."

"Yes. That's what Gaspard said." He looks at me, eyes narrow and filled with suspicion. "How did you know him?"

"I didn't. He was a double agent embedded in a group I worked with." I wave my arm around. "Before I went to London. Before all of this. He betrayed a friend of mine and sent him to Dachau."

"And your friend. Is he . . . ?"

"I don't know." Garrow survived his imprisonment, but I fear it's too much to hope that O'Leary will too.

Hubert says nothing. He is giving me the opportunity to make my case. So I continue.

"Neveu came from Montluçon. We know that he was sent to find Gaspard, then locate me. And I have every reason to believe that those instructions came from a German officer named Obersturmführer Wolff. I've seen him twice with my own eyes. Once, eight years ago in Vienna. And then again in Termes. Wolff was the one who ordered the gutting and execution of Gabriel Soutine's pregnant wife."

I can see the muscles tighten along Hubert's jaw. "He's the one I had to stop you from going after?"

"Yes. And he's the one who shot our radio operator in Bourges."

"Denis's lover?"

I nod. "I am certain that he's the one who sent those scouts to the farmhouse several days ago. It's obvious there has been a shift in

Tardivat's group. They are growing by the hundreds every week. They are better armed than they were a month ago. They are going on the offensive."

"Which means that Wolff knows you're here."

"Or he suspects it, at least." I stretch my neck, rolling it from side to side. Sleeping in a barn isn't all that different from sleeping on the ground, and my body has started to complain. "The attacks won't stop. Not unless we cut the head off that snake."

"He'll just be replaced with a different head."

"Then we cut the neck off as well."

Sometimes, being right isn't as satisfying as I would like it to be. Hubert and I stand beneath the overhang of the barn, quite literally up to our ankles in old manure, looking at all the different pins pushed into the map we have spread out on a makeshift table. We can hear Denis Rake up in the hayloft, listening to the latest radio transmission, tapping out his messages in Morse code.

I watch Hubert's face as he ponders how we would even pull off such an operation. "We'll need intel from Tardivat," he says, and I am about to suggest sending Jacques to collect him immediately when three things happen in quick succession.

There is a distant boom, followed by a momentary silence, then a rumbling tremor that rolls through the ground at our feet. It shakes dust from the barn rafters and rattles the timbers.

After that comes the faint crackle of machine-gun fire and the sound of shouting.

And finally, Louis comes stumbling through an adjacent field, one arm bloody and the other hanging limp at his side. I watch, strangely paralyzed, as he lurches, falls, and is swallowed by the tall grass.

"Where did they come from?" Hubert shouts beside me as he rips the map off the table and heaves Louis's gangly body onto it.

Louis's teeth are clenched together. He's whining, like a dog in pain, and I am grateful for the noise. It means he's lucid and angry, and that might just keep him alive.

"Montluçon," I tell Hubert. It may as well be a curse word for the way I spit it into the air between us.

"Status?" Hubert demands as Jacques trots up to the barn, carbine slung over one shoulder.

"We're s-s-surrounded," he says.

"And why the hell didn't we see them coming?"

"We d-d-did." He nods at Louis. "Just not in t-t-time."

"How many?" Hubert presses the heel of his hand into the bullet wound in Louis's shoulder, stanching the flow of blood, and is rewarded with a yelp of pain. Hubert looks at Denis, who has climbed down from the loft, and barks out an order for bandages.

Louis lifts his head from the table and speaks between clenched jaws. "A few hundred. With six thousand more . . . ggggrrrr . . . on the way."

Hubert snarls. "Then it should have been easier to spot them!"

"They were already in position," he pants, grinding out the words. "I think the scouts came ahead and—*merde* that *hurts*!—" he screams as Hubert presses harder into his shoulder.

"—the bullet's still in there—"

"—they've been narrowing down . . ." Louis takes a deep breath, eyes rolling back. "Our location . . . since we retreated . . . from . . . the . . . farmhouse." He drops his head to the table with a thump, unconscious.

Our group of maquisards, with Anselm in the lead, has wasted no time setting up a perimeter around the barn and field where we are camped. Eighty men, in groups of two, each armed and ready to fire a bazooka at the first German they see. The line won't hold against cannons or tanks, but it will buy us several hours against infantry.

Hubert has his fingers pressed to the side of Louis's throat, searching for a pulse.

"How much time do we have?" I ask.

Hubert glances at me. At the perimeter. At Louis. "I don't know."

The machine-gun fire is growing closer, and directly to the west I hear the first rumbling bang of a bazooka go off, followed by a plume of dirt exploding airborne at the far edge of the field. It is followed by the shrieking of men, though I can't be certain whose.

I take the bandages and medic pack from Denis when he returns. Hubert helps me roll Louis onto his side and I tell him, "We need reinforcements."

"We're on foot. And Tardivat is an hour away," Hubert says.

We work in silence for a moment. I dig through the pack, looking for a pair of surgical tweezers. Nothing. "Dammit," I cuss. "How am I supposed to find that bullet?"

Hubert uses his free hand to grab a knife from his pocket. He hands it to me without comment and I unfold the utensils. Because it belongs to Hubert, it is clean, oiled, and sharpened.

I'm not a doctor. I'm not even a nurse. I don't know the names of any muscle, ligament, or tendon in the shoulder. But I do know that I shouldn't go digging around in the human body with a folding Sheffield knife.

Hubert pulls his hand away from the wound and points. "It isn't deep. You can see part of it, right there, lodged in the muscle. Be quick."

I decide on the marlinespike, then spread Louis's bullet wound open with two fingers. He groans on the table but doesn't wake up. My fingers are slick with blood, but I hold the spike steady as I insert it into his shoulder and set the pointed end beneath the lead slug. I flick upward, and the bullet dislodges. We pack the wound, then wrap it with bandages.

Once the crisis is averted I tighten my belt, wipe my bloody hands on my trousers, grab my pack, and turn to the north.

"What are you doing?" Hubert demands.

"Going for reinforcements."

I am yanked back before I can take two steps.

"N-n-no," Jacques says. "My turn."

I am about to argue but Hubert nods. "Let him."

Without a word Jacques slings his carbine over his shoulder. Tucks revolvers into the holsters at either side of his belt. Grabs four extra cartridges and shoves them into his pocket. Then he is bounding to the edge of the field like a deer. In one fluid movement he crouches and disappears into the tall grass.

"He didn't like it last time," Hubert tells me. "The entire three days you were gone on that bike he paced the camp and cursed himself. The stuttering drove me *crazy.* I can't take it again."

I hold a finger in his face. "Don't make fun of him."

"I'm not! Just telling you how it was. Jacques feels it's his job to keep you alive."

I listen to the distant *rat-tat-tat* of gunfire. "How long do you think before the remaining troops reach us?"

"Not long enough."

"And Jacques won't get to Tardivat for at least an hour?"

"Right. And then he'll have to bring reinforcements." Hubert scans the field, looking for our men. Occasionally Anselm pops up and runs to another location, then dissolves into the grass. "They'll need more ammunition."

"So let's get it to them," I say.

Denis Rake is standing beside Louis, eyeing him cautiously.

"Do you have your pistol?" I ask him.

Denis pats the Welrod in the holster at his thigh. "Yes."

"You shoot any German who comes near this barn. Understand?"

His face turns red and he whispers, as though confessing some mortal sin, "I don't think I could shoot a man unless I was drunk, Duckie."

I have no brandy. I have no bourbon or whisky or scotch. Not even any rotgut bathtub gin. All I have is a bottle of pure rubbing alcohol in the medic's kit. I dig around in the bag and give the bottle to Denis, along with two warnings. "Only a few sips. Much more than that and you'll go blind, then die." I point at Louis. "If he wakes up, pour that into his wound. He'll hate you for it, but he'll stay conscious."

Hubert and I have carried seventeen cases of ammunition—mostly AT116 rockets, each filled with three and a half pounds of explosives, for the bazookas—to various groups along the perimeter, when we hear the rumble of motors, the static of machine guns, and artillery shells to the southeast.

"Tardivat?" I ask.

"Did he come in from their rear?"

He nods. "Trying to draw them away, I think. Give us time to retreat."

"Then let's not disappoint him."

I bolt for the barn.

"What are we going to do with him?" Denis asks, pointing at Louis, who, though now conscious, looks as though he might not be for long.

"We'll have to carry him."

I wonder if it is possible to crack open my chest and pour the bottle of pure rubbing alcohol directly onto my heart. It's not that I want to die, but rather that I never want to feel anything again. I don't know how to get through the rest of this damn war while caring for so many people.

The surrounding fields are quiet now, thanks to Tardivat and his ferocious strike on the German battalion. They dissolved shortly after his reinforcements arrived, expecting a group of less than one hundred and being ambushed on three sides by over a thousand.

Hubert and Tardivat find me sitting on the ground beside Louis, whom I have wrapped in a blanket because he's shivering uncontrollably. Beside him are the bodies of seven other maquisards who were killed during the skirmish. Two of them are mine. Five are Tardivat's.

"It is time to go," Tardivat tells me.

"We have to bury them first."

He peers at the sky and scratches his head. "It will be sundown in an hour."

"So?"

"There is a churchyard a few kilometers from here. We can sneak in once it's dark."

We bury the seven maquisards along the high wall of a small, Protestant churchyard in Les Cernes. The little cemetery has only one exit, and we place Anselm at the gate, Sten gun at the ready, to ensure that we're not ambushed by a passing German patrol. We give them rocks for headstones and all the military honors that we can under the circumstances.

I am quiet as Tardivat drives Hubert and me to our next camp in the Forêt de Tronçais—a well-hidden area, closer to Tardivat, and protected by one of his groups. The car is so quiet I can hear his stomach rumble.

"Jacques arrived with your message," Tardivat tells me, patting his belly, "while I was eating lunch."

I lift an eyebrow and try not to smile. It feels wrong to smile with grave dirt still on my hands. "Was it good?"

He shrugs. "It was food."

"A Frenchman walked away from a meal? I'm astonished."

"It is a thing that would only happen for you, Madame Andrée."

I sent Denis ahead, with Jacques and two of Tardivat's men, to get Louis to a small hospital in Ygrande that is run by a religious order and does not ask too many questions. By the time we reach our new camp in the Forêt de Tronçais Denis Rake is waiting for us, an enormous grin on his face.

"Good news, Duckie!" he shouts the moment I step out of Tardivat's Renault. "I've just been on the radio. The Allies landed in Toulon and Cannes this morning! Three hundred thousand troops! Americans. Brits. Canadians. This is what we've been waiting for!"

This changes *everything*. The first Allied landing at Normandy was meant to put the Germans on the defensive. The second landing, in the south of France, is meant to end the occupation entirely, cutting off their reinforcements and avenues of retreat. Now it is time for the Maquis to nail the coffin lid shut.

Anselm trots over to join us, grinning like a bona fide madman. "You know our targets?"

"Yes," I tell him. I carried them with me, in the lining of my purse, all the way from London. Two sets of targets: the first to be destroyed immediately after D-Day in order to cripple supply lines and infrastructure, and the second to cut off any means of retreat for the Germans. We intend to hunt them down one by one.

Anselm is bouncing on the balls of his feet, wanting nothing more than to put his explosives to use. "When do we start?"

I spend most of the night assigning targets for Tardivat's men to raid. There are bridges, roads, tunnels, and railroad tracks that must be destroyed. Of particular importance are a number of potential escape routes near the garrison in Montluçon that must be demolished so the German troops cannot move north. Fifteen different groups are sent out with land mines and mortars to render these routes impassable by vehicle. Anselm I send, along with forty Maquis on the Allied team, to take control of a synthetic petrol plant in Saint-Hilaire. Originally we were instructed to destroy it. But Tardivat suggested we seize it instead as a source of fuel for ourselves.

"And for me, Madame Andrée?" Tardivat asks. "Surely I won't be left out of the fun."

I look at Hubert and he nods.

"*Non.* Of course not. You and your team are coming with Denden, Hubert, Jacques, and myself to Montluçon."

MONTLUÇON

Hôtel d'Orcet, August 16, 1944

Montluçon is secluded and beautiful. It was, I am told, built on the slope of a dormant volcanic hill and is home to a medieval abbey and the somewhat infamous Dukes of Bourbon Castle. It is skirted by the River Cher, which empties into a large reservoir nearby. It is the largest town in the area, home to over forty thousand people, and given that we have come on market day, is bustling. But the crowds provide good cover and give us an opportunity to survey our target.

Hubert and Tardivat flank me on either side of the market while Denis follows three paces behind. We are scanning the market for German officers wearing civilian clothes. For snipers. Checkpoints. Any form of trouble at all. Jacques is tucked away on the top floor of a post office across the square from the Nazi-occupied hotel. He is my best sharpshooter and I am relying on him to protect us from capture should this ambush go wrong. We left one maquisard near the truck to guard our escape route, and several others are stationed at the rear exits of the hotel to prevent any German officers from slipping away.

"Remember, Nance, this is not a full-on military assault, but rather a precision strike. We'll have one shot, and then it's a hasty exit," Hubert tells me.

"I know," I say, my eyes on the top floor of the hotel.

Tardivat has assured us that the Gestapo have taken over the entire hotel and installed their senior officers in the rooms.

"They meet in the top-floor suite, every afternoon at twelve thirty, for drinks. It is their prelunch ritual," he told us earlier as we packed the weapons and explosives we would need.

"What about security?"

"Minimal, at noon, given the allure of a midday aperitif. But guards are still posted at the front and back entrances, along with the stairwell and elevators."

"They won't let five armed Resistance soldiers waltz into the hotel," I said.

"No. But they are known for having... *ah*"—Tardivat hesitated, the end of his nose turning pink—"female *company* on occasion. A woman dressed in civilian clothes could make it to the front entrance before being questioned. Beyond that she would have to use her wits."

"And fists?"

"A knife would be better," he told me, drawing one finger in a straight line across his throat.

Given this bit of information, I'd made the decision to wash quickly and change into civilian clothes, and I am glad that I did. The skirt and blouse help me blend into the crowded marketplace.

I was able to fit only three grenades into my purse, so they will have to be enough. Hubert has more in his pack, as does Tardivat, but Denis insisted on bringing nothing but his Welrod pistol, so he will bring up the rear.

Tardivat joins Hubert and me as we move through the crowd. He speaks quietly so only the two of us can hear. "At one o'clock sharp we pull the pins."

We drift apart, again, as we each move toward different entrances. Tardivat, Hubert, and Denis to the rear. I will be going through the front door.

It is 12:45.

I climb the hotel steps, purse slung over my elbow, letting my skirt swish along my calves. There are two Gestapo guards on either side of the front doors and their eyes settle on me as I approach. I know that across the square, on top of the post office, Jacques has me in his sights. And I know that, if either of these men gives me an ounce of trouble, he will pull the trigger and give me a few precious seconds to escape. The knowledge that he is there is the only reason my heart is not racing.

The guard to the left of the door steps forward. His hand moves to his waist and settles on the grip of his pistol.

"This hotel is not open to the public," he says.

"I was invited."

"By?"

For the first and only time in my life, I am pleased to hear the faint tremble in my voice. "Obersturmführer Wolff."

He looks me over and offers a base, male grunt. After a moment he steps aside and opens the door. I did not realize I was holding my breath until I let it out between pursed lips. The lobby has marble floors and a small reception desk manned by an older, distinguished gentleman with silver hair and a weariness around his eyes that no amount of sleep could erase.

I look at him and nod, once, willing him not to ask questions as I walk toward the elevator and the guard posted there. He looks me over with great sadness and I think he makes an assumption about my presence in this hotel at this particular time of day. Clearly, I am not the first woman to have joined the Nazis' prelunch celebration.

I have no way of knowing whether Tardivat, Hubert, and Denis have dispatched the guards stationed at the back entrance. None of us can use our guns. We cannot warn the German officers that we are here. We need them massed, in one location. We need to catch them unaware at one o'clock when we pull the pins. And if I am the only one to make it into the building, then so be it. Jacques will take care of any Gestapo trying to escape after that.

Once across the lobby, I approach the elevator. I grip the handles of my purse in both hands and keep my eyes down, staring at my knuckles. They are white from the strain, but this is the only way to keep my hands from shaking.

I have made it into the building, so he has less reason to question me, but still the guard asks, "What is your business?"

I let him assume that my cheeks are red from shame instead of anger and excitement.

"You know my business," I say, not looking up.

"Lass sie sein."

The voice behind me is male and guttural and I do not understand a word of it. But the guard does, because he steps aside and salutes. A hand reaches beyond my shoulder and presses the button for the elevator.

I rotate my wrist and note the time.

12:50.

I am afraid to turn and look. Instead, I listen to the pulleys sliding behind the closed doors. I hear the carriage lower, and then finally the groan as it stops. A bell rings and the doors slide open to reveal an empty carriage. I step inside, and only then do I turn and face the man behind me.

There is nowhere for me to go. Nowhere to turn or run. I am frozen in place as he steps into the elevator. His face is like the inner workings of a watch. Oddly shaped gears and widgets. But it does not take them long to shift into place, and when they do, I know that he recognizes me as well.

I wait until the doors close behind him before I say, "*Bonjour,* Obersturmführer Wolff."

Nancy Fiocca

LONDON, ENGLAND

August 1943

The trunk that Henri packed was waiting for me in Barcelona. And a good thing too. Because by the time we arrived, weeks later, I looked—and smelled—as if I'd been living under a bridge for several years. My clothes were filthy. My hair limp, greasy, and knotted. It was the scabies that nearly broke me, however. Well over half my body was covered in the red, oozing sores, and it took three hours, countless gallons of hot water, and a scrub brush to remove the mites from my skin once we were delivered to our final safe house.

Retrieving the trunk at the post office in Barcelona was complicated, given that I no longer had identification papers. But since I was the only person who had tried to claim it and I knew the sender and return address, they reluctantly handed it over.

God bless Henri. Not only did he send a sufficient replacement wardrobe, complete with my favorite little luxuries, but also enough cash—in single banknotes, stuffed into waistbands, stockings, and shoes in the event the trunk was searched—to get me into a hotel and, eventually, out of the country. Not to say that it was easy, of course. I was arrested and charged with illegal entry as soon as I applied for a new identity card in Barcelona. But the British vice consul intervened the moment he was notified that a subject of the Crown was being harassed. The appropriate bribe was paid. My papers were issued. And a notification of my pending arrival was sent ahead of me to London.

Barcelona to Madrid to Gibraltar. Vehicles and trains and lengthy stops that only wasted time. One delay after another. I nearly crawled right out of my skin with frustration before boarding the British ship *Lutsia* and joining a convoy of seventy ships bound for the United Kingdom. We sailed through the Strait of Gibraltar, into the Atlantic Ocean, up to the Bay of Biscay, and into the Celtic Sea. It took ten days, and I am told that had we tried to go through the English Channel we would have been sunk by German U-boats. As it was, we were still escorted by one British destroyer, three warships, and a rotating series of air patrols—mostly American Liberator bombers. So, once again, my route was circuitous. Once again, I had to sit and wait and trust that safety was more important than speed. Finally, however, we docked at the Scottish port of Greenock. One train to Glasgow. Another to Edinburgh. A third to London, and by the time I stepped onto the platform in the city of fog, I felt as though half my life had been wasted by travel.

Henri will meet me in London. That was our arrangement. And I have made arrangements of my own as I wait. I find us a small, furnished flat in the Piccadilly and St. James's Street area. It's dirty, needs to be painted, and the parquet floors could use a good sanding and polish, but it hasn't been bombed like so many others nearby and we'll make do. I apply myself with vigor to these domestic duties my first months in London and by the time I'm done, our little flat gleams. Funds are limited, but I do buy Henri a pair of pajamas, slippers, and a dressing gown. I also buy a bottle of French champagne and an expensive bottle of brandy so we can properly celebrate when reunited. I keep them in a cupboard and look at them longingly each night before bed. I miss the scent of brandy on his breath. I miss the heat of his skin beside me as we sleep.

I cannot call Henri because the lines in our Marseille flat and in his office are tapped. I cannot write to him because our mail is being intercepted. I have no safe means of getting a message to him. So I wait. And I wait. And I wait.

The thing is, I've never been good at waiting.

LONDON

Headquarters of Charles de Gaulle's Free French Forces, October 5, 1943

"What do you mean you are 'declining my services'?" I demand of the older, portly French recruitment officer sitting across from me. His name plate reads "Colonel Passy" and his expression "unamused." He is trying not to yell at me, I think.

"I have already been working on your behalf for three and a half *years*," I tell him. "I helped establish the Resistance network in Marseille."

"What I mean," Colonel Passy says, as though I am a very stupid—and possibly hard of hearing—child, "is that we do not need your help."

"The hell you don't! I've just come from France and the whole damn country is going to hell."

"We have the situation handled," he tells me.

It is a monumental struggle not to stand and slap the man senseless. "France is overrun," I tell him. "Your citizens are being jailed and slaughtered by the thousands for the mere *suspicion* of working against the Germans. The entire infrastructure is destroyed. It is a fallen country under enemy occupation and you have the nerve to sit here, in *safety,* hundreds of kilometers away, and tell me you have it *handled*?"

"If you are so eager to help the war effort, madame, I suggest you buy a ladle and go volunteer at a soup kitchen."

"Be grateful I don't have a ladle now, Colonel, or I'd beat you over the head with it." I collect my purse and see myself out.

* * *

Henri

Fort Saint-Nicolas, Marseille

Paquet points at him. "Get dressed."

Henri lifts his manacled arm as though to say, *I can't.*

Paquet nods at Marceline and she moves forward with the key. Once free, Henri's arm drops to his lap with a thump. It has long since gone cold and numb and he worries that—should he survive this ordeal—his circulation will never be right again. It begins to tingle after a moment as the blood courses more easily through his veins. Then his arm begins to cramp.

They watch Henri as he struggles into his clothing. It is an ordeal with broken fingers on his left hand and his right arm unable to obey commands. Each movement is stiff and agonizing. In the end he doesn't bother to tuck in his shirt or lace his shoes. Marceline clucks her tongue.

"Surely you can do better than that," she says. "Do make yourself presentable." Marceline ties his shoes, then tucks in his shirt.

"Where are we going?" Henri asks from between clenched teeth.

"On a field trip."

*

The Société Marseillaise de Crédit does not open for another hour. The door is locked and the windows shuttered. No one has swept the front step this morning or turned on any of the lights save those on the first floor. But Paquet in his full officer's regalia strikes an imposing figure, and the bank manager rushes to unlock the doors when he bangs on them with his fist.

Henri is dressed and as tidy as can be expected under the circumstances with his hands cuffed behind his back and the pained movements of a man who is clearly injured. He has known the manager for decades and appreciates the look of dismay upon his face.

"We are not open for another hour," the manager says.

"I don't care," Paquet says, and then, "Where are your safe-deposit boxes?"

The manager looks between them, alarmed. "In the vault."

"Take us there."

"I cannot—"

"You can. And you will. Because if you choose not to

cooperate, we won't even bother to put you in the cell beside Monsieur Fiocca, we'll just shoot you in the street and leave the dogs to clean up the mess."

If Henri's hands weren't cuffed, he would set them on his friend's shoulders to reassure him. All he can do instead is say, "It's fine. Do as they tell you."

The manager leads them through the marbled lobby of the Société Marseillaise de Crédit. Henri's grandfather banked here. His own father still does. He's been traversing these hallways since he had curls at the nape of his neck and dimples on his knuckles. He knows the way to the vault by heart. But he drags behind instead, hoping that there is still some way to prevent Marceline from taking anything else from him.

The vault door is made of solid steel and weighs one thousand pounds. The keys required to unlock it are numerous, and the combination complicated. The manager gets it wrong on the first two tries because his hands are shaking. Henri did not realize that, at some point after entering the bank, Paquet drew his gun, and just as he begins to mutter curses under his breath the giant door swings inward.

Marceline steps into the room first, surveying all the boxes, large and small, along with a second, smaller vault door where Henri assumes the bank keeps cash and gold.

"Which box is yours?" she asks.

He nods at a medium-sized box along the far wall. "Number seventy-five," he says. "But I do not have the key."

And then she gives him the smile he's grown to hate as she reaches into her pocket and removes the keys she took from him weeks ago. "I do."

Office keys. Home keys. Mailbox key. Car key. And safe-deposit box key. He's never been concerned about keeping them together and on his person because he and Nancy are the only people who know which boxes they rent. This scenario never crossed his mind.

Marceline steps in front of box seventy-five, slides the key into the lock, and turns it. He watches, in mute acceptance, as they begin to plunder his life.

"What do you want from me?" he asks.

"Your money, of course," she says. Henri's entire life savings in gold, cash, and bonds are pulled from the box and stuffed into a bank bag. "Among other things. Not the least of which is information on the whereabouts of your wife. The Germans are willing to pay handsomely for that."

"You won't find it in that box."

"Maybe," she says, tying the knot on the bank bag. "Or maybe not."

Once she has rendered him penniless, Marceline begins doing the real damage.

Henri's birth certificate is lit with a match. He now has no way to prove his citizenship. The deed to the building that houses his family's shipping company. The lease to their flat. His marriage certificate. These all burned to ash right before his eyes as well.

Only when the box is empty does she turn to him again.

"Now," she asks, "which box belongs to your wife?"

* * *

LONDON

The brassy, metallic clamor of a ringing telephone startles me from sleep. The sun is high, and light bounces off bright, bare walls. I don't know who I am or where I am or what is happening, and that infernal ringing just won't stop. It doesn't help that I came home and drank a good bit of the brandy I bought for Henri when the Free French rejected my services. He'd be so disappointed in me if he knew. Angry drinking is dangerous drinking.

It takes a moment to settle into my own body, to remember.

And then another to scramble out of bed and stumble to the other side of the room and yank the receiver off the wall.

"Hello?" I sound awful. Like I'm hungover. Which I am. But I won't apologize for it, because I hate everyone right now. Except for Henri. Him I miss so much it makes my stomach hurt.

"Nancy Fiocca?"

The use of my married name is strange and the cautious instincts that I have honed over the last few years kick into gear. I feel the adrenaline whoosh through my blood. My heart rate ticks higher.

"Yes," I say.

It is a male voice. So generic and blandly English that I cannot place the region, and therefore I know it is either fake or being controlled. Whoever this is does not bother with further pleasantries.

"What were you doing in central London at the general's headquarters yesterday?"

"General . . ." It is neither a question nor a statement.

"De Gaulle," he says, and waits in silence while I decide on an answer.

"I think you must have confused me with someone else."

"No, Mrs. Fiocca, we haven't. You were wearing a blue dress, belted at the waist. You arrived just after three o'clock in the afternoon and were gone by three twenty. You were back home in Piccadilly at ten minutes to four."

Well, I'll be buggered. I'm being followed. Again.

"What's it to you if I did visit them? I volunteered my services to the Free French—because I lived in France for the last *nine years*—and was rejected without cause. That's hardly an offense worthy of an interrogation at"—I glance at the clock. *Eleven? Really?*—"so early in the day."

"My superior would like me to inform you that if you are similarly interested in serving the British cause against Germany, you should report to fifty-seven Orchard Court, Portman Square, promptly at two o'clock this afternoon."

I am confused. I shake my head. Rub my dry, scratchy eyes with a fist.

"And who, exactly, is your superior?"

He repeats the address. "Two o'clock this afternoon. Fifty-seven. Orchard Court."

MARYLEBONE

57 Orchard Court

I wear the same dress so they can see me coming. I've always liked this one. Navy, with a scoop neck and mother-of-pearl buttons down the front. Black leather belt. Black leather pumps. New stockings. Lipstick. Attitude.

I stand on the sidewalk looking up at the six-story apartment building. Cream-colored stone. Flat edifice. Plain windows. Nothing fancy or ornate about the thing. There is no indication of what lies within. But I've been pondering my circumstances since the mysterious call this morning and I think I've got an idea of what might be going on. My unsolicited arrival at the Free French headquarters garnered immediate suspicion. I am a British subject, after all. So they rejected me out of hand in the belief that I'm a pawn, sent by the British. But my visit was also noted by the Brits, who are, in fact, spying on the French, though not with any help from me. They saw me come and go. Followed me home. Ascertained my identity. Given that the British vice consul alerted London of my departure from Spain, it wasn't all that hard for them to connect the dots. Nancy Fiocca, Resistance figure, back in London.

I step through the front door, into the lobby, and walk toward the stairwell. An elevator would be nice given my choice of footwear, but I'll make do. I smooth the front of my dress and take a deep breath once I've reached the fifth floor. It's not like I'm out of shape, but really, they should install an elevator. High heels weren't made for *climbing.* I look for number fifty-seven. Eight doors down, on the left. I knock.

"Come in!"

I enter the sprawling flat and see a young, pretty woman at a desk in what I assume—under other circumstances—would be the living room. She has blue eyes and blond hair and she reminds me so much of Stephanie that I can hardly look at her.

"Can I help you?" she asks as I close the door behind me.

"Yes. I think so, at least. I was told to come for an . . . *appointment* . . . ? At two o'clock." I check my watch. Right on the money.

"Name?"

"Nancy Fiocca."

She doesn't glance at a notebook or check a list. Simply gives me a curt nod and points at a door down the hall. "He's waiting for you."

"*Who* is waiting for me?"

Her only answer is a smile.

I do love a mystery. And truth be told, I have nothing else to do today, so I follow her slender arm and the pointed finger at the end of it down the short hallway.

The floors are carpeted, the walls beige, and the doors solid oak. I knock again and am instructed to enter. A man sits behind a desk in what was once a bedroom. The plaque on the polished wood surface indicates one *Major Morell*.

"Nancy Fiocca, I presume?" he asks, then steps out from behind his desk and offers his hand. "Please, have a seat."

I shake it. Sit down. "You are the one who called this morning."

He raises an eyebrow.

"Your accent," I explain.

"What about it?"

"Wherever it is you come from, you're trying very hard to hide it."

This wins me a grin. "Experimenting."

"On?"

"You."

I grunt. "Seems a waste of time, honestly. Why not say, 'This is Major Morell with . . .'" I wait for him to supply the answer. It takes a moment, but he finally obliges me.

". . . The Special Operations Executive . . ."

"'. . . with the Special Operations Executive'—what the hell is that anyway?"

Another grin. "We'll get to that in a moment."

"Right. Morell. With the . . . ah . . . SOE . . . and I'd like to chat. By the way, I'm from Bristol." I catch him blink, quickly, several times, and I know that my guess hit home. "That would have done the job. I would have come. Why all the secrecy?"

Major Morell has been standing through all this, looking at me as if I've grown feathers out of my nose. Finally, he shakes his head, astounded, and sits down opposite me at his desk.

"He did say you were sharp."

"Who said?"

He ignores that question but answers the other. "The thing is, Mrs. Fiocca, the SOE is a covert organization and I can't just go announcing it when I call."

"And why did you call?"

"You were recommended to us."

"By?"

"A mutual friend."

Now I'm just frustrated. "Recommended. For. *What?*"

"I apologize. You've been out of country, so of course you wouldn't know. The Special Operations Executive was formed three years ago to conduct... shall we say... *clandestine*... operations in occupied Europe. We engage in sabotage. Reconnaissance. And a bit of..." He searches for an acceptable word that will not frighten me.

"Spying?"

"Yes."

"Excellent. How do I join?"

He blinks at me. "Well, that is why we would like to speak with you. We've heard of your work in France. Forging documents. Smuggling downed British pilots and Jews across the border into Spain. We have been told that you and your husband financed a great deal of the work yourselves. We believe you would be an excellent fit for our organization."

If he'd told me he wanted to make me queen of the British Empire I couldn't be more pleased. But I still have questions. "You keep saying 'we.' Who do you mean? *Exactly.*"

"Myself, of course," he says. "And Maurice Buckmaster."

"And who the flaming hell is he?"

Major Morell is a *blinker.* If you impress him, he blinks. If you astonish him, he blinks. And if you offend him? His eyes flutter at such a rate you'd think they were in danger of falling out.

"Maurice Buckmaster is the head of the French Section of the SOE."

"He's in charge?"

"Yes."

"Where is he, then? Why isn't he conducting this interview?"

"The interviews are my job."

"And have I got it? The job, I mean?"

"That depends on how you do with the admissions tests."

I wave the idea of *tests* aside. As far as I'm concerned, I've proven myself ten times over. "I will accept the position on one condition."

Poor Major Morell. He may have been told of my arrival, but he has absolutely no idea what to do with me. "And what condition is that?"

"That you send me back to France."

"Why France? Do you think it will be glamorous?"

"*Glamorous?* If I wanted *glamour* I'd go back to New York. Or take up residence at Buckingham Palace. France is occupied by the Nazis, for God's sake. There is nothing glamorous about it. Why would you even ask such a question?"

He shrugs. "I just wanted to see your reaction. It's my job to gauge your reactions."

"Then gauge this. *Record* it somewhere so I don't have to say it again. I want to go back to France because my husband is there. Because half my friends are there. My *dog* is there. Because the damn Nazis have turned it into a hellhole, and I can't live with the idea that they could do the same with the rest of the world." I stand up. Square my shoulders. Clutch the handles of my purse so tightly my knuckles turn white. "Where am I supposed to report for duty?"

KENT

"The Mad House"

As much as I dislike tests, I am unable to avoid them. And I am certain that I fail the first one. But it can't be avoided. I despise psychiatrists, and I suspect the feeling is mutual.

I sit in his office, the day after my interview with Morell, on the bottom floor of a manor home outside Kent that I am told is called "the Mad House." And no wonder, given this first bit of bizarre intellectual prodding. I do not ask his name, but I assume he has mine because there is a file open on the table before him. He scribbles something in the margins before holding up another inkblot.

"What kind of test is this, anyway?" I ask.

"It is called a Rorschach test."

"It sounds German."

"It's Swiss," he tells me.

"Do you really think the Nazis are going to tie me down and show me inkblots when I go back?"

"Please answer the question. What do you see?"

"An *inkblot.* Like I said with the last one."

"What. Does. It. *Look.* Like. To. *You?*"

It's a stupid game and I can't see how it tells him anything about my mental state. He lifts up one card, then another, and I answer honestly each time.

"Blot . . . blot . . . blot."

On and on we go. He probably shows me fifty before stopping. "Surely you can see *something?*"

I nod. "Yes. I see that someone has thrown an ink bottle on a pile of cards and you were charged with picking them up."

It's the most spectacular thing. There is no expression on his face whatsoever. I can read nothing as he collects the cards and taps them back into place.

"How about a different line of questioning?" he asks.

"By all means."

"Do your parents have a happy marriage?"

I can't see how this has anything to do with espionage or is, in fact, any of his business at all, so I make sport out of finding creative answers to his questions.

"Quite happy. They've been married over forty years and have six children."

"Do you want children?"

"I find them rather smelly."

"Have you ever run away from home?"

"Not unless you count one failed attempt at joining the circus."

"Have you ever put yourself in harm's way for attention?"

I answer this one truthfully. "No. That would be an absolutely stupid thing to do."

My thoughts on government, nutrition, exercise, labor unions, agriculture, feminine hygiene products, train schedules, and technology are likewise explored. By the time he's done I am so bored that I have resorted to picking at a patch of dry skin on my nose.

"That will be all, Mrs. Fiocca. Someone will meet you in the hallway shortly."

"For what?"

He closes my file. "Your next test."

Another young, pretty, nameless woman finds me in the hallway and hands me a blouse, a pair of trousers, and British army boots. The sizes are approximate, and I don't look attractive once dressed, but she leads me out of the manor home, through a manicured garden, and into the woods.

"Where are we going?"

"To the obstacle course," she says.

I slow, mid-step, and curse under my breath. Athletics have always bored me.

"Do you see those two gentlemen at the bottom of the hill?" she asks.

"I do."

"Go to them. They will take it from here."

And then she turns and retreats to the comfort of the house while I traipse on alone.

The men in question could not be more different. The first is tall, thin, and in his mid-thirties, with a receding hairline. His nose is straight, his eyes are blue, and he has the fine bones of a gentleman. He extends his hand the moment I reach them.

"Maurice Buckmaster," he says. "And you are Nancy Fiocca."

"I am."

"And a fellow journalist, I hear. I was a reporter for *Le Martin* in France."

"Former journalist," I tell him. The Special Operations Executive has done a great deal of research on me in a short amount of time, and I can't decide whether to be impressed or unnerved.

The second man is my height, roughly my age, with brown eyes, dark hair, and an aristocratic set to his mouth. He's holding a clipboard in one hand, but he extends the other.

"Denis Rake," he says. "I am one of the instructors."

"Pleased to meet you both."

"I hear that you had opinions about the psychological exam," Buckmaster says.

"Did you? That was rather fast. But yes, it was an *idiotic* test."

He chuckles. "A lot can be communicated while an applicant is in the changing room."

"And I suppose your good doctor gave his negative opinion of my performance?"

"On the contrary. He said you will make an excellent candidate for our program."

I turn to Buckmaster, plant my fists on my hips, and search his face for dishonesty. "I was sure I'd failed."

"You wouldn't have been sent on for the next round of tests if you had." Buckmaster tips his head to the side, trying to identify whatever his psychiatrist saw in me, I suppose. "As unreasonable as that test may appear to you, Mrs. Fiocca, he can tell as much from a stubborn, churlish interviewee as he can from an eager, compliant one. The point is not to get the correct answer, but to determine the kind of *person* one is dealing with."

"And what did he determine?"

"That you are... *spirited*."

Denis Rake is watching me through this exchange, looking me over, determining, I think, whether that same stubborn, spirited streak will get me through his obstacle course in one piece.

I survey the wide swath of country estate before me. Water-filled ditches crisscross the field. There are enormous tractor tires half-buried in the ground. Platforms with ropes hanging from them. Barbed-wire fences. Rope netting that stretches across a slimy pond. Barrels. At the far end of the field is a woman climbing a tree in a pair of men's trousers.

"Who is she?" I ask.

"An applicant," Buckmaster says.

"She's French."

"How can you tell?"

I shrug. "I just can. They all have a *look*." By which I mean that she is entirely flat-chested and has an arrogant set to her mouth. I watch her shimmy to the top, ring a bell, and climb back down the tree. Once finished with the obstacle course, she trots over to us.

"Well?" she demands.

Denis Rake nods but betrays no indication of his thoughts. He presses his clipboard to his chest. "Thank you, Miss Sainson. You may return to the house."

"Did I pass?" she demands.

"We will notify you of your score shortly. Please wait inside."

She glares at him. Glares at me. Does everything within her power *not* to glare at Buckmaster. Then she flicks her hair over her shoulder and returns to the house with chin held high.

"What is the point of this?" I ask.

"To see how fast you can think. How fast you can move," Rake says.

"I moved fast enough the last time I had to escape the Germans."

"And *how,* exactly, did you escape them?" Buckmaster asks.

"I jumped off a train and ran through a vineyard while they shot at me," I say. "An entirely unpleasant experience, if you want to know the truth."

Buckmaster and Rake glance at each other. Something—I cannot tell what—is communicated in that quick flash of their eyes.

"No one is going to shoot at you today," Rake says. "But you will be graded. Each obstacle on the course has been assigned a point value. There is a placard next to it, indicating how many points you will receive if properly completed. There are eighty-five total points that can be accrued, but you will pass if you score a minimum of fifty. You can start anywhere, and you only have to complete the obstacles you choose. Which one would you like to attempt first?"

I answer honestly. "None of them."

He laughs.

"How many obstacles did that last woman complete?" I ask.

He smiles but says nothing.

I leave Maurice Buckmaster and Denis Rake and jog toward the trees if for no other reason than the Frenchwoman saved them for last. Honestly, who climbs trees past the age of ten? That is what I'm thinking as I climb up the low-hanging branches. It isn't difficult, but it does feel somewhat awkward. Up, up, up and I ring the bell.

Down is harder—it requires a different set of muscles. I reduce my speed and focus on where I place my feet. Then I'm off again once I reach the ground. I jump over ditches. I climb the net and almost drop into the pond but save myself at the last second by pure stubbornness and quick reflexes. I take a running jump at a wooden slat wall, make it only halfway up, fall off, and have to go again. Dammit. Whatever. I get over the thing in the end. I crawl through a trench covered in barbed wire. I climb over and through tractor tires. I jump off a platform, grab a rope, and swing to the other side. I hate every second of it. But I finish every obstacle, then jog back to where Buckmaster and Rake are standing.

"How did I do?"

"You took to it like a duck to water," Rake says.

"My score?"

He laughs. "Eighty-five points."

"So, I can go back to the house and change?"

Rake shakes his head. "No. Next come the group exercises."

"But you sent that Frenchwoman back to change!"

"She didn't pass the test," he tells me. "Climbed one tree and gave up."

The group exercises are worse. I am assigned to an all-male group that has, apparently, been waiting on me before they can continue. One of them—a tall, pale chap named John Farmer—stiffens the moment he sees me.

"What?" I demand.

"You're the holdup?" he asks.

"Not my fault I had a better time slot than you did."

Before we can get into it further, Rake gives us our instructions. We are to search the basement—which, for the purposes of this test, will be considered an imaginary room—for imaginary papers.

We look like ridiculous mimes stumbling about the empty room as Rake shouts at us. "Ho there, Duckie! You've just walked straight into a wall!" or "Farmer! You won't find anything while standing on the sofa!" There is no beginning or end, and I finally stand up and march over to Denis Rake.

"Here!" I say, grabbing his hand and pulling his fingers flat, "are your damn papers. I found them in the toilet. I hope you have a bit of soap because whoever was in there last messed the bowl up properly."

"Now," Denis Rake says, strapping a pack onto each of our backs as we stand at the edge of the obstacle course, "you need to do it in the dark."

"What the hell did you put in here?" I ask, shifting the weight of my pack from one shoulder to the other, only to realize that it isn't comfortable either way.

"Four tins of Spam," he says.

"I detest Spam."

"You don't have to eat it, Duckie. Just carry it."

John Farmer notes this pet name, looks from Rake to myself, and makes some calculation that I cannot read.

"But," Rake announces, "that's not all. Find a partner."

Given that I am the only female and Farmer is the tallest among us, we are left to one another. Everyone else pairs up instantly. Rake hands out three neckties.

"What are these for?" Farmer demands.

"A bit of fun. You will do the course again, in the dark, with a partner, while wearing a pack, and your legs will be tied together."

"Why?" I demand.

"To see how you work together and if you'll help one another." Denis Rake steps backward into the shadows. "Begin when I blow the whistle."

"I hate him," I hiss to Farmer. "This is bullshit. We won't need a bit of it in France. The Nazis don't care about obstacle courses or Spam. They just want to cut your throat while you sleep."

"You've been there?" he asks.

"I just *came* from there."

"Okay, then," he says, setting the tie at our knees instead of our ankles and pulling it tight. "We get through this—it has to be together, though, or we'll fail. And I hope to never see you again. Deal?" He sticks out his hand.

I shake it. "Deal."

Denis Rake blows his whistle. It tears through the darkness and John Farmer and I move very carefully through the obstacle course. We aren't the first to finish but we are the only uninjured pair.

By the time I'm allowed back into the Mad House, I am exhausted. I am filthy. I want to go home. And thanks to that last midnight run through the obstacle course, I'm fairly certain there is pond scum in my bra. Possibly my underwear as well. The thought of what I'll find when I get to the shower makes me a little uneasy. But I strip off my clothes in the locker room and scrub myself clean regardless.

When I emerge, Denis Rake is waiting for me.

I glare at him. "If you tell me I have failed this test I am going to wring your neck."

He looks at his clipboard. Tries not to smile. "I was instructed to wait here, not give you the results."

"Why?"

"Because," says a voice behind me, in the door, "I wanted to give them myself. I recommended you for this program after all."

I cannot hide the smile on my face at the sound of that voice. The pure elation. The *relief.* I mean, what are the odds? A million to one? I turn and, despite my best efforts, burst into tears.

"Well," I say, "if it isn't Simón Bolívar, alive and in the flesh."

He grins. "Welcome to the Special Operations Executive, Nance."

Denis Rake straightens his back, lifts his hand, and salutes. "Lieutenant Colonel Garrow, sir!"

Madame Andrée

MONTLUÇON, FRANCE

August 16, 1944

Wolff and I stand facing each other. I am stunned to find that he is shorter than me, that I have to tilt my chin down to meet his dark, sunken eyes. I've never before seen eyes so soulless that the pupils are swallowed whole. The outer corners are pulled tight with recognition and I know that I have run out of time.

Wolff utters a single, guttural word. But German is a language I do not speak. And honestly, there is nothing he could say that I would care to hear. I have watched this man commit unspeakable acts without a hint of remorse.

I am not sorry for what I do. And I spend no time debating. I take a quick breath and lay my hand flat against my collarbone, as though afraid. Then I let that hand fly flat and hard through the air until it strikes the side of his throat, two inches below the ear, where, I have been taught, the spinal cord is most vulnerable. I feel the crunch and collapse of Wolff's windpipe. It is so different, in reality, than it was in training, when we sat in the library at Inverie Bay and banged our hands against the wooden tables for hours at a time.

Wolff's airway is demolished beneath the force of my hand. The impact hurts but not so much that I can't bend my fingers. I am startled by the way his neck flattens, and how he begins to claw at his Adam's apple. The simplicity of it is breathtaking.

I allow myself one moment to be amazed. It worked! Then I place that same hand on one of his shoulders and drive up hard, with my knee, right into his crotch. He drops to his knees, then on his side, thrashing on the elevator floor.

Wolff's lips are turning blue. His face red. His eyes bulge as small capillaries begin to burst. But I am not done with him yet, and I do not care if he cannot understand English. I will speak in my mother tongue and it will be the last thing he hears.

"That is for Janos Lieberman. And for the old woman in Vienna who you tied to that waterwheel and whipped within an inch of her life." A deep breath as my own pent-up rage begins to boil, then spill over. "It is for Olivia Soutine and her unborn child and the little girl you left without a mother—for the man you left without a wife. That is for every person you have killed. For every child you have left an orphan. For every Jew you've carried off to your slaughterhouses. For Patrick O'Leary and for Alex." I take a step toward Wolff and put my foot on his neck, then press harder, hastening the process. "That is for *France*."

When Wolff stops jerking and the foam fades from his lips, I realize that the elevator hasn't moved, that I never pushed the button for the top floor. I am strangely elated by this, by the fact that I still have work to do.

"Going up?" I ask, stepping away from his still form and pressing the pad of my thumb to the number eight.

It is 12:57.

The elevator opens to reveal a short hallway—maybe thirty feet long—with a door at the opposite end leading to the stairwell and a second door, on the right wall, leading to the suite. A Gestapo agent is posted outside the suite, spine straight, hands folded. His head swivels to look at me even as one arm goes up in salute, and I think he must be expecting Wolff or another officer. Finding me instead, he drops the arm and gapes. It takes me two full heartbeats to realize that his eyes are not on my face but on the body at my feet. I can hear the din of conversation and laughter in the suite behind him. I can hear the hammering of my own heart.

His mouth opens, and I see the word *Halt!* forming on his lips when there is the creak of hinges and the blur of movement in the doorway at the end of the hall. He turns as Hubert and Denis step from the stairwell, guns drawn.

It takes only a fraction of a second for Hubert to assess the situation, and I see him mouth the word *down.* I drop even as Denis Rake moves forward, his Welrod pistol extended at the end of his long arm. My knees hit the elevator floor and Rake's pistol makes a tiny crack—not much louder than the sound of knuckles being popped. The guard stumbles backward into the wall and begins to slide down as a red splotch, the size of a saucer, spreads across his chest. A thin stream of smoke rises from the long barrel of Denis's pistol and he looks startled, as though he can't believe he pulled the trigger. It is the quietest gun I've ever heard. It suits Denis Rake perfectly.

I keep one hand pressed to the elevator door to keep it open as Hubert sprints down the hall to catch the guard before he crashes to the floor and alerts the officers in the room behind him. He grabs the man under his arms and lowers him to the floor. The soldier's mouth opens and closes like that of a dying fish. Blue lips. Clenched fists. His face turns gray. He twitches at Hubert's feet.

Denis Rake skirts them and rushes to me.

"Are you okay?" he hisses.

The entire thing has taken ten seconds. Maybe fifteen. But it played out in such excruciating detail that I feel as though I am caught in slow motion. "You shot him," I say.

"I never said I *couldn't* shoot. Just that I don't like to."

"But you're not even drunk."

"Don't worry, Duckie, I will be soon."

I move aside to show him the body on the elevator floor. "Wolff." I nudge his body with one of my feet. "I promised you I'd kill him."

His eyes are locked on the gruesome corpse. "How . . . ?"

Denis helps me up and I hold my hand out flat and make the chopping motion he taught me.

"I told you it would work," he says in a strangled voice as tears of gratitude flood his eyes.

"Quite effectively at that."

Hubert is kneeling beside the dead guard, pulling a grenade from his pack and setting it on the floor. He glances at us, then to the body in the elevator, and offers a quick nod of approval.

"Where is Tardivat?" I ask Hubert.

"Guarding the stairwell. Come on, we don't have much time."

And then there is nothing left but the job we've come to do. It is 12:59.

Hubert and Denis move to either side of the door to the suite. I set my purse on the floor and carefully pull out a grenade. Hubert holds up one hand and begins counting down with his fingers.

Five.

Four.

Three.

Two.

One.

Then he kicks the door open. There is a moment of startled silence as the Nazi officers within stare at him. They freeze, drinks in hand, cigarettes dangling from open mouths. Then bedlam. But there is only one door into the suite, and Hubert blocks the way out.

"Vive la France!" Hubert screams, and pulls the pin on his first grenade.

He tosses it into the room and turns away so Denis has room to do the same. *Five seconds* before it detonates. Shouting. Curses. Furniture being knocked over. Dishes breaking. *Four seconds.* Denis lobs his grenade directly into a group of men standing beside a buffet table. They swat at the device, then scatter. *Three seconds.* I pull my pin. I roll my grenade so that it lands three feet within the room and blocks the path of anyone lucky enough to escape. And then we run like mad toward the stairwell. *Two seconds.* The sound of four dozen grown men cursing, screaming, and crying is the last thing I hear before the ear-shattering *boom Boom BOOM* comes in quick succession. The windows explode outward and the air reverberates. Dust fills the hallway but no coughing, gurgling, or cries for help can be heard from within the room. For ten seconds we are surrounded by morbid silence and the salty, iron smell of blood.

Then I hear the sound of distant gunfire as Jacques begins picking off Nazi officers as they try to escape from the lower floors of the Hôtel d'Orcet.

FRAGNES

August 30, 1944

With the Nazi headquarters in Montluçon destroyed and the Germans facing assault from all directions, we decide to move our camp to more comfortable accommodations. But no sooner have we taken up residence in an empty château in Fragne, a few kilometers from Montluçon, than we get the news that Paris has been liberated.

On August 30, the morning of my thirty-second birthday, I wake to the blaring sound of a trumpet. I thrash out of bed, thinking that we are under attack, only to find Denis Rake standing in the doorway, face solemn.

"What is it?" I demand.

"Gaspard is here," he tells me, one eyebrow cocked at the sight of my blue satin nightgown. "Get up. Get dressed. Meet me out front."

I lie back for a full ten seconds, allowing myself to simmer with rage. That *man*! What the *hell* is wrong with that man? It seems as though every time something starts to go right, Gaspard steps in to ruin it. Tardivat's Maquis have waged full-on war with the Germans stationed in and around Montluçon. Without their leaders they are unorganized and demoralized. Without escape routes, reinforcements, or a weapons supply, they are all but defeated. The maquisards have had more victories in the last two weeks than they have in the last two years combined.

Cursing, I pull off my nightgown. Yank on my underclothes. Trousers. Boots. Blouse. I run the brush so hard through my hair that I rip out knots. Scrub my teeth and leave my gums sore. Mine is a level of fury that requires two coats of lipstick and a fully loaded revolver.

Men run out of my path as I stomp through the château, murder in my eyes. Hubert and Denis stand on either side of the double front doors and they both take a step backward at my approach.

"Nance—" Hubert says.

"I don't know what Gaspard has done this time," I interrupt, "but I've had enough. I'm going to *kill* him."

There is no time for further explanation, so he and Denis each grab a door handle and pull them wide. I am greeted by blazing sunshine and another blast from the trumpet.

It takes a moment for my eyes to adjust to the light. And I see that Gaspard is indeed standing in the front drive. So are Fournier and Tardivat, along with Judex, Louis—newly released from the hospital and with his arm in a sling—Anselm, and every lieutenant in the French Resistance whom I have worked with over the last six months. My eighty maquisards are there as well, along with at least one hundred other men, all of them standing in the large circular driveway, straight as pins, arms at their sides, waiting.

"Happy birthday, Duckie," Denis says, and then he and Hubert walk down the steps and join the others.

They turn sharply on their heels and stand at attention. There is one last trumpet blast, then every man before me raises his hand in salute. It is a show of respect. Of honor. Deference. They are acknowledging, one and all, that I am their leader.

MARSEILLES

September 1, 1944

"The Germans have evacuated Vichy! They are on the run!" Louis shouts two days later, stomping into the kitchen the moment I sit down to eat.

We gather our eighty maquisards and give them the news. Vichy is only an hour away, so we free them to go join their countrymen in taking back the last German stronghold in France.

"Aren't you coming?" Louis asks when I don't immediately run off with the others.

"No." I shake my head and look at Hubert, Denis, and Anselm, daring them to defy me. "I am going to Marseille."

"Your husband?" Louis asks.

I nod.

Louis lifts his chin and I see that he is trying not to cry. "He will be very proud of you."

I say good-bye to Tardivat, Jacques, and Louis on the front steps of the Château de Fragne. I watch as my maquisards drive away, hanging out the windows, whooping and hollering, and I think that I have never loved any group of men more than I do right now.

"Are you sure you want to go?" I ask Hubert.

"Yes. We go where you go, Nance."

Hubert, Anselm, Denis, and I drive south together, but the roads are clogged with countless other vehicles and it takes us twice as long as it should. It is a haphazard journey at best since the Allied air forces have destroyed every major bridge and the Resistance has taken out most of the Routes Nationales. But we move forward through highways and byways the best we can, and I stare out the window in silence as Hubert drives. I am afraid to think. To speak. To hope. I am afraid of what I might find—or might *not* find—at home.

At sunset we reach the outskirts of Marseille and I do not even recognize my beloved city. The harbor has been bombed again and the boat docks are empty. Most of the buildings—the one that houses Henri's shipping company included—are nothing but rubble. The streets are quiet. Half the lights are out. Everything is overgrown and unkempt.

"Where do you want to go?" Hubert asks, hands tight on the steering wheel.

"Just find somewhere to park," I say, and he does.

And then my friends follow me as I begin picking my way through the broken streets toward the Hôtel du Louvre et Paix.

There are no swastikas hanging above the front columns. No Germans in the lobby. No Brownshirts in sight at all. But Antoine's is full, and I can hear the sounds of celebration even from a distance. I wonder what we look like as we enter the bar. Warriors? Refugees? How ragged and weary and dirty. We clearly make a scene, because all conversation fades.

Heads turn.

Mouths drop.

And Antoine, my friend and coconspirator, looks up. He is not used to seeing me like this and it takes him a beat to recognize me. One long second. Then he tosses his towel onto the bar and grins. He limps his way toward me, arms outstretched.

"Madame Fiocca!"

"Where is Henri?" I ask. "Is he okay?"

Hélène

INVERIE BAY, SCOTLAND

October 15, 1943

Ian Garrow escorts our little group to Scotland. It's me, John Farmer—much to my chagrin as we had agreed to part company—and four other men, none of whom have decided how they feel about my presence. It takes sixteen hours by train and Garrow and I talk the entire time. Of Patrick O'Leary. He can't get any news out of Dachau and doesn't know whether our friend is still alive. It grieves us both that we failed him when he risked so much for us. We speak of Françoise. Bastian. Of Jean and Pilar. Garrow's own journey across the Pyrenees, which, while not enjoyable, wasn't quite as miserable as mine. No snow or scabies for him.

At some point, late in the evening, after nursing a glass of single-malt scotch, Garrow lays his head against the window and drifts off to sleep. He looks like himself again. He's gained weight and the whites of his eyes are no longer yellow. His ribs aren't showing. The bruises are gone. But something is different. It can't be seen or even named, but no one can endure what he did and not come out changed on the other side. Will this happen to me as well? I wonder. I am trying to identify what this thing is so I will know it when I see it in the mirror, when John Farmer speaks.

"You were the one who got him out of Mauzac, weren't you?"

He has been watching and listening this entire time, putting two and two together.

"How did you hear about that?" I ask.

"Everyone has heard about the woman who broke Garrow out of a concentration camp. You're a legend."

"No. I'm not."

Farmer's words make me uncomfortable. I didn't do any of it alone. Henri gave me the money. O'Leary and Françoise did their part. The operation cost each of us dearly. The idea that it's now some story told around campfires during SOE training rankles me. I turn away from him and close my eyes. Count my losses. Try to ignore every savage emotion that presses in on me.

The estate where we conduct the next phase of our training looks like something out of a painting. It sits right at the edge of Loch Nevis on Inverie Bay. Above it are hills covered in gray heather and, beyond them, snowcapped mountains. The house is built of startling white stone and has ten chimneys that rise above the roofline, smoke curling from the tips. All the lights are on and it glows with a deep, golden warmth. It looks like the very place one would want to spend Christmas. We tromp up the front steps after midnight and are shuffled off to sleep, each in our own bedroom.

* * *

Henri

FORT SAINT-NICOLAS, MARSEILLE

October 16, 1943

Henri has lost all track of time. It was easy, at first, to keep the days straight. But when they began regularly interrogating him, the pain took over and his mind . . . *shifted.* It's a protective measure, he thinks. A way to survive. Seconds. Minutes. Hours. Days. Weeks. Months. They're one and the same to a mind that is trying not to break. He has not seen the sun since the day he was taken to the bank. Great lengths of time go by before he sees Marceline or Paquet. His cuts and bruises heal. His hair and beard grow longer. But other times they are in and out of his cell on a near-constant basis. Asking questions. Demanding information. Knocking him around. He says as little as he can. He breathes through the punches. Counts backward silently as the kicks land. Paquet used his baton during one of these interrogations, but Marceline stopped him after the first excruciating blow to his head.

"We still need him," she said.

Henri lay there, afterward, blood trickling from the cut in his temple, and prayed for an infection. He knows it's possible under these conditions. The filth. The hunger. Pain and fever and unconsciousness. But he isn't so lucky. The wound oozed, then scabbed, and now there is a puckered, pink scar near his left eyebrow.

So, yes, he's been here for months. How many? That is a question he cannot answer. Unlike the others, which he *chooses* not to answer.

"Where is your wife?"

"Who are her accomplices?"

"What cities did she travel to?"

"Who funded her operation?"

"Who supplied her with travel documents?"

"When did she begin her treasonous activity?"

"What is the extent of your involvement?"

On and on and on they go. Sometimes Paquet brings a chair into his cell and sits while Marceline barks out questions. But usually it is her sitting there, smoking a cigarette, looking at him as though she cannot understand his choice. Nancy over her. It always comes back to this. That single question burns in her eyes continually. How could he choose a foreigner? An *Australienne*?

Henri thinks that the season has changed again. The stone walls have grown colder recently. By a few degrees only, but it is enough to make him shiver as he sleeps. It is enough to heighten his sense of misery. He is awake when he hears footsteps approaching his cell again.

Low voices.

A key turning in the lock.

The groan of rusted hinges as the door swings outward.

He stares at his bare feet. Marvels at how long his toenails have grown. How dirty they are. He decides this will be what he focuses on through whatever comes next.

A gasp. "Henri."

He is expecting her voice. Or maybe Paquet's. But not his father's.

His head snaps up.

"Papa?"

Henri tries to get to his feet, but he is weak. He is hungry. One arm is still chained to the wall. And his legs give out. He slides back down the rough stone and lands on the floor with a thump.

Ranier Fiocca has never been a tender man. Proud. Exacting. Arrogant. Stubborn. Impatient. Determined. So many things that make an excellent businessman and so few that make a good family man. And yet, they have always had each other. They are family—even if an odd one.

His father turns on Marceline. "What have you done to my son?" he demands.

"He has done this to himself."

"Chained *himself* to a wall? Stripped *himself*? Beaten *himself*?"

No, not a tender man at all, Henri thinks. But he can stoke a rage like few people he has ever known. It is a pity his father and his wife never got along. Had they ever found themselves on the same side of a cause, they would have made a terrifying partnership.

"Your son didn't just conspire with a known traitor"—she looks at him as though to suggest he could have prevented this—"he *married* her. He funded her operations. And now he is hiding her."

Henri has never seen his father cry. Never seen his face twist with anguish or his fists pound his thighs in fury.

"I knew it!" he hisses. "I knew that woman would ruin you. Look what she has done."

"*Noncee* did not do this to me, Papa." He lifts his free hand and points at Marceline. "She did."

"*Non!* That woman trapped you. Seduced you. Addled your mind. Spent your fortune to support her treachery. And now she has abandoned you!"

Henri watches as Marceline stands beside his father and sets a comforting hand on his shoulder. Watches those wicked, snakelike fingers spread across his shirt.

"All we need is her whereabouts," she says. "And then we can release Henri. It isn't hard. But he refuses."

Her voice is dripping with deceit, but his father hears only what he wants. He cannot see through the fake mask of concern.

"Henri, please." Ranier Fiocca moves forward and drops to his knees before his son. Grabs Henri's good hand and pulls it to his face. Kisses the knuckles. "I had to beg and bribe my way in here. I had to plead with them so I could see you. Please. *Please.* It isn't too late. That woman does not deserve you. Tell them where she has gone and they will release you."

Henri doesn't want to spend another moment in this cell. He doesn't want to shield himself from one more punch or kick or whip. He wants a warm bed and a hot meal and the comfort of his wife's body. He wants to taste her kiss and hear her laughter and be free of this place forever. Henri Fiocca has no idea if those things are possible. He has no idea how this war will end. But he is absolutely certain of three things: his wife is the bravest person he has ever known, his father is a fool, and Marceline is a liar.

Henri pulls his hand away. *"Non."*

"Son! Don't do this! Don't throw your life away for *that woman.*"

"She has a name, Papa. *Noncee.* She is my wife and I love her. Go now. Leave me alone."

It pains him to wound his father in this way. So he does not watch Marceline lead him from the cell. He spares himself the knowledge of whatever expression is etched on his father's face. The door bangs shut. The key turns. The footsteps retreat.

Then Henri Edmond Fiocca begins to weep.

*

When the door is opened again Henri startles awake from the first deep sleep he has had in weeks. The grief of seeing his father, of sending him away, pulled him deep beneath that fold and he is grateful for the rest.

Marceline and Paquet enter his cell. Paquet kicks the sole of Henri's bare foot with his boot. The pain evaporates all tendrils of drowsiness that were swirling around in his mind.

Henri gasps and pulls his feet under him.

"That was a very stupid decision," Paquet says. "But I will give you one more chance. Where is *la Souris Blanche*? Where is your wife?"

When Henri speaks a moment later, it is the absolute truth. "I do not know."

Marceline looks at Paquet.

He nods.

She crosses the small cell and squats beside Henri. She rocks back on her heels and once again looks at him with disappointment. She pushes a lock of hair away from his eyes. "It is clear we will get nothing from you. You have made up your mind. And we have made up ours."

"What are you going do?"

"The job that I have been given."

"You are going to kill me?"

"That is only a task," she says. "A thing that must be done before I can go to bed. But my job—my real job—is to find your wife and kill her. Be assured that I will not fail."

Henri is startled by the growl that rises in his throat.

Marceline sets one finger against his lips. "She isn't worth it, you know. Any of this. Not your loyalty. Your fortune. Your love. Her cause will be destroyed. Her name will be forgotten."

"Not by me."

"Alas, you are not enough to keep her memory alive."

Marceline reaches her hand into her pocket and pulls out the key to his manacle. Two swift turns and she has released him. She grabs him beneath one arm and Paquet takes the other. They drag him from the cell and dump him in the hallway.

Henri does his best to push himself onto his hands and knees, but one arm is numb and the other hand healed badly from the break, so he collapses, twice, before pushing up onto his knees and then to his feet. He wobbles, but he remains standing.

"Kneel," Marceline says.

"Non."

Paquet punches Henri in the small of his back and he collapses, knees hitting the hard, stone floor, pain exploding through his field of vision in the form of a thousand little white lights. He groans. Bites his tongue. Tastes blood.

Henri looks up at Marceline. She holds out her hand, palm up. Paquet pulls a pistol from the holster at his waist. He hands it to her dispassionately and she takes it without comment. But Henri sees her swallow. He sees her hesitate, before wrapping her fingers around the handle. This is harder for her than she wants it to be.

Henri closes his eyes. He thinks of Nancy's face. He summons the memory of her laughter. The curve of her lips. That one perfect dimple. He thinks of how she plays with his earlobe when they kiss. The taste of her tongue. Henri summons courage from her memory. He cannot stand, but he straightens his back. He clenches his jaw. And he drowns out the sound of the hammer being drawn back on Paquet's pistol with a single word.

"Noncee," he says.

* * *

INVERIE BAY

October 16, 1943

I wake with a scream lodged so deep in my throat that I begin to gag. I am thrashing in the dark. Kicking at my blankets. Clawing the air in front of my face. Something has gone terribly wrong. It's as though an elephant is sitting on my chest. As though there are snakes beneath my skin. As though my soul is being ripped in half.

A nightmare.

A nightmare.

It's only a nightmare.

It's slipping away from me and I remember nothing but shadows and warnings. Something malevolent. I gasp for air. My satin nightgown is glued to my breasts, belly, and thighs with a thin film of sweat. I sit up. Leave my room. Walk trembling, down the hall, to the bathroom and peel off my nightgown. Toss it on the floor and step into the shower. I stand beneath the lukewarm spray, my senses slowly returning to me. I am in Scotland. I am alive. Nothing is wrong.

Over and over I repeat this to myself. I repeat it until I believe it. Until I am no longer shaking from that strange, foreboding dream. I repeat it until the water runs cold and I am shivering. I turn off the tap and stand in the shower, dripping. I steady my breath. I watch the water trickle down my skin and run into the drain. I let the sound of a leaky faucet erase the sound of my racing heart.

I pull a towel from the hook on the bathroom door, wrap it around my damp skin, and go back to bed. I lie there in the dark, eyelids growing heavier, and I mutter the incantation that always brings me peace.

"Henri. Edmond. Fiocca."

A long, calming breath through my nose.

"Henri. Edmond. Fi..."

Breathing. Fading. Darkness.

"Henri. Edmmmffff... Henr... Hen...."

And the great mercy of an unknowing sleep falls heavy on me once more.

Madame Andrée

MARSEILLE, FRANCE

September 1, 1944

I weep into Antoine's chest, gasping for air, trying to push away even as his arms are locked around me in a rib-crushing vise.

"I am so sorry, I am so sorry," he whispers, over and over again. "I could not help him. I tried everything. Begging. Bribes. Not even Françoise could get me into that prison. Paquet gave his orders and no one dared to cross him."

"Paquet?"

I feel Antoine's head nod beside mine.

"I was chasing devils everywhere else. How could I have missed the one living right beside me?"

"It's not your fault," he says. "Don't you dare blame yourself."

After a while my tears slow and my breath comes in hitches. "Where is he now?"

"Somewhere in Marseille. I do not know. Many of the Vichy officers have gone into hiding since the Germans retreated. They fear reciprocation for what they did to French citizens."

We stand in the far corner of the bar, in the very place where Henri and I sat one afternoon, listening to France and England declare war. My friends form a loose circle around us, daring anyone to intrude.

Now that I am no longer thrashing against him, Antoine's arms loosen, and I step away. "Would you do me a favor?" I ask.

"Anything."

"See that my friends get a room and a change of clothes."

"Where are you going?"

"Home." I shrug, then begin to cry once more. "But I will be back tomorrow."

I take a step toward the door, but Denis steps in front of me. "Wait," he says.

"What?" I gasp, voice raw, eyes overflowing.

"I am so sorry, Duckie." He pulls me into his arms and lets me soak his shirt with my tears.

My friends do not know how to let me go. But I need to do this alone. So I return to the flat that I shared with Henri. The keys he sent in my trunk still work, but our home has been ransacked. Every valuable item stolen. My stockpiles of food, cigarettes, and liquor confiscated. The furniture broken. Dust and cobwebs everywhere. There is no sign of Picon. I know Henri is not here, has not been here for a very long time, but I search for him anyway. Opening cupboards and doors. Looking in closets. Smelling his clothes, desperately searching for the faintest trace of his scent. But I find nothing.

I walk into our old bedroom, crawl into the bed that I once shared with my husband, and scream into the pillow for so long that my throat becomes raw and I can taste blood in my mouth. I pound my fists against the mattress. I weep and curse, allowing myself to break, finally and completely, into a thousand jagged pieces. Then I cry harder, grinding those pieces into dust.

I'm not sure if it is sleep that finds me. Or some other all-consuming thing. But I wake, late the next morning, my emotions no longer reckless and violent. My mind feels very still. And though I dread it, I know what to do.

There are still a few items of clothing in the closet and thrown about on the floor. They are dusty and wrinkled but in far better condition than what I'm wearing. I turn on the shower and wait until the water is no longer rusty. It never gets warm but I've long since given up being picky about things like that. I scrub my body in a way that I have not been able to do since the public baths in Chaudes-Aigues. I get dressed in a black pencil skirt and the green cashmere sweater that Henri loved so much. They are at least two sizes too big now, and I have to dig through the remnants of our closet for a belt.

I look in the mirror. My hair has grown past my shoulders. There are fine lines and circles around my eyes. I am the same but different, and I greet this new reflection with a nod of acceptance. There is metal in my spine and there are fractures in my soul. I resemble Garrow now. I have been changed by war.

I comb my hair and dig through the medicine cabinet until I find a tube of mascara that hasn't gone completely dry. A bit of blush. Powder. And then I pick through my purse and pull out the tube of red lipstick. With a shaking, unsteady hand I apply my armor.

Then I go in search of Ficetole.

Hélène

INVERIE BAY, SCOTLAND

October 16, 1943

Training begins that first morning.

I am woken by the cheerful, melodic voice of Denis Rake, who, I learned on the way up, took a turn through both the national theater and the circus and can project his voice impressively.

"Wake up, Duckie! No time to lie in."

A quick shower. A quick breakfast. And we are led outside beneath a sky so heavy and gray I fear it will break open at any moment. Our group of six is led to the water's edge, around the shore, and into the hills, where an extraordinary stockpile of weapons, along with one very short man, is waiting for us.

"My name is René Dusacq," he says, "and I will be your weapons instructor on this course."

His accent is American, but the name is French and his words are peppered with the familiar purr of a native speaker, so I wonder where exactly he's come from. Dusacq has a full, neatly trimmed beard. The lightest brown eyes I've ever seen and sandy-brown hair that wants to curl but is kept too short.

He paces back and forth. "How many of you have never fired a weapon in your life?"

I am the only person to raise my hand. The rest are, apparently, all former military.

"Excellent! I have a week to make you proficient in the use of handguns, rifles, explosives, grenades, bazookas, Sten guns, Bren guns, and land mines."

The low rumble of thunder announces a pending storm and Dusacq looks heavenward, grinning like he's been given a gift.

"Perfect timing!" he says.

"How so?" I ask.

"We've had complaints from the neighbors about the explosions. Thunder will help mask the sound. Now." He claps his hands twice. "Pick a weapon."

It's not so scary once you realize the thing in your hand is just a machine. No different than a vehicle, really. Those can kill a man too, under the right circumstances. As it stands, my weapon of choice is a .38-caliber Webley British service revolver. Given that my five colleagues are all familiar with small arms, they move off to start target practice while Dusacq instructs me on the basics.

"There are ten parts to this weapon and you must learn them all. Become familiar with these parts and what they do and it will no longer be intimidating to you. Understand?"

"Yes."

He holds the revolver up to me, at eye level, and points at them in turn. He starts at the end of the barrel and works his way around. "Front sight. Cylinder. Rear sight." He runs his finger from sight to sight along the cylinder. "Line your target up between these two points and you won't miss. Next is the hammer. Then the latch. The grip. Trigger. Cylinder stop. Barrel. And extractor rod."

"What about the bullet?"

"Very important, but not part of the actual gun."

René Dusacq sits down beside me on an oblong boulder, beside the gray waters of Loch Nevis as the rain begins to fall, and teaches me how to disassemble and reassemble my revolver. We do this over and over, saying the names of each part, until I no longer have to ask questions.

By the time he declares me competent, we are both soaked to the skin and I am no longer afraid of the weapon in my hands. It is almost a relief to join the others for target practice. Dusacq leads me to a copse of trees where my teammates lie on their bellies at one end and fire into bales of straw at the other.

"Why does my target already have holes in it?" I ask.

Dusacq laughs. "Ask the man to your right."

John Farmer glares at me.

It is less frightening to actually fire a gun than to think about firing one. And after the first time I squeeze the trigger, I realize that I actually like the exercise. What's more, I'm good at it. An hour later, with numb fingers, cold nose, and forearms that are buzzing from the recoiling of my Webley, Dusacq blows his whistle, collects our firearms, and instructs us to go get our targets. I didn't hit it every time, but I never went high and am declared a "crack shot" as a result.

By now it's well past lunch and I think we might be allowed to go back and warm up, but no, we are piled onto a boat and taken onto the water for explosives training. Before any of us can ask why we're in a boat instead of on land, Dusacq lifts a grenade from the locker at his feet, pulls the pin, and launches it, overhand, as far as he can into the bay. A plume of water gushes skyward with a gentle thud seconds after the grenade falls beneath the surface.

He hands the next one to me. "Your turn," he says.

Everyone is watching, so I open my palm and receive the heavy, pineapple-shaped little bomb. "Like this?" I ask, pointing to the pin.

He nods.

I pull and launch but, much to my dismay, have only a fraction of the upper-body strength that Dusacq has, so the grenade clears the ship by only ten feet. Six grown men throw themselves to the deck of the boat and I am left alone, standing, to be drenched by the spout of water that ensues.

The next day we are educated in the use of both Bren guns and Sten guns and their three main causes of failure. We load them. Fire them. Clean them. Dis- and reassemble them. We learn how to carry the semiautomatic rifle. How not to dislocate a shoulder or break a jawbone from the recoiling. How to run and leap with one strapped to your back. And it rains on us the entire time. I envy my male colleagues. Their comfort with the weapons. Their physiological advantages: strength, speed, balance. Even their short hair that does not constantly drip into their eyes. But there is no time to feel sorry for myself, because the week is consumed with training. With rain. And the unrelenting enthusiasm of Dusacq. I have never before met a person who so enjoys the destructive power of weaponry.

On our final day in weapons training, Dusacq introduces us to his favored way of causing damage.

"This is a bazooka, a rocket-propelled grenade launcher," he says, stroking its long pipe as though it were a woman's thigh, "and if the very sight of it doesn't make your nethers tingle, then you aren't worth knowing. Because this baby can blow a hole through a building, destroy a vehicle, or, in the right circumstances, puncture a tank."

Sadly, there are no spare tanks to be blown up in the highlands of Scotland, but there are countless piles of rocks and, after very careful instruction, we each get a turn. It's a two-man job, and once again I'm placed with John Farmer. He sets the launcher on his shoulder and I stand behind him, loading the explosives through the tube so that they connect with the ignition, while Farmer aims and fires. I am alarmed at how much I enjoy the simple act of destroying things, of watching rock piles explode into dust. And though John Farmer is generally one of the most painfully boring men I have ever met, I do appreciate the fact that he is capable of working in companionable silence.

The most physically grueling aspect of our training comes next. Self-defense, hand-to-hand combat, and silent killing.

"I don't understand what this has to do with anything," I tell Denis Rake one afternoon as we sit in the library, banging the flats of our hands against the antique tables. It's been less than thirty minutes and I can already feel the bruise blooming from the tip of my pinkie to the bone in my wrist.

"Do you know how to crush a man's throat?" he asks.

"No."

"Well, you don't do it with your thumbs. You do it with the fleshy, flat part of your hand. A hard, ferocious blow to the side of his neck"—he sets his fingers against my throat to show me where—"two inches below the ear, where the spinal cord can be snapped. You'll crush his windpipe and, if you are lucky, paralyze him."

"I only weigh eleven stone," I tell Rake.

Denis Rake offers me his hand and I take it. He pulls me up.

"Your size doesn't matter," he tells me. "Nor does your weight. If you hit a man at exactly the right angle, with the right amount of force, and a hand hard as brick, you can kill him."

He lifts my hand to his throat, to the spot he indicated. Then he puts both of his against that spot and mimics gasping for breath. Given his theatrical past, he goes all in. Stumbling and flailing. And when he has everyone's absolute attention, he pauses, then says, "If you were to knee me in the groin now, I would gasp from the pain and it would collapse my lungs. And just like that, your assailant is not only incapacitated, but hopefully paralyzed and dead in less than three minutes from suffocation."

We each have to practice this move. Over and over again until Rake feels confident we could pull it off in the field. And then he sends us back to the tables and has us pound our hands on the table once more.

"You will do this every day for an hour," he orders. "Until that skin is thick and that muscle dense. There will likely come a point when the only weapon at your disposal will be your bare hands."

After our third day of self-defense instruction I am somewhat overwhelmed and not a little exhausted. We are dismissed early for the day—dinner isn't for another hour—so I decide that a long, hot bath is in order. My body hurts. All the muscles and ligaments feel like they're about to snap. I have punched and wrestled and dodged for eight hours straight. I peel off my boots and socks and trudge to the third floor of the manor house barefoot. The bathroom that I am supposed to have all to myself—but have ended up sharing with

Rake—is at the end of the hallway. I knock, just to be sure. This is the arrangement we've made. He doesn't have to go downstairs to use the loo and I don't have to live in fear of walking in on him while he's on the pot.

The bathroom is empty, and I give a silent prayer of thanks. Lock the door. Peel off my sweaty clothes. Run the tap. At some point I drift off, because I wake to find myself submerged in cold water. I dig through the linen closet, looking for a clean towel, and stumble on something that makes me smile.

A small rubber duck.

The plan forms as I dry myself off. It's just a bit of fun, really. And Rake would do the same if given the opportunity. So I decide to sneak into his room and leave the duck on his pillow as a calling card. Just a gag. A way of letting him know I was there. The pet name he adopted in London has stuck. He's not called me Nancy a single time.

Rake is in his room. Sound asleep. But he's naked as a jaybird and I cannot, under any circumstances, wake him. I am wearing nothing but a towel and I never wanted to know him this well anyway. But it's just too good of an opportunity to pass up now. I tiptoe toward the four-poster bed, as quietly as I can, and set the rubber duck on his pillow, directly in his line of sight, so that it will be the first thing he sees when he wakes up.

Denis Rake never even stirs.

And I am laughing to myself as I close his bedroom door.

The problem is, when I turn, Maurice Buckmaster is standing there, ready to knock. He looks at me. He looks at the towel. He looks at the door I have just closed. And I can see him reassess every single thing he thinks he knows about the both of us.

"Aaahhhh . . . ," he says, unable to formulate a proper sentence.

"It is not what you think." I'm scrambling now, desperate to explain myself. This sort of thing could get me kicked out of the program. "I left a duck! A rubber duck! Because of the nickname he gave me. It was just a bit of fun. He had it coming. Really! I mean, you've met the man. He's incorrigible."

My voice must be growing louder than I think, because I can hear a thump on the other side of Denis's door, as though something, or someone, has fallen off a bed. A curse, and then, "I'm going to kill her!"

God bless Maurice Buckmaster, he's trying not to laugh.

I bolt down the hallway, holding my towel in place, muttering every single French curse word Henri ever taught me.

Madame Andrée

MARSEILLE, FRANCE

September 2, 1944

I find Ficetole in the small home he shares with his wife and daughters on the outskirts of Marseille. The house is humble but it is clean, and I steal my courage to knock on the door.

"Hello!" I call. "Monsieur Ficetole! It is Nancy Fiocca."

There is no answer, at first, but then I hear scuffling and sniffing on the other side of the door.

"Hello?"

And that is when the most wondrous howling begins. Picon. He barks. He snaps at the door. He still recognizes my voice. He scratches and whines and begs to be let out. I'd forced myself not to hope. I'd forced my heart to bury him too. But there is no mistaking the sound of Picon's frantic joy. Finally, I hear footsteps and the sound of a chain being pulled aside.

"Madame Fiocca!" Ficetole says, that one gray eye brighter than ever.

But I see him for only a moment because Picon is bounding at my feet, licking my ankles. I pick him up and pull him to my chest. Then I bury my face in his fine white hair.

"How did you find him?" I ask.

Ficetole sets one large, warm hand on my arm and says, his voice etched with sadness, "Your husband told me to care for him until you returned."

My safe-deposit box is empty. Well, not *entirely* empty. I learn this an hour later when I stand inside the vault at the Société Marseillaise de Crédit.

I lift the delicate gold necklace out of the box and hold it in my palm like some tiny, dangerous viper that must be kept at arm's length. The dainty letter *H* rests on the heel of my hand. Picon hears my sharp intake of breath and looks up at me from where he is sniffing something in the corner.

"Marceline," I say, and hate that my voice cracks on the last syllable.

"What of her?"

I spin around, only to find Ranier Fiocca standing in the doorway to the vault. His arms are crossed over his chest and his jaw is clenched. Fury radiates from his entire body.

"What are you doing here?" I demand.

"I bank here. My father banked here. My *son* banked here." He looks at the open box, at the key dangling from the lock. "Come to plunder the spoils of war, have you?"

"*Henri* told me to come here. He made me promise. In case anything happened to him."

He takes one menacing step toward me, finger pointed and accusing. "*You* killed my son. *You* do not get to speak his name."

"Marceline killed him. Not me." I hold the necklace out with a trembling hand, and something in the tone of my voice makes the hackles on Picon's back rise. He barks once, in warning.

Ranier Fiocca looks me over head to toe, then snorts in disgust. "If not for you, my son would still be alive."

The reason his words cut so deeply is because I know them to be true. But there is nothing I can say to Old Man Fiocca that will ease his grief or mine. So I pick up Picon and walk from the vault, tears streaming down my face. I throw Marceline's necklace in the trash on the way out.

There is nothing left worth keeping in our flat besides a few pictures and Henri's Victor Hugo collection. Everything that I care about fits into a single box and I bring it with me to Antoine's. I will stay at the hotel until we leave Marseille and head back to Fragnes, where we must complete our work with the Maquis.

My friends don't recognize me when I walk into Antoine's. And why would they? Not a single one of them has ever seen me dressed up, with a full face of makeup, and a little dog beneath my arm. They don't look half bad themselves, sitting at that corner table, relaxed, showered, shaved, and in clean clothes. Grief has hollowed me to the point where I don't mind being invisible for a little while. I go to the bar before joining them.

Antoine limps over the moment he sees me, then looks at the bar as I slide a small pillbox across the scuffed surface.

"What is this?" he asks.

"A gift from me for Monsieur Paquet, should he ever dine in your establishment again."

Antoine opens the lid and sniffs the contents. "Almonds." He looks up sharply. "Cyanide?"

It has been inside the second button on the left sleeve of my blouse since flying into France. Pity to let the thing go to waste.

"I am told it will dissolve easily in any liquid," I say.

"You have my word." He slides the pillbox across the counter, puts it into his pocket, and gives me a small bow. "Can I get you a brandy?"

I think for a second but shake my head. "No. A French Seventy-Five, please."

We eat on the house that night and my friends let me grieve the death of my husband, alternately laughing and crying as I tell them stories of our marriage. I tell them what happened at the bank earlier in the day and they allow me to confess that Old Man Fiocca gave a voice to my greatest fear: that my involvement in the war cost the life of my husband.

"You will never know that for sure," Hubert tells me, and I love him for not dismissing the possibility out of hand. I love him for blinking back tears and clearing his throat as he leans across the table and says, "But I do know that there are thousands of people—literally *thousands,* Nance—who wouldn't be alive right now if you'd stayed out of it."

Hélène

INVERIE BAY, SCOTLAND

December 15, 1943

I was taught, as a young girl, to brush my teeth twice a day. And I have never been more grateful for this bit of maternal instruction than I am when Maurice Buckmaster brings a dentist to Scotland. We are British agents for the Special Operations Executive but we are being sent back into Nazi-occupied France. We have to speak French—not an issue with this particular group, given that we are all fluent in the language. We have to look French—a bit harder, if I'm being honest, given the stiff upper lips of my companions. We have to smell French and move French and never, once, give the enemy any reason to doubt our nationality. This has been drilled into us from the first day of training.

"Everything that you do will be French in manner," Buckmaster tells us. "You will comb your hair like the French. You will hold your forks and knives like the French. The way you answer the telephone or call a waiter will be, exactly, as a Frenchman"—he looks at me then—"or a Frenchwoman, would do."

What none of us had anticipated, however, was that he would take his commitment to authenticity to an extreme level. The morning we are to begin our coding lessons with Denis Rake, Buckmaster walks into the library.

"I would like a show of hands as to who has fillings in their teeth," Buckmaster says.

Everyone but me raises their hands.

I've never been more grateful to be singled out when he adds, "Nancy can stay. The rest of you, come with me."

John Farmer hazards a question. "Why?"

"Because the French don't have lead fillings. They have gold. You'll be given away as English with a single glance in your mouth. So we're having them replaced."

Buckmaster may as well have said the five of them needed to be circumcised, judging by the terrified expression on their faces.

"Do you really have no fillings?" Farmer hisses at me as he passes.

I open my mouth to show him a perfect set of pearly-white teeth. My mother had many faults. But her commitment to oral hygiene wasn't one of them.

The room grows very quiet, once Rake and I are left alone, however. I glance in his direction and he is grinning like a fox left alone in the henhouse.

"I imagine you think you are very clever," he says.

"Listen, I'm sorry—"

"All is fair in love and war, Duckie. I'll get you back. One way or another. Just know that."

"I think, perhaps, that you are not hearing my apology."

"I don't hear an apology." His grin widens, and I think he is enjoying this a great deal. "Nor would I accept one, if I did."

"Denis—"

"I've been charged with teaching you how to code messages and communicate in Morse code. And that is exactly how we're going to spend the rest of this day, *Duckie*."

MANCHESTER, ENGLAND

February 15, 1944

We leave Scotland as a group. Buckmaster has gone on ahead of us without a word of what's coming. Denis Rake and René Dusacq have joined our group but are not in our train compartment.

"Do you think we'll be sent back now?" I ask.

Farmer shakes his head. "No."

"What could possibly be left?"

"Well, we aren't swimming to France, you know."

"What's that supposed to mean?"

His mouth curls down at the corners. "Parachute school, most likely."

"Oh surely not."

Farmer is right. On our first night in Manchester we are loaded into hot-air balloons and flown over the countryside. Our instructor for this particular exercise is a battle-hardened, retired RAF pilot known as Simmons.

"Your mother told you everything you need to know in order to survive this," he tells me once our balloon is hovering five thousand feet above the earth.

"I doubt that," I tell him.

"Elbows in, legs together."

My mother never once told me to keep my legs together. But then again, she never tossed me out of a hot-air balloon in the middle of the night over the English countryside either. We float in the darkness, without sound, and the instructor tightens my pack.

"We're going to do this," he says, "so you may as well accept it. Do you remember the instructions?"

"I count to five and pull the cord. I keep my elbows in and my legs together. Bend my knees on landing. Try not to snap my ankles."

He looks at my army boots and grunts. Then he undoes the latch in the door of the wicker basket so that it swings out. All I have to do is step over the edge. It's a small movement. Babies do it. Anyone can do it. But I am paralyzed. The idea of stepping from a functional balloon into thin air has sucked all the breath from my lungs.

"What's wrong?" he asks.

"I just need a moment."

"You don't have a moment," he tells me as he grabs the collar of my shirt and forces me to the edge so that my heels hang over the rim. "If you don't jump, you don't go to France. And if I have to push you, I'll take some off your score."

He pauses to let the next words sink in.

"For cowardice."

Well, I have been called a lot of things in my life, but *coward* has never been one of them.

"I really hate you."

"Everyone does," he says, but the words are swallowed up by silence as I step backward over the edge.

Absolute, utter quiet. That is all I hear as I fall, feetfirst, through the darkness toward the earth.

One.

Two.

Three.

Four.

Five.

I pull the rip cord and a slim silver balloon flies out of my pack. But it seems an eternity before that balloon triggers the chute itself. And I have not taken a single breath the entire time. A whoosh and tug and then the moon is hidden by the silver rectangle of my parachute. I am told it will be different when they fly us in. That falling from a balloon and hurtling from a plane have very little in common. The point of this is simply to get us used to stepping out.

I couldn't clamp my knees together harder if I was trying to prevent a pregnancy. It's a perfect, clear, windless night and I drift to the ground in a field populated, below the balloon, by Buckmaster, Rake, Dusacq, Farmer, and the rest of my team who have already gone before me. They hoot and holler when I land. Slap me on the back. It is the first time I feel as though they consider me one of their own.

Nancy Grace Augusta Wake

One Year Later

64 BAKER STREET, LONDON

August 15, 1945

"Congratulations on your promotion to colonel," I tell Buckmaster once we are comfortably seated in his office.

He called me this morning and asked me to come in. I returned to London nine months after the liberation of France, after we had chased the Germans from all their dingy little holes. I brought Picon with me. And I have done my best to begin life anew.

"Thank you," he says, "and welcome back."

I shift in the chair. "It feels strange. I don't know what to do with myself now that I'm not busy every moment of every day. I haven't learned how to be alone."

He winces. "I am sorry about your husband. Truly, I am. If we'd only known, maybe we could have…" Buckmaster lets his words fade away, unwilling to speak something we both know would be a lie.

"Even if you had known, there's nothing you could have done." I look him square in the eyes so that he won't have the opportunity to feel guilty. "I'd do it all again. Every bit of it."

"It's a loss, though, and a terrible one."

"One of millions. Henri just happens to be *mine*." I am still surprised at the sudden waves of grief that threaten to drown me. I take a deep breath and give Buckmaster half of a smile. "Henri once told me that when the war was over, we would remember our friends and count the dead. That time has come due, I suppose."

There is a flicker in Buckmaster's eyes then, just a flash of mischief, but it does not escape my attention.

"It is rather hard to count amidst the chaos, though. People slip through the cracks." He holds up one finger and reaches for the phone on his desk. Dials, waits a beat, then says, "You can send them in now."

"What are you doing?" I ask.

"I told you on the phone this morning that I had news."

I turn in my seat as the door to his office swings open and Hubert enters, followed by Anselm, Denis Rake, and Ian Garrow. I haven't seen them in months, not since we arrived back in London. We've all gone our separate ways, trying to rebuild new lives on old foundations.

"What's this about?" I ask, rising from my chair.

"Your friends thought it was high time you all celebrated together," Buckmaster says.

I am about to hug them each in turn when I see a man in full military regalia standing in the doorway. He is walking with a limp and leaning on a cane. His beard is full and dark, peppered with silver, but neatly trimmed. He is smiling at me, as though we are old and dear friends. The man takes off his cap and tucks it beneath his arm.

"Good to see you, Nance," he says.

And then I recognize the warm brown eyes. The strong, straight nose. I step forward and mean to throw my arms around him, but he looks a bit unsteady on that cane—his left leg is badly misshapen, and he is quite thin. So I stand in front of him instead, cover my face with my hands, and begin to weep.

"I thought you were dead."

Patrick O'Leary pulls me close with his free arm and says, "No. Just delayed."

"The Americans liberated Dachau in April," Buckmaster tells me. "We made contact with him as soon as we could."

I turn an accusing stare to Garrow. "Did you know?"

"We wanted to surprise you," he says.

"I'm so sorry—" It's all too much. I let the tears flow freely.

O'Leary sets a hand on my shoulder. "Enough. You have nothing to apologize for."

"I should have—"

"You did the thing you needed to do. And so did I."

I pull away. Dry my eyes. Dry my nose. Look him over. He looks positively *distinguished.* There is no sign of the reckless Belgian soldier whom I traipsed across France with.

Once I've composed myself I say, "You know, there is one thing I have always wondered about."

"What's that?"

"Your real name."

The man I know as Patrick O'Leary laughs so long and so hard that Buckmaster and the others join him. And I stand in their midst, swiveling my head, as though I have been left out of some great joke. And I suppose I have. When O'Leary gets control of himself he straightens his body, snaps his heels together, and salutes me. Then, very gently, he extends his hand like we are meeting for the first time.

I take it and he says, "Major General Comte Albert-Marie Edmond Guérisse. I am pleased to *officially* meet you, madame, and I remain, eternally, at your service." Then he turns my hand over, brings it to his mouth, and kisses my knuckles.

I can think of only one thing to say. "You big Belgian backhander! You never told me you were a count!"

Hélène

SOE HEADQUARTERS, LONDON, 64 BAKER STREET

February 20, 1944

"What's this?" I ask as Buckmaster hands me a small, wrapped present.

"A gift," he says. "For completing training. Go on, open it."

I peel back the paper to find a small box, and inside that a silver compact with mirror. It is lovely. Too nice, in fact, and I am overwhelmed. I press it against my chest and look at him, blinking back tears.

"Thank you," I say.

"You've earned it. And besides, I know you like nice things. I can't imagine sending you back to France without a token of my respect."

Maurice Buckmaster's office is as spare and unassuming as the man himself. It is only a few blocks from where I first interviewed on Orchard Court, and I look around the room trying to find any personal items. Nothing. I know he got married a couple years ago because Rake mentioned it in training. But there are no pictures. He doesn't wear a wedding ring. There is nothing to identify him as the *man* as opposed to the officer.

"You're sending me back? So I passed?"

"You did. In spectacular—if not unconventional—fashion. Put all the men to shame, as a matter of fact."

"When do I leave?" I ask.

"Soon," he says. "All you have to do between now and then is memorize the details of your mission."

"Which are?"

"To finance, equip, and train the Maquis d'Auvergne. We will be sending you ahead, into the Auvergne, to help arm the French Resistance ahead of the Allied landing. They must be prepared for battle."

"Am I going alone?"

"No. You will be accompanied by Denis Rake—he will be your radio operator, known to you as 'Denden'—"

"I bet he'll love that."

Buckmaster taps the file in front of him with one long finger, then lifts an eyebrow. "He petitioned for your code name to be 'Duckie.' I overruled him."

"What is it, then?"

"Hélène."

"Well, he's never once called me anything but Duckie. Good luck getting him to change now." I draw a long breath through my nose and let it out of my mouth. "Me and Denis? I can live with that."

He snorts. "Another of your fellow trainees will accompany the two of you to France. I have assigned him to be your partner."

I hesitate. "Which one?"

Maurice Buckmaster smiles, proving once and for all that he does in fact have a rather wicked sense of humor. "John Farmer. But to you, he will be 'Hubert.'"

BENSON MILITARY AIRFIELD, ENGLAND

February 29, 1944

The night is crisp and clear. The air smells of frost and diesel fuel, and the acrid scent tingles the inside of my nose. The Liberator bomber is waiting for us on the tarmac. Denis Rake was flown in by Lysander a week ago, so it's just Farmer—no, *Hubert*—and myself on this mission. Somewhere, back in the hangar, René Dusacq and the others are drowning the remnants of a blistering hangover in a pot of burned coffee. We have said our good-byes. I am packed. Armed. I have memorized all my targets and coordinates. The job before us is overwhelming. The odds of success minimal. The enemy deadly and unrelenting. But out there, across the English Channel, deep in the heart of France, thousands of brave, patriotic men are waiting for our help. And we cannot leave them to fight this war alone.

I am ready.

Hubert goes into the belly of the Liberator first, but I turn and look at Buckmaster.

"Thank you," I tell him. "For sending me home."

Author's Note

Reader, beware.

As with all of my novels, the following pages are filled with explanations, backstory, anecdotes, and spoilers. If you begin this journey here, your reading experience will be altered. It will be a bit like watching a magic act after you've learned how the rabbit is smuggled into the hat. You'll never see the rabbit the same way again. You also might end up disillusioned with the magician. Trust me on this, start at the beginning and let the show proceed as planned.

But, if you choose to keep reading…

Don't say I didn't warn you.

I first heard of Nancy Wake in October 2015. I was sitting in a hotel room in Buffalo, New York, waiting for an event, when I got an email from Sally Burgess, a woman I consider to be a second mother. She told me, in no uncertain terms, that if I didn't write about Nancy next, we could no longer be friends.

The thing is, I have never been good at doing as I'm told (just ask my real mother). I wrote *I Was Anastasia* instead. But I do know a good story when I see one. So a year later I turned my attention to Nancy Wake, and I *knew,* the way I *always* know, that I had found my next novel.

I'd never read any story like it—much less a true one!—in which it was a woman who went off to war while her husband stayed behind to hold down the fort. A woman who stepped onto a battlefield and was not only treated as an equal, but was revered and respected as a fearless leader. A woman who killed a Nazi with her bare hands. In all my years researching and writing historical fiction, I have never come across such a bold, bawdy, brazen woman. The fact that she really lived, and I had the honor of telling her story, is something for which I will always be grateful.

At this point I have spent three years reading and writing about Nancy Wake, and I never cease to be amazed by her exploits. While I read countless articles about her, my primary research materials were *Nancy Wake: A Biography of Our Greatest War Heroine* by Peter FitzSimons, *Nancy Wake: SOE's Greatest Heroine* by Russell Braddon, *The Women Who Spied for Britain: Female Secret Agents of the Second World War* by Robyn Walker, and, most important, *The White Mouse* by Nancy Wake.

In these books I discovered a remarkable young Aussie expat who bluffed her way into a freelance reporting job at the European branch of the Hearst Newspaper Group in Paris. According to Peter FitzSimons, one of Nancy's first assignments was interviewing the newly elected German chancellor Adolf Hitler. I worked for *months* to find that article, to no avail. As a matter of fact, I could not get my hands on a single article written by Nancy Wake in her three years at Hearst. And I don't think I am alone in this because not a single one of her biographers quoted from her articles in their books. After reaching out to a university librarian, I was told that Hearst does not make their articles available digitally and that, were I to visit their archives, I likely wouldn't find Nancy's articles regardless. Apparently, at the time, Hearst did not print the names of its female journalists—or, when they did, the articles were often not filed under those names. "It's just the way it was," the librarian said. However, it is worth noting that I did not reach out to Hearst to confirm this. I had a looming deadline, a busy family life (four kids in four different schools across two school districts), and tens of thousands of words left to write. So I abandoned my pursuit of the articles and got back to work. It would have been incredibly *helpful* to have them, but it wasn't *necessary*. I know that the articles exist in some dusty archive. I just don't know if she ever got credit for them. It is quite possible that Nancy Wake was being erased from history even as she was writing it.

Where names, dates, details, and accounts of Nancy's life differ in these biographies, I have deferred to her version. It was her life, and I believe that she knows what happened. For instance, in her autobiography, Nancy says that she parachuted into France on February 29, 1944 (a rather memorable day—and quite easy to confirm, given that it rolls around only once every four years), but FitzSimons describes her being dropped into France on or around April 28, 1944. It's a small detail but maddening when you are trying to get your facts straight. So whenever choices had to be made about whose account to believe, I chose hers.

When at all possible I used Nancy's descriptions of events in her own words and have sprinkled them liberally throughout the book. Some of the dialogue and many of the descriptions of people and events are taken directly from her autobiography. But other details are taken from interviews, articles, and even obituaries in *The New York Times* and *The Independent.* I have also included details she gave to her biographers (both of whom were able to interview her at length before she died in 2011). A few such examples include the following:

Nancy's account of parachuting into France and describing the landing zone as though she were about to "descend into the rimfires of Hell, complete with a control tower to guide us in," as told to biographer Peter FitzSimons in his book *Nancy Wake: A Biography of Our Greatest War Heroine* (page 193).

Nancy's opinion that Henri's wealth was "more pleasantly unimportant than if he had none" was found in Russell Braddon's biography *Nancy Wake: SOE's Greatest Heroine* (page 17).

The details of Nancy's job interview with Hearst and how she bluffed her way in by pretending to read and write Egyptian was found in *Nancy Wake: A Biography of Our Greatest War Heroine* by Peter FitzSimons (pages 44 and 45).

I read about my subjects extensively and, in the drafts that I turn in to my publisher, footnote every single detail that I find. These footnotes obviously do not make it to the copy you hold in your hands. But they help me (not to mention my editors—my copyeditors, in particular) throughout the process. I set a personal record with *Code Name Hélène.* Of the 612 pages in the final draft pages, fifty were footnotes.

Code Name Hélène is a work of fiction. It is not a biography. That bears repeating here because I have altered, condensed, and/or changed some details of Nancy's life to fit my needs in this particular novel. If Nancy were still alive, I would beg her forgiveness. Instead, I must beg yours. As with any historical novel of this size and complexity, creative license had to be taken in a few places to ensure narrative drive. I never change the details of a person's life flippantly. There is always a reason. And I believe that in the instances where I have done so here, I have, at the very least, remained true to the spirit of Nancy's story. A few examples of the changes I have made include the following:

Nancy's initial trip to Vienna happened in 1934, but I bumped it up to 1936—the year she met Henri Fiocca—to condense the timeline. Nancy met Ian Garrow and Patrick O'Leary in 1941, but I have them meeting in 1940, under fictional circumstances. In real life she met them separately over several months, and in the company of her husband. However, Nancy did in fact bribe the guard at the Mauzac concentration camp, ensuring Garrow's release. And he did recommend her for the SOE program in England. The rest, as they say, is history. Or, if you prefer, *her story.*

Nancy's escape from France actually took three months and seven attempts. She spent three additional months in Spain waiting for an exit visa to sail for England. And while she had any number of fascinating adventures during that time, I did not have room in this novel to include them. I recommend finding a copy of Nancy's autobiography, *The White Mouse* (if you can; it's currently out of print), or any of the biographies written about her, and reading them for yourself. I have taken the most exciting moments from those various attempts (the scabies and the three-day hike, for instance) and combined them into a single escape for the sake of narrative flow. Much of Nancy's time was spent in the "hurry up and wait" category, and while that is far more accurate to covert activities, it's also far less interesting to read. Please forgive me on that point.

I greatly condensed Nancy's SOE training. The details of those months she spent in Scotland are lengthy and fascinating. (I could write an entire novel about that time in her life.) But in this particular book, I wanted her time with the Maquis to take center stage. There were many female spies in World War II, but there were only a handful of female military leaders. It was her time with the Maquis that made Nancy one of the most decorated women of that war, and I wanted you, the reader, to understand why. Her path to recognition was a bit rocky, however. After the war she was recommended for numerous medals in Australia but was turned down because she did not officially fight for the Australian army. Many years later the government apologized and offered to give her the medals, but she refused and is famously quoted as saying, "The last time there was a suggestion of that I told the government they could stick their medals where the monkey stuck his nuts. The thing is, if they gave me a medal now, it wouldn't be for love, so I don't want anything from them." In the end, however, she was properly honored and by the time of her death was appointed a chevalier of the Legion of Honor by France, and later promoted to officer of the Legion of Honor; she was made a companion of the Order of Australia; and she was awarded the RSA Badge in Gold, the Royal New Zealand Returned and Services' Association's highest recognition. Other honors include the George Medal (United Kingdom), the 1939–1945 Star (United Kingdom), the France and Germany Star (United Kingdom), the Deference Medal (United Kingdom), the War Medal 1939–1945 (United Kingdom), the Croix de Guerre (France), the Medal of Freedom (United States), and the Médaille de la Résistance (France). All of Nancy's medals are currently on display at the Australian War Memorial.

A few other miscellaneous notes:

About Picon: yes, he's real. (Nancy called him the great love of her life.) And yes, he survived! My readers are consistently worried about the animals in my novels, and I am delighted to report that, in this case, our sweet little pup had a happy ending. He lived for another seven years after the war, and when he eventually passed, of natural causes, Nancy wept for days. As she told Russell Braddon in an interview, "If you love dogs you'll know the reason [why she cried]. The other part is that when Picon died, the last of my youth died too" (Braddon, pages 15 and 16).

About the men: with the exception of Louis, they are all real. Hubert. Denis Rake. Ian Garrow. Patrick O'Leary. Tardivat. Anselm. Fournier. Jacques. Every one of them lived and fought like bears to free France from German occupation. Gaspard and Judex were also real. And very flawed.

About Nancy's dream: yes, it really happened. She woke up in a cold sweat in the early morning hours of October 16, 1943, and she *knew.* In her autobiography, *The White Mouse,* Nancy says, "In the middle of October I had a terrible nightmare and woke up convinced that Henri was dead... it was foolish to allow a nightmare to upset me in this manner but the doubt I had in my mind continued for days, until at last I thought I was being unrealistic" (pages 101 and 102). As it turns out, she wasn't. And that, my friends, was one of the hardest parts of this novel to write.

About the profanity: yes, I know, there's *a lot.* And there's a huge debate among readers and writers about how much is too much. When it's overkill. When it's vulgar—and which *words* are unforgivable. But here is what you need to know: Nancy Wake used profanity. Liberally. Unapologetically. And with *flair.* It was one of her greatest weapons in gaining dominance and respect with the maquisards of the French Resistance. If she was to lead those men, she could not appear weak, delicate, or easily offended. And there is no honest way to write the character of Nancy Wake without the use of profanity. If anything, I toned it down.

About the drinking: yes, I know there is *a lot* of that, too. So. Much. Brandy. It is important to note that all negotiations with the Maquis for supplies and arms were done over a bottle of brandy. They meant to use this tactic to take advantage of Nancy, but she repeatedly turned the technique against them. As John Farmer, a.k.a. "Hubert," noted in an interview many years later, "It was absolutely incredible. I had never seen anyone drink like that ever, and I don't think the Maquis had either. We just couldn't figure out where it all *went,* and how she could stay conscious! In my long life, it remains one of the most extraordinary things I have seen" (FitzSimons, page 211).

About the red lipstick: yes, she wore it, often, and as a badge of honor. It's a small, frivolous detail. But somehow that one thing has come to characterize Nancy for me. She was a devoted fan of Elizabeth Arden cosmetics, and I am certain—though I cannot prove it—that she wore Victory Red, the shade commissioned by the U.S. military for female service members.

About Marceline: no, she is not real. Her character, as written in the novel, did not exist in real life. She is a composite of the women Henri so famously dated prior to meeting Nancy and the woman Nancy sent before the firing squad. Those faces merged in my mind and became Marceline, the living embodiment of French collaborationists who threw their lot in with the Germans.

This is a novel about marriage. Yes, of course it's also about war and friendship and bravery and tragedy and one of the most important conflicts of the twentieth century. Yes, to *all* of that. Particularly the friendship. But to me, at its heart, this is a novel about a woman and her husband and the sacrifices made by both in the midst of extraordinary circumstances. Marriage is a subject I am perennially fascinated with—particularly good, healthy, lifelong marriages. I wish there were more good marriages portrayed in print. And I believe that all good marriages have one thing in common: sacrificial love. Which brings me to Henri. Yes, reader, he was killed for refusing to turn Nancy over to the enemy. The details of his father coming to the prison and begging him to give Nancy up are true. In real life it was a Gestapo agent who pulled the trigger. I am so sad. For Henri. For Nancy. And for myself. (I so badly wanted them to have a happy ending!) I will be heartbroken for a good long time, I think. But I am also inspired by their courage, and I want to live that kind of love. My holy book says, "Greater love has no man than this, that he would lay his life down for his friends." I believe that Henri Fiocca displayed the greatest love possible.

Honestly, I could spend the rest of my career writing about

Nancy Wake. I could write about her life after the war. Her political aspirations in Australia. Her wistful return to England and how Prince Philip (yes, that Prince Philip!) numbered among her admirers and supporters. The thing is, books are never really done. They are only due.

Acknowledgments

To give thanks in solitude is enough. Thanksgiving has wings and goes where it must go. Your prayer knows much more about it than you do.

—VICTOR HUGO

To give thanks in solitude might be enough, but (no offense to Victor Hugo) I think it is better to give thanks in public. And I have many people to thank for helping me bring this book into the world. So bear with me for a moment while I try to properly express my gratitude.

My agent, Elisabeth Weed, has, for eight years, made this writing dream come true. I don't know how she does it, but I am grateful that she continues to work her particular brand of magic. In addition to being an advocate, she is also a friend, confidant, and, on occasion, therapist. She has untangled the knots in my mind—and in my manuscripts—more times than I can count. Everyone at The Book Group is a delight to know and work with. Each and every woman there has encouraged me and made this industry a better place to work. Hallie Shaeffer, in particular, has stopped me from letting countless things fall through the cracks—all while sounding chipper as a jaybird. Faye Bender, Julie Barer, Brettne Bloom, and Dana Murphy all deserve a round of applause as well. If you know them, you know what I mean.

My editor, Margo Shickmanter, has the patience of a saint (I might have had her watching the clock a few times throughout the writing of this book) and the editorial eye of Maxwell Perkins. She is *really* good at what she does, and I am fortunate to work with her. *Hélène* is a much better novel for having been set beneath her red pen.

Marybeth Whalen is the kind of friend every woman needs. She celebrates with me, but she also listens to me bleat when things go wrong—in life or in work. We've been friends for over a decade, and I can't imagine what I would do without her snarky texts or constant prayers. She keeps me sane, and she makes me laugh. And occasionally we get to run off and have crazy adventures. You're the best, MB.

Blake Leyers is like a weighted blanket for the writing process. And—bonus!—she's also a great friend with excellent taste in literature and margaritas.

JT Ellison and Paige Crutcher have a knack for inviting me out to "lunch" (by which I mean vats of queso, because cheese is my love language) at exactly the moment I'm about to shred my current work in progress and turn it into cat litter. I am so grateful for their friendship. For their faith in me. For that chance meeting seven years ago.

Lisa Patton always appreciates the fact that I suffer from Inappropriate Laughter Syndrome. Sometimes she's the cause of it.

Kristee Mays is my oldest friend, and I don't deserve her. She's never once given up on me, even when I go dark or get overwhelmed or forget to respond to a text. I don't know what I'd do without her.

The publishing wizards at Doubleday are the best in the business. I couldn't be more fortunate to work with Todd Doughty, or more grateful to call him friend (blankets up!). Judy Jacoby is a marketing maestro. Bill Thomas and Suzanne Herz have been longtime champions, and I am so deeply thankful for their support. Emily Mahon (jacket designer), Nora Reichard (production editor), Lorraine Hyland (production manager), and Pei Koay (text designer) all bring immense talent to the very real and laborious process of turning a Word document into a tangible book. Thanks for all you do! And I would be remiss if I did not thank the Penguin Random House sales team for their unrelenting enthusiasm and support of my novels. Because of them, you can, quite literally, find my books wherever books are sold. Special thanks go to Jessica Pearson, Valerie Walley, Christine Weag, Ann Kingman, Emily Bates, Lynn Kovach, Beth Koehler, Beth Meister, Mallory Conder, Chris Dufault, Ruth Liebman, David Weller, Annie Schatz, Jason Gobble, Nicholas LaRousse, and Stacey Carlini (even though she's moved on, I still adore her).

Thanks to every single independent bookstore that has hosted me over the years. Thank you for inviting me in, for introducing me to your beloved customers, and for hand-selling my novels. I would not be able to do this job without you. I am particularly grateful for Parnassus Books, Page & Palette, Foxtale Book Shoppe, Watermark Books, Books & Company, Northshire Books, Square Books, Interabang Books, An Unlikely Story, Novel Bookstore, Murder by the Book, Excelsior Bay Books, Valley Bookseller, The Little Bookshop, and Litchfield Books. I know that I've forgotten some. (Please forgive me!) And I know there are other, incredible stores that I haven't had the chance to visit (I'm trying to get there as fast as I can). Thank you so, so much!

My friends and family are the foundation of all I do. The real people in my real world care for me, support me, lead me, pray for me, mentor me, challenge me, and make me a better human. There are not enough pages in this book to express how much I love Josh and Abby Belbeck (we're in this together, come rain or shine), Emily Allison (you're the best, Mom), Tayler Storrs (I'm so freaking happy for you!!!), Dian Belbeck (I'm trying to be better than I am, Gigi), Jerry and Kay Lawhon (thank you for always making me feel welcome), Blake and Tracy Lawhon (I love you guys), Andy and Nicole Kreiling (can't wait for the beach!), Jannell Barefoot (man, have you saved my bacon on more than one occasion!), Michael Easley (thanks for the wise words, Doc), Kayle Storrs (please move back), Chris Wilson (we did it!!!), Traci Keel (you could totally fix it), and Christine Flott (I'm sorry they eat you out of house and home, but thank you for loving my kids!).

The great thing about this job is that, eventually, your friends in publishing become your friends in real life as well. In particular, I adore Patti Henry, Karen Abbott, Denise Kiernan, Laura Benedict, Deanna Raybourn, Greer McAllister, Helen Ellis, Anne Bogel, Joy Calloway, Joy Jordan-Lake, River Jordan, and Niki Coffman.

My husband, Ashley, is, and always will be, the best thing that has ever happened to me. He makes me laugh every single day. He is the person I miss most when I travel (sorry, kids). He is my best friend, my biggest champion, my coffee maker, my green-eyed Texan, my wine buyer, my baby daddy, my laundry folder, my dinner date, my morning person, my handholder, my joyful singer, my music maker, my partner in crime, and my project finisher. Mine, mine, mine. He is MINE. And of all women, I am most fortunate.

Together, Ashley and I have brought four amazing boys into the world. We usually refer to them as the Wild Rumpus (unless they're misbehaving, in which case we call them the Barbarian Horde). The moniker fits. They are loud, boisterous, strong-willed, intelligent, compassionate, independent thinkers who will—eventually—take the world by storm. I am so proud to be your mom. London, Parker, Marshall, and Riggs, I love you with my whole heart.

Mostly I am thankful to God for this wondrous life that I get to live. I am thankful that Jesus loves me. I am thankful for the great privilege of growing old. I am thankful for my scars, stretch marks, gray hairs, wrinkles, and crow's-feet. I'm even thankful for my bum knee. Because every bit of it means that I have lived and loved and survived. Thank you, Lord, for this good life.

ALSO BY

ARIEL LAWHON

I WAS ANASTASIA

Russia, July 17, 1918: Under direct orders from Vladimir Lenin, Bolshevik secret police force Anastasia Romanov and her family into a damp basement, where they face a merciless firing squad. None survive. At least, that is what the executioners have always claimed. Germany, February 17, 1920: A young woman bearing an uncanny resemblance to Anastasia Romanov is pulled shivering from a canal and taken to the hospital, where an examination reveals that her body is riddled with countless horrific scars. As rumors begin to circulate through European society that the youngest Romanov daughter has survived, old enemies and new threats are awakened. This thrilling saga is every bit as moving and momentous as it is harrowing and twisted.

Fiction

FLIGHT OF DREAMS

On the evening of May 3, 1937, ninety-seven people board the *Hindenburg* for its final, doomed flight. Among them are a frightened stewardess who is not what she seems, the steadfast navigator determined to win her heart, a naive cabin boy eager to earn a permanent position, an impetuous journalist who has been blacklisted in her native Germany, and an enigmatic American businessman with a score to settle. Over the course of three champagne-soaked days, their lies, fears, agendas, and hopes for the future will be revealed—and one in their party will set a plot in motion that will have devastating consequences for them all.

Fiction

THE WIFE, THE MAID, AND THE MISTRESS

One summer night in 1930, Judge Joseph Crater steps into a New York City cab and is never heard from again. Behind this great man are three women, each with her own tale to tell: Stella, his fashionable wife, the picture of propriety; Maria, their steadfast maid, indebted to the judge; and Ritzi, his showgirl mistress, willing to seize any chance to break out of the chorus line. As the twisted truth emerges, Ariel Lawhon's debut mystery novel, now with a new epilogue, tantalizingly reimagines a scandalous murder mystery that rocked the nation.

Fiction

"A spellbinding work of historical fiction. . . . *She is real, this really did happen* is the mantra you may find yourself repeating, in awe at every page."
—*BookPage* (starred review)

In 1936, Nancy Wake is an intrepid Australian expat living in Paris. She has bluffed her way into a reporting job for a Hearst newspaper when she meets wealthy French industrialist Henri Fiocca. No sooner does Henri sweep Nancy off her feet and convince her to become Mrs. Fiocca than the Germans invade France and she takes yet another name—a code name.

Told in interweaving timelines organized around the four code names Nancy used during the war, *Code Name Hélène* follows Nancy's transformation from journalist to one of the most powerful leaders in the French Resistance, known for her ferocious wit, her signature red lipstick, and her ability to summon weapons straight from the Allied forces. But with power comes notoriety, and no matter how careful Nancy is to protect her identity, the risk of exposure is great—for herself and for those she loves.

"Fascinating." —*New York Post*

"A compulsively readable account of a little-known yet extraordinary historical figure—Lawhon's best book to date."
—*Kirkus Reviews* (starred review)

Cover design by Emily Mahon
Cover photographs: front © Mark Owen/Trevillion Images; second page © Max Right/Alamy and © STOCKFOLIO®/Alamy
Author photograph © Kristee Mays Photography

@ariel.lawhon @ariellawhon
@ArielLawhonAuthor

www.ariellawhon.com
www.anchorbooks.com

Reading Group Guide available at www.ReadingGroupCenter.com

U.S. $16.00 Can. $22.00 Fiction
ISBN 978-0-525-56549-9
51600
9 780525 565499